MW01067938

Golden Boxty in the Frypan

Pat Spencer

Golden Boxty in the Frypan by Pat Spencer
Copyright © 2023. All rights reserved.

ALL RIGHTS RESERVED: No part of this book may be reproduced, stored, or transmitted, in any form, without the express and prior permission in writing of Pen It Publications. This book may not be circulated in any form of binding or cover other than that in which it is currently published. This book is licensed for your personal enjoyment only. All rights are reserved. Pen It Publications does not grant you rights to resell or distribute this book without prior written consent of both Pen It Publications and the copyright owner of this book. This book must not be copied, transferred, sold or distributed in any way.

Disclaimer: Neither Pen It Publications, or our authors will be responsible for repercussions to anyone who utilizes the subject of this book for illegal, immoral or unethical use.

This is a work of fiction. The views expressed herein do not necessarily reflect that of the publisher.

This book or part thereof may not be reproduced in any form, stored in a retrieval system, or transmitted in any form by any means-electronic, mechanical, photocopy, recording or otherwise-without prior written consent of the publisher, except as provided by United States of America copyright law.

Published by Pen It Publications in the U.S.A.
713-526-3989
www.penitpublications.com

ISBN: 978-1-63984-469-2
Edited by Jen Selinsky

DEDICATION

Kathleen Marie Ryan (Parker)
1923 — 2008

Golden Boxty in the Frypan is dedicated to my mother, Kathleen Marie Ryan. She grew up knowing the fear of being locked in dark places and abandoned by those who should have cared for her. As an adult, she protected herself from further hurt by packing away these emotions and carrying on.

I also dedicate this story to the millions of other orphaned children. While many benefited from the kindness of caretakers and community, that was not true for all. My research revealed the horrors many vulnerable youths experienced in the hands of those entrusted with their care and wellbeing. Personal stories recount the good and the bad. The media focuses on incidents of abuse. My mother shared personal stories of both kinds. And like many orphans, she carried emotional scars to her grave.

As a child, I remember my mother saying, "God helps those who help themselves." I continue to seek the answer to a larger question: "Who helps those who can't? Who keeps them safe until they can?"

The absence of a satisfactory answer keeps me awake at night.

ACKNOWLEDGEMENTS

I thank my wonderful husband Mike for his support during the writing of *Golden Boxty in the Frypan*. I greatly appreciate the housekeeping, laundry, and grocery shopping he did to give me more time to write.

I owe a special thanks to my cousins. Since the characters in this novel passed before I began writing, the documents, photos, and remembrances contributed by Carol Moran and her son Mark Moran, Kathy King, Sharon Goodman, Paul Ryan, and Rusty Ryan enriched and enlivened the history of our parents' lives and the era in which they grew up.

Where would a writer be without librarians? Judy McGinnis, Library Director of the Pueblo County Historical Society, conducted records searches and provided important information that enriched the telling of this story. I was also fortunate to benefit from the expertise of several fabulous Oceanside and Carlsbad librarians: Nadine Buccilli Spano, Erin Nakasone and Lisa Ferneau-Hayne, Cathy DiMento, Hillary Holley, Monica Chapa-Domercq, Marie Town, and Liza Blue.

This story benefited from the experience and skills of the members of the Orange County Write On author critique group. They patiently and steadfastly read and offered suggestions for character and plot development, as well as rooting out those pesky typos. Many friends and fellow authors contributed by reading and offering feedback as I worked through the many drafts of this novel and its book cover description: Marlis Manley Broadhead, Anita Downing, Mallory Eaglewick, Helen Gould, Joyce Hayes, Patti Johnson, Josephine Strand, Diana Pardee, and Trisha Vernazza.

I am grateful to Nicole Mullaney for her support and for choosing Golden Boxty in the Frypan. Pen It Publications for appreciating my work and turning my manuscript into a beautiful novel.

I appreciate each and every one of you!

Other Works of Fiction and Nonfiction by Pat Spencer

Novels
Story of a Stolen Girl (International Thriller)

Short Stories
Oceanside: A Healing Place
Winner Write On! Oceanside Library Literary Festival
Isibambiso (Literary Yard)
Passing On (Potato Soup Journal)
Bittersweet (Scarlet Leaf Review)

Anthologies
Ouija Sleuth: 13 Mysteries
California Writers Circle

Upcoming Novels
Sticks in a Bundle Trilogy

Nonfiction Columns
Good Looks (The Press-Enterprise, Riverside, California)
Dear Pat (Inland Empire Magazine)

Nonfiction Articles
Inland Empire Magazine
Beauty Education
National Beauty School Journal

Nonfiction Book
Hair Coloring: A Hands-On Approach

Praises for Golden Boxty in the Frypan

Katie is an incredibly strong individual who strives to keep her increasingly smaller family together through untold tragedies and losses. Heartrending and absorbing, reading more like a memoir than a novel. Intriguing descriptions— bring the time period to life.
— *The BookLife Prize.*

The inspiring true-life story of a plucky girl's determination to rise above poverty, hardship, and abuse in order to assure her family's survival.
— *Sandra Homicz, California Writers Circle.*

THE HOSPITAL ROOM
KAISER PERMANENTE: RIVERSIDE, CALIFORNIA, 2008

Hospitals are notoriously cold. Each shiver whisks me back in time to the wintery chill of my family's two-room tenement. Like a spirit overhead, which I will soon be, I see myself peep out from under our threadbare blanket.

I watch Mam stuff the firebox, then hold a match to the tip of a tightly rolled newspaper. The twigs crackle and shoot out tiny fireworks. In anticipation of its warmth, the corners of my lips turn up as they did then.

I smell the oily mattress where I slept on the floor, squeezed between my parents' and grandparents' iron-framed beds. Even though the hospital bed in which I now lie measures barely thirty-six inches wide, it is luxurious because I am free to stretch my arms and legs instead of curling up small enough to fit between my older siblings, Joe and Ed at my back, and sister Mary in my face.

My childhood was difficult beyond what any young person should bear. I lost more than most. Over the years, I evaded further hurt by padlocking my feelings into the right-hand bottom corner of my soul. In my last moments, the pain is great as those emotions break free.

My daughter sits in a metal chair beside my hospital bed, staring at the wall. I can't read her face. I never taught her to share her feelings. How could I teach her that which I cannot do myself?

Now, it is too late.

The doctor explains, in addition to pneumonia, my old heart is giving out. My daughter has a copy of my DNR, but since I survived two heart attacks before, she doesn't realize I am dying.

My heart aches to share the remorse I feel, but I no longer have the breath. As I lie in this bed, childhood memories flow like water in a river, a torrent coursing through my brain. I sense not all are true remembrances. I suspect some are images of the way I wish my life had been. Others likely reflect the terror I felt as a child rather than the actual danger.

They say a heart attack crushes like an elephant sitting on your chest. For me, it is the hand of regret squeezing with all its might. But if I close my eyes, unclench my fists, and breathe slowly, deeply, my mind escapes this weary old body.

Then, once again, the year is 1929. I am six years old this frosty January day when I return to our tenement flat in Swampoodle, Philadelphia. My worn flannel nightgown scratches my chilled skin. Hunger pangs keep me awake. Yet I don't complain.

Is it possible that even as a child, I sense these inconveniences are insignificant when compared to what comes later? The loss of most everyone I love? Abandonment by those who should have stayed and cared for me?

Still, I have much for which to be grateful. My heart flutters as light as a butterfly at the possibility of speaking up and sharing the hardships of my early life with my daughter. But as fate would have it, the hand of regret returns to squeeze one final time as the echo of feet stomping up the cement stairwell outside our tenement door returns me to the tragic events that altered my young life.

CHAPTER ONE

JANUARY 1929: SWAMPOODLE, PHILADELPHIA

A sharp rap on our door startles me. I peep out from beneath the worn flannel blanket as Mam opens the door to a man I've never seen before. He wears a suit as black as the leather bag he carries in his bony hand. His hat brim casts an eerie shadow across the deep wrinkles in his cheeks. From the mattress on the floor, I can't see his eyes. Prickly hairs rise on my neck.

Since Da, Granda, my brothers, and sister have left for work and school, I ask Molly if she thinks it's safe to let this strange man inside. But I set her age at five, the same age I was when Nana gave me this cloth doll, who was also her childhood friend. And since Molly isn't six like me, she isn't old enough to know if this thin, dark man might hurt us.

Mam gives this stranger the sweet, grateful smile she saves for Father Logan after he blesses our family. Still, I scoot to the bottom of the mattress so Molly and I can keep our eyes on him.

My skin creeps when Mam closes the door behind the man. How will we escape?

"Thank you for coming, Dr. Doyle."

The man is a doctor! I squeeze Molly to let her know she's safe and strain to hear his soft voice.

"Let's see what I can do to help, Mrs. Ryan. I've seen more patients with chest problems this winter than any previous year."

When the doctor moves out of sight, I rise from the thin, lumpy mattress. Our third-floor flat is so small I need only tiptoe two steps then

I am in our other room, the combination kitchen and living room.

Dr. Doyle removes his black felt hat and sets it and his leather bag on our supper table. He glances at the long-legged, icy triangles forming inside our window's corners, shivers, and rubs his arms.

"I warm the place as best I can," says Mam. "Bought a bit of coal, but we burned it last night."

My Nana, wrapped tightly in her shawl, sits in her rocking chair. I think she's asleep until a cough, as hoarse and raspy as the bulldog that roams our alley, growls up her chest.

Dr. Doyle rummages through his bag until he locates a black tool with a tiny bright light attached. He opens Nana's eyelid with his thumb. His eyes bore into hers.

I face my doll toward the doctor. "You may watch now, Molly. He didn't poke out her eye."

The doctor presses two fingers against the tender inside of Nana's wrist and stares at his watch. I can't imagine what good that will do. When he takes out flaccid black tubes shaped the same as a forked water witch and guides the rounded end inside my grandmother's nightgown, I know she won't take fondly to that, so Molly and I inch closer in case Nana needs our help.

"Mrs. Ryan, did your mother work in the textile industry? I inquire because her symptoms align with those of weavers diagnosed with consumption. We believe the disease spreads as women suck thread through the shuttle."

"No, Doctor. She worked on our family-owned potato farm in Ireland until we immigrated to America."

"No harm in that." He removes a brown glass bottle with a metal cap from his bag. "One ounce every four hours will soothe your mother's cough."

"And the cod liver oil and whiskey?"

"Ah, Mrs. Ryan, you didn't mention whiskey. This syrup contains a great deal of alcohol. Yet a little extra in her tea will induce sleep, and rest builds strength. Cod liver oil won't hurt her either. Make your mother as comfortable as feasible, but none of this is a cure."

"Will she get well?" whispers Mam.

This question scares Molly. I cuddle her next to my chin so she won't be frightened.

"She should improve. This spring, on days the air is not heavy with coal and manufacturing smoke, have your mother take hours of outdoor relaxation. For now, keep the room warm and dry. After this storm clears, open the window and air out your place."

I lift my doll up to the doctor. "Molly says our window won't open. She asks if that means Nana will die."

The doctor frowns, then glances away.

"Can my children catch this?" asks Mam.

"They need fresh air, Mrs. Ryan. Outdoor play."

I give Molly a happy squeeze. We've wanted to play outside so we can find a friend, but Mam says our neighborhood is too dangerous. Now the doctor says we must. Surely, she can't disobey.

"Mrs. Ryan, consumption spreads through touch. Scrub extra well with carbolic soap, especially beneath the fingernails. Rinse your mouths with Listerine to kill germs. Contact my office if your mother takes a turn for the worse."

"How much do I owe you, Dr. Doyle?"

"Not a thing."

Mam selects a small red and white Maxwell House Coffee tin off the shelf. "Please, take this dollar seventy-two. But don't let on. Just give my father, her husband, the lower price. I'd prefer the men not know I'm holding back."

"Mrs. Ryan, spend it on cleaning supplies. Your father, Mr. Maguire, agreed to payments."

My mother's eyebrows pinch, and she bites her lower lip. Last night, she screamed at Da that by month's end, we won't be able to afford a rusty nail if he keeps spending his paychecks on bootleg. And that was before she knew of this promise to give the doctor our money.

When a wet, croupy cough rattles Nana's chest, Dr. Doyle twists the lid off the brown glass bottle. "A spoon, please, Mrs. Ryan." He gently opens Nana's lips, and the syrup trickles into her mouth.

I hug Molly so she'll know this doctor is a nice man and will stop being afraid.

"What else can I do?" asks Mam.

"Nothing short of leaving the state."

"Oh, my. Leave the state? Doctor, I don't know how we'd manage such a move."

CHAPTER TWO

FEBRUARY 1929

My family argues a lot. When I tell my big sister Mary shouting upsets my stomach, she pats the top of my head. "Don't worry, Katie. We'll be fine."

I'm not sure she's right. Da says if big brother Joe keeps picking fights at the Bell in Hand Tavern, he'll get himself killed, the same as the young fella who used to shovel coal alongside my father at the railway yard. But tonight's fight centers on Mam wanting a job.

Da bangs his fist against the wall. "Yeh can't type, so what the bloody hell will yeh do?"

"I guess you'll find out, won't you?" My mother glares until my father sinks behind his newspaper and pretends to study every written word.

Molly and I keep our eyes on the end of the sofa in case we need to hide. But when Mam grabs her broom and sweeps our spotless floor as if it has never been swept before, I believe their disagreement, what Granda calls a parting of the minds, is resolved.

Yet the very next morning, I have a new problem to worry about. My mother pales, grips the sink, and heaves. When Nana tells Mam she should eat the last farl to settle what's growing in her belly, I fear a horrible creature might be inside of her.

"Hush. Don't care for anybody knowing yet." Mam stabs a fork into the warm soda bread, takes a bite, then offers me the rest. My mother burned the bottom, but she can't be blamed. It's because of the bad creature in her tummy. I tell Molly the next time Dr. Doyle comes to care for Nana, we must be brave and ask him to take the tiny monster out.

Before Joe, Mary, and Ed left for school, they gathered the tree branches that now spark and flare inside the oven firebox. Feeling sorry for myself because they didn't allow me to tag along, I climb into my grandmother's lap. "Nana, they always leave me behind."

"That's the nice thing about family, lovey. They never leave for long."

Not being one to give up, I ask, "May I go outside and make snow angels?"

"You'd freeze into a block of ice." Nana chuckles and slaps her thigh. "I suppose we could defrost you by hanging you in the church vestibule alongside the angels peering down upon us sinners and let your toes drip on Father Logan's head."

Molly and I agree Nana's joke's not the least bit funny, so we follow Mam into the bedroom.

My mother selects her Sunday dress from the closet. I love to watch her get ready for church, but today is Wednesday. Mam says a blush of pink gives the impression a woman is young and virtuous. Since we're not going to worship services, I don't see the need for the lipstick she's rubbing on her cheeks.

"Katie, get dressed. I'm set on finding a job today."

"I should stay with Nana."

"Mrs. O'Shea will check on your grandmother."

"But Mam, I'd rather stay with Mrs. O'Shea."

"Truth be told, Katie, I'm nervous. Never applied for a job before, and I'd appreciate your company."

Molly messages me, *Your mother needs our help!*

I hike up my long cotton stockings and wriggle into my new flour sack dress. Mam made my other two dresses from scratchy potato sacks. I worry she will make me change, but since she's setting out Nana's medicine and spooning brown leaves into a cup of boiling water, she's too busy to notice. Yesterday, the flowery scent smelled so good I took a sip of Nana's tea. Chamomile must be a fancy name for dead weeds. But today, when Mam adds a spoonful of golden honey, I force a dry cough.

"Put on your coat, Katie. If we dawdle, other women might get the high-paying jobs."

Once on the bus, I stare out the window until Mam says, "First stop, Bell Telephone Company."

"Can we buy a phone?" The possibility excites me even though I have no friends to call.

"No, silly." Mam taps the newspaper ad circled in red. "Applications are taken in the rear."

My mother and I scuffle forward each time the women move ahead. The hour stretches into two before a man steps out. "Thank you, ladies. That's all the applications we're accepting."

I feel terrible for my mother when her shoulders slump. She spins me toward the street. "Back on the bus. Campbell's Soup is next."

My spirits rise. "Will you make tomato soup and bring it home?"

"No, I'd work the assembly line."

Nothing is going right. As the bus rolls along, I count twenty-three cars parked curbside, then begin again because that's as high as Mary taught me. I'm up to fourteen for the second time when my mother jabs me in the ribs with her pointy elbow.

As we step onto the street, I crinkle my nose.

Mam explains, "The oily stench of manufacturing—enormous choppers, conveyor belts, giant steamers."

Inside the building, my mother fills out a form and hands it to a man seated at a desk. "On Friday, I'll post a list on the outside wall. If your name is on it, you're hired."

Back on the city bus, we eat the quarter-sized boiled potatoes Mam wrapped in a towel to keep warm. After we stop at every place marked in the newspaper's classified section and the sun touches the horizon, my heavy eyelids glide shut until Mam nudges me. "Katie, take a gander at that line. Driver, we want off."

"Next corner, ma'am."

I struggle to keep up with Mam's heels clicking against the asphalt. When she jostles me forward in the line, I jerk back into the enormous burlap handbag carried by the woman squeezing in behind us. Before I offer my apology, she hisses, "Move up, girl."

A man with oily black hair blocks the entrance. "Do you have sewing experience?"

"Yes, sir," answers my mother.

I believe the dress Mam made from a flour sack, with white ducks printed on royal blue, will impress the man, and help her get this job. I open my coat so he will notice the one-inch wooden buttons and hand-sewn buttonholes.

"Aren't you a pretty little thing?"

I recoil from the stink of his rotting teeth.

"Lady, fill out this form. Room on the left. No children allowed."

"Sir, my daughter can't stay alone."

"She won't be alone." His lips stretch into a thin wet line. "I'll keep an eye on 'er."

I shudder.

"Make up your mind, lady. Plenty others want these jobs."

"Can I take the form home and return tomorrow?"

"Not hiring tomorrow."

When Mam kneels to face me, the skin between her brows folds like the accordion Mr. Walters plays at church. "Katie, I don't feel right leaving you, especially when it's getting dark."

"I'm not afraid." I suck my bottom lip inside my mouth so she won't see it quiver.

The man motions impatiently. "Lady, move aside. Let the next woman by."

"It's okay, Mam."

"I'll hurry, Katie. Stay where you are."

The man questions the two remaining women; one he sends away. The other, he follows inside and slams the heavy metal door behind them.

A dog howls in the distance. I pull my frayed coat collar higher on my neck, but it offers little warmth. There are no streetlights. A single yellow ray breaks through the rectangular dirt-caked window above the door. A bang as loud as a gunshot frightens me, but it's too dark to see what's happening.

I bolt halfway up the street before I hear, "Katie! Stop!"

I squeal with happiness, scamper back, and bury my face in my mother's coat.

"I'm sorry, Katie. Never imagined that man would leave you alone in the dark."

"I can take care of myself. I'm a big girl."

My body magically stops trembling when my mother bends and kisses my runny nose. "Yes, you are. Time to go home."

I lean against my mother's arm and settle into the bus's gentle rock until I hear her voice.

"Wake up, Katie. We're home."

My head is foggy as we climb the steps. When Mam opens our door, the heavenly scent of Mrs. O'Shea's fresh-baked wheat bread clears my mind.

"Your men came downstairs, wondering where you were and fussing because no one was fixing their supper. They got me worried about what was taking you so long, so I started cooking."

"I appreciate it, Mrs. O'Shea. Didn't expect we'd stay out this late." Mam kneels alongside Nana's chair. "Mom, are you okay?"

When Nana nods, Mrs. O'Shea pats her left breast, where she hides a tin flask inside her brassiere. "Made a dose of me special medicine, a tablespoon of the syrup Dr. Doyle prescribed with an equal portion of honey and a generous dose of Old Fitzgerald. Eases the cough so your mother's little body can rest and heal. That's why they call whiskey the water of life."

"You can't have much left," says Mam.

"I don't, thanks to the dry crusade. Makes me so mad I might take to the streets with those protesting to change the law." Mrs. O'Shea lowers her voice. "Did you find employment?"

"I believe I did, but one more ad such as this and I'd 'ave thrown in the towel." Mam plucks a crinkled flyer from her pocket and balances her reading glasses on the bridge of her nose.

Wanted, respectable, steady young woman as servant of all work. Must be a good plain cook and have twelve months' character from her last situation. No Irish need apply.

"I've heard it said in Los Angeles, nobody cares if you're Irish. Hundreds of jobs await everyone." Mrs. O'Shea plops a huge pat of butter into our cast-iron skillet. "I'm a lucky lass. Me mother left me the trust fund. Of course, only because my brothers died. Tell me about the job you found while I fry up these boxty."

"I was beat." Mam unbuckles her two-inch square-heeled shoes and wiggles her swollen toes. "Then, we came upon a line of women clear around a block in the garment district."

Mrs. O'Shea pats my cheek. "You were tired, weren't yeh, darlin'? Such a good girl. I bet you got off the bus without complaint."

I lean against the soft body of this woman I love as though she were my second mother. "A creepy man scared me."

"Oh, darlin'. Hearing that puts me out of sorts. You did good, though, helping your mother get a job."

"Yes, she did. Now, Katie, go read the book Mrs. O'Shea bought you."

I settle on the sofa and prop Molly against my stomach so she can read along. We admire the cover, a rabbit wearing a light blue coat and running on two legs as if human. This is the only book I've ever owned, not borrowed from the library Mary walks me to on Saturdays. I open *The Tale of Peter Rabbit*.

"Tomorrow, I take a sewing test," says Mam.

"May the wind be at your back. You sewed the Gingham Girl flour sack you're wearing as stylish as the flapper dresses in my new Sears, Roebuck catalog." Mrs. O'Shea leans toward Mam. "My daughter-in-law's boss fired her the minute she showed. Won't happen to you. Dropping the waist to the hipline was a bonny good idea—nobody can tell."

Molly and I agree Mrs. O'Shea is whispering about the monster inside Mam's stomach.

Granda raises the radio volume. "Our incoming president, Herbert Hoover, vows he'll block the stock market decline."

My father growls at the announcer, "It's about bloody time."

Mam glances at him, then turns to Mrs. O'Shea. "Brings me to the favor I wish to mention."

"No need to ask." Mrs. O'Shea winks at me. "Caring for Katie and your mother is my pleasure."

"Only till Mary gets home from school. I'd be grateful. And by the grin on Katie's face, I believe she'd be happy to have your company. No more charity, though. I'll pay you from my wages."

"There yeh be again, offending me. Couldn't accept pay for spending the day with my little friend." Mrs. O'Shea smiles so big her cheeks puff as if there are ripe plums beneath her skin. "We'll have a grand time, won't we, darlin'?"

I love going to Mrs. O'Shea's flat because we always fry up a skillet of boxty. She says no one grates potatoes as good as I. Now that she'll be taking care of Nana and me while Mam works, I hope we can make another Irish pound cake using her special recipe. Mrs. O'Shea fills her jigger with the Old Fitzgerald from the tin tucked inside her brassiere. She lets me mix the golden liquid with vanilla extract and ground mace, then stir it into the flour. I am sworn to secrecy when she adds a second jigger, but the way Mam's eyebrows rise when sampling the cake makes me think she suspects.

Molly and I glance up hopefully when Mam says, "Please, Mrs. O'Shea. Won't you stay and eat with us?"

"I thank you, but I sampled plenty making sure my boxty suits the men's taste. Couldn't take another bite. I'll return in the morn. Goodnight, gentlemen." Mrs. O'Shea closes the door behind her.

Da clicks off the radio. "We're starving. When do we eat?"

Mam turns her back on him and murmurs, "Katie, don't mention the sewing test. Never tell a man what he doesn't want to hear until his stomach is full."

Last week, we ate boiled cabbage sprinkled with pepper and salt, but yesterday, on the way home from the sewing test, Mam bought a tiny hen. It's simmering in a sea of chopped carrots, yellow onion slices, and small brown potatoes with white sprouts my mother calls eyes. I pick off the eyes. I don't like them looking around inside my tummy.

Only Molly and I know Mam passed the sewing test. We also know she added a slice of thick chopped Irish bacon because it's Da's favorite and will bring his good favor to her.

"A fine meal, Mam." Da swigs his whiskey. "Best we had in a month of Sundays."

"Must agree." Granda pats his belly. Mary bobs her head, and Ed tips his bowl to his lips and slurps the last drops.

"Thank you, gentlemen, glad you enjoyed it. Tomorrow, I begin my job, so dinner might be a wee bit late."

I nearly leap from my chair when Da slams down his glass. "Sweet Jesus on a stick! That's the damnedest nonsense that ever came out your mouth."

I slump, hide behind my water glass, and tuck Molly deeper into my pocket.

Da snarls, "Who's gonna corral these hallions while you're working?"

"Mrs. O'Shea offered to mind Katie until Mary and the boys get home from school."

"Who'll cook supper? And our lunches? Mary? Yeh remember she's only ten?"

"Eleven, and we need the money."

"Malarkey! Granda and I put food on the table, clothes on your back, and a roof over your head. Only an ungrateful woman expects more."

Mam's eyes turn the steely gray that warns everyone she won't back down. "How many more years can you shovel coal? On top of that, Granda's seventy-six cents an hour and your fifty-three won't buy rail tickets to Los Angeles."

"Jesus, Mary, and Joseph, why would we go to Los Angeles?"

"I told you why."

"Woman, you yammered until my ears sealed up."

"Dr. Doyle said leaving the state is our only hope of decongesting Nana's chest. He recommends a dry, sunny clima—"

"Holy shite! You can't finance a move across the country with the piddly bit you'll earn."

"I'll earn fine wages, especially for an Irish woman. Nineteen dollars and twenty cents a week."

Granda sets down his fork. "Your wife might have the right idea. Won't be long until they electrify all trains, and you find yourself without a job."

Da glares at Mam. "How many years of saving will it take? And on the pie-in-the-sky idea that we get to California, how would we live while both Granda and I locate jobs?"

"Haven't figured that out yet."

"No, woman, I didn't think yeh had."

"Son, you might as well whistle jigs to a milestone. Yer woman decided, and I believe she's bang on." Granda kisses Nana's hand. "I need me girl to get well, and this might be the ticket."

When Mam strains to stand, I hop off my chair and support her elbow. "Is the creature in your stomach heavy?"

Mary flicks my arm. "Annoying as an itchy nose, you are."

Nana's laugh brings up a wet craggy cough. "Leave Katie be—high time she knows another brother or sister is on its way."

I look into Molly's eyes and send her a secret message. *There's a baby in Mam's stomach, not a monster! Let's pray it's a girl. Then we'll have someone to play with.*

CHAPTER THREE

———— ∞ ————

NOVEMBER 1929

I hide in the space between the wall and the sofa's end and pick at the green paint peeling off the wall. Mary's busy washing our breakfast bowls, so I motion for my brother Ed to join me. He edges toward the door, poised to bolt each time our mother screams.

A baby brother named Jimmy died in 1922, the year before I was born. If he were here, he'd hide with me and Molly—and we wouldn't be afraid.

Nana shoots Ed a squinty-eyed expression that means he'd better not leave, so he slinks to the sofa, lets his hand drop over the armrest, and yanks my hair.

Mrs. O'Shea enters in a flurry. "Heard the shrieking clear downstairs."

I hug Molly so she knows everything's okay now. I run to Mrs. O'Shea but scurry back and peek around the sofa's arm when Mam shakes a fist toward the ceiling. "Holy Mother Mary. I beseech you, strike me dead if I let that lout in my bed again!"

Mrs. O'Shea winks. "It's good yer Da's at work. He doesn't need his ears filled with the names your Mam's calling him."

Ed shrugs. "He's heard 'em plenty."

Mam presses against her stomach and groans.

"I believe the time has come. I'll boil water." Mrs. O'Shea scrubs her hands with our Sunlight soap. "Where's Joe?"

Nana struggles to rise from the rocking chair. "Only the good Lord knows where that boy goes."

"Sit, yer shaking like a leaf. And appear to weigh about the same," says Mrs. O'Shea. "Mary, help your mother into bed."

My mother's face twists until I hardly recognize her. "My insides are ripping out."

Nana slaps her knee. "You might consider how much it hurts before you get yourself in this state again."

I have no view of what's happening in the bedroom, so I creep from my hiding place and join Ed on the sofa.

Mam braces against the wall, rests her forehead, and pants like a dog. "Damn that bodach. If he comes near me again, I'll yank his langer over his head and tie it around his neck!"

I ask Molly if we should run for Dr. Doyle. Her tiny glass eyes send a message. *We don't know how to find his office.*

Mrs. O'Shea yells, "Mary, get more towels."

Mam grunts and strains as if forcing a boulder off a cliff. "Holy shite! It's coming."

Mrs. O'Shea says St. Joseph's Orphan Asylum keeps children whose parents don't want them, and her friend's daughter brought home a baby girl. I tell Molly that's how we'll get ours.

"Get ready for the big push." Mrs. O'Shea leans over my mother. "Mary, take Katie and Ed to my place and check on my bread pudding."

Mam's hair, drenched in sweat, flies when she throws back her head. "Get this child out!"

I tug my older sister's sleeve. "Mary, is Mam dying?"

"No, it's just bloody hard work giving birth."

"Let the bread pudding cool," yells Mrs. O'Shea as we step into the hall. "We got enough problems without you scalding your tongues."

Sweet maple scents waft up the stairwell. Wanting to be first to the fresh-baked treat, I jostle Ed and careen into the downstairs flat, then stop to check the wall behind the sofa. Mrs. O'Shea pinned my last drawing next to the sunflowers growing in a field, above last year's snowman, and beneath the white horses from the stories I make up. Molly will be proud, so I scoot her in my pocket, just enough that her little eyes can see my art.

Mary grabs a dishtowel and removes the pan from the oven. The pudding's edges are crispy brown. An angry volcano of sugary syrup spews from the center. My mouth fills with saliva as she scoops heaping spoonsful into three bowls.

Ed slurps noisily. "Is there cream?"

Mary snorts, "Boys. Always wanting more."

I roll my eyes to let my brother know he's dumber than mud. "That's why I've been praying for a girl."

As Mary washes dishes and Ed digs into his trouser pocket for the yellow swirl marble he won from an older boy who lives on the other side of our alley, Da bursts in. "Come meet the new wee one."

I sprint upstairs to where Mrs. O'Shea is hanging wet towels on the wooden rack. "Go on, darlin'. Your mother's ready."

No one ever waited so long or prayed as hard as I did for a baby sister. I squeal with delight to be first inside the bedroom. The room reeks of sweat and the metallic tang of blood. A gurgle arises from the green knitted blanket in Mam's arms.

Nana sits on the bed's edge. "Grandmother to five. I couldn't be prouder."

Mam, eyes half closed, sinks against the pillows. "Katie, come meet your new brother, William John. We'll call him Billy."

Purple veins crisscross his hairless head. Red eyelids, puffy as a frog's, bulge from his blotchy face. Yellowish bubbles gather in the corners of his lips. Overwhelmed with grief, maybe anger, or perhaps a mix of both, I dash to my hiding place and remove Molly from my pocket. She has a tear in her eye, just like the one in mine. I prayed for the Holy Virgin Mother to send a girl so we'll have a friend. And what did we get? A boy as ugly as ground beef.

In the morning, I roll off the mattress where I sleep with my sister and brothers and glide in my socked feet past Mam toward the leftover farl on the counter. Billy nuzzles and slurps louder than if there were a litter of puppies inside my mother's floral duster robe.

"Molly said it was a bad dream, and we still had a chance for a baby girl, but she was wrong."

"Katie, you should be ashamed. This child is family. That's more important than whether it's a girl or boy."

I get used to Billy being a boy, even look forward to cuddling and rocking him to sleep. Nana explained babies need extra attention so I shouldn't be jealous when Mam spends more time with him. But I don't envy my new brother. All he does is eat and sleep, poop and blubber. I don't even mind that he's on the bus with us because I'm the only kid who knows our mother's secret.

I feel special when she pats my knee. "Your father and Granda didn't believe I could earn enough. Won't they be surprised?"

We're on a different bus than the one we take to St. Francis Xavier Church. The Tasty Bake Bakery sign catches my attention. A sweet, doughy scent drifts in the bus window, but the set of my mother's jaw makes it clear there's no point in asking, not even for a single freshly baked, icing-covered, cinnamon bun we could share.

A few buildings are sparkling clean as if just built. Others appear old yet well-kept. Traffic slows when we turn onto North 29th Street. As we pass an abandoned, four-story building with Bergdoll & Psotta Brewery 1875 painted in thick black letters on its cobwebbed red brick wall, I imagine ghosts calling for Molly and me. I hug her tight.

Mam tsks, "Crying shame, a beautiful building left in ruin. Prohibition caused businesses to fail and put hardworking folks out of jobs. Teetotaling maggots shouldn't make decisions for the lot of us."

A few days ago, Mam bought a small rump roast at a reduced price. Bad words flew out her mouth when she unwrapped the paper. I saw the disgusting white maggots squirming in the meat, yet now I don't understand the word teetotaling or what maggots have to do with making decisions. But my mother's face wrinkles up in irritation, so I don't ask.

As the bus turns onto Market Street, she points to a ground-floor window display. "Strawbridge & Clothiers Department Store sells the coats the other seamstresses and I sew."

"Will you buy one for the trip?"

"Too expensive. I'd rather have the black cloche hat with the tulle rosebud."

"See the girl in the white dress? Molly and I want bows like hers tied around our waists."

"A bow is all you want? My supervisor allows us to buy bolt ends for a penny or two. I'll sew you a sash."

"Molly too?"

"Of course. How could we forget her?" Mam clutches Billy against one shoulder and hangs her handbag over the other. "There's the depot."

As we step off the bus, a whistle shrieks, and Mam says, "Let's get a gander at the train."

I run through the ticket office and onto the wooden platform to keep up with my mother's long legs. A steamy white trail spews from the smokestack. The engineer leans out the locomotive's open window and rings his bell.

Mam fumbles with her handbag then shoves Billy into my arms.

"He stinks to high heaven."

"He's a boy, Katie. Were you expecting rosewater perfume?"

"How many tickets will we buy?"

"Eight. Billy rides free because he'll be on my lap."

"We could get seven. I'll sit on Nana's lap."

"For two thousand miles? Nobody wants that, especially Nana. She hasn't the strength."

"One of us kids should stay with Mrs. O'Shea."

"Who do you suggest?"

"She likes me best."

"Can't spare you." Mam motions toward Billy. "Need your help with this stinky rascal. I love all my children, each their own special person. Couldn't decide who to leave behind."

I'm on the verge of suggesting Mary until it hits me, that'd make me the only girl left to deal with the boys. "Definitely Joe. He makes you angry."

"We love Mrs. O'Shea too much for that."

"She could come with us."

Billy gurgles up sour milk. "Good Lord. Take your brother to the restroom and wash him up. I'll get our tickets."

When Mam and I return home and step inside, Mary glances up from her homework. "Where've you been?"

I smirk and keep the secret.

"Where's your brother?" asks Mam.

Ed scuffles his feet. "Um, well, Joe got detention."

"Again?" Mam lays Billy on the bed alongside Nana. "She's sleeping soundly."

"I gave her a dose," says Mary.

"Good. Peel the potatoes."

Mary huffs then makes her *ha-ha* face when Mam says, "Ed, get the broom. I want this place sparkling clean before the men get home."

Red-hot flickers rise when Mam pokes the firebox coals with a long metal fork. She hums while opening two cans of dried beef. "Katie, get the milk. We're having creamed chipped beef on toast." Mam snaps open her handbag, removes the envelope holding the railway tickets, and sets it at the head of the table.

I feel obliged to warn her. "Da doesn't care for surprises. Remember when you brought home the lamp he says is as ugly as a horse's langer?"

"Watch your language. This is better gotten over fast."

I sense doom and ugliness, the same as when Joe doesn't come home at night. Confident Mam will thank me because Da won't yell as much if he eats first, I cover the envelope with a napkin then pile Da's silverware on top.

Joe straggles home an hour later. He hangs his flat cap and cringes as if expecting Mam to grab his ear. "What's going on?"

Ed shrugs.

Mary mutters, "Trouble's brewing faster than bathtub gin."

Da flings open the front door. "Me shoulder's killing me."

I'm still lying low, so I straighten Molly's skirt.

"Bone tired." Granda sets his lunch box on the table and rubs his back.

The men splash water on their faces, scrub grime off their hands at the kitchen sink, and take their seats. Da's silverware clatters when he yanks his napkin. He grapples with his spoon then takes up the envelope. Eight railway tickets spill out.

"Jesus, Mary, and Joseph! You haven't a *baldy* notion what you've done. Thirty days? Have you lost your mind?"

Molly hates shouting, so I nudge her down in my pocket to protect her ears.

Granda's voice is deep and calm. "Son, I'd appreciate it if you don't wake my wife. But Mam, this is a bit sudden."

"Nana's wasting away. Barely eats. Wouldn't change out of her nightwear this morning. Dr. Doyle says a move to Los Angeles or Colorado Springs gives her the best chance of recovery." My mother's glare locks on Da. "That was our agreement."

"Sweet Mother of Christ. You decided by yourself."

I scrunch in my chair and message Molly that we should hide.

Mam slams Da's plate down so hard the creamed beef goes airborne. "We decided ocean air and LA's temperate weather are best because Nana's always shivering."

"Where the bloody hell was I when we came to this agreement?"

"Right where you are now," Mam hammers the table with her index finger, "at this table stuffing your mouth. Besides, the way men are getting laid off, you or Granda might be next."

"Not a chance, woman. We're good employees."

CHAPTER FOUR

―――――∞―――――

DECEMBER 1929

Laundry day is hard. I help my mother hang clothes on the wooden drying rack. Then, we sweep and mop. Our flat smells fresh and clean, and it looks especially nice today because Mam flipped the Marshall Brothers calendar to December. The picture is of a young man at the base of a blue-gray mountain capped with snow, gaping toward an approaching grizzly bear.

"Mam, do bears live where we're going?"

"Only in the zoo."

"We'll be safe?"

"So safe you can play outside and enroll in school. You'll make those friends you've been praying the Holy Virgin Mother will send you."

Mam circles our departure day, Monday, December 16, in black ink.

I use my red crayon to draw a star over the 25. "Will we buy Christmas presents in Los Angeles?"

"Sorry, there won't be any. The trip and buying a house will take every penny I saved. Thank the Lord, I kept my earnings in a jar instead of investing. We might have lost it in the stock market crash."

The door flies open and crashes into the wall, jarring loose more green flaking paint. Mam rubs her forehead and stares at the indention made by the doorknob.

"The worst happened," announces Da. "Reading Railroad cut departures and laid off me and fifteen more. Can you imagine? The years I've given—"

"Should've seen it coming," says Granda. "Trains leaving the station half filled. Rumors flying. I might be next."

"Proof this move is best for you *and* Nana. Plenty of good jobs out west. Being Irish isn't quite the stain, given less respect than a mule."

Since Molly hears what I say without me speaking, I peer into her eyes. *Do you think it's the same for Irish children? Will kids want to be our friends?*

The woman on the second floor purchases our sofa. The man who shouts because his wife doesn't cook him bangers surprises everybody by buying our wooden supper table to replace the warped door he propped on a pile of bricks. Mam gives him the ugly lamp Da never liked for no extra charge.

With the money, she buys battered brown tweed suitcases from the secondhand store. When the largest is open, another is stacked inside, and another, and another.

The day before the train trip, Mam hands me the smallest.

"Not fair. Molly and I can't get our belongings in such a tiny suitcase."

"Listen, Katie. Except for Billy, you're our smallest person. That makes it plenty fair." Mam spins me toward the door. "Wipe that sourpuss off your face. I'm busy packing Da's clothes. Appears he forgot how."

That night, I flip and flop. My eyes burn, and my head throbs as if I've been awake the entire night when Mam says, "Joe, put the trunk out on the landing." Then, in a louder voice, "Time to get up, kids. Mrs. O'Shea is waiting breakfast for us."

I'm excited, but Molly's been anxious ever since Mam said we were moving in thirty days, so I tuck her into my coat pocket and message her not to worry. But the truth is I'm terrified and sadder than I thought I'd be. I swallow repeatedly but can't get rid of the lump caught in my throat.

Mrs. O'Shea makes the best Irish pancakes. She whips mashed potatoes with buttermilk instead of regular and melts a pat of butter in with the oil. While she adds grated potatoes to the mashed, I whisper my worried thoughts to her. Mrs. O'Shea sets aside the wooden spoon, bends, and cups my chin in her hand. "You're heading out for a great adventure. Sure, darlin', a matter or two might go wrong, but my little friend, you're the strongest girl I ever met. No need to look so glum. Everything looks better when golden boxty are frying in the pan."

Our tummies are full when a horn honks. Mrs. O'Shea quickly stacks our plates. "Me boy, Connor, is outside. Take care going down. After last night's storm, the steps are icy."

Mrs. O'Shea's son tips his hat to Nana and Mam then shakes hands with the men.

Da points toward *Edwin A. Smith & Son* painted in tall gold letters on the truck's wooden side. "Please thank your employer for his generosity."

Ed and Joe propel the battered steamer trunk into the truck.

Granda helps Nana into the passenger seat and wraps her shawl snug to her neck. "You okay, me auld dear?" His breath billows white. "Katie, you're shivering as if we're at the North Pole. Come up front with Nana."

"Thanks, but I'll climb in the back. I must show Mrs. O'Shea the Old Maid deck we bought at the secondhand store so we can play on the train."

"Darlin' Katie, I'm not traveling with you."

"I don't leave my friends."

"I love yeh as much as my own, darlin', but I can't go."

"You must come." I grit my teeth to stop my voice from quaking.

Mam points to the back of the truck. "Enough nonsense, Katie. Get in."

Ed, Joe, and Mary scramble into the panel truck, but I drop my suitcase on the ground and jab my fists into my waist the way my mother does to let people know they dare not argue with her. "I'm not moving without Mrs. O'Shea." *Please, Holy Virgin Mother Mary, make my parents listen.*

Da tips back his flat cap and scratches his head.

Joe heaves me by the armpits. "Get your puny arse in this truck."

I kick and scream. "I won't leave Mrs. O'Shea!"

Da climbs in. "Knock it off, Katie, afore I give you a smack worth bawling about."

I collapse into Mrs. O'Shea's extended arms. "Many adventures await you. Rise, darlin'. Be strong. You're breakin' my heart."

"Please, you must come." I sense my heart being ripped from my chest. When I try to catch my breath, hiccups break through my sobs.

"Glory be, you know half of me wants to. But I must stay, and you must go." Mrs. O'Shea uses her thumbs to wipe the tears streaming from my eyes. "We'll still be best of friends, darlin' girl. Write as soon as you get settled, and I'll answer right away."

Mary pulls me from Mrs. O'Shea's arms. I try to jump out, but my sister holds strong. I elbow her and moan, "This is just wrong."

As the truck rolls forward, Mrs. O'Shea calls out, "May the road rise with you!"

I scream, "We can't abandon you!"

"Don't that beat all," says Da. "A six-year-old knowing a word like *abandon*."

Connor barrels the delivery truck through the intersection of 15th and Market. The wig-wag warning signal clangs and startles me. Filled with dread and mesmerized by the swinging red light, I watch until an enormous black engine hauling a coal car and red caboose rumbles past and the light stills.

"Get out." Mary prods from behind.

I swat her then slump out of the truck. As if a magnificent church, the red brick depot looms higher and wider than I remember from the day Mam and I bought the tickets. I lean back, as flexible as a limber sapling, and fix my gaze on its lofty spire, then slowly step backward, feeling like a sinner sneaking away. "I want to go home."

"Nobody cares," snarls Joe. He and Ed grab suitcases and sprint toward the depot entryway. They dodge a trolley, and the driver clangs his bell. After stacking the suitcases, the boys run back and grasp the steamer trunk's leather handles.

Ed loses his grip. "Sorry, Nana."

"That battered trunk traveled just fine from Ireland. Yeh can't hurt it."

Rows and rows of wooden benches inside the depot remind me of ribs. I feel as if I'm inside the belly of the great fish God sent to save Jonah from drowning, only instead of darkness, sunlight filters through the windows.

Mam speaks with a man behind the counter, then waves. "The train is on time. Go on out."

I help myself to a postcard from a circular wire rack. "Mam, I need this for Mrs. O'Shea."

"For the love of Jesus, Katie, that's the Liberty Bell. All the years Mrs.

O'Shea lived in Philly, I'm pretty sure she's seen it a million times."

"Three for a penny."

"Don't you think she'd prefer a picture of palm trees and the sparkling blue sea?"

"It shows the crack really well."

"Katie, I'm gonna *crack you* if we're still here arguing when the train departs. Put it back."

"You said I could write whenever I want."

Mam yanks my collar and hurls me toward the platform. Coal smoke stench hangs in the air. The chug of the train engine and clackety-clack of the steel wheels slow. Vibrations shimmy through my feet and up my legs. After the brakes screech to a halt, I weave between grunting porters unloading the baggage compartments. A woman's blue wool skirt, softer than any fabric I've ever touched, swishes against my hand.

When a racking cough nearly knocks Nana off her feet, Granda helps her step into the coach. We sit on two wooden benches facing each other in the cabin car's center row.

I scramble for the window seat then gasp when a train on the next track rolls by close enough to rip my arm off if I stuck it out.

People from around the world board. I have been transported somewhere strange and wonderful. One man's head is wrapped in a turban of black cloth, and a thin mustache rides above his equally thin lips. A white linen robe flutters around another's ankles. The piece draped over his head and past his shoulders reminds me of Nana's Easter Sunday tablecloth. Many men wear tailored suits, others denim overalls. The swish of women's colorful dresses reminds me of peering through Mrs. O'Shea's kaleidoscope. Some passengers wear hats. Others have silk scarves or colorful fabric wrapped around their heads. Tall, thin, short and bulky; pale as snow, as dark as a lifetime in the sun; hair of every color.

"Nana, what if these people buy all the houses before we find one?"

"Don't worry, lovey. Many will get off before we arrive in LA."

Our Swampoodle landlord was too miserly to install indoor toilets in our 1860s tenement, so we shared the wooden jacks with five other families.

Because I feared the rims that might be damp from the night air, or somebody's pee, Mary hovered me over the seat.

Now as the train rattles and shimmies, I pinch my knees together. When I can wait no longer, I ask for Mary's help. The stall is small and narrow, but the toilet seat opening is large. Mary clutches my waist.

Terrified, I lock my hands behind her neck. Wooden track slats form a moving blur inside the toilet, and a chilly wind whips against my bare bottom. The train wheels clack as if they'll crack and send metal slivers flying up to cut me. I'd ask the Blessed Virgin Mother for help, but this doesn't seem the proper time. But as we reclaim our seats by the window, I tell Mary how grateful I am to have her for my sister. When she smiles down at me, a warmth rises in my chest.

Dingy smoke billows from the chimney stacks perched on the roofs of soot-covered factories. We pass through towns of rundown houses with dirt yards and a field of old cars and stacks of tires.

"Yeh kids are seeing America's backside," says Granda.

"Who lives in these old homes?" Mary peers out the window.

"Immigrants, some Irish, same as us, many from Italy, Poland, South America—well, from nearly everywhere."

Like a picnic on wheels, the train rolls past cities, rivers, and fields as we eat thinly sliced beef and thick layers of cabbage slathered with Mrs. O'Shea's special mustard sauce and sandwiched between slices of homemade rye bread.

"Mam, where do we sleep?" Mary glances toward the rear.

"Curl up as best you can."

"Folks in the forward coach have beds," says Ed.

"We'll make do." Granda pats the seat. "No sense wasting money better spent on a new home."

Joe covers his ears. "How're we supposed to sleep with the metal wheels clanking? Besides, this bloody bench is too hard. Hurts me bum."

"Lap of luxury compared to our sailing ship." Nana covers her mouth and coughs. "May the Lord shine His mercy upon us if we ever again travel on a coffin ship."

"What's a coffin ship?" Ed wipes mustard off his mouth.

Joe snorts. "Carries dead people, eejit."

Granda chokes and spits a spray of black coffee.

"Desperate Irish ran from one kind of death to another." Nana shivers and rubs her arms. "All searching for a better life, but powerful waves washed many overboard into seas so frigid, heart attack took 'em afore they felt the cold. The term coffin ship has survived since the 1840s when thousands escaped the potato famine only to die because of the horrible conditions on the ships."

"Many starved to death. All our passage came with was salt pork and bread as hard as flint." Granda gulps his last bite of sandwich. "Nothing as good as Mrs. O'Shea's homemade rye."

"Many died of dysentery."

"Nana, what's diss-en-tary?"

"Begorrah, lovey. Given your fear of toilets, we best leave that out of the story."

Goosebumps rise when Granda strolls two fingers up my arm. "Typhus and cholera left many an unholy soul dooterin' around the deck at night."

Nana smacks his hand away. "Stop now. She's gonna have dead folks wandering through her dreams. While some say unclean habits and low morals of the Irish caused these diseases, that's bunk. Cholera took my father, and he was meticulous in his habit, never missed a service and never swore. Though, he drank more than his share."

By the next afternoon, I imagine myself a sardine crammed into a teeny can. I walk the aisle, stretch my legs, then stare through the window into the coach behind. My nose makes an oily smudge on the window as I imagine myself as one of those passengers, relaxing on a soft cushion and enjoying the snacks passed out by a woman wearing a white apron.

A girl who looks six, like me, unwraps a large cookie, takes a bite, and grins at her mother. When chocolate crumbs tumble and catch on the white lace surrounding the pearl buttons on her blouse, I pray, *Dear Holy Virgin Mother, just one cookie would be nice.*

As I return to my seat, the train emerges from dusty neighborhoods of tiny homes and smoking factories graying the sky. Our second day is nearing its end, but for now, the sky remains clear and blue as we pass through fields of tall grass swaying in the breeze.

I tell my mother, "I could hide in there, even standing up."

"Winter wheat. Men harvest the golden stalks and grind the wheat berries into the flour I use in my farl and freckle bread."

"But your flour is white."

"They bleach it."

"Same as Da's underwear?"

"Sort of like that, silly goose."

Mam hands me a strip of dried beef. I take it hesitantly. "Can we have a warm dinner tomorrow if we behave?"

"Can't afford to waste the food we brought." Da pats Mam's knee. "Your beef jerky tastes grand, especially when I wash it down the ole pipe with a nip from me flask."

Not ready to give up, I employ my method of batting my eyelashes at Granda that usually gets me what I want. "I smell roasting meat."

"Begorrah. I do too. Now, ladies, if you'll excuse us, Da and I will join the gentlemen's card game in the smoking compartment."

Mam feeds Billy his bedtime bottle then pats his back. He obliges her with a sour burp.

In the distance, the tall buildings' lights twinkle like hundreds of stars falling from the sky. Butterflies flutter in my stomach when the world darkens as if the train entered an enormous cave.

I curl up with my head on Mary's lap. "I miss Mrs. O'Shea." A single tear tickles my cheek as it makes its escape. I sleep soundly until the slowing chooga, chooga disrupts my dreams. Then, I rub my eyes and squint into the morning sunlight. The sign hanging from the platform roof reads, *Kansas City Union Station*.

A lean man wearing a dark blue uniform saunters the coach aisle. Nestled in his palm is an ornate timepiece attached to his belt by a long gold chain. "Train stops for fifteen minutes." The conductor winks at me. "Be six days until we roll this track again. Best not be late getting back on."

Families gather on the platform. Three children, dressed in their Sunday best, watch their father's finger trace the red, blue, and black lines on the enormous map inside a glass case on the wall. Other passengers inspect paper train schedules then step back when the coach doors open. Flared skirts swirl around women's calves as they board. Young girls in ruffled dresses flounce and scurry after their mothers.

When Joe and Ed career off the train, Da grumbles, "I'll make sure the boys don't make a holy show."

I smooth my wrinkled flour sack dress. "If you don't mind, Mam, I'd rather wait here."

"I'll stay with her," says Mary.

A man wearing a brown suit and yellow necktie motions to our grandfather. He pumps the man's hand so hard I worry he might yank it off.

"Granda made a friend."

"I believe you're right, Katie. That's the man he plays cards with, the one who gave him the manky cigar," says Mary.

Granda leaps off the platform, onto the coach steps, and hurries up the aisle. He waves as if he hasn't seen me and Mary in days. "Where'd everybody go?"

I point toward the exit.

"My news won't wait. Girls, the wind is at my back. I've got a job, and a fine one at that."

"I'm proud of you." That's what Granda tells me when I do something that pleases Mam. What he's done is even better. "Now will we get the house with a large window facing the morning sun so Nana can warm herself while drinking her morning tea?"

When Granda nods, I reach into my pocket and give Molly a gentle squeeze to message her all this will make Nana well.

As my family returns, Nana takes Granda's arm. "What's making you so blessed happy?"

"Behold the new supervisor of making bricks for construction projects and steelworks at the Colorado Fuel and Iron Company."

"You mean California," says Mam.

"I said what I meant. And the job pays more than your husband's and my Philly salaries together."

"Are there palm trees in Colorado?"

Mam swats my leg. "Hush, Katie. I'll sort this out."

"But you promised I could buy Mrs. O'Shea an ocean postcard."

Mam grits her teeth. "*Katie*, I said *hush*."

Nana wheezes. "But we're headed to sea air."

Granda sets his feet as if bracing against a storm. "Dr. Doyle also recommended elevation to clear your lungs."

"You can't change our plan without a family talk." Mam glares at Da, who appears unable to meet her eyes because he's counting his shoelace holes.

"Captain Lambourn, the company's vice president, says Pueblo is known for its clean air and sanitariums to treat consumption. This and the promise of a high-paying job makes Colorado the best choice for my wife and me. He guarantees Da employment as well. Not as a supervisor same as me, but a decent wage, enough to support you and your kids, if you can avoid having more. Daughter, when the cat lets go of your husband's tongue, you'll realize he wants it too. I hope you'll come with us, but either way, Nana and I will transfer to the Pueblo train at the next depot." Granda puts his arm across my grandmother's shoulders and pulls her to him as if she agrees.

"Nana needs sun and salty air," says Mary.

I'm feeling brave, so I join my sister's effort to persuade. "Seaside picnics and—" I scoot out of reach of the hand Mam swings toward my thigh.

"*I speak* for this family." Mam's known to slap people who say words she doesn't want to hear, so I hold my breath until Da finally raises his eyes.

"People are losing jobs faster than a dog sheds hair. Here's me and your father, offered good positions from a man we didn't even know before last night's poker game." Da abruptly stops speaking and inspects his shoelace holes again.

"That's a fact." Granda pats my father's back. "What's more, the banker in the smoking coach said thousands empty their accounts and leave for California, but jobs are scarce. Another fella saw men hawk their cars to buy food. In fact, he witnessed entire families living on the streets."

"Husband, can I speak with you in the back?"

Heads swivel. Mam stabs a finger into Da's chest so many times I fear blood will spurt out. Then, my father motions toward us and talks up a storm. Surprisingly, Mam stops poking him and appears to listen.

Billy, long fed and burped, waves his chubby baby hand when my parents return. The clench of my mother's jaw warns she's in no mood to appreciate Billy, no matter how cute his baby antics. "You know I can be difficult to persuade."

Da mutters, "Amen to that."

Mam ignores him. "I'm not totally convinced, but Colorado may be best, all things considered."

I rise to protest this terrible decision.

Mary rips me back into the bench seat and shoots me the *don't-be-stupid* evil eye.

CHAPTER FIVE

DECEMBER 21, 1929

The wheels clank slower as the train chugs up the mountain. The whitest snow I've ever seen blankets the ground. Unlike Philadelphia's dingy gray roads with potholes and mud-filled ruts, not even an animal track blemishes this immense coverlet of fluff, sparkling in the sun. Only stately dark-green pines interrupt this quilt of white.

Granda draws Nana close. "She's got a chill."

Da groans as he pushes up from the bench. "I'll find the conductor. The radiator's not getting enough steam."

I slide my doll inside my sweater, wriggle out of my coat, and tuck it around Nana's lap. "I have my flannel nightgown underneath, so Molly and I are plenty warm."

"Mam, you raised a fine young girl." Granda blinks his reddened eyes and clears his throat. "I have an announcement."

Mam snaps, "Another one?"

I think, Oh, dear, this is going to be bad.

"This announcement yer gonna enjoy. Tomorrow morn, we'll pull into Pueblo. Tonight, to celebrate our good fortune, I made reservations in the dining car. My treat."

The polished cherrywood walls glow beneath the lighted ceiling fans. Four sets of sparkling silverware lie upon each tablecloth, as white as fresh milk. Red velvet curtains, tied with black braided cord, frame each window.

"You kids sit together." Mam points to a table across the aisle. "Don't make me regret it."

I crouch and peer at Ed through the center of my tent-shaped napkin. As I giggle and stick my tongue into the tunnel, my napkin flies.

"*S'il vous plaît.*" A handsome dark-haired waiter in black pants and vest snaps my napkin in the air and lays it atop my lap. "*Mademoiselle.*" The menu he places before me is printed in ebony script inside an embossed border. I'm so excited I can barely hold still, but I do because I'm embarrassed to have this waiter think I'm a total child.

SPECIAL SUPPER 75¢

INCLUDES ROLLS, BUTTER, DEMITASSE
CHOICES
FRESH SHRIMP CREOLE WITH RICE
CHICKEN LIVERS & BACON ON TOAST
SMALL TENDERLOIN STEAK, MUSHROOM SAUCE
& LONG BRANCH POTATOES

Joe smacks his lips. "Steak for me."

"Men's food." Ed sits taller in his chair. "Me too."

I say, "No on the chicken livers."

Mary points to the shrimp and steak. "Want to share?"

I've never tasted either, but I think these are foods rich people eat every day, so I eagerly bob my head.

"*Tres bien. Excellente,*" croons the waiter then fills our glasses from a crystal water pitcher.

I feel the heat of Mam watching our every move, so I'm careful when I take a sip. I watch her from the corners of my eyes, and when she gracefully lifts the crisp linen napkin from her lap and dabs the corners of her lips, I do the same.

Mary grins. "If this is a sign of what our new life will be, I'm gonna love Pueblo."

The following morning, as Granda and Da drag suitcases from beneath the bench seat, Molly's head peeks out the neckline of my sweater, and we stare out the window. Long jagged icicles hang from the Pueblo Union Station sign. Tiny ponds of melted ice shimmer in the sun. Huge droplets drip off the dingy asbestos roof and slither down the brick depot walls. Red-nosed reindeer smile, and black-hatted snowmen wave from the windows on which they are painted. I wave back as if they are real.

"Are these people getting off, or not?" Joe bullies his way through the other passengers.

"Not a palm tree in sight."

"Katie, I'm in no mood for complaints." Mam adjusts Billy on her shoulder, steadies Nana with her free hand, and bumps me forward.

I grumble out to the street and kick a mushy snow pile. "This can't be good for Nana."

"According to Captain Lambourn, Pueblo has the least snowfall of any Colorado city," says Granda.

Mam yanks my collar. "You're gonna make us miss the trolley."

I scramble to get a seat by the open window.

Mary twists my head toward a dress shop. "When I get babysitting jobs, I'll buy the grandest dresses."

"For me too?"

"Sure, why not?"

The trolley driver stops after only two blocks and announces the Vail Hotel. Da grumbles, "Guess we wasted money on this ride."

Granda nods toward Nana. "Not a waste at all."

She raises her head from his shoulder, "Pueblo's a younger town. I like the look of it."

"Our lives will be different." Granda beams and helps Nana navigate the trolley's steps.

Dangling my suitcase from one hand and clutching Molly in the other, I step toward a tall building the color of a baby fawn.

"Behold the Vail Hotel, Captain Lambourn's recommendation." Da tips his flat cap to Mam. "Isn't it grand?"

My mother's eyebrows pinch together. "I fear a bit too grand."

Atop the roof, an enormous American flag flaps in the frosty breeze. Inside, golden light from the crystal chandeliers bounces off windows as enormous as any storefront. After counting the rows of smaller windows so high they appear black, I announce, "Six stories tall."

"Clean air. A perfect blue sky." Nana draws air deep into her lungs. "Exactly what Dr. Doyle prescribed."

"You'll be your former spunky self in no time," says Granda.

"We'll all breathe better." Mam bounces Billy as he starts the wup, wup that precedes his wails. "Here, here. No reason to twist yourself inside out. We're spending the night in this lovely hotel."

I peer through the double door's oval windows. Flames dance in the fireplace. Two women perch in blue brocade upholstered chairs on each side of a delicately carved table. The woman closest to me wears a blouse the color of the clotted cream Mrs. O'Shea and I made to spread on the scones she received from a friend who now lives in Britain. Her pencil-thin skirt is the color I imagine the inside of a seashell to be.

I smooth my skirt. How could I stay in a place where people wear such fine clothes?

The lady wearing a heavy pearl necklace that drapes to her waist pours from a rectangular china teapot painted with a cottage surrounded by flowers. Steam rises off the golden-brown liquid. I smile, even though I feel sad remembering my last tea party with Mrs. O'Shea and drinking from the delicate, gold-rimmed cups she inherited from her mother.

When the heavy door closes behind the adults, my oldest brother, Joe, lifts Ed as if he's the baby and heaves him off the porch.

Ed tumbles and raises his fists. "Want a knuckle sandwich?"

Mary picks up her suitcase. "Come, Katie. There'll be hell to pay when Mam catches the boys acting the maggot."

I move to a window as far from our brothers as I can get. My breath makes a fog circle on the glass. In the lobby's center stands an enormous fir tree. Tiny white lights sparkle and reflect off red and silver bulbs. Cotton puffs perch on dark green branches as if snow fell through the hotel's roof. Beneath the graceful boughs sit boxes wrapped in colorful Christmas paper and tied with red velveteen bows.

I'm pretending the two largest gifts are for Molly and me when the adults step out and Ed throws a snowball that hits Joe's head.

"Yeh puny gobshite! Hope yer fond of hospital food 'cause I'm comin' after yeh."

Da's eyes bulge from his angry red face. "Knock it off, boys. People will think we just got off the boat."

I place my hand on the hotel's ornate brass door handle.

Mam's face looks sad when she spins me away. "We won't be staying."

We walk several blocks before halting at a red brick building. A soggy newspaper lies in a muddy puddle near its base. Mary reads the writing on the wall. "Walter's Market. Dr. Henchal, Dentist. Max's Shoe Repair."

"The hotel clerk said this tenement is more likely what we can afford." Da points toward black letters painted high on the four-story wall. *Rooms for Rent.*

"Not as run-down as our place in Philly," says Mary.

We wait curbside until Da comes back out and waves us in.

I feel the urge, so I ask, "Where are the jacks?"

"Our flat has an indoor toilet."

"Da, I love this place."

"The elevator's out, but the manager is getting it fixed." Da hands Joe a key. "We're on the fourth floor. Ed, help me with the steamer trunk."

Mam repositions Billy on her hip and lifts her suitcase. Joe stuffs a small case under his arm, hefts a large one in each hand, and grunts on every stair.

On the second-floor landing, Granda gasps, "Nana needs a rest. We'll catch up shortly."

Da calls back, "From what the manager said, I think this flat is twice as big as ours in Swampoodle."

"Do Joe and I get our own room?" asks Ed.

"Son, it's not that big."

"I'm sick and tired of sleeping with the girls."

"Sweet Jesus. Tell yeh what. Sleep outdoors. Tomorrow, let me know if you've changed your mind regarding sharing a room with yer sisters."

"Sorry, Da. I didn't mean it."

When we reach the fourth floor, Joe unlocks the door. "This place is a kip, a bleedin' dump. Smells like the toilet overflowed." He drops the suitcases and storms out when Mam raises her hand to him.

"Can't go anywhere without a fight," mumbles Mary.

Nervous, I brace myself, "Mam, is this the new home we've been talking about?"

"No, Katie, it's not, and please don't whine. I'm plain worn out." Mam skims her hand over the scratched iron countertop. "Kitchenette is small, but I can clean it."

Granda grasps the front doorjamb and grips his knees. "We made it."

Nana inhales like a balloon with its mouth stretched tight. "Oh, my. What's that smell?"

Da hangs his head. "Appears the toilet overflowed."

Granda helps my grandmother sit in the closest chair. "Not to worry. Given our new higher wages, we should dooter about tomorrow and shop for a house."

Mary and I beam and leap out of the way of Mam's flying feet when Da lifts her and spins like a merry-go-round. "Darlin', I promise you a finer life."

CHAPTER SIX

---✦---

CHRISTMAS 1929

The solitary reason I don't demand to be returned to the depot so I can catch a train back to Philadelphia is Mam says I've grown enough to enroll in school. Finally, I'll make friends. But even that doesn't stop me from letting everyone know this is our worst Christmas Eve ever.

"No tree, no bulbs, no fairy lights. Mam left our decorations in Swampoodle. We don't even have popcorn to string. I'm asking to spend our savings on a Christmas tree instead of a house."

Mam glares around the corner. "Get out of bed. We're going house hunting."

Joe shoves Ed off their bed, and Mary whisks the blanket away from me.

As I touch my bare feet to the frigid floor, Mam hollers, "Change of plans. No sense house hunting until these men bring home the paychecks they've been bragging about. But Da and I have an errand that needs doing. The rest of you are staying home."

Two hours later, when our parents walk in, Mam orders us to our bedroom.

We scurry as told, then Joe smashes his ear against the closed door. I wriggle in and press mine too.

"What's going on?" whispers Mary from where she and Billy sit on the bed.

"Quit flapping your gums so I can hear," mutters Joe. "Da asked Mam what she expects for fifty cents."

"Shush," I say. "Paper's crinkling."

Joe backs away. "Somebody's coming. Act normal."

The hinges rattle when Da pounds our door. "We know yer listening. Come on out."

A scraggly three-foot tree stands on the sofa table. Four pocket-sized boxes wrapped in shiny red paper nestle in the folds of the white terry towel wrapped around the tree's base. With a devilish grin on her face, Mam reveals a thin packet of construction paper and the red metal tin of Jolly Time popcorn she was hiding behind her back. "We'll make our own decorations."

Ed and Mary beam, but I sniffle.

"Glory be, child," says Mam. "You cried because we didn't have a tree, now you're blubbering because we do."

I hug my mother. "Thank you, Mam. Will you help me write to Mrs. O'Shea? I must tell her how wonderful this Christmas is."

Six days later, Mam announces it doesn't matter that we barely know our neighbors; a New Year's potluck is tradition, and she already invited them. I'm thrilled, so excited I wriggle with joy until my mother hands me a bucket.

"Mam, we should mop after the party. People have dirty feet."

"Cleanliness is next to godliness—guarantees a fresh beginning." Nana hobbles to the kitchen counter and grabs yesterday's loaf of bread. She braces against the sofa arm and gives the door three whacks. Chunks fly and crumbs tumble. "Can yeh feel it? The negativity moving out?"

"Nana, I'm trying to clean this floor."

"Now the good spirits know they're welcome."

Mam points to the far side of the sofa. "Katie, bread hunk."

Mary holds the edges of the white tablecloth Nana embroidered fifty-eight years ago, in 1871, for her wedding trousseau and unfurls it over the supper table.

Mam says people who buy bootleg alcohol end up in the clinker, so she hides ours behind the oatmeal bag, but now she sets the tall bottle at one end of the table.

I arrange water glasses around the whiskey in a perfect circle then sniff the raisin and spice porter cake. "Beer? Will I get drunk?"

Mary ruffles my hair. "Nah, silly. You'll be fine."

Mam lifts the lid from the stockpot that's simmered all day. Corned beef, sugar, and garlic aromas tickle my nose.

As the wall clock chimes nine, someone kicks the door. When Da opens it, Ruby from across the hall bustles in. He says only a Mack truck can stop her hips once they commence jiggling and joggling, but he never says it when she's around.

"Couldn't knock, hands are full." Ruby carries a Christmas tree-shaped platter piled high with shortbread biscuits drizzled with red frosting. Her low-cut neckline shifts as she sets the platter on the table.

Joe leans as if reaching for a glass and ogles down Ruby's blouse. His eyes bulge, then he gasps when Da hooks his index finger inside my brother's collar and jerks him upright.

"Sweet Jesus, Da. You're choking me."

"Coleen's at the rear of me with plum pudding," says Ruby. "Don't know who's following her, not her bag-of-shite husband. Be glad for that. The bum would eat half the table before anyone else got a bite."

Coleen swishes in wearing an emerald-blue chiffon dress. Her Eau de Cologne assaults my nose. "Meet my Bobby."

The tall redheaded man offers two bottles of pink wine. "May the thorn in your New Year's hangover be a Wild Irish Rose."

Ruby takes the bottles and winks at Coleen. "Glory be, we like your new man better than the former."

"Look who arrived. The Kozaks." Da towers over dark-haired Moshe and pumps his hand. "Esther, let me take that heavy pan."

I sidle up and gape. Yam cubes and long fat leeks float in the juices of a big-breasted, golden-brown roasted chicken.

"Seasoned with thyme and chopped fennel," says Mrs. Kozak. "Makes a festive bird, don't you think?"

"My mouth's a'watering," says Da.

Nana tightens the shawl around her shoulders. "The Espinoza family's coming in the door."

I'd spotted the girls in the hall a day ago but wasn't brave enough to speak.

"Meet the twins, Elena and Elizabeth," says Mam.

Elena opens her palm, revealing a brown ball the size of the dough balls Mam uses to make Irish Whiskey Caramel Thumbprint Cookies. Elizabeth spreads her fingers to reveal the five metal jacks in her palm.

After a year of praying for a friend, the Holy Virgin Mother sends two. Granda was right. Pueblo is a better place than Los Angeles. I present Molly to the twins. "We want to play."

Minutes before midnight, Granda motions toward the table. "Please, help yourselves to a measure of whiskey."

"Apple cider for the children." Mam carries a gallon jug.

Mr. Espinoza opens the brown paper sack he had placed on the counter. "My wife cut grapes into bunches of twelve each. *Las doce uvas de la suerte*. Eat a single grape with each chime of the clock and you will have good luck."

"I can use that," laughs Coleen.

Ruby tips her glass toward Bobby. "I'm thinking you've got all the luck you need."

"As long as my husband stays away."

Mr. Kozak lifts his drink. "*Sláinte mhòr!* My wife and I wish you and yours a blessed year."

Mr. Espinoza drapes his arm across his wife's shoulders. "We come together, full of hope and good wishes, to share our traditional dishes. *Feliz años nuevo*."

Da raises his glass. "We toast this new year."

Granda clinks his glass against Da's. "Remember to forget the troubles that pass your way, but never forget to remember the blessings that come each day."

"And say a prayer for the millions who lost their jobs after the stock market crash," says Mam.

"And may the Colorado State Insane Asylum take my Uncle Oisin back." In the awkward silence, Coleen adds, "As janitor...Not inmate."

Ruby's eyebrows rise. "So you say."

Redheaded Bobby bends Coleen over his arm until her hair touches the floor and kisses her. Ruby swoons, but Ed and I scrunch our noses.

While the women collect empty dishes and pans, the men shake hands and pat each other's backs.

When I ask Elena and Elizabeth, "Will you play tomorrow?" the twins smile and nod.

After the door closes behind the last guest, Nana picks up our carving knife. "Thirty minutes into the Day of Buttered Bread, and for the first time, we can be honest as to our situation. Good fortune will follow us throughout the year."

Granda stretches like a cat. "Can't this wait until morning?"

"It cannot. Katie, get the butter." Nana slices two, inch-thick slabs off the freckle loaf, spreads a generous coating, and slaps the bread together.

"Do I eat the sandwich?"

"No, lovey. Put it on a plate and set it outside our door so everyone knows we won't be hungry during this bonny new year."

My stomach is full of party food, but I haven't forgotten the times hunger pangs kept me awake. I glance back inside our flat. Mice will eat the bread and the creamy butter before our neighbors awaken and note the message it sends. Nobody would know if I took a quick bite, but what if I bring bad luck when our lives are going so well?

I'm the last child in bed. I'm proud because I only ate a raisin, yet Mam's upset voice turns my smile upside down.

"It's been hours since Joe snuck out. Only the good Lord knows what that boy of yours is up to."

"He's celebrating with his new friends," says Da. "It's only a few minutes after one."

CHAPTER SEVEN

JANUARY 1930

When the clock strikes eight, I drag my sleepy self out of bed. Mam isn't speaking to Da. Somehow, it's his fault Joe didn't come home last night. Us kids don't want the blame for setting off a fight, so we spend New Year's Day quietly playing games. Even Billy seems aware of the danger of letting out a wail. When he wants a bottle, he raises his pudgy hands and grunts.

After eating party leftovers for supper, Ed plays marbles while Mary washes dishes and I sweep the kitchenette floor.

As soon as we finish, Mam points toward our bedroom. "I'm in no mood for any guff. I'm going to St. Francis Xavier Church, and you kids are going to bed."

We change into our nightclothes. Mary rocks Billy and tells me and Ed the story of the headless horseman. We squeal and hide beneath the blankets until Granda commands, "Keep it down in there."

Determined to witness the fight when Joe comes home, I flap my hand against my thigh, wiggle my toes, and hold my eyes open until they burn. Then, I lose the battle to stay awake.

But early the next morning, I perk up when Mary says, "Joe spent the night in the clinker."

"Zip it." Ed draws his hand across his lips. "The fight's getting good." Mary and I join him and press our ears against the bedroom door.

"Da, I deliver a bottle or two to my boss's friends," says Joe. "Pete says the country's headed into the worst depression ever. Not everybody's as lucky as me, to have a steady job."

"How do your mates buy their pints?"

"Two or three different jobs, a few hours here and there. Da, I'm the new fella. Need to impress my bosses. This delivery was a personal favor so I could get on their good side. Yeh needn't rile yerself."

"Coppers don't stake out a lad unless the favor stinks of breaking the law."

"Nah, that's not it. Carlinos lost their farm. Honest family men trying to make a living."

"Yeh think I'm stupid? You're delivering bootleg. I read the newspaper. Carlinos built hundreds of stills from here to Denver."

"Nah, I mean, sure, Da, a few. No news on that front. Pete and his brother Sam are business folks."

"So why didn't these upstanding business folks pay your bail?"

"It was an accident that I was in the wrong place at the wrong time. A rival tipped off the beat cop because Pete infringed on his territory. Don't think Pete or Sam even know I was arrested. Wasn't nothin' against me personally."

"Doesn't sound like nothing. Yeh kids are starting new schools. Get a record and you'll find yourself on a work farm."

"School will never know."

"You're a bigger fool than I thought," says Da. "Half the block knew before I got to the station and bailed you out."

"I'm fourteen. No reason to stay in school. I'll get a full-time job and my own place."

"Your mam spent half the night at St. Francis Xavier. Kept me awake the other half mumbling Bible verses about stoning rebellious sons. Wasn't even dawn when she headed back to light more candles and pray Saint Christopher brings you home with all your body parts."

"She needs to understand, I'm an adult."

"Joe, you're the one who needs to understand, staying in school is the only way your mother's gonna let yeh live. Don't let me catch yeh with them Carlino thugs again."

"I'll approach Captain Lambourn," says Granda. "A few part-time jobs are coming up at Colorado Fuel and Iron."

"Thanks. I'll find my own. Gonna meet up with the lads who hang around Benowitz's hardware store."

"Joe, yeh stink. Did somebody wipe the floor with yeh? Clean yourself. Mam should be on her way home." Da yells toward the bedroom. "I know you kids got your ears glued to the door. Peel 'em off. Show's over."

New Year's morning tradition is Mam serves a stack of golden boxty. It didn't happen yesterday because of the ruckus Joe caused by not coming home. Remembering Mrs. O'Shea says every little problem looks better when golden boxty are frying in the pan, I hope Mam will cook them today.

Da tosses a box of Muffets Shredded Wheat on the table as I enter the kitchenette.

"None of us likes Shredded Wheat."

Da points to Granda and himself. "None of us cares."

Ed walks up behind me. "Can't we wait for Mam's boxty?"

Mam tromps in and slams the front door. "Where have you been?"

Joe cringes. "All fixed. I explained it to Da."

She pokes him in the chest. "Try telling me."

That afternoon, Mam acts as if the incident with Joe never happened. She even hums "When Irish Eyes Are Smiling." Her knife clangs the beat as she halves the mayonnaise, lettuce, and peanut butter sandwiches lined up on the iron countertop. When we finish lunch, she announces, "The girls and I are going shopping. Peoples Drug Store is discounting notebooks and pencils."

I squeal and twirl with delight. Not only have we girls never gone shopping without at least one of the boys, today we will buy my very first school supplies.

At Peoples, we select eight marbled composition books, two for each school-age child. Mam lets me choose a pink pencil box. I feel giddy just thinking about using these on my first day of school.

As we walk back to the bus stop, Mary peers into the beauty parlor window. "I'm sick of this childish long hair."

Mam points to a flyer taped to the window. "Can't afford five dollars. I'll bob your hair."

"Me too? A big girl style for my first school day?"

My big sister glares. "We are *not* wearing the same hairdo."

"Enough, Mary. I'll cut bangs on your sister. Besides, Katie's hair has more curl, so the cut will look different on her."

Later, Mam snips Mary's hair then pats the chair to signal it's my turn. She combs my hair smooth, pressing so hard the plastic teeth scrape my scalp, but I don't complain. I remain as still as a statue as Mam saws the dull scissors through my thick brown hair.

Mary twists a strand around a finger and crisscrosses two rippled-metal bobby pins on the fat curl as Joe struts in. "Yeh birds look like boys. No self-respecting man will marry yeh. Don't be thinking I'll support you two old maids the rest of yer lives."

The four days until January 6 pass slowly. I'm frenzied from debating what should be the first words I write inside my new composition book with my freshly sharpened #2 pencil. Yet I'm as happy as a bumble bee sucking nectar while walking to school with Mary and Ed until they peel off toward their classrooms and leave me alone in the hall, remnants of this morning's eggs, fried in bacon fat, rise in my mouth.

I pat the fringe of my newly bobbed hair. Even Da complimented me, saying I am now a young lady rather than a girl. Still, a terror tingle runs up my neck. But Molly's nestled inside my skirt pocket, so I step into the classroom.

Children pivot and stare.

A spindly woman glares over the tops of her gold wire-rimmed glasses. "I am Miss Carter. Who are you?"

"The new girl." I smile big so the teacher will think I'm happy to join her class.

"I received no notice."

A brown-haired boy in the second row snickers, "Leprechauns appear out of nowhere."

I ache to belt him in his big fat mouth, but making a good impression on the teacher is more important. So, when Miss Carter beckons me forward with one long bony finger, I say, "Yes, ma'am."

"Write your name on the chalkboard."

My hand quivers, and the letters squiggle as if the room is biting cold. When I return the chalk to the tray, it falls and shatters, sending white flakes onto Miss Carter's black Mary Jane shoes.

I'm wishing my shoes weren't scuffed lace-ups when she says, "Good Lord, girl. Are you always this clumsy?"

I intend to apologize, but first I bend to wipe chalk dust off the teacher's shoes.

"Stand up, girl. Tell your classmates about yourself."

"My parents and grandparents came from Ireland on a huge, old wooden sailing ship." I strain to still my knocking knees and act as if I don't notice the students snickering. "But I came to Colorado on a long, sleek train."

Miss Carter harrumphs and lifts a book off her desk. "Students, please open your *Pathway to Reading* primer to page fifty-five."

The children open small blue and gold books.

Was I supposed to bring my own? I panic until Miss Carter hands me the finest book I've ever held. I run my finger over the embossed cover picture of a boy running with his dog. The boy wears a soldier's helmet and balances a sword on his shoulder. His dog's tongue dangles as if he's excited to join his master on a grand adventure.

"Children, the new girl will read aloud."

The lines blur. Letters move on the page. I squint at one student then the next. Will they know if I tell the story I pretend to read from Mary's schoolbook, my made-up story about white horses that fly higher than any bird, horses with rainbow-colored ribbons flowing in their manes? Cold sweat pools in my armpits. "Miss Carter, I don't know this story."

"Just read the words."

"I haven't learned all these. May I begin on page one?" A small tremor strikes my hand. The pages flutter.

"Didn't you learn these simple words in your previous school?"

I drop the book, hightail it outside, and hide behind a schoolyard tree. A deep, rhythmic voice reminds me of Father Bertram preaching the word of God. The heavy-set woman looking down on me looks blurry through my teary eyes.

"My, my. Is school goin' that bad for you?"

I sniffle and nod.

"The kids call me Mama Louise. Come with me to the cafeteria." Once inside, she steps behind the counter and hands me a small milk carton. "Did those sassy boys abuse you, darlin'?"

My heart swells to the size of a watermelon and crushes against my ribs. Mrs. O'Shea is the only person who ever called me darlin'. "I couldn't read the words."

"Ah, yes. I heard the principal forgot to tell a teacher about the new student assigned to her. That means you ran afoul of Miss Carter. Lousy luck on your part."

"She hates me."

"Don't let her hurt your feelings, darlin'. Miss Carter doesn't care for me either. Speaking to negros is beneath her. But mostly, she's cranky on account of turning thirty with nary a marriage proposal. It's true she's tough, but not as tough as a strong Irish girl such as yourself. Throw that empty milk carton in the trash, and I'll walk you to your classroom."

In the hallway, I release Mama Louise's hand because the big-mouthed boy will tell everyone I'm a baby. But first I give it a squeeze, so she'll know I'm grateful.

"Remember, Katie, life's a cup of tea. Some teas are strong and bitter; others weak, no flavor to speak of. Either way, it's for you to add the honey. Don't let those hooligans ruin the sweetness of your life. And if you come upon a situation you can't handle, you know where I am. Now, hold your chin up and march yourself into that classroom."

I'm too timid to speak for the remainder of the school day, but it doesn't matter because nobody pays me any attention. When the bell rings, I fiddle with my new yellow pencil then tug my sagging white knit stockings up over my kneecaps. When I'm the only kid left in class, I plant myself before Miss Carter's desk.

"Katie, can you not see I am grading papers? I do not tolerate students who interrupt my work."

"This is my first time to attend school."

"You should have begun in September, wherever it was you lived."

"Mam made me wait until we moved to Pueblo. I was too small, and Swampoodle too dangerous."

"Swamp-oodle? Where on Earth is that?"

"Philadelphia, ma'am. If you let me borrow the reading book, my older sister will teach me the words. Tomorrow, I'll read as good as any other kid."

"Students are not allowed—"

"I'll clean the erasers and stack your papers." I straighten my shoulders so Miss Carter can't see me squirm.

"Oh, all right. But bear in mind, you'll pay if you lose that book."

Then, the following morning, Miss Carter requests a volunteer, so I raise my hand and wave as if to a long-lost friend.

She asks Robert to stand and read, but the instant he finishes, I thrust up my hand, only to be ignored as if I don't exist.

The called-upon girl, dishwater blonde curls tied neatly in a yellow bow, flounces her store-bought skirt. Her voice is as smooth as butter spread on warm bread.

When Julia closes her book, I raise my hand again. "Please, Miss Carter, may I read?"

"You couldn't read a word yesterday. Why should I call on you today?"

"My sister taught me last night."

"Nonsense. You couldn't learn that fast."

The boy in the back row snorts. "Irish kids got mashed potatoes for brains."

Big brother Joe speaks inside my head. *Ryans don't let no fool give us guff.* I shoot the boy my *don't-mess-with-me* glare then still my shaking hand and raise the primer to my nose. "Page 65. 'On down the road went Billy Boy and his friends. Just then a pony came by and said...'" I deepen my voice the way the horse in the book might sound. "'Where are you going, Billy Boy?'"

Miss Carter peels off her wire-rimmed glasses. "I misjudged you, Katie."

My knees quit quaking. I square my shoulders and tilt my chin. "'I am going to seek my fortune, and my friends are going with me, said Billy Boy.'"

The next morning, Miss Carter calls me to the front. A creepy tingle behind my ear warns me something is about to go wrong.

"Children, raise your hand if anyone ever judged you unfairly."

"My brother said I couldn't eat an entire apple pie," calls out the redheaded boy. "But I did. He judged me wrong."

The children snicker, but I don't even smirk. I've suffered under their ridicule and won't take part.

"Thank you, Roger, but that's not what I meant. Katie demonstrated a first impression is not always correct. Because she wears a homemade potato sack dress and scuffed shoes, we judge this poor immigrant as not smart enough to read."

My face is on fire. I want to run. Instead, I stiffen my spine and lick my lips. "Excuse me, Miss Carter. I'm a citizen, born in the United States."

"Ah, well, children, Katie speaks a common Irish dialect, yet that makes her no less smart than you."

"Miss Carter, I read just fine. I was nervous because I'm new."

"Ah, yes, but I'm speaking now. I'll let you know when I want to hear from you. Students, we must lend a helping hand to Katie and others such as her."

I slink back to my chair. I should have stayed on the train. Surely nicer people live in Los Angeles.

Julia wears a dress more ruffled than yesterday. "My mom has a red, flowered flour sack. I shall bring it so your mother can sew you a better dress."

"A generous offer," says our teacher.

I fume, smooth the multi-colored rickrack Mam spent hours sewing on my hem, then chomp off my pencil eraser. The moment Miss Carter dismisses class, I snatch my lunch tin and scurry to the cafeteria. I have no money, but that doesn't stop me from peering over the counter of steaming food. An aproned woman bustles toward the refrigerator, and another serves. The janitor pushes his broom. When my classmates file in, chatting and laughing, I can't take any more.

The janitor glances up from the food scraps he's swept into a pile. "Sho'nuff, little girl, don't believe you should leave."

"Why not?"

"Teachers don't cotton to that none. I reckon you best wait."

"I'm searching for Mama Louise."

"Not working today."

I sit at a table in the rear corner, pluck a small, boiled potato from my lunch tin, and sulk.

Julia peels an enormous orange and shares juicy pieces with the girls who surround her. I tell myself they are twits. Still, I wish they'd invite me to their table. If I had the same lunch period as Elena and Elizabeth, I wouldn't have to sit alone. It takes every bit of my willpower not to watch Julia and her admirers sashay past.

I enter the classroom last, but Miss Carter doesn't notice because her attention is on the multiplication problem she's writing on the blackboard.

The lad across the aisle keeps his voice lower than the chalk's screech and leans toward Roger. "Hey, Tomato Head. Does Santa know you stole his suspenders?"

Earlier, as students waited in line, Roger confided he has no belt. I'm sympathetic to his plight because I don't own a belt either, yet I have problems of my own.

When Miss Carter releases the class for recess, I scramble to meet my only friends.

Elizabeth swings one leg over and steps off the teeter-totter, dropping her twin to the ground. She thunks on the ground. "*Casi me matas! Creo que me rompiste la pierna.*"

"*Silencio, por favor.* Elena, your leg is fine. It's our friend who's hurt. See her tears."

"Nobody likes me."

Elizabeth pats my shoulder. "Not so, *mi amiga*. We like you."

The black-haired boy who sits in the last row with a scowl on his face signals three others to follow. When he snatches up a mud clod, the boys do the same. "Look what we have here, fellas. Two bean heads and a potato breath."

"Leave us alone." My heart races, yet I square my feet, raise my fists the way Joe taught me, and throw a punch that misses the fella completely.

The lads laugh, and the black-haired boy says, "Ooh, I'm sooo scared."

Elena swings and clobbers him.

The twins' teacher, Mrs. Napoli walks up behind and grabs the boys. "Girls, go to my classroom. I shall join you after I escort these gentlemen to the principal's office."

As we wait, I admire the brightly colored pictures of lions, tigers, and other wild animals tacked onto Mrs. Napoli's bulletin boards. I especially fancy the *Welcome Students* banner above the chalkboard. Miss Carter's banner is the ABCs.

As our teachers enter the classroom, Elizabeth and I hold very still and fold our hands in our laps. But Elena rubs her leg as if to remind everyone she's suffering from the fall.

"Miss Carter and I assure you, no one will treat you girls badly again."

"That's much appreciated, Mrs. Napoli. How will you stop them?"

"Not your worry, Katie. We have the issue in hand."

At the school day's end, I bolt to where the twins wait near the schoolyard gate with Mary and Ed.

Elena motions me over. "Tell your brother what those boys did to us."

Ed hunches into his boxing stance and pummels the air. "Show 'em to me. I'll take 'em out."

"We'll be okay as long as they don't get us alone," says Elizabeth.

I ask Mary if I should tell Mam what happened.

"Nah, some things are best left unsaid. This is one of those times. She was hanging over the toilet this morn, face as green as spinach."

CHAPTER EIGHT

MARCH 1930

Pueblo streets bustle. Store owners open doors to entice customers and gentle puffs of spring air to enter. A signboard on the sidewalk reads,

Used Red Eye Treadle
50% Discount

I beg, "Please, Mary. Let's go look."

Ed steps toward a parked car and whistles. "Niagara Blue 1928 Phaeton. First year it came in any color other than black. Wonder who owns this beauty? Need me a job like his. Crack on, girls. I'll wait on this curb, admiring this automobile."

Inside, fabric bolts line the walls: plaids, stripes, and flowers. I brush my fingers against crisp cottons and wools as soft as bunny ears. "Imagine the clothes we could sew, blouses with butterfly sleeves, straight skirts that flare at the calf, and a reversible housedress for Mam."

I don't tell my sister everything because the last time I complained Da wouldn't give me money for a new dress, big brother Joe said, 'Toughen up. Everybody's got it rough.'

But before I realize what's happening, my words blurt out of my big mouth. "Mary, I got slagged because of my underwear."

"You showed your unders?"

"On the monkey bars. Nobody gets across as fast as me. Two girls threw down a challenge, so I showed them a thing or two. But I swung my feet too high, and they saw the 100-pound weight printed on my bottom."

"I guess you *did* show them a thing or two. Lots of kids wear homemade underwear. Wear your whites and you'll be fine."

"They called me crybaby."

"Lordy, Katie."

"I tried holding back. Honest, Mary."

"Didn't realize the girls were so hard on you."

As we stroll outside, Ed rams his hands into his pockets.

I ask, "Who'd you wave to?"

"Uh, nobody. Just the most incredible automobile I've ever seen."

"That was Joe, wasn't it?" Mary shoots our brother the *you'll-be-sorry-if-you-lie-to-me* squint. "Is the car his?"

"Nah, his boss let him drive it to deliver crates of Sugar Moon."

During the bus ride home, my mind whirls around the idea of owning a Singer and making beautiful dresses. I'm imagining how Julia and the other girls will want me as their friend when Mary says, "We both need new clothes. I'll do some babysitting."

"I'll find a job too."

"That's sweet, Katie, but there's not a lot available for seven-year-olds."

Saturday morning, Mary rips lined paper from her composition notebook. We make flyers to tuck under neighborhood porch mats and into doorjambs. At the last house, a frantic woman opens the front door with a howling baby balanced on one hip and another kid's pajama neck gripped in her free hand. As two more thigh-high children peek around her legs, Mrs. Murphy glances at the flyer and offers Mary a job. Wilted leaves hang over the sides of starting pots near the picket fence. I offer to plant her broccoli and dig up weeds for a nickel and am delighted when the frazzled mother agrees.

At supper, we chatter happily about how much money we will earn, until Ed interrupts. "If yer not hungry, slide your stew my way."

"Not a chance." Mary fills her spoon with lamb, fresh peas, carrots, and leeks floating in a rich brown gravy. "This is better than any meal we ate in Philly."

Granda wipes his mouth. "There's only one way to go from here, and that's up. CF&I increased employee salaries by five percent. And Captain Lambourn complimented me on running a tight ship, says brick production is up twenty percent, and so is my paycheck."

The adults click their whiskey tumblers together.

We kids raise our water glasses and cheer.

"Guess we'll be having lamb stew every day." Ed pokes out his pink tongue and sloppily catches the gravy dribbling out the corners of his mouth, reminding me of the giant lizard at the city zoo.

"Thank the Lord for our good fortune," says Mam. "When I pass soup lines wrapped around city blocks, I think, there but for the grace of God.... Men, heads hanging, women with children huddled at their feet, more than a person can bear."

"Hundreds applying for a single job. This family is blessed." Da pats Mam's belly. "And now we need a larger house."

I wriggle with excitement. Six children are a bunch, but surely this will be the sister I ask the Holy Virgin mother for every night.

Joe swaggers in, but no one calls him out for being late.

"I want an electric stove," says Mam.

"A separate bedroom for us lads, please, Da."

"Ed, I'll do what I can, but bear in mind, we're buying a house, not the Queen's castle."

Granda pats Nana's knee. "Most important is a coal furnace to keep my girl warm."

"This should help." Joe smacks a stack of dollar bills onto the table.

Da's face reddens. "How'd yeh get your hands on so much money?"

Molly gets frightened when Da shouts, so I dip my hand into my pocket and cover her ears.

"I made special deliveries."

Mam wrinkles her nose. "I don't like the smell of this."

"On the square, just helping my family." Joe kisses our mother's cheek.

Da refills his glass but never thanks Joe for the money. Everyone knows after his third whiskey comes the fourth and the point at which Da upsets easily.

Ed shuffles a deck of cards as the adults meander into the living room. "Knock Rummy?"

I jerk my head toward Da. "Knock quietly."

With each card Ed deals, Mary's frown gets deeper, and I get more excited. I inspect my tenth card and chuckle under my breath. All I need is to swap out the ten of spades for a six of diamonds and I will triumph. But before I draw my first card, Billy lunges across the highchair tray, grabs the upcard, and yowls when Ed rips it from his slobbery mouth. I jerk my head around to watch for what Da will do.

"Blast yeh to hell! Can't a man have a peaceful drink in his own home?"

"Now you've done it," mutters Mary. "Haul your butts to bed. I'll offer our apologies."

We gather around the supper table. Before anyone takes a bite, Granda clangs his knife against his glass. "I've got another announcement. A young fella at work lost his wife."

"Beastly news," moans my tenderhearted Nana.

"Sweet Jesus, that's not my announcement. His wife dying is a terrible circumstance. My news is the lad wants out from under the payments, and he's selling his house."

My grin stretches across my face and spreads as wide as Granda's.

"Mam, you need to go to the bank," says Da.

"Tomorrow's wash day. Can it wait?"

"Best not. Thousands are closing their accounts. By day's end, the banks might not have enough to give us our hard-earned savings, and we need to make a payment to secure that house."

"I'll catch up with you and withdraw me and Nana's funds," says Granda. "As soon as I get my crew set to the work needing to be done."

The following evening, Mam glances up from mending Ed's ripped trousers. "Good fortune that I left early for that spool of thread 'cause I ran into a line of people two blocks long."

Da hesitates with his whiskey glass an inch from his mouth. "Big sale on thread?"

"You're not paying attention."

Da pushes up from his chair. "Is this gonna be a long story?" He whisks the whiskey bottle off the counter. "I'd offer you a bit if there was more than a wee nip left."

"Do you want to hear what I have to say or not?"

I consider hiding. Sometimes when my mother gets angry with Da, she screams at us kids as if it's our fault.

Da holds his back, grunts, and lowers himself into his chair.

"Word comes, it the bank's line, not Singer's." Mam slips off her shoes. "My feet hurt like two whining dogs. Still, I inched along and struck up a conversation with a woman ahead who stood in line all day yesterday without getting inside."

Granda removes a flask from his shirt pocket. "I'm legging it toward Mam when a man pokes out his head and shouts, they're only taking ten more customers. We were lucky to be sixth in line, on account of that's when the cursing and shoving began."

I sense Molly's worry, so I ask, "Mam, did you get shoved?" When she shakes her head, Molly and I are relieved because the sister growing inside my mother's tummy didn't get hurt.

"Been donkey years since I got stuck in a group so riled. Had to duck a few flying beer bottles." Granda pats Mam's hand. "I felt like a coward, being too old to be much good at protecting you."

"Sorry you went through that," says Da. "I should have gone instead of sending you."

I'm caught by surprise. As Granda says, an apology from Da is a rarified event to behold.

"We withdrew our savings, and that's what matters," says Mam.

A month passes before, on a sunny April day, my family climbs the three red brick steps of the front porch that runs the width of our new house. "If we got a bench, I'd do my homework outside on warm days."

Joe winks at Ed. "Any bench will be for us fellas to watch for bits of fluff who foot it this way."

My father sets his cardboard box on the wooden porch and inserts the key in the lock.

I wriggle past and through the open door. "Da, the owner forgot his furniture."

"Ours now. Should be beds upstairs, one for you girls and another for the lads."

Having never experienced a bed of my own, much less how one can own the flat above their heads, I ask, "Doesn't another family live there?"

"First upstairs claims the best room," shouts Mary.

Joe grabs her waist. "Won't be you."

"Run, Katie!"

I thunder up the stairs, but my excitement sinks into dismay. Feeling as if I have been tricked, I stomp my foot. The identical rooms are large enough that Mrs. O'Shea could have lived with us, if she had come.

Word of Mary's babysitting skill spreads, and as mothers learn she celebrated her twelfth birthday, they hire her for longer stays. Mrs. Murphy pays me a nickel each time I tend her vegetable garden. My sister and I save our money in a Mason jar hidden in our closet's deepest, darkest corner, where neither Da nor the boys will find it.

Several weeks later, Mary brings home two shopping bags, one from Leeds Shoe Store and another from H.S. Kress. She slides her feet into black and white shoes, ties the laces, and extends a foot. "Saddle oxfords, all the rage."

I'm a bit steamed when she removes a blue plaid skirt from the second bag. Mary spent the money we agreed was to buy a Singer, which means I can't sew a new Easter dress. I fight the overwhelming desire to call my sister a selfish maggot because I fear she might quit sharing the Baby Ruth candy bars she also buys. I can't risk that, so I tell Nana, "I'm not going to Easter services."

"Got to admit, Father Bertram goes on and on in the name of our Lord. The more important the occasion, the more he builds up steam. But Katie, there's an egg hunt afterward, both chocolate and the hard-boiled kind."

This news makes me twice as sad.

Nana pats her thigh. "Sit in my lap, lovey, and tell me why you'd stay home."

"My classmates brag on their Easter dresses."

"And..."

"The girls poke fun at what I wear."

"Bloody bints. Haul me up from this chair."

Nana is as unsteady as Billy trying to learn to walk, so I support her elbow until we get into the bedroom. Her joints crackle like tinfoil when she kneels to open the steamer trunk. She brings out a white cotton dress with long satin ribbons radiating from its waist. When my grandmother drapes it over my shoulders, and the folds gather gracefully around my legs, I feel like a princess.

Mam pokes her head into the room. "What are you two up to?"

"My wedding dress isn't doing anybody any good setting in this old trunk. We could use your help making it into a new Easter outfit for Katie."

"I'd be happy to help," says Mam. "The pearl buttons will show off her cute shape. Everyone will think it's store-bought."

"Remember the young ladies strolling the upper deck?" asks Nana. "So grand, swishing their skirts all the way to the New York shore. Offering a peek of their corded petticoats, as if that might catch a man's eye."

"I remember it well, Mother. And the pretty gal who was so busy watching the young men watching her, she tripped on a coil of wet anchor rope." Mam spreads two sheets of *The Pueblo Chieftain* on the living room floor. "Lie down. I'll cut around your body." When I giggle with anticipation, she pokes my ribs. "Hold still, wiggle worm."

Nana smiles as if reliving her special day. "Warms my bones to behold my wedding dress free of that musty old trunk."

"You aren't mad at me for being selfish? Letting Julia and her snooty friends get the best of me?"

"Don't think that way, lovey. I'm as happy as a clam at high water. Fabric this fine deserves to be worn and admired."

Mam cuts the newspaper along the curve of my hip. "Plenty for two dresses. Those girls will die of green-eyed envy."

"I'm eager to witness that." Nana's hands tremble as she picks the seam between two skirt panels. "But I'm worn out."

Mam and I each take one of Nana's arms and help her shuffle toward her bed. A croupy cough racks her body. She wheezes, "I'm freezing."

My mother presses a palm against Nana's forehead. "You're on fire. You need another dose of morphine. Katie, bring Mrs. Winslow's Soothing Syrup and another blanket. We'll sweat this fever out."

When Nana snores, Mam says, "Mrs. Odell bragged about a doctor who healed her youngster of a bad flu. You know, the girl next door you met the other day. I'm going over and ask the doctor's name."

"Molly and I'll sit beside the bed." I gaze deep into my doll's eyes so she will understand we both need to pray for our grandmother. We wait patiently until Nana awakens, then I coax her to eat three spoonsful of homemade chicken soup. "Would you like me to read to you?"

She nods weakly, so I open my book. "Mrs. Kozak gave me *A Girl of the Limberlost* by Gene Stratton-Porter. Her daughter doesn't read it anymore because she's older now. I haven't learned all the words."

"Make them up. I won't know the difference."

"It's about a poor girl who lives near a swamp. She wants an education, but her parents can't afford it, so the girl, her name is Elnora, collects moths and sells them."

"Smart. And determined."

"I am too, Nana. Nothing will hold me back."

"Good girl. Life is hard."

I skip a few words, but what I read makes sense until in the third paragraph I come to Onabasha. Frustrated, I flip the page and begin my own made-up story. "Once upon a time, there was a princess. Nana, her name was Katie, same as mine. She owned beautiful dresses and wore a different one every day. Her best friend, who she loved very much, was poor because she had lots of brothers and feeding them cost a lot. Not only that, they tore their trousers because they played rough, then their mother had to buy more. Princess Katie brought her friend to the castle and let her choose ten dresses to place in a golden trunk. Her brothers obeyed her every command, so they loaded the trunk into her carriage, pulled by four white horses. Then, the princess took the reins and drove the beautiful dresses to her friend's cottage in the woods."

A soft smile appears on Nana's face, and her breathing slows. When Mam steps in, I put my finger to my lips. "She's asleep."

"Keep reading, Katie. Your voice soothes her."

As my mother closes the bedroom door, I wonder if I should confess that I told Nana a pretend story because the book is too hard. But I quickly set my worry aside and continue on. "The Princess decreed that anyone who spoke ill of her friend would face beheading in the castle square. The two girls lived happily ever after and stayed best friends their entire lives."

Later, everyone except Nana, who still sleeps, gathers around the supper table. Mam says, "Mrs. Odell's doctor will pay us a visit on his way to the hospital in the morn. Such a kind man."

Granda smiles, then a frown flits across his face. "Should I stay?"

"Nah, you best not show up late so soon after your boss was nice enough to give you such a hefty raise. I'll tell you what the doctor says."

The following morning after Joe, Ed, and Mary leave for school, I shake the wooden rattle to entertain Billy. I'm expecting Rose because we pinky swore to walk to school together every day. But when I answer the knock, a man carrying a black medical bag tips his hat.

"Doctor Newell here. Is this the Ryan home?"

"Yes, sir. We need you to make my grandmother well."

Dr. Newell tilts his chin to Mam, then leans Nana forward and puts his stethoscope against her back. "Breathe deeply, please."

"Are my grandmother's insides okay?"

"Young lady, would you like to listen to her lungs?" Dr. Newell gently tucks the ear-tips into my ears.

"Sounds like our new cereal, Rice Krispies."

"Doctors call it apical crackles. This tells me your grandmother has more than a cold."

Nana rests back against the chair. Her breath sounds like gravel scraping through a narrow pipe, and her hand drops as if clenching a heavy rock rather than a cotton handkerchief splattered with dried blood.

"You're exhausted, aren't you?" When Nana struggles to raise her head and meet his gaze, Dr. Newell asks, "How would you describe the pain?"

"Like a knife."

He shakes a thermometer and guides it into my grandmother's mouth. "Mrs. Ryan, how much weight has your mother lost?"

"I'd guess twenty-five pounds. Always been slight, but now she's a wisp of her former self. I fix tasty meals, but she has no appetite."

"Night sweats?"

"Most nights."

When Dr. Newell removes the thermometer, it sticks to Nana's dry, wrinkled lips. "Mrs. Ryan, how long has your mother had this fever?"

Mam's lips turn down in a worried frown. "Months, on and off. The Philadelphia doctor said Colorado's fresh air and higher altitude would help."

My fear rises when a chill vibrates Nana's body like a breeze against a dried leaf. I know Molly is worried about what the doctor will say next, so I pat her in my pocket, hoping that will comfort her.

"No one else has symptoms?"

"My youngest, Billy, had the croup. I set him in the highchair in front of the open oven door, and the heat dried his cough right away."

"Young man, may I place my stethoscope on your back?" Dr. Newell nods as he listens. "His lungs are clear. Your boy is fine."

Mam holds her palms out as if she wants the doctor to inspect them. "We scrub our hands extra well. I wipe the counter and sink with Lysol, like the Philly doctor said."

"Continue those measures, but this disease spreads more through air than touch. Position your mother near an open window or outside on the lawn. Instead of cloth handkerchiefs, have her use tissues and dispose of them immediately. Mrs. Ryan, may I speak with you in private?"

"Katie, wait on the porch."

I take my lunch tin and step just outside the door, close enough to make out what the doctor says.

"Mrs. Ryan, your mother has tuberculosis."

"Dr. Doyle said consumption."

"That is the common term for tuberculosis, especially at its onset."

"Oh, Lord, what have I done? I should've gotten a better doctor, a different medicine."

"Mrs. Ryan, this is not your fault. Science provides no cure for TB."

I peek in around the doorjamb. Mam's face pales, a sign I know means she's as panicky as Molly and I. Still, in fear of making her mad and the punishment I'll receive for disobeying, I resist the urge to run back inside.

"Doctor Newell, will my mother die?"

"We need an x-ray to inform us of the severity."

I'm unaware of Rose's approach until my friend asks, "Why are you crying?"

I explain what I overheard as we walk to school. The weight in my chest grows heavier with each step. The school day passes in a blur. I'm sure I will never smile again.

But as we walk toward home, Ed meets us on the corner, pushing a clanging, banging metal mop bucket on wheels. "Did you steal that?"

"Nah, found it in a vacant field. Good place to store my bolts and nuts and other supplies. Stand on the rim. I'll give yeh both a ride."

The wheels wobble. Rose and I squeal each time the tub hits a crack in the road. We lose our grips when Ed jerks to a halt at Rose's house. "I'm going ta hide my bucket behind the shed until the right minute comes along to tell Mam about it."

Later that night, Mam, Da, and Granda head out to the back porch. I creep up, worrying Mam will find Ed's bucket and make him return it. She sees me with the eyes in the back of her head and sends me inside. I slam the screen door, then hide in the shadows where I can still hear.

Granda growls, "Damn it, we'll get that x-ray. Never should have bought this house. My money would have been better spent on a sanitorium."

I hug Molly because the word sanitorium scares her, then step back from the door, hustle past Billy, who is leaving a trail of cracker crumbs across the kitchen floor, and slip into Nana's room. "Are you awake?"

"I am. Cuddle up. Keep me warm."

The arms my grandmother wraps around me feel cold and clammy, but that's not what I complain about. "Nana, your ribs are poking me."

"I'll be putting my weight back on when I beat this cough. How was your day, lovey?"

"I'm sad. I want you to take me for walks like before you got sick. If Mrs. O'Shea had come to Pueblo, she'd mix her special medicine and get you well. She took good care of us."

"Don't be sad, lovey. I'll be up and pecking around like a mother hen in no time at all. Besides, you have Mrs. O'Shea's letters. She's in your heart, and you're in hers. I doubt we're ever going back to Swampoodle, so those letters will have to be enough."

CHAPTER NINE

─────── ⟨∞⟩ ───────

SEPTEMBER 1930

My grandmother's cough doesn't worsen. I almost forget about her illness, especially when Rose and I go swimming at the public pool or downtown to visit the twins, Elena and Elizabeth. Now that summer break is over, I'm excited to return to school, until the night before classes begin again. Then I toss and turn, worrying my second-grade teacher might be as hateful as last year's Miss Carter.

By the day's end, I realize I fretted needlessly. Rose and I have the good luck to be assigned to Mrs. Buttons' class, and she's nice and has a cheerful smile, even if we students don't know the correct answer. When she dismisses us from class, she says, "Tootle loo. See you tomorrow, my chickadees."

Rose and I chat happily as we skip toward Miss Betsy's Sweeter Than Sweet Candy Shoppe to spend the two pennies Mam gave us to celebrate our first day back at school. We select anise hard-candy squares wrapped in red cellophane.

The melted candy sprays purple when Rose speaks. "Have you seen where they lock up children?"

"What children?"

"The ones without parents."

"Their parents died?"

"Some, Katie. Others don't want their kids, so they leave them with the nuns. Around the corner. Not much farther."

"Why would nuns want other people's kids?"

"They make the boys move boulders from one side of the yard to the other and hire them out as farmhands, then keep their wages. Not a penny goes to the boys. The girls scrub miles of stone floors on their hands and knees, clean forty bathrooms, and a gigantic kitchen."

"Doesn't the orphanage have a janitor, like at school?"

"Nope. Every day, the orphans wash a hundred pounds of bedclothes and towels and the nuns' big white underpants in leaky whiskey barrels filled with cold water and lye. Kids who complain get locked in a closet for days."

"Nuns wouldn't do that."

"Yep, they surely do. The ladies who play bridge with my mum gossip up a storm. Mrs. Grady says the nuns work the orphans hard to build their character. Otherwise, they'll end up in a life of sin and no-good. When the nuns aren't slaving those poor kids, they have them kneeling and praying the Lord takes their souls when they die."

Sacred Heart Orphanage looms before us. The building's lower level is grey, the upper three floors dingy red brick. Heavy draperies fill each rectangular window. On the fourth floor, perhaps it is an attic, three windows perch on the roof. A tall spire reaches toward the heavens. The air is heavy and quiet, without a hint of movement inside.

"Rose, have you seen the orphans?"

"Just one. My cousin was with me." My friend's eyes widen. "The annoying pox banged a stick against this fence, made a terrible racket. A big ole nun stormed out screaming and waving her arms, her black gown flapping like bat wings. Scared the piss out of us. That's when I saw the girl, stringy brown hair and wearing a raggedy white nightshirt. Pale as the dead, surely an orphan ghost, except she talked."

"What'd she say?"

"*Help me...*" Rose mimics the ghostly girl by stretching her arms as if to grasp my neck. "But when the nun waved a fist at me and my cousin, the girl disappeared."

Rose's story creeps me out. I feel as if Ghost Girl now watches our every move and reads our thoughts. "Where'd she go?"

Rose shrugs. "Back to heaven? Or maybe behind a tree?"

"What tree? All I see are rocks and weeds."

"No trees?" squeaks Rose. "Run!"

Ten minutes later, chests heaving, we wipe our sweaty brows and hug goodbye.

I conjure Ghost Girl's face as I climb the porch steps. Her lips move. Does she beg for help because she's hungry? I know how that feels. Granda and Da now earn enough for food and a house, but it wasn't always so. Is that what Ghost Girl wants? But living with nuns is as close as a kid can get to living in the house of God, so that makes no sense. I close my front door then nearly jump out of my skin.

"You're late."

At least Ghost Girl doesn't have her mother sneaking up and scaring her to death. "Sorry, Mam. Rose and I had a hard time deciding which candy to buy at Sweeter Than Sweet."

Holy Virgin Mother, leaving off the rest isn't a lie, is it? Probably is. Please, forgive my sin. I'm too worn out to face Mam's measuring stick.

"Where's Ed?"

I pretend not to hear.

"In the Lord's eyes, withholding from your mother is a sin as serious as lying."

"A mortal sin?"

"Not quite, Katie. But all sins add up. Where's your brother?"

"Since it's not a mortal sin, I'd rather he tells you himself. He only got detention because he was sticking up for me."

"Detention? Best you tell me the rest."

"Like I said, Mam, I'd rather you hear it from him."

"You're in too deep for that. Or should I get my measuring stick?"

I gauge Mam's anger as at a three-swat level and spill the beans. "After Mary headed toward Central High, me, Rose, and Ed were walking across the play yard, minding our p's and q's, not doing a thing wrong, promise, Mam. When we split up to go to class, this great big fella, I don't even know him, tripped me and called me an awful name."

"What did this great big fella call you?"

"A hoor."

"And what did your brother do?"

"Ran back and knocked him flat. A teacher yanked Ed off the brute and drug them both to the principal's office."

"And what did you do?"

"Rose and I ran to class like a banshee was coming to announce our death."

"Were you hurt?"

"No, Mam. Just my feelings."

The front door creaks. "Get in here, Ed. I've something for you."

If Ed had a tail, it would be between his legs.

"My stomach's tied in knots." Mam pats her growing belly. "Thought I'd settle it by eating bread."

My eyes bulge as she scoops a thick pat of Bossie's Best. I was with my mother when she scolded the market owner because the butter cost fifty-six cents.

"Now, I'm a' thinking you deserve this slice of fresh-baked freckle bread with sugar sprinkled on top."

Cautiously, Ed raises his head. "Aren't I in trouble?"

"For protecting your little sister? Nah, but don't get it in your head that I'm giving you a free pass to fight. Don't want you ending up like Joe, spending more time in the principal's office than in class."

"Um, there's another bit of trouble."

Mam gives Ed the squinty eye.

"The principal didn't believe me. He said setting me on the correct path is his duty."

"It is, but I believe you, and that matters most."

"I'm sorry, Mam, but I got to tell yeh, I have detention again tomorrow."

"Not a problem, Son." Mam presses her lower back and bends over the kitchen sink. "Sweet Jesus, that's a cramp."

Ed yanks my sleeve. "We'd better give our mother some lady time. Me mates are gathering outside. Let's take a go at Kick the Can."

This was an honor of the highest regard. I stood there like a dummy. "Me?"

"Sure. Run get your friend so yeh won't be the only girl."

A week later, the back door slams so hard the windows rattle in their wooden frames. Mary and I spring from bed. Even though it's still dark, we scurry downstairs.

"Where's Da?" asks Nana.

"Out back smoking a cigar," answers Granda.

Mam shouts, "Tell that stinking gobshite to haul his arse in here or he'll be spitting tobacco back up his throat for a very long time to come."

I whisper, "Mary, is our sister getting born?"

"Yep. Get the towels. I'll boil water."

Feet pound down the stairway. "Sounds like it's happening again. I'm outta here."

Granda grabs Joe's arm to stop him. "Could be your new brother coming."

"Don't need another. Already got more of the puny beggars than we need."

My mother clenches her teeth. "Joe, get Mrs. Odell!"

"I'm late, Mam. Can't stay."

"Get her, or you'll be wishing you were the one never born."

"Aye, aye. On my way."

My mother kneels on the bed and grips the iron headboard. "Holy Mother of Jesus."

Nana applies pressure against Mam's back. "Hang on. Your body knows what to do."

Stationed near the bedroom door, arms filled with frayed towels, I focus on the stairs while wishing Billy would bawl and give me an excuse to leave until startled by Mrs. Odell's orange and green flowered housecoat flapping around her ankles as she dashes in the front door. After she snatches the towels from me, I huddle on the sofa and stick my fingers in my ears.

Mam screeches and calls Da a good-for-nothing filthy wanker.

I motion toward the ceiling. "How can Ed and Billy sleep?"

Mary tosses two bloody towels into the kitchen sink. "They're faking. The entire neighborhood's awake."

We spin toward a shrill, "Ahhhhhhhhhhhhhhh...Holy shite!"

A jolt of fear runs up behind my ears. "Did Mam die?"

"No, ninny." The words no sooner escape Mary's mouth than the baby wails.

"Is the coast clear?" Ed carries Billy, who is fighting to get loose.

I smile happily. "Yep, we're waiting to welcome our new sister to our family."

Thirty minutes later, Mrs. Odell pokes out her head. "They're ready for you."

Da and Granda come back into the house, and we line up alongside the bed. Nana stands near the headboard and beams. The bundle in Mam's arms emits a soft *waah, waah.*

"Meet your baby brother, Thomas Joseph."

"That's it. I'm done praying to the Blessed Virgin Mother."

Mam brushes wet strings of hair from her face. "Mary, take Katie out."

My sister shoves me toward the stairs. At the top, I shout, "I prayed for a girl!"

I crawl into bed and snuggle under the covers, but three hours later, my cough awakens Mary. She bumps my shoulder. "Go sleep on the sofa."

Trying to make it look like an accident, I kick my sister as I roll out of bed wearing our blanket like a floor-length shawl. "Sofa's no place for a sick person."

"I need sleep." As I stomp down the stairs, she shouts, "Bring that blanket back!"

Alone and sick, I peek in on Mam talking sweetly to the tiny bundle in her arms. And when he gurgles and coos his response, I forgive Tommy for being born a boy, snuggle with Molly on the sofa, and fall asleep thinking about detouring past the orphanage again after school to find out if Ghost Girl needs my help.

Not only do I cough throughout the night, but fever brings on a sweat. As the sun climbs, I head to the kitchen for a cool glass of water. Pain slices through my belly and bends me over. Orange chunks coated in yellow slime splatter the wall.

"Holy mackerel," says Joe. "That hurl outdid all my drinkin' buds."

Mam scurries from the bedroom and grabs a wet dish towel. "Glory be. Saint Raphael answered my prayers. I was worried sick that cough meant you had TB, but it's the flu."

Monday, I ignore my clammy forehead and claim to be in good health. But I'm sorely disappointed after I knock on Rose's door and her mother appears instead. I would have stayed in bed if I'd known my friend also had the flu. Rather than admit my lie, I drag myself to school.

My new teacher, Mrs. Buttons, treats every student with respect, even when they don't deserve it, like the two stupid boys in the back row who call her Mrs. Butts. I always do my best for Mrs. Buttons, but this morning, I'm too weak to concentrate, so I lay my head on the desk, until my teacher says, "Katie, please solve 8x9 on the chalkboard."

Out of habit, I slide my hand into my pocket to give Molly a comforting squeeze. But now that I'm in third grade, I leave her home. None of Julia's friends carry dolls around.

I solve the math problem, but as soon as I'm back in my seat, my mind wanders to the time Nana said a person shouldn't draw attention their way when it pertains to unearthly beings. Perhaps going alone to the orphanage is a serious mistake?

"Katie, I called upon you twice." Mrs. Button looks at me kindly, but questioning. "Please spell citizen." The know-it-all who sits behind me snickers, but I pretend not to hear. I hold my head high and recite, "C-I-T..." He won't be laughing when I rescue Ghost Girl.

Still, I'm uneasy when I reach the rickety orphanage fence. I should go home, but my feet move forward. The gate latch creaks. What was I thinking, coming alone? I brace against the gate until my heart pounds its way back down my throat, then sneak toward the lone ground-level window with its drapery pushed aside.

When I spot the girl, I think my brain is playing tricks. Yet I wave. The girl's enormous black eyes sink deeper into her deathly pale face, and the heavy brown drape closes. My heart leaps into my throat, and I bolt. The gate clangs, but I don't stop to check if it closed properly. Four blocks away, I slow to a jog. Was the girl alive or dead? Should I go back and help her?

That night, the girl's pale face floats behind my closed eyes. Did the nuns jerk her away from the window? Or did she enter the afterlife right before my eyes?

I yank the blanket over my head, curl into a ball, and swear not to return to the orphanage until Rose is well.

CHAPTER TEN

MARCH 1931

After I finish my Saturday chores, I scamper to Rose's. The house is quiet, the kind of quiet that tells you nobody is inside. Still, I knock then sulk home.

I help Nana hobble to the wicker chairs that Da carried from the porch to the lawn because the brisk spring air is what both of Nana's doctors prescribed. The way her wasted muscles shift when I tuck the blanket around her thin legs gives me the willies, but I don't let on, not even when she pats my hand.

"Be glad you're not tall like Da and the boys. Husbands prefer wee wives."

"I'm not interested in a husband."

"Has a boy kissed you yet?"

"Oh, Nana."

"Lovey, the blush rising in your cheeks tells me one has. Spill the beans."

"Fourth grader."

"Irish?" When I nod, Nana says, "Don't be holding back."

"His name is Francis. Boys poke fun, say it's a girl's name."

"Did you like the kiss?"

"I guess. I hardly know him. Happened fast, like a butterfly on my cheek." I stare as if I've never seen my grandmother before. Why did it take so long to realize she's the best friend I could have? Someone who listens to my worries and secrets and loves me no matter what.

"You might want to get to know him if you want another kiss." The rhythm of Nana's raspy breathing slows. The sun warms our entwined hands, and my heavy eyelids close.

When the weekend arrives, my tulip bulbs shoot up tender sprouts as if they have no fear, even though the weatherman predicts frost. Billy makes engine noises as he propels his small wooden car, a gift for his third birthday. On the top porch step, Mary balances Tommy on her lap and tickles his lips with the baby bottle nipple to coax him to drink while Mam takes a much-needed nap. Ed's lying on his back, blowing into the grass whistle he made instead of digging up weeds. As usual, nobody knows where Joe is.

When Da finishes mowing, I scoot our wicker chairs to the yard's sunny side. I have an hour to bring Nana out before Rose's mother takes us to a rerun of *The Love Trap*. I'm hurriedly wiping dew off the chairs when Granda's wail shoots through the air like an arrow to my heart.

"No! Please Lord, no!"

The mower handle thuds to the ground as Da leaps onto the porch. The screen door slams behind him.

I don't understand what is happening, but punishments spread from one child to another, even the innocent, the way fire skims dried leaves, so I stay put. Then, I realize Granda's high-pitched scream sounds as if he's calling someone far away.

"Come back, my love. Come back."

As I follow Ed into the house, Mary hands me Tommy.

Billy cowers against the sofa.

Mam lifts the receiver of our new phone. "I'll call Dr. Newell."

"Too late. The love of my life is gone." Granda clamps onto the bedroom doorjamb. His shoulders cave forward as Da guides him back to his wife.

I nuzzle Tommy's baby-soft neck. When he pats the tear on my cheek with his pudgy fingers, I murmur, "Let's pray."

Ed captures Billy as he tugs the doily beneath Mam's favorite glass lamp then plunks next to me on the sofa.

Molly is in my pocket, but the exertion required to bring her out is too much. "Ed, I feel sick. I should have taken Nana outside more often to take in fresh air."

"Katie, that didn't kill Nana." Ed's twelve, yet he sounds like an adult.

I want to believe him, but the giant hand squeezing my heart means he's wrong. I set Tommy on the yellow bunny quilt Mrs. Parker made when he was born then creep toward the bedroom door.

Mam perches on the edge of the bed, caressing Nana's lifeless arm.

Granda, hunched in the armchair, hides his face in his arthritic hands.

"May I come in?" I walk into my mother's extended arms. After a long hug, I wipe my tears and break our embrace. The frayed rope rug muffles my footsteps. Granda doesn't notice me, so I rest my palm atop his enormous hand.

Mam exhales a long, painful sigh. "Stay with him while I call McCarthy's Funeral Home."

I whisper, "I loved Nana so much. Granda, I don't know what I should do."

His jaw sags. Dark skin puckers like wrinkled cloth draped below his vacant eyes. A violent sob wrenches up from his ribs. I remove a hanky from the bureau, wipe his eyes, then dab mine. He rolls off the chair, onto the bed, and molds his body to Nana's.

I feel like an intruder. So, I step outside the bedroom, close the door, and sit cross-legged to block those who might violate my grandfather's last moments with his wife. When I close my eyes to pray, no words come. As Rose and her mother open the front door, I realize I should greet my friend, but I can't even raise my head. I don't acknowledge anyone until a large presence looms over me.

"Young lady, I'm the coroner. May I go in?"

When I open the door, my grandfather's shattered breath fills the bedroom. Two men squeeze by me with a gurney. Even Tommy and Billy watch until they leave with Nana lain out beneath a white cloth. Granda stays at his wife's side until the men slide her into the hearse.

"Will you bury my grandmother now?"

"No, dear." I am comforted when the coroner's expression softens. "I'll return her to you tomorrow morning for the wake."

The antique wooden wall clock chimes. Mary returns the hands to 11:45.

"Why stop the clock?" asks Ed.

"Tells guests the time of Nana's death."

I blink to soothe my burning eyes. "Not a good time for guests."

Mary points toward the gold-framed oval mirror. "Ed, help me flip this against the wall."

"Why?"

"If Nana's soul leaves through the mirror, she could wander into another world."

"What other world?"

"Sweet Jesus, Ed. I don't know. We're helping Nana find heaven."

I murmur, "Thank you."

"Lots needs doing." Mary rubs her forehead. "You up to helping?"

I feel my head nod, but my brain is so foggy I'm not sure how it did. I retrieve the mop from the closet and the bucket from beneath the sink. Mary thrusts Bon Ami cleanser, a Lysol bottle, and a thick square sponge at Ed. He snatches the supplies and stomps into the bathroom.

Mary dampens a washcloth. "Let me wipe this table before you mop. People will bring food."

"Why? We have our own."

"Katie, it's for Nana's wake. More than we can feed will come to pay their respects."

"But she rarely went farther than the yard. The Parkers and Rose's mom were her only friends."

"Granda is an important man at Colorado Fuel and Iron. The owner and other men who work with him will attend. And neighbors and friends from church, market clerks who know Mam, the knit shop lady where Mam bought Nana's yarn, the folks who came to our New Year's Eve party, and the women whose kids I babysit will surely show up."

Butcher knife in hand, Mam marches up to the small table beneath the living room window and digs at the sill, sending dried paint flakes flying. Then, she shoves it open with a bang. "It's freed. Katie, clean this mess. Arrange Nana's favorite belongings on this table. They'll draw her soul to the open window so she won't get bound to Earth."

I prop Nana's small black Bible against the sill. The sinking sun glimmers off the gold letters on the cover. Nana's pink kid-skin gloves, the first birthday gift from Granda after they arrived in America, I drape across the Bible's lower edge. As if dreaming, I see Nana admire her gloved hands and say, *Such a thoughtful man. Nineteen cents, an extravagance we could ill afford.*

I touch the blue booties Nana knitted for the baby named James who died the year before I was born. My hand trembles as I set Molly beside the tiny booties. "I have more chores, but you must stay and help Nana get out the window."

I excuse myself after our very late dinner and head to bed. My sleep is restless until Da shouts, "I'll not have their bootleg whiskey in my home."

My father never refuses a bottle, so I tiptoe to the stairs.

"I don't want the Carlino brothers near my home. People die when they're around."

"Da, Pete and Sam understand. Besides, they're hiding out. Sent the whiskey as a sign of respect."

I lean over the rail and catch a glimpse of the angry purple veins bulging like worms on my father's forehead. "A rival gang bombed their house! Want ours blown up next?"

Mam glides out of her bedroom as quiet as a shadow. "Joe says the Carlinos protect him."

"They can't protect themselves. What makes you think they'll protect him? Or us?" Da shakes his fist in Mam's face. "My ears are waiting for your answer."

"I don't have an answer, but you might as well let the whiskey stay. It's better quality than the bootleg I bought, and there'll be plenty of drinking at the wake. Over and above, I don't believe the Ryans want to be the ones to insult the Carlinos."

Da rubs his head the way he does when it hurts.

I creep back to bed.

Parked cars line the street. About four o'clock, guests stream in for Nana's wake. Guinness beer bubbles around hunks of lamb, carrots, onions, and potatoes in Mam's aluminum stewpot. Two bread pan-shaped wake cakes, dripping with powdered sugar icing, await slicing, and the ornate platter Nana brought from Ireland holds four dozen Irish Whiskey Caramel Thumbprint Cookies. Yet the warm, sugary scents fail to entice me.

I sense a pull, as if my grandmother beckons. The thought of even a single peek inside the casket causes painful goosebumps to rise on my neck. But I never disobey Nana, so I move to her side. She wouldn't approve of the maroon tint the coroner painted on her thin lips. I glance over my shoulder, remove a handkerchief from my sleeve, and blot. Then, wearing my most innocent expression, I face the guests.

I recognize Granda's and Da's boss from CF&I. The strange men who follow make me nervous. My grandmother won't take kindly to them eyeing her lying down. But when the Parkers, Mrs. Odell, and Rose arrive, I'm glad. Nana's happy when they visit.

Each woman who enters hugs my mother. Will I ever have that many friends? Mrs. Murphy brings ham and red currant jelly sandwiches made with wheat bread. The knit shop lady brings a bologna casserole. Other guests place shepherd's pies, vegetable platters, and potato wedges on the supper table.

Unsure what to do, I squeeze into a corner and watch through the haze of cigarette smoke. I'm terribly grateful when Rose takes my hand and leads me to the sofa.

Mrs. Kozak hands Mam two odd-shaped bottles. "Kosher wine—when it comes to bootlegging, you gentiles have nothing over us Jews."

Mam fills four cut-glass wine glasses to the brim. "Too good to share with just anyone." As she hides the kosher wine in the cupboard behind the Quaker Oats, Mrs. Espinoza sets a tamale platter on the counter.

"*Mis amigas*, you weren't leaving me out, were you?"

A chilly breeze riffles the pages of the open Bible and blows Molly over onto the blue booties.

Rose's mother gives Mam a goodbye hug and tugs my friend toward the door.

I have never felt so alone, yet our living room is still packed with people, talking, moving, even laughing, as if they are one giant, fuzzy blob. I can't stand the thought of them touching me, or watching me weep, so I work my way through the crowd and climb the stairs.

When I peek in the boys' room, Tommy snuffles like a kitten.

Billy quit sucking his thumb a month ago. He must sense our sadness and has taken up the habit again to soothe himself. Of all my brothers, he tugs my heartstrings the most. With his tender emotions, he's always crawling into someone's lap. I fear what he'll face when he attends school, especially if assigned to Miss Carter's class. At least for now, he's safe.

I enter the room Mary and I share and change into my pajamas. My swollen eyelids are heavy, but an hour later, I'm still awake. I need Molly. So, I tiptoe downstairs, weave amid glasses clinking and people saying goodbye, and make my way toward the table that holds Nana's favorite things.

You did well, my friend. Come to bed.

Granda and Da take their places at the head of the casket, Joe and Ed in the middle, and two men from Colorado Fuel and Iron at the foot. They grasp the gold handles and lumber toward the long black hearse.

My eyes burn as if singed with hot coals, and my arms weigh as much as logs. I'm supposed to get into the car CF&I provided. I even hear my mother say, "Come, it's time." Nothing I tell my body compels it to move.

Joe sweeps me into his arms. "It's okay, Katie. I got yeh."

He sets me in the automobile beside Mary, then Ed climbs in. I am comforted when they each take one of my hands in theirs.

We enter St. Francis Xavier Church's viewing room. "Danny Boy," the song Nana sang while rocking in her chair, drifts from the choir to the mourners. My Sunday school teacher says the dead live in a lovely place where clouds glimmer in the sun as if touched by the hand of God, and every soul finds peace and happiness. But Nana's face is pale and lifeless, without a hint of her sweet smile, the smile that might tell me she is in a better place.

Well-wishers pause and murmur words of respect. Others nervously move past the casket then approach my family and express their sympathies.

A somber, black-suited man speaks to Granda. "If you are ready, we may move into the nave."

The first notes of "The Mountains Mourne" fill the air as mourners approach the church. Father Bertram stops the procession at the entrance and spins the aspergillum, a silver ball attached to a wooden stick. Holy water sprinkles out its tiny holes. The casket is blessed.

Pallbearers follow the priest to the altar. Mam and Da set their pace to Granda's, prepared to steady him should he stumble. My family slides into the front row pew. The air is heavy with the scent of flowers and despair.

Bagpipe notes float in the open door and fade as the pallbearers position the casket, but I turn my attention to the scuffle of shoes and the click of high heels against the tile floor as people fill the pews.

Father Bertram steps up to the ambo. "Please, open your Bibles to the Wisdom of Solomon 3:1. 'The souls of the righteous are in the hand of God, and there shall no torment touch them.'" When he asks if anyone wants to speak, Mam leans against the pew and works her way toward the aisle.

The priest steps from the ambo and offers my mother his hand. She clutches the lectern's wooden edges. Her knuckles whiten. Her voice is weak.

Mourners lean forward in their seats.

The microphone amplifies the air Mam sucks into her lungs. It sounds like wind rushing through tree leaves. "My mother will walk with me and never leave my side. When she speaks, her words come directly to my heart. As tiny as she was, and as frail as she became, my mother, Katherine Caroline Busby Maguire, Carrie to her friends and Nana to her eight grandchildren, was the strength of our family. Now, she rises and takes her own long-passed baby James, and my infant son named for him, to her bosom, into her loving care until I join them at our Lord's feet."

I balance on the edge of my seat, expecting Mam to need support. But her hands are still, her breathing calm, when she returns to us.

Granda steps up. The microphone, perched on a silver stand that accommodated Mam's shorter stature, crackles when he bends close. His deep voice fills the void of the church ceiling and the niches in which statues of saints reside. "My soul is a bird that has flown away, never to return."

The pain piercing my chest brings a sob to my throat.

"I fell in love with my wife the moment she spoke my name—her voice as smooth as silk. I knew she was the woman I should spend my life with, if I could convince her to marry me."

Tittering ripples throughout the church.

"She didn't say yes the first time I proposed, and I don't blame her. I can be a bit irritating."

"Amen," rings out from a rear pew. Even though my heart swells with affection for Granda, I can't suppress a giggle.

"I spent our sixty years of marriage doing my darndest, sorry Father, to convince my wife she hadn't made a mistake by marrying me. I can only say no other woman could have loved me more."

The handkerchief in my hand is damp and wadded into a knot. I pull a thread from the flowered border Nana crocheted for me. With each tug, my heart unravels more.

Granda reaches inside his suit jacket and removes his reading glasses and a folded sheet of paper. "I'd like to read a bit of a sermon given by a priest, a Mr. Henry Scott Holland, at St. Paul's Cathedral in London in 1910. He's an Englishman, but we won't hold that against him."

When mourners chuckle, a soft smile crosses Granda's face. The microphone broadcasts the crinkle of the paper he unfolds and the ahem of clearing his throat.

> *Death is nothing at all.*
> *I have only slipped away to the next room.*
> *I am I and you are you.*
> *Whatever we were to each other,*
> *That we still are.*
> *I am but waiting for you.*
> *For an interval.*
> *Somewhere. Very near.*
> *Just around the corner.*

Granda steps down from the microphone and places his hand on the casket. His voice quakes.

I lean over the kneeler, leverage the pew's bookrack to pull closer, and strain to catch his words.

"Save my place, my love. I'm an old man, too weary to continue without you." He bends and kisses the casket above the blanket of white roses, where Nana's head would be.

When the church falls as silent as a vacant room, Nana speaks to me. *I'm here, lovey. I promised I'd never leave you, and I never will. When we have our private conversations, you must be very quiet because the world will drown me out.*

Mary breaks my trance by nudging my foot. "We're done."

People gather outside the church. I search for Rose, but before I find her, Mary drags me by the hand.

"Where are we going?"

"Roselawn Cemetery. Get in the car."

Da starts the engine and follows the hearse. I lean against the window and search for a sign of heaven between the tree branches and fluttering leaves. The motor's hum and the car's gentle rock lull me to sleep as Da slows to the pace set by the hearse's driver.

My mind is still hazy as the men place Nana's casket on a low brass stand at the grave's dark and shadowy edge. My family sits in metal folding chairs on the opposite side. Mourners form rows shaped like a fan.

In voices that flow as smooth as fresh honey, three women from the church choir, white robes fluttering around their ankles in the breeze, sing "Toora, Loora, Loora." When the choir comes to the lyric of remembering the lullabies sung to them as a child, my head, too heavy to hold up, rolls toward my chest. I can't even raise my hand to wipe the tears streaming down my cheeks.

CHAPTER ELEVEN

———— ⧖ ————

MAY 1931

A soft golden ray peeks between the curtains as I lie in bed and listen to the quiet. Nana's cough had become background noise that barely registered in my mind. Now, I miss the sound. Even though two months have passed, loneliness still attacks like a pointy stick jabbed in my side. I wrote Mrs. O'Shea a letter because she's the person with whom I share my deepest emotions, the only person who will understand what I must do to quit crying. Every night, I pray for a speedy reply.

I pad down the stairs, thinking about how our mother hadn't slapped any of us since the funeral until last night, but Joe deserved it. Acting uncommonly kind, Mam had said, "Joe, I'm making beer-baked beef for Sunday supper. I'd be pleased if you invite your girlfriend."

"Nah. She's a geebag, not me girlfriend."

Mam's hand flew so fast Joe couldn't duck.

I sense, like me, my mother craves to throw a glass or plate, make them shatter into a million pieces, and hurt them as she has been hurt. Joe provided her an easy opportunity. I believe Mam's grief has burrowed into her bones, just as it did into mine. So, I'm careful about what I say and distract the boys with food or a game of catch in the yard when their loud voices or mischievous antics threaten to push our mother over the edge. But Joe's unexplained absences and drunken behavior are beyond anyone's control.

I feel sorry for Da when Mam glares at him, and he hides behind his newspaper and waits for her to leave the room.

Tonight, Joe's making deliveries. Mary is babysitting the Murphy kids. Ed's in the street between the makeshift goal of two metal garbage cans, ready to dive, bat, or hurl the sliotar ball at the neighborhood boys.

I'm nervous because I don't know how to ease the sorrow setting Mam's nerves on fire. I can't even do it for myself. But my problem for the here and now is I'm the only child left in the house who's old enough to become the victim of her misery.

I lift my brother's undershirt and blow a raspberry on his bare belly. "Bath time, Billy Boy."

"Wanna play boats?" Billy's eyes sparkle with anticipation.

Our round-bottomed, cast-iron tub is my favorite thing and the one place in this house of nine human beings where I find a moment of peace. On these occasions, I soak until the water cools, or my brothers bang the door until it almost rattles off its hinges. Now, relieved to escape to this quiet place, I help Billy into the warm water.

As I close the bathroom door, Mam glares at Da and releases the fury she's been harboring inside. "You must stop our son! Our house might be the next one bombed by the Carlinos' rivals."

I imagine my father searching for the newspaper he usually ducks behind. He won't find it tonight. Mary crammed it beneath the washing machine to catch the oily residue leaking out its back. His second line of defense is to head to the back porch and smoke a cigarette, but I doubt even he has the nerve to do that given the sharpness of my mother's voice.

Billy jams his rubber boat underwater. When he releases it, water sprays our faces. He squeals with delight and sinks it again.

"Shush, Billy Boy. I want to hear the fight."

"What do you expect, woman? I've threatened and punished. He's fifteen, and like you, got a strong will."

"Listen to me. We're talking about dangerous men. The Carlinos' rivals are not average bootleggers. They're killers."

"You think I don't know that? Told Joe a hundred times to quit that job."

I pick up the tin box of Canthrox then change my mind. Billy screams when the tiny grains get into his eyes, and once he's wound up, he flails, slides, and sucks dirty bathwater up his nose. There's no way to put a lid on the racket he makes. To avoid all that, I wipe his head with a damp washcloth until the yard dirt melts.

I'm sure Rose and her mother next door hear Mam shout, "Their rivals didn't just blow up Carlinos' house. They were bent on killing the entire family!"

"I'm trying to listen to this radio," says Granda. "The reporter claims unemployment sits at sixteen percent and economists predict two thousand businesses will close this year. The drought's gonna make it worse. Folks leaving Great Plains farmlands in search of city jobs that are no longer there. CF&I laid off another twenty men last week."

Da glowers at the radio. "Do yeh think they'll lay us off?"

"Radio be damned." Mam's voice escalates. "What's wrong with you two? Our family is in danger. Joe could be the next person killed in these gang fights."

"I'll talk to him again, dear, for all the good it'll do. Your son's head is as thick as a fireplace wall."

I wrap Billy in a towel and lead him into the living room as my mother rushes past.

"Men! Holy Mother of Jesus, I'd be ever grateful if you'd put brains in their heads before you send them down to Earth."

At midnight, Joe's heated tone awakens me. "Nobody's blowing up our house. It wasn't a rival gang. Coppers found the trunks where Pete stashed his valuables and determined he did it for the insurance money. I thought he was smarter than that."

"You're telling us not only is your boss dangerous, but he's stupid too?" Da growls, "A deadly combination. Son, you won't be going back, not for a single day."

"How yeh gonna pay bills without the money I give you?"

"Either break your association with the Carlinos or move out. It's my responsibility to keep this houseful of kids safe."

In the tense silence, I inhale and hold the air until my lungs burn.

Finally, Joe says, "Have it your way, Da. I'm thinking I should leave town anyway until this mess quiets down."

"Coward. Any son of mine would face the man."

"Better a coward for a minute than dead the rest of your life," says

Granda.

"Fine. Leave by morning."

"Noooo!" Mam wails, "He's our son."

I whisper, "Mary, are you awake? We should say goodbye."

"Stay in bed. We don't need Joe's shite spreading to us."

I leap up and smash my nose against the window.

Joe disappears into the night.

I whisper, "Mary, he's gone."

"Nah, just another of his fits. He'll be back."

But by month's end, I'm still praying for Joe's return.

I'm outside near the fence, planting bell pepper plants I started by seed, when the neighbor's dog barks. He's a good watchdog. If it's the postman, he barks twice and whines. That's what he does, so I dig another hole.

But when Mam knocks on the window and shouts, "You've got mail," I run inside.

"For me? The only package I receive is Mrs. O'Shea's Christmas present."

"The return address says her son sent this. Remember Connor?"

"Why would he send me this little box?"

"Let's open it and find out." Mam slips a carving knife between the twine and brown wrapping paper.

I lift the lid and unfold a piece of stationery. "This is Mrs. O'Shea's flowered writing paper but not her handwriting."

"How about a cup of tea? We'll read it together."

I unwrap the crinkly tissue paper. "A velvet pouch. Touch it, Mam. It's as soft as the bunny's tummy at the petting zoo."

"Such a lovely royal blue."

"Can I open it?"

"Katie, let's read the letter first."

I smooth the stationery flat while Mam fills two cups one-third full with milk. "Second time I've warmed this pot. It's brutally strong. What can you read?"

"Most, if I go slow."

Dear Katie,

    This is the most difficult letter I have ever written. My mother never stopped speaking of you and retelling stories of cooking and playing games with you. She told me every letter you write ends with, 'I miss you. Love, Katie.'

Mam slips on her readers and bends over the letter. "Oh, my. This is not good."

"Not good?"

"Oh, Katie, take a sip of tea. I'm afraid this will break your little heart."

"You're scaring me."

"I'm sorry. Let me read the rest to you."

    Before my mother died two weeks ago, she made me promise I would write you. She was seventy-two and appeared healthy. She never complained. In the end, I'm sure my mother suffered no pain. She died in her favorite chair with a sweet smile on her face. Her heart simply stopped. The drawings you made for her still hung in her flat. She would have wanted to take your artwork with her, so I hope it comforts you to know I put them in her casket. A piece of you will be with her forever, and I find comfort in that because my mother loved you so. Please feel free to write. My address is on the reverse side.

My deepest sympathy, Connor O'Shea

The words blur and move on the page. My eyes are on fire. I can't blink; the pain coursing through my body is too great. I open my mouth to scream, *No, no, you can't go!* No sound comes out.

"Shall we open the pouch?" murmurs Mam.

Holy Virgin Mother, why did you let this happen? I tremble as I tug the black braided string then tilt the pouch. A necklace flows into my hand.

Graceful swirls adorn the tiny gold cross.

"It's lovely. Uncommonly delicate," says Mam.

"Like love. She said when God saw her wearing this cross, He sent His love to her, even though she wasn't worthy."

"And now," Mam's voice wavers, "it brings God's devotion to you."

"And Mrs. O'Shea's love."

Mam's been so angry she frightens me, like when she swears she's going out back and dig Da's grave. Yet I've never seen my mother shed tears.

"Connor cried too." I caress the raised spots, each the size of a fingertip, sprinkled across the stationery. "These are his tears."

Mam sniffles. "I'm surprised you're not sobbing your heart out."

"She's with Nana. She took her special medicine to heaven, and Nana's better already."

I fall into my mother's embrace and cling as if I can take strength from her wiry body. Mrs. O'Shea was full and soft. Her arms drew a person in as if absorbing them beneath her skin.

If only I could hug you one more time, my dear friend.

CHAPTER TWELVE

SEPTEMBER 1931

Once again, Mam's belly is as big as a watermelon, but I don't bother the Holy Virgin Mother with my request for a younger sister. I've abandoned all hope. Besides, Mary says it's too late, that God decides everything regarding a child before the mother realizes she's pregnant.

I swoop up Tommy, balance his plump bottom on my hip, and make a beeline out before Mam can tell me to mop. He needs changing, but I'm not going back. I set him down and wipe the damp spot his soggy diaper left on my skirt.

We crawl on the grass and push the orange and white wooden matchboxes I sneaked from the kitchen drawer. Tommy squalls if he loses a race.

Since I don't want to give our mother any reason to call me in and shove the mop in my face, I trail my matchbox inches behind and jokingly complain about eating his dust. I mimic a radio announcer, "World famous race car driver, Thomas Ryan, crosses the finish line. The crowd roars! Fans are on their feet, waving American flags."

Tommy laughs and claps his little hands until a car screeches to the curb. Da jumps out and leaps the front porch steps.

I grab Tommy and enter to find Mam leaning on her broom, glaring at Da. "Wasn't expecting you for several hours."

"Been at the hospital."

Tommy runs his matchbox across my shoulder. "Zoom, zoom."

"Your father ran smack dab into a wheelbarrow full of bricks, knocked himself over, and broke his hip.

"Oh, my." Mam's brows pinch together.

"The doctors are undecided, either a cast from his chest to his knee or surgery that inserts a metal pole into his hip and leg. He's in a foul mood. CF&I loaned me a car so I could drive you to the hospital before he threatens a nurse again. Since Nana died, you're the only person who can calm him."

Mam unties her apron and grabs her pocketbook. "Katie, watch the boys. Brisket's in the pot. Chop the carrots and potatoes and add them in three hours." Mam grabs the washcloth and dabs a grease spot on her lilac cotton housedress. As she and Da rush out, Mam hollers, "Don't let the broth dry up."

I crumple into the chair. "Well, Tommy. What else can go wrong?"

"Zoom, zoom." Tommy runs his matchbox up my arm as Billy bumbles in with a bloody lip.

For the first two weeks after surgery, Granda sleeps most of the day. When he's awake, he complains the bolts and rods some fool doctor rammed inside his leg burn like the devil stabbing him with a pitchfork. He's exasperating. Still, I force a sunny smile when I deliver meals to his room. He's embarrassed when he needs help to sit on the toilet, so I'm quick and quiet, the way I imagine a nurse might act. I get emotional when he pats my hand and gives me a shy grin.

After school, I bring Granda a cool glass of water and the morphine pills prescribed for his pain. Long before he's allowed another dose, he becomes short-tempered, but a swig from the laudanum bottle improves his mood. Mam says a man gets cranky because his ego deflates when he must depend on a woman for necessary things.

While I'm sorry my grandfather's in pain, I'm really tired. And when, "Jesus Christ, I'm a kid, not a trained nurse," slips out, Mam washes my mouth with carbolic soap.

As I rinse the stinging bubbles from my mouth, I pray. *Holy Virgin Mother. I'm working hard to make up for the care I didn't give Nana. Could you please speak with God about forgiving me for what just popped out of my mouth?*

The opposite of Granda, Billy, turning two in a little over a month thinks he can do everything for himself. I mutter, "Give me fortitude," as he races from the bathroom waving a stream of toilet paper over his head. I wrestle him, kicking and screaming, to the ground, and plunk him at the table with a coloring book. He scribbles, making no effort to remain within the outline of a Thanksgiving turkey with our only unbroken crayon—Olive Green.

Baby Tommy fusses in his crib. Sometimes, he dozes off on his own, so I lie on the sofa and prop my feet on the armrest until Mam screams.

Billy tosses his crayon and scrambles to my former hiding place behind the sofa arm.

I run to Mam. Blood flows down her leg. She moans, "Too soon!"

Granda hollers, "What the bejaysus is the hullabaloo?"

Mam presses against her stomach and writhes in pain.

I lower her onto the floor near the kitchen sink. "I'll get Mrs. Odell." When I reach her door, I fling it and scream, "We need help!"

Rose, her mother, and I rush back to my mother.

Rose's mom kneels on the floor and peeks under Mam's skirt. "Oh, my. Girls, step into the other room."

Panic flows through my veins. I still feel the guilt of not helping Nana as much as I should have. "I'm staying with my mother."

"Well, I suppose you're old enough. Dampen a dishtowel." After Mrs. Odell wipes Mam's legs, the towel is soaked in red. "Any more pain?"

"None. Help me up."

"I will not. Lay there and relax. How far along are you?"

"Seven months, plus a week or two."

"What does the doctor say?" asks Mrs. Odell.

"I'm fine."

"You haven't seen a doctor, have you?"

"I arranged for a midwife."

"Fine, but now you need a doctor." Mrs. Odell wipes Mam's forehead with a clean damp cloth. "Mr. Parker's home. He'll drive us to the emergency room. The girls can handle the boys. Katie, when your father gets off work, tell him we're at Corwin Hospital."

By the time Mr. Parker arrives and helps Mam out to his car, Tommy's bawling his lungs out. Rose slips into Mam's bedroom, hefts him from the crib, and coos, "What a good boy you are." He gurgles and vomits a stream of curdled milk.

After I refill his bottle and hand it to my friend, she asks, "You want me to feed him this so he can upchuck again?"

"That's what boy babies do."

"It's good to be an only child."

"Rose, you have no idea...."

Ed traipses in after completing his evening paper route and heads upstairs. "Got homework."

"Of course, you do, you slimy worm. And I don't?" I rub my pounding forehead. *Holy Virgin Mother, could you please check on my mother?*

Mary lets the front door slam behind her. "What's going on?"

"Mr. Parker drove Mam and Mrs. Odell to the hospital. Her privates bled."

"Is she having the baby?"

I shrug. "She's never bled like that before."

Da opens the door. "Don't smell my dinner cooking. Girls, where's your mother?"

Of course, he wants his dinner, but I can't handle anymore. Tears roll down my cheeks.

Granda hollers from his room. "Yeh better hustle over to Corwin. Your wife's got woman troubles."

Hours later, Mrs. Odell returns with a large pot she sets on the stove. "I brought leftover soup. The doctor says your mother lost too much blood, but she'll recover fine. Your father can tell you more when he comes home."

Long after Mary and I wash the dishes and tuck the boys in bed, when the house is pitch black, I curl up on the sofa to wait. But I leap, prepared to attack a burglar, when the front doorknob clicking awakens me.

The shadow moving in the hazy dawn speaks. "Your mother's doing well. And you have the baby sister you've been wanting."

I hug Da and barrel up the stairs, whooping wildly. "Mary, wake up! We have a sister!"

"Not another boy?" Mary rubs her eyes and rises from our bed. "Glory be."

I dart into the boys' room. I had put Tommy with his brothers instead of his crib so he wouldn't be alone, and now he's curled against Billy's side. "It's a girl!"

Ed rolls his back toward me. "Can't yeh see we're sleeping? Leave us be."

I run back downstairs as Mary asks, "Da, are they coming home?"

"Not yet. Doctors gave your mother a transfusion. She needs another."

I ask, "Can we visit?"

"Not today. Mam wants Mary home with Granda and the wee lads. Katie, you and Ed, off to school with yeh."

"Please, Da. I've waited a long time to be a baby girl's big sister."

"She's in an incubator."

"A what?"

"Incubator, same as hatching chicken eggs. The lights warm her. Theresa is frail, and your mother's not strong enough to care for her."

"Theresa?"

"In St. Theresa's honor because she suffered many illnesses and still lived a long and useful life devoted to the Lord."

"Our Theresa is frail? Is she a changeling?"

"Good Lord, she's not a fairy child. Our baby is as human as you and me. The doctor says her tiny lungs make it hard to breathe." Da yawns. "Was a long night. I could use a nap, but I'd better return to your mother and our baby girl."

I awaken alone in bed then tiptoe to the boys' room. Billy snores softly. Ed sounds like a train. There's no school today, so I let them sleep. But when Tommy stuffs his big toe into his mouth, I scoop him up. "I'm sure those are delicious, but I'll fix you a better breakfast."

The woodsy scent of black tea meets me on the stairway. When I enter the kitchen, Mary says, "Good, two of you are up. I'm fixing oatmeal."

"With raisins *and* brown sugar?"

"Of course, silly."

"We didn't have both in Philly."

"Da and Granda are making more money here. Listen, I've got a babysitting job in thirty minutes. Take this mug into Granda then haul our lazy brothers out of bed."

Still riding Tommy on my hip, I yell from the foot of the stairs. "Ed! Get your butt down to breakfast and bring Billy with you."

"I meant go up, not stand there and scream bloody murder," scolds Mary.

I motion toward the overhead thumping of bare feet. "It worked."

"I'll come home around noon, and we'll go to the hospital."

"I'm starving in here," booms Granda.

"Take over. You're the mother till I get home."

"You remember I'm eight?"

"Plenty old to dish oatmeal." Mary hands me the wooden spoon and hurries out.

I cringe at Billy's blood-curdling shriek and bump-bump-thud when he lands at the bottom of the stairs.

"Is my breakfast ready?" Granda's shout from the bedroom is as loud as Bill's scream for help.

Holy Virgin Mother Mary, I've lost my grandmother and Mrs. O'Shea. Mam and my baby sister are sick. I don't want to fall short on my responsibilities. Please forgive me, but I can't go on.

Rose sticks her head in our front door. "My mom's wondering if you need help."

Thank you, Blessed Mother. That was quick work.

An enormous white cross perches on the spire atop Corwin Hospital's roof. I pass beneath the Holy Virgin Mother standing in the alcove above the entrance and make the sign of the cross. *Thank you for watching over Mam and my new sister.*

In the waiting area, the stale stink of sweat churns my stomach. The metallic reek of blood and sickly sweet smell of carbolic acid burn my nose. When we pass a grizzled man with his left trouser leg cut off, revealing his swollen knee, I sneak a gander at the pus oozing from the circle of rust-colored blood.

Granda, Billy, and Tommy are at home under Mrs. Odell's care. But

Mary and Ed join the line at the check-in counter. I wander over to the gift shop window. From between a pot of artificial tulips and two leather-bound poetry books peeks a pink rabbit with brown glass eyes the shade of toasted walnuts and a tail as fluffy as cotton candy.

Ed taps my shoulder. "Mary says to come over by her."

"The bunny, Ed. We don't have a single toy for our new sister." I wave for Mary, but she ignores me and heads through oversized double doors. Ed and I rush to catch up. Our shoes tap against the hard, shiny floors, echoing in the dimly lit hall.

A nurse peers over a clipboard. "Quiet, we have sick people in these rooms."

Ed mutters, "Guess we're too stupid to know—"

Mary smacks his arm, enters the room at the hall's end, and speaks with a nurse who points down the aisle bordered on both sides by ten iron-framed beds. Even a quick glimpse at the women lying beneath the white bedcovers seems a violation of their privacy. I avert my eyes until a young woman across the aisle moans like a wounded animal. "My baby, my child."

Square glass containers shrouded with white gauze sit on steel trays alongside most beds. Narrow tubes connect to the women's arms. The huge needle piercing Mam's hand must be terribly painful. She is as pale as Nana when the coroner closed the casket lid. She doesn't move when I brush my fingertips along her clammy forearm.

"Are you awake? It's us, your kids."

Her eyelids flutter. "Have you seen Theresa?"

We shake our heads.

"She's an angel, eyes as green as spring grass and a precious face." Mam pinches her lips into a pencil-thin line. "Skin as delicate as a butterfly wing and the color of fresh churned butter."

I ask, "Can I hold her?"

"Not yet. I fear Theresa's skin might tear at the slightest touch."

"Will my new sister get better?" It's a strain, yet I smile, hoping to cheer my mother.

Mam's face remains sad. "Her every breath is a mere wisp of air, but the saints watch over her. And nurses tend her around the clock."

"Can we see Theresa now?" asks Mary.

"Your father is with her. The nurse will show you the way."

A woman, her dyed black hair combed slick beneath a white cap the shape of a miniature cardboard tent above a face wrinkled like a prune, inspects the unconscious woman in the bed before her. When Mary inquires about directions, and the breath Prune Face expels sounds like Tommy's little baby farts, Ed coughs to disguise his laugh.

"Children, I am busy."

"Could you point the way?" asks Mary in her kindest voice.

"All work falls to me," says Prune Face.

I give Molly a squeeze in my pocket. "We are sorry to burden you."

"Only the Good Lord knows what might happen while I'm parading you children through the hospital."

Prune Face halts before a viewing window. "The Ryan child is in there. I am unaware of the whereabouts of your father. You may wait in this hall."

The tiniest versions of children lie inside the boxes encased with domed glass lids. Black knobs and a gauge, not unlike the speedometer in Mr. Parker's car, line the base. Silver latches secure the lids.

I say, "There's no reason for the locks. These babies are too tiny to climb out."

One child is red and swollen, and two are gray and parched. Da steps up behind us and points at the far-left incubator. That child has old-man skin, shriveled and translucent. The heat of panic burns my face because I think it must be a boy until I notice a pink bow on the card that reads, *Theresa Marie Ryan.*

"She has my middle name?"

"Your mother decided months ago, if this child was a girl, it's only fair we name her after you. You prayed for a girl, and Mam's confident you will protect your sister, no matter what."

"May I hold her?"

Da draws me to his side. "Nah. See the tube up Theresa's nose? She must breathe on her own before the nurse removes her from the incubator."

"I'd like to kiss her."

"We have too many germs. Possibly tomorrow when our baby's stronger."

"But Da, I must tell her I love her and am praying she'll get well."

"She knows, Katie."

Later that night, after my brothers settle in their room and Mary's breath falls into the soft rhythm of sleep, tears flow from the corners of my eyes and patter onto the pillow like soft summer rain. I lay Molly on my chest and make the sign of the cross.

Hail Mary, full of grace, the Lord is with thee. Blessed art thou among women, and blessed is the fruit of thy womb, Jesus. Holy Virgin Mother Mary, please hear my prayer. Things aren't going well on Earth. I thank you for my baby sister, but she came too soon. Her tiny lungs don't work right. Her name is Theresa Marie, and her nametag has a pink bow on it. She's in an incubator at the end of a long hall and around the corner in a small room with three other babies.

I swallow hard and press against my lips but can't block my sobs. *I've asked for a lot, like a new dress after those snotty girls made fun of me and to make me Joe's favorite so he'll treat me better. You know, I'm older now, almost nine. Those were the stupid prayers of a selfish child. I understand why you didn't approve of them. But if you grant this request, I promise I'll pray only for others who are sick and in need, and never again for stupid things. And I apologize for taking up your valuable time. Amen.*

I wipe Molly's eyes, then mine. "The Lord is my shepherd; I shall not want. He maketh me lie down—"

"Hush. People are sleeping around here."

"Sorry, Mary."

"I'm sorry too. That's a good prayer, but could you keep it inside your head so I can get some rest?"

After ten days in the hospital, Da is bringing Mam and Theresa home. Yesterday, Mary and I finished the laundry. Today, I cleaned the kitchen and mopped every floor. As a special welcome home, I filled the crystal candy dish with creamy homemade fudge and set it on the side table. I bubble with excitement, and after I fan out the burnt freckle bread odor, the house will be perfect for Mam's return.

When I raise the window, Ed's voice shatters my thoughts. "First base, yeh scut! Never would have chosen you if I knew yeh run as slow as a bird."

Bottom in the air, Billy pushes his firetruck in circles around my feet. Baby Tommy stirs on his yellow bunny quilt, yet doesn't wake until his brother screeches, "Fire! Eeeee-uuuuu-eeeee-uuuuu."

CF&I's owner gave Granda the watchman's job so he can hobble on his gammy leg and work at his own pace. The pain in his broken hip flared today, so he's home, yelling from his bed for the boys to quiet down.

I scoop up Tommy and whisper, "He's like having another brother."

Billy pats his stomach. "Hungie."

I hand each boy a saltine cracker. But the relief is temporary. By the time the sun sinks behind the Mayday tree, both Billy and Tommy's clothes need changing. Then, Ed straggles in with torn trousers and a bloody knee.

When Mary finally steps through the front entryway, I give her my most severe squinty-eyed glare. "You said you'd help make supper."

"The Murphy kids were wild today. I needed a break. Went for a soda with a fella from school."

"You were making a holy show of yourself with some stupid boy instead of helping me get everything ready for Mam and Theresa? You're selfish."

"Relax. I boiled carrots and lima beans last night. Rip the stale bread and smash it in with the last egg and a cup of milk."

"Mary, that's a terrible meal for Mam's first night home."

"It's all we've got, so stick it in the oven and cut the whining."

I run upstairs, flop onto the bed, and wait for my sister to apologize. But it's a loud noise that awakens me. The room is dark, and Mary's side of the bed is cold. Her voice travels upstairs.

"Da, let me help you."

I tiptoe to the banister and lean until I see my father sprawled on the bottom stairs shouting, "Get the bottle from my sock drawer."

Granda pokes Da with his cane. "Go to bed, Mary. I'll deal with this fool."

Ed leans out the boys' bedroom door. "What's going on?"

Mary frowns. "It's Da, doing what Da does. Nothing you can do. Are Tommy and Billy asleep?"

Ed snaps his fingers. "Out like lights and sucking their thumbs."

"Mam and Theresa aren't coming home, are they, Mary?

"Not tonight, Katie. Maybe tomorrow."

I awaken to squeals of delight and squeaking springs. Irritated, I shout, "Stop jumping on the bed! It's time for breakfast."

The boys nearly knock me over scrambling to be first downstairs. Bowls, spoons, and Grape-Nuts and Raisin Bran boxes sit on the kitchen table. "This is swell, Granda. I'll get the milk."

Granda slams the teapot onto the burner grate then bangs his palm against the on-off dial. "How the devil do yeh light this blessed stove?"

Mary snatches a matchbox off the shelf above the stove while I fill the cereal bowls. "Granda, are we going to the hospital?"

"I'm borrowing Mr. Parker's car. We'll bring Mam and the baby home around noon. Damn your father. He should be the one telling you what's going on."

We spend the morning tidying. When we finish, Mary feeds the boys a lunch of peanut butter and grape jelly sandwiches while I curl up in a chair with a view of the street. The time passes slowly, but finally, two hours later, I shout, "They're home!" and rush to Mr. Parker's car as Da opens the passenger door.

Mam's eyes are dull. She doesn't move, and neither does the tiny bundle in her arms.

I gaze up through the opening between two enormous fluffy white clouds. *Holy Virgin Mother Mary, something's wrong.*

Granda kicks open the rear car door, grunts, and balances on his cane.

After Da takes Theresa, Mam clenches the doorframe, heaves herself from the car, then climbs the porch steps as if carrying a hundred-pound load on her back. "Give us a few minutes, children."

The bed springs creak. The soft thump, thump sounds as if a pillow is being fluffed. After Tommy was born, Mam positioned herself on the sofa the way the Queen of England might sit on a jeweled throne. *"Mary, I need tea. Katie, bring my lap blanket."* Today, she waits silently while we gather around the bed.

I shake my arms to throw off my unease. The lamp casts a long beam, shrouding the room in shadows. Granda says I have a lovely smile. I want Theresa to have one too, but her thin straight lips appear drawn on with a purple crayon. Her eyeballs protrude from the clingy skin surrounding the sockets. I will her to move.

When Theresa raises her perfect little hand as if to show off her perfect little fingernails, it is as if the house exhales.

Afraid to speak in my normal voice, I whisper, "May I hold her?"

Mam pats the mattress. "Sit by me. Theresa's not well. Tell her you love her. Kiss her tiny forehead. This may be your only chance."

I'm terrified to ask why this might be my only chance. I must concentrate, or my tiny sister, as light as a feather, might float away.

Mary's voice cracks. "Is Theresa dying?"

"Why would you ask such a horrible question?" I brush Theresa's forehead with my lips and sniff her powdery scent.

Mam's sob jars the metal bedframe. "Hand her to Mary. Everyone should say goodbye. We don't have long."

Even though Mary cuddles our baby sister as gingerly as if the infant were a delicate flower, Theresa expels a tiny puff of air, and her hand falls limp.

Every sound is quiet and loud at the same time. The pounding between my ears threatens to split my head in two. *Holy Virgin Mother, is this my fault?* I bow my head. *Punishment for my sins? I apologized for calling Mary a bad name and prayed for forgiveness. After I used Jesus' name in vain, I promised never to swear again.* I cross myself then grip the bedside table. *Please, don't do this. Punish me another way. I'll try harder, be better. I beg of you, please, make my baby sister breathe.*

Through the blurry mist that fills my eyes, I watch Mary kiss Theresa's cheek.

Then, Ed takes our frail bundle in his arms. "Goodbye, baby girl. I'm sorry you must fly to heaven."

I flee and let the back door slam then shake my fist at the star-filled sky. "Lies and more lies. You don't care about us. I did exactly what Father Bertram said. Read a million Bible verses, prayed, and watched my mouth."

My legs buckle. My knees hit the damp ground. "Maybe I didn't do everything the way you wanted, but you're the Holy Virgin Mother, you watch how hard I try." My shoulders slump when there is no reply. "Are you listening? I did my best to love my enemies, even when they were terribly mean."

I fall forward and dig my fingers into the ground. "I took care of my brothers, kept them safe, and you know how difficult that can be. You had a son."

When I roll onto my back, unchecked tears stream the sides of my face, pooling in my ears. The evening dew seeps through my dress. I shiver. "Please, please, tell me why you let Theresa die."

Two days later, I smooth my skirt and await our friends and neighbors' arrival. Mr. Parker drops off a transparent glass casserole dish of chopped red peppers and ground beef floating in a lumpy beige sauce. He mumbles apologetically, "My wife made this," then leaves. A few minutes later, Mrs. Odell slips in the back door with scalloped potatoes topped with a thick Corn Flake crust, whispers in Mam's ear, then disappears.

I abandon my post near the front door. "Mam, when is everybody coming?"

"I'm not expecting anyone."

"When Nana died, people came in cars, on the bus, by foot, and brought food and made speeches about her life."

"It's not the same. There's no celebration. This child barely had a life."

"Her name is Theresa. Theresa Marie barely had a life."

CHAPTER THIRTEEN

———— ∞ ————

NOVEMBER 1931

Glass shatters. I bolt upright and blink in the dark when Mam screams, "I'd rather die!"

"You can't deny me. I'm your husband."

Mary motions to follow her into the boys' room. Sleepy Billy mumbles, "I want a cookie," then snuggles against Ed's back. We squeeze into the bed, lean against the wall, and tuck the blanket under our chins.

"I told you, six is enough!" shouts Mam. "But no, you wouldn't listen. Theresa lived ten days. I can't suffer through that again."

I exhale as if a heavy weight propels my last breath. Oh, Mam, I can't either.

"The good Lord decides how many is enough," snarls Da.

"No... *I decide*. I don't want another child."

I grab Mary's arm at the sound of what might be a chair crashing into the wall then squeeze Molly against my chest. "Don't be afraid. I won't let him hurt you."

"What about what I want?" yells Da.

"Eight pregnancies wore out my insides."

"Damn it, woman. Use something." A bottle clanks against the trashcan's metal bottom and echoes throughout the house. I strain to hear Mam's lowered voice.

"You know that's a sin."

"You're my wife. You have no choice."

"Oh, I have a choice."

Heavy feet stomp across the hardwood floor. The front door slams.

Windows rattle.

When I ask if we should go down, Ed cautions, "He might come back. Stay in your room while I check on Mam."

Mary puts a trembling arm around me. From the floor's creak, we can tell Ed is helping our mother into bed. His voice is firm, but Mam's is muffled with sobs.

A moment later, he barrels up the stairs. "She's okay, but the wall didn't fare so well. I'll go down and keep watch. You girls sleep up here with the lads."

"I'm too scared to sleep."

"You're safe, Katie. Nobody's getting past me." Ed squares his shoulders and puffs his chest. I realize he's trying to look like a man who can keep us safe. To me, his posture makes him look every bit a child just as frightened as I.

A metallic bang startles me awake to a sun-filled morning. Curious about the burnt smell, I creep downstairs while watching for danger with every step.

"About time you got up." Mary closes Mam's bedroom door. "The boys are doing me in. Ed said he'd make breakfast, but he dropped the cast-iron skillet. Go find out what he's doing to those poor eggs while I change Tommy's diaper."

"Is Mam okay?"

"She's fine. Just wants a day of rest. Gave me money for miniature golf, so don't dawdle."

Smoke pours out of the toaster. The bread encased between the open wires is burned to a crispy black on one side yet still white on the other. Ed rips the plug from the wall, and with vengeance, smacks an egg against the cast-iron frypan. Eggshell shards spray the stove.

I consider telling him Mam bought several slices of Irish bacon, but frying eggs appears to be all he can handle. I leave him be and set the table.

After a flurry of dressing and face washing, we make the hour-long trek to Pueblo Mini-Golf. We fall in line behind three nuns dressed in white-collared, black habits. The nun with long fingernails pinches

Tommy's cheek. "Aren't you cute?"

When he swats her away, her face retreats inside her veil.

A second nun, whose apple-red cheeks and short, chubby body resemble Tommy's, chatters with him in baby talk.

When Billy steps between them, she says, "My name is Sister Anne Beatrix. What is yours?"

"Billy." He extends his hand. "Nice meeting yeh."

"What a polite young man." Sister Anne bends and shakes hands. "Your father must be very proud."

"The Lord shines His love on children such as you," says the nun who pinched Tommy.

I ask, "Nuns play golf?"

"Yes, dear, I suppose that might surprise most people." The third nun's blue eyes sparkle when she winks. "I much prefer baseball."

Mary and I restrain Tommy, new at walking unassisted, from toddling off as we hit golf balls through barrels, down drainpipes, and into trashcan lids. Billy cackles and snatches the balls before they drop into the hole. Ed laughs and tells him to run faster.

My sister uses her babysitting money to purchase two orange Nehi sodas. The competition for gulping soda is as great as making the most holes in one. When Ed empties the first bottle in a single, long swig, Mary smacks him between his shoulder blades. "That's enough, yeh little shite."

"Ahem." The pinching nun peers out from her fluttering veil and tsks her disapproval. But when they finish their mini-golf round, the nuns smile and wave. I welcome that sign of forgiveness.

Even Tommy flaps his arm in a happy goodbye.

Mary prods Ed toward the street. "Quit limping along. You could go to hell for making fun of the poor nun who dragged her foot."

The farther we get from Pueblo Mini-Golf, the more Ed irritates me. "Catch up, you laggard. You're gonna make us late."

My brother extends one leg and hops until a hickory-handled putter slides out of his trouser.

"Better not let Mam catch you with that," says Mary as Ed swings the club and lops the top off a weed.

The house is quiet when we enter. I head for the kitchen and hand Billy a hunk of soda bread. He thanks me with a wide grin of sparkling white teeth.

"I'm hungry too." Ed snatches an orange and slams the back door behind him.

Suspicious, I peek out.

Ed spits on his handkerchief and cleans the stolen putter's metal face then whacks the orange across the yard.

"Billy, big brother's having all the fun." I take his hand and step out the back door.

"Go back in," snarls Ed. "You'll bring Mam out here."

"She's resting. Can't we play?"

Ed hands me the putter. When I smack the orange, its skin cracks, juice sprays, and he grumbles, "Look what you've done."

"Yes, Katie, look what you've done." From where Mam stands on the porch, she seems ten feet tall as she scowls down upon us. "That's how you thank me for giving you Da's hard earned money to spend on fun?"

Billy squeals and runs toward Mam.

"It's his, not mine." I toss the putter to Ed. He hides it behind his back then scans the yard as if searching for an escape route.

Mam jams her fists against her waist. "Get up here."

Ed climbs the three steps as if marching to the guillotine. He swerves, but Mam grabs his ear. "Poor man, trying to support his family, and you steal from him?"

"Ah, Mam. This club's pretty beat up, ready for the trash bin."

"Did the owner say he was throwing it away?"

Ed leans back in a weak attempt to loosen Mam's grip on his reddening ear. "He didn't say exactly that."

"Return it and ask for his forgiveness."

I know well the smirk on Ed's face. He'll dump the putter in the weeds.

"Since none of you put the kibosh on your thieving brother, you'll all go apologize. I want a signed note thanking me for making you return his property, or your punishment will be a four-week restriction rather than two."

The smirk slides off Ed's face.

"We may not have much, but no child of mine steals. The minute you return, go to your rooms. Consider the orange you wasted as the dinner you wish you had. Perhaps you'll think twice about stealing again. Don't show your faces or say a word until church tomorrow morning."

When Ed groans, Mam gives his ear a final twist that propels him into the house. "Take Mary with you."

The following morning, we tiptoe to the bottom of the stairs, peer around the doorjamb, then cautiously enter the kitchen. Hungry from missing dinner, we don't want to upset Mam for fear she'll extend our punishment, and we'll go without breakfast too.

"Wang Wang Blues" plays on the radio. I have no memory of our mother ever dancing, but there she is, sashaying to the music's rhythm and flinging out her leg as she tosses the mixing bowl into the sink.

Mary shrugs at me. "Mam, can we help?"

"Take the carrot marmalade buns out of the oven, but don't put them near the flowers your father brought. The heat will wilt my lovely bouquet."

I whisper, "What's with her?"

"Appears Da apologized, and you know how unusual that is." When Mary opens the oven door, the kitchen fills with the scent of sugary dough.

"My mouth's watering," says Ed.

"Mam, Katie and I saved enough for the Singer that's on sale, if it's agreeable with you."

"Lovely. I'll give you sewing lessons."

"Me too?"

"Of course, Katie. You're plenty capable."

I visualize my first new dress as I coax Tommy to slide his legs into the highchair. When he pounds his hands on the tray, I set a Shredded Wheat cube before him, and he pounds it too. Strands fly and fall upon the floor I swept clean the night before. He shouts, "More, more!"

Ed laughs then cringes as if expecting scolding words for encouraging Tommy's bad behavior, but Mam says, "Somebody help Granda. He's hobbling like a three-legged mule and scratching my polished floor with his cane."

Relief creeps into my chest. It appears Mam resolved the stealing incident in her mind, and now Granda is her source of irritation. I tap up every crumb and a stray drop of carrot marmalade so as not to leave a mess that might send her anger back at me.

"Dress Tommy in his new blue creeper," says Mam. "Ed, you and Billy wear your matching bow ties."

Ed groans, deep and low, a mad dog growl.

Mary kicks him under the table.

I flash my sweetest smile, hoping to win Mam's favor. "What should Mary and I wear?"

"You girls know how to dress for church."

I stick out my tongue at Ed as Mam shoves away her plate. "Anyone want my bun? Smelling it makes my stomach roll."

After services, Mam taps the bus window. "Next stop—Singer Sewing Store."

Billy slumps in his seat and Ed harrumphs, "We'll miss the game."

Their dour faces wash me with guilt. Sunday afternoon baseball with the neighbor lads is my brothers' favorite activity. Ed either pitches or plays first base. The boys tell Billy he's the water boy. His chest puffs each time the older boys sip from the ladle he dips into the rusty bucket.

As the bus stops at the corner, I consider speaking on the boys' behalf, asking Mam if they can go home. But it's easy to get on my mother's cranky side when her stomach is upset.

Inside the store, foot-pedal sewing machines housed in hardwood cabinets line one wall. Mary points to a portable Singer sitting atop a display counter. Its gold lettering sparkles on the polished black machine. "Take a gander at this beauty."

1919 Singer Portable Electric
Model 128 with Bentwood Case
Used—As Is—$25

I ask, "Twelve years old? Is that too old?"

"Runs like a champ," says the perky peroxide-blonde clerk. "Completely refurbished. Stitches as smooth as a professional machine. The matching case is sturdy, yet lightweight so you can carry it home yourselves."

Red and gold swirls follow the machine's curves. I rotate the wheel and watch the needle bob up and down then spin the thread sitting on the spool dolly.

"My manager allows me to reduce the price one dollar."

"Seems a good deal." Mam slips a saltine into Tommy's hand to distract him from yanking her hair.

"Very good, indeed," agrees the clerk. "One hundred percent guaranteed for thirty days."

"We'd have money left over." Mary pats her pocketbook.

"Please, can we buy it?" My mind swirls with thoughts of sewing ten new dresses. A pink with a full skirt, a sky blue with puffy sleeves, and others with brightly colored prints. More dresses than that snooty Julia owns. She'll be sorry she didn't invite me into her group of friends. She can take her fancy bows and that juicy orange and—

"Katie, I asked you a question," says Mary.

"Sorry, didn't hear you."

"What color do you prefer?"

I lift a bolt of navy-blue fabric with white quarter-sized polka dots from the new arrivals table.

"We all love that fabric." Mam brushes Tommy's slobbery cracker crumbs off her shoulder. "But we can't afford cloth that fine."

The clerk waits as Mary digs into her pocketbook for the dollar bills and coins wrapped in a handkerchief. After paying for the machine, $2.32 remains. We select a Simplicity pattern with three dress styles for twenty-five cents and four yards of fabric off the sale counter.

Mam buys two spools of J&P Coats thread and a packet of ivoroid buttons with a raised flower design. "An extravagance, but I can't resist this pale cream color. Nobody will suspect they aren't real ivory."

Ed shifts the Singer, one arm to the next, and grumbles all the way home. "Lugging this machine is stretching my pitching arm."

"Should help you throw farther," says Mary. "Guess you'll be thanking us."

As we approach our house, I'm first to spot Joe on the porch. I run and hug him. "I thought you might never come home."

"Had my own doubts for a while."

"Nice of you to drop by." Mary pokes his biceps.

Joe rumples Ed's hair. "I believe you're a foot taller."

"This blasted machine is killing my arm. Let's go in."

Billy cocks his head as if trying to remember Joe.

Tommy stares blankly. I'm sad to realize, at one-year-old, he has no memories of this young man who is his big brother.

When Mam sets Tommy on the floor, then reaches for her eldest son, Joe bends to our mother's height. She clings then breaks the embrace and pats his cheek. "I'm not a hundred percent. Need a few minutes rest."

As she closes her bedroom door, Joe removes his flat cap. "She plugged again?"

Mary shrugs. "She's not saying."

Joe makes airplane noises, hoists Tommy, and swoops him through the air.

"Me, me." Billy yanks Joe's trouser leg. I think he's remembering the good times they had together.

While the boys reacquaint themselves, Mary lifts the Dutch oven lid and places the corned beef in the center. She covers the meat with water and measures two tablespoons of Mam's homemade pickling mix of allspice berries, black peppercorns, mustard seeds, cloves, and coriander seeds.

I peel and cube potatoes and carrots, slice a large cabbage, then set them aside until the meat is an hour from being done. It's as if Joe never left until he stops playing with the boys, scratches his head, and paces the room. Then I sense his tension. I'm also nervous about what Da will say.

Mam emerges from the bedroom. "Nice beefy smell coming out of that oven. Hope I can keep it down."

"Mam, I'm sorry I had to be away so long."

"A letter, a card, would have been nice, Joe."

"I know." Appearing truly sorry, my eldest brother wears what Granda calls a hangdog face. "I couldn't risk someone tracking me."

"Save your explanation for the men."

Within thirty minutes, Granda hobbles in and pats Joe's back. Joe takes his grandfather's elbow and steadies him over his cane.

Da stomps into the kitchen and yanks out his chair. His fork and knife clang when he slams his arms on the supper table.

I sit Tommy in his high chair then silently take my seat.

The creak of Mary opening the oven door is the only sound until she speaks in a calm voice. "Da, will you carve?"

"No, don't want to cut the damn meat."

Mary slices off the white fluffy fat cap and sets it aside. She spins the corned beef and slices through the grain. Her hand jerks when Da raises his voice, and the knife knicks her thumb.

"Joe, while yer eating the food I put on this table, yeh best say why you chose now to come back."

"It's been more than a month since the coppers found Pete's body dumped under Siloam Bridge. Carlino's reign is over. Nobody's interested in me."

"The newspaper said the gang that shot Pete used bullets poisoned with garlic." Granda slaps his knee. "How the bejaysus does garlic kill a person? If that were true, there wouldn't be a single Italian left on the planet."

"Yeh drill the tips and stuff fresh garlic into the cavity—causes a deadly blood infection." Joe glances toward Da to see if he will object to him holding out his plate for a slice of beef. "It's insurance, in case the bullet fails to do its job."

"Are you safe now?" asks Mam.

"The higher-ups either left the state or joined Little Caesar's gang."

Da slams his fork against the table. "Sweet Jesus on a stick. Who's Little Caesar?"

"He's taken over bootlegging in Colorado. I'm not joining his operation. Set my sights on fighting fires. I'll find part-time work nights and weekends and finish my last year of school, if you'll let me sleep here."

Mam signals Da with her squinty eye. Everybody knows he'll leave Joe hanging until the boy squirms in his skin, but I'm not worried. Mam won't let him kick Joe out again.

Mary and I store the leftovers as the others move into the living room.

Joe hides behind the newspaper as if it will protect him from Da's wrath, so I'm surprised when he has the nerve to speak. "No construction or farmhand jobs, but Colorado Fuel and Iron is hiring."

I stop drying dishes and wait for the blowup. Da won't want Joe working the same place as he, so I'm surprised when Granda says, "CF&I is one of the few companies not laying off. I'll put in a good word for yeh with my boss."

"Paper says 2,291 banks have failed," says Joe. "Guess I'd better keep my earnings in a jar, like Mary and Katie."

When the kitchen is clean, Mary says to me, "Let's lay out the chambray. There's enough we should each get a dress."

"I want a white collar like Julia's."

"Who's Julia?" asks Mam.

Mary snorts, "A rich goody-two-shoes Katie wants to be her friend."

Mam tsks, "You can use the white leftovers from the underwear I made."

"No collar for me," says Mary. "People will think we're the Bobbsey twins."

Da slams his hand on his chair arm. "Mary, quit blathering nonsense and fill my glass."

"Sorry, Da. Bottle's empty."

"Bleedin' Drys. A hardworking man deserves a drink. I'm not buying O'Sullivan's deadly brew—mostly creosote and embalming fluid. Joe, get yer lazy arse down to skid row and buy some whiskey worth drinking off yer bootlegging friends."

Joe lowers the newspaper and grinds his teeth as if biting back his words. "Da, it's not safe. Little Caesar's lackeys will recognize me."

"Yeh said they're not interested in you. That's the only reason I'm letting you move in. So, which is it, Son? You've put this family in danger? Or your gang mates don't give a damn about you?"

The knot in Joe's jaw rises and falls.

"No answer?" snarls Da. "Then, get a bottle, or be on your way."

I squeeze Molly so she'll know to remain quiet.

When Mam steps between the two men, Joe clenches his fists and storms out.

"Woman, you can't be coddling that boy. This ain't no charity house. One misstep and I'll send him on his way again."

CHAPTER FOURTEEN

DECEMBER 1931

On this last day of school before Christmas break, a gale howls and rattles the windows. Hailstones splat on the street and clatter against the house. I search for a sunbeam to cut through the gray clouds tumbling in the sky.

Jesus, Son of God, Father Bertram says you can't answer every prayer. But if you have a break in the demands placed upon you, I'd be grateful if you'd stop the hail while Rose and I walk to school. In return, as your humble servant, please call upon me for anything you might need done on Earth.

Repeated honking disrupts my prayer. I peer out the living room window and watch marble-sized hail ping off Mr. Parker's shiny black Ford. He's a patient man. What the heck could make him pound his horn? But it's Mrs. Odell who leaps out of the driver's seat and jogs toward our door.

Mam rushes from the bedroom, an umbrella in her hand. "Grab your coat. Let's go."

"Where?"

"Mrs. Odell's driving me to my doctor's appointment. We'll drop you and Rose at school."

I set Molly on the table beneath the window to await my return and raise my eyes toward the ceiling. *Thank you, Jesus. This is even better. Remember what I said, I'm here if you need anything done.*

The hail barrage slows during arithmetic. By the time geography ends, a steady downpour converts the schoolyard into a sloshy swamp, but nobody cares. We're on our way to the cafeteria for a Christmas party.

Each grade level made a different decoration. My class shaped paper mâché into snowmen to hang on the tree. The kids in the grade below made snow with water and laundry flakes. From where Rose and I stand singing "Here Comes Santa Claus," the snow is as white and fluffy as real. But the far side is bare because the boys flung the soapy snow at each other rather than the tree.

"What did the teachers expect from grade two boys?" asks Rose.

After a rousing round of "Dashing Through the Snow," we file past the counter and help ourselves to a cup of red fruit punch, a star-shaped sugar cookie with silver sprinkles, and a gooey lemon bar. I scan the room for Mama Louise as I follow Rose to our table in the back.

"Hello, darlin's." Mama Louise slips up behind. "Good to be inside, isn't it?"

We nod, but our eyes are on the hand Mama Louise slides into her large apron pocket. She removes a white cotton napkin, glances around the cafeteria, then unwraps two golden squares. The fragrance of sweet baked corn is strong.

"Don't tell anyone my secret ingredients, a generous pour of honey and a solid pound of fresh-churned butter." Mama Louise cups her mouth with one hand. "Never use that new-fangled oleomargarine, nothing but animal fat, ruins the taste. My Alfred says nobody makes better cornbread."

I open my lunch tin. "We have a gift for you too."

Mama Louise fusses over the cutout bells as the cornbread melts in my mouth, much like my fondness for her melts my heart. But there's also an ache as I remember Mrs. O'Shea giving me, and only me, crumpets fresh from her oven.

"You okay, darlin'?" Mama Louise gently pats my back.

I want to explain, but my throat closes up, preventing me from speaking, so I nod.

When the party ends about three o'clock, Rose and I stroll home. We are deep into a discussion of the snow-throwing boys' juvenile behavior when Mrs. Odell steps out my front door and waves. "Yoo-hoo. Rose. Over here." As we step inside, she places a finger against her lips. "Mam's under the weather."

I ask, "What did the doctor say?"

"Your mother's out of sorts, nothing serious, likely to sleep through the night."

"The only time she sleeps during the day is when we're having another baby."

"Ah, no baby coming. Woman problems, honey. There's a bottle of Dr. Bonker's Egyptian Oil on the counter. Every half hour, give her ten to twenty droplets in molasses. She'll be fine in a few days. I whipped up my best ground beef, cabbage, and rice casserole for your dinner. Rose and I must go, but I'll check on your mother in the morning."

An hour later, when the men arrive, I glance up from my arithmetic homework. "Don't disturb Mam. She's in bits."

"Who's making my supper?"

I cower from the bite of Da's whiskey breath. Mary shoves him away. "It's in the oven."

As Mary dishes the casserole, Mam surprises everyone by appearing at the kitchen door. I support her elbow until she sits in her chair at the table. But when she raises her fork, her arm falls limp. "I can't eat. Must be the flu. Help me to bed."

When Da supports our mother as she rises, I give Mary the *what's-up-with-him* stare.

After we finish eating, the fellas move into the living room. I clear the table and set the dishes in the sink, but it's Mary's night to wash and mine to dry. So, when I hear the washing machine, I investigate why she's doing laundry at night instead of helping me.

"Holy, shite, Katie. Quit sneaking up." Soap bubbles thicken into a pink foam as the agitator jerks the bedclothes back and forth.

"Is that blood?"

"Yeh, a rotten bit of luck, flu and monthlies at the same time. Listen, I don't think Mam should be alone. She certainly can't take care of the boys. I sit for the Murphy kids tomorrow, so we'll postpone shopping for a tree."

"But Mary, you promised—"

"We've plenty of time, six days until Christmas Eve."

But for the next two days, we barely think of Christmas. I take on more responsibility for the boys so, every day, Mary has time to strip Mam's bedclothes and wash out the blood. While they dry, Mam sips homemade chicken broth. I pour her a dose of Lydia E. Pinkham's Vegetable Compound. Almost immediately, she falls back asleep.

On the third day, I ask my sister, "Is the medicine working?"

"The label says unicorn root and black cohosh. No idea what they cure."

"There's no such animal as a unicorn."

"No, Katie, but there's fifteen percent alcohol." Mary peers into the half-empty bottle. "Guess that's why she sleeps so much."

A twinge runs down my neck. "Will she die?"

"Of course not. Mam's bleeding less, but there's some white sticky stuff that's got me worried. Might be pus."

"Shouldn't she go to the doctor?"

"She says she's feeling better."

The next day, when Mary returns from babysitting, she removes a glass container from a small brown paper bag. "I told the pharmacist at Peoples Drug Store how tired Mam is, and he recommended Mastin's Yeast Vitamon Tablets. He said her energy should return in a week. But I've a bit of cruddy news."

"No tree?"

"Aye, Katie, I think it best we skip the tree and gifts this year. But we can cook a Christmas goose."

"Goose? We've never had one before."

"The ladies tipped me extra this week. I bought a nice fat bird and ingredients for plum pudding."

On the evening of December 31, Da lifts Mam as if she were a sleeping child and carries her to Mr. Parker's car. Molly and I snuggle on the sofa and watch snowflakes collect in the window's lower corners. We pray to the Holy Virgin Mother to ask God to heal Mam. God took Nana and Mrs. O'Shea to heaven. Doesn't He understand we can't bear to lose our mother too?

I wake up at one in the morning when Joe stumbles past me. As he staggers upstairs, I slip Molly into my pajama pocket to keep her warm, step onto the porch, and watch for headlights. I haven't given up hope my mother will come home tonight, but gooseflesh rises so high on my arms and legs it hurts, so I climb the stairs and crawl into bed.

When I lean my pillow upright against the bedframe, Mary elbows me. "Hold still. I'm worn out."

"I'm waiting for Mam."

"Katie, it's too late. The doctors must be keeping her for the night."

"Can't sleep until I know what the doctor said. I'll wait up for Da."

"Go to sleep, Katie. Doubtful he'll come home either."

CHAPTER FIFTEEN

JANUARY 1, 1932

Billy balances an old broom handle over his shoulder as if it is his rifle and marches the living room's perimeter. "Soldiers don't eat cereal. I need pancakes."

My head pounds from staying awake most of the night, and my leg is numb from bouncing Tommy on my lap. When I set him down, his squeal is like a knife in my brain. I'm grateful for the fog that fills my mind as he settles with his toys on the living room rug. But when Mary tosses a handful of spoons onto the table, and Ed shouts, "Give me that," as he bats at the CoCo Wheats box Joe waggles above his head, I cringe.

Da wanders in and leans against the doorjamb. "God almighty!" His hands shake, and his legs wobble. "Can't you stop these hallions from running amuck?"

Mary slams down the milk bottle hard enough to make the spoons clatter again. "We're doing our best. A little help from you wouldn't hurt."

Joe backs out of the room. "I'm off to work."

Ed grabs his jacket. "I've got papers to deliver." He slams the door on his way out.

"Is Mam coming home today?" Seconds drag like minutes as I wait for my father's response.

"No. She's got septicemia."

"How'd she get that?"

"From the surgery I told your mother not to get."

Da doesn't abide folks going contrary to his will. I brace for his anger, knowing he won't like my next question either. "Surgery? For a stomachache?"

"Ask your mother. Fix me breakfast."

Loose skin bags beneath Da's eyes, and his hair lies in dark, oily strings. When I set a peanut butter and mayonnaise sandwich before him, he peels apart the spongy slices of Tip Top bread. "What's wrong with you, girl? A man shouldn't have to eat this shite."

"Sorry, Da."

"Fry me some eggs, Katie."

I'm afraid to tell him what I must say next. "Sorry, Da. We don't have any."

As if Mary is not in the room, he asks, "Didn't yer sister go shopping?"

"You haven't given me any money." Mary is as tall as Mam, but even at fourteen years and five feet, four inches tall, she's not big enough to stand up against Da's wrath.

"Jesus, Mary, and Joseph. If anything's getting done, I guess it's left to me." He crams the sandwich into his mouth.

"We're doing a lot." I cringe because I expect my father to shout. Instead, he closes his eyes and rubs his forehead.

"Da, we're going to the hospital," says Mary. "Are you coming?"

He snatches his flat cap off the side table. "I'll wait on the porch."

I help Billy and Tommy into their jackets, hand-me-downs from Joe and Ed, then lead the boys outside. Powdery snowflakes ride the breeze and melt on our eyelashes.

"Where's yer sister?" Da grinds his cigarette into the porch floor.

Before I can say—She's behind you—the bus slows at the corner, and Mary shouts, "Run, Da!"

He waves and hollers, but the driver continues. I scoop Tommy off his stubby legs, and Billy bolts ahead. We scream, "Wait! Wait!"

Passengers gawk as Da bangs on the side of the metal bus. The brakes screech, and the door opens. We pant as we board. I prop Tommy on the seat behind Mary and Billy and pretend not to notice our father sulking in the rear.

Downtown, people stroll the streets, stepping around pools of melted snow that glisten in the sun. A grocer stacks softball-sized oranges in a bin beneath a blue and white striped awning. I inhale as if I can take in their scent, then cough from oily exhaust fumes.

We pass men lined two deep under the Sunshine Diner's banner. *Free Soup, Coffee, and Doughnuts.* A few men wear suits, but most are dressed in work overalls. A tall young man tucks his tattered, yet neatly ironed, shirt into the waistband of stained trousers that pucker under the belt cinched around his waist. But it's his blue and white striped tie, loose and hanging as if a flag lowered in defeat, that makes me sad.

Last week, I prayed the Holy Virgin Mother would send a new father, one who wouldn't drink up his wages. I glance back. When I catch Da's eye, shame burns my cheeks. At least he brings home enough that we're not begging for food.

The bus halts at Corwin Hospital. We're a somber bunch as we enter the large double doors. People sit in rows of metal chairs, many holding their heads or pressing against bleeding wounds. A pint-sized boy screams and grabs his leg as two men in blue scrubs assist him into a wheelchair.

We follow Da down a long hall. Florescent tubes cast unearthly shadows. I have walked this way before, still I shudder, a combination of cold and horror, until my father points. "She's in this room."

"Mam, Mam." Billy rushes in.

I shush him and reach for his arm, but he slips away.

Our father halts at the door. "Goin' for a cup of joe."

Mam leans off the bed and clings to Billy as if he's the lifeline she desperately needs.

"Too tight." Billy wriggles free and climbs onto the metal chair.

"I'm glad you came. My heart's pounding." Mam presses against her breast and shivers.

Mary unfolds the flannel blanket hanging over the foot railing and spreads it over our mother.

A metallic rattle draws our attention. A nurse pushes a device about her height that resembles a tin streetlight on wheels. She hands Mam darkened goggles and frowns. "Step away, children. Time for your mother's sunray treatment."

The frowning nurse plugs the long black cord into the wall, adjusts the beam, then leaves when a patient calls from the farthest bed.

I ask, "Mam, will the light make you well?"

"It cures inflammation, but last night, it gave me a fever."

Mary fluffs the pillow and places it between our mother's bony spine and the iron headboard frame.

When Tommy fusses, Mam says, "Let me cuddle my youngest son."

Nestled in her arms, he sweetly hums, "Ma, Ma, Ma."

"Mam, what's wrong with you?"

"Katie, I made a mistake. Mary will explain later."

"Please, tell me now."

"Unplug the light. I'm having a hot flush." Our mother's limp hand doesn't make a sound when she pats the bed. "Don't need everybody hearing my business. I just couldn't do it again."

I want to demand, What couldn't you do? But Mam's eyes close as if she's sinking into a heavy sleep.

"I told you Mrs. Odell was taking me for a doctor's appointment. That wasn't true. We had an appointment with a woman who performs abortions at home."

"Abortions?"

Mary elbows me. "Hush."

"Every day, I live with the pain of having James and Theresa for such a short time before our Lord lifted them into His heavenly arms." The tear teetering in the corner of Mam's eye breaks loose and glides the curve of her cheek.

I caress my mother's hand. "We miss our babies too."

"When I carried them, they didn't settle inside me just right. My body can't bear a ninth child, so it seemed a better way."

Mary picks up a tin water cup from the bedside table. "Take a sip. Then, you must rest."

"Can't sleep." Mam's lower lip quivers. "I'm haunted. Too many worries."

"A woman took our baby out of you?"

"Enough, Katie," warns Mary. "Let Mam rest."

"Is that why you bled?" A scream pushes against my tongue. Was this baby the sister I prayed for?

"The doctors say the woman wasn't clean and scraped too deep. That caused blood poisoning or septicemia."

"Can you come home?"

"Not yet, Katie." Mam shivers.

"You're as cold as ice." Mary wipes sweat beads from our mother's forehead. "I'm flipping on the sunray lamp again."

"Girls, it's important you understand, we scarcely feed and clothe the six of you." Mam pauses to catch her breath. "Your father said Mary should quit school and get a job. I said no. She has three more years. Both my girls will earn diplomas."

The nurse returns with a bottle and pours a large spoonful of reddish-brown liquid. "Mrs. Ryan, the doctor prescribed laudanum to help you sleep."

Mam's nose crinkles as she swallows.

The nurse clanks the spoon against the bottle and frowns. "Visiting hours are over."

Mary takes Tommy from Mam's arms and kisses her on the forehead.

I whisper, "We'll be back."

As we march to the coffee shop to find Da, I ask, "Are the red spots on Mam's arms and chest contagious?"

"Don't know, Katie."

"I'm not worried for myself, but Tommy's not even two, and she hugged and kissed him. Billy too. They both touched the red spots."

Two days later, Mary rummages through Joe's pockets while he's asleep and finds enough for two round-trip bus rides. She tells the boys they'll wait at home for a report on how Mam is faring.

In Mam's hospital room, we come face to face with the frowning nurse. She harrumphs and blocks our way. "Where do you think you are going?"

I stand tall. "To visit our mother, Mary Isabelle Ryan, wife of Edward Joseph Ryan."

"I don't care whose wife she is, young lady. Your mother is in ICU. No children allowed."

I shrink under the nurse's disdain, but Mary says, "I don't understand."

"Intensive care unit." Frowning spreads her arms and herds my sister and I toward the exit as if we're sheep. "Your mother needs more care."

I protest, "We haven't seen her for days."

The rapping of Frowning's pencil against her clipboard echoes like a buckshot in the quiet hall. "Bring your father. Perhaps the nurse will give you a moment if you're under his control."

"Our mother will think we don't love her anymore."

Frowning swivels on the heel of her black Mary Janes. "Don't bring your brothers. We can't have a bunch of rowdy kids roaming ICU."

In the early morning, Mary throws open Da's bedroom door. "We're leaving for the hospital in...Good Lord. He's gone."

"Can I go in his place?" asks Ed.

"Frowny nurse says you're not allowed. Stay with the boys."

I sit beside my sister in silence for the entire bus ride, remaining deep in my worried thoughts. Inside the hospital, she requests directions to ICU.

"Floor three," says a cherub-faced woman dressed in so much white she could be mistaken for an angel.

We exit the elevator and stop in front of a long white counter. The chilly room smells like disinfectant. A doctor studies a chart, and four nurses shuffle papers.

Mary announces, "We're here for Mrs. Ryan."

The nurse with a manly black mustache rises, leans over the countertop, and squints. "Relatives?"

"Yes, ma'am," says Mary.

Beneath the glare of the mustached nurse, I feel like an intruder.

"Follow me."

The nurse leads us to the fourth cubicle in the semicircle behind the nurses' station. Mam doesn't stir. A tube connects a boxlike machine to her nose. The only sound is our mother's rapid breath.

On a contraption similar to a metal coat tree hangs a small empty bottle. The nurse replaces it with one filled with blood as red as Tommy's firetruck. A white-coated doctor removes the needle from Mam's arm, pours alcohol on a gauze pad, and wipes.

She flinches when he punctures her skin. "Nurse, where is the husband?"

"Haven't seen him, doctor. These are Mrs. Ryan's girls."

The doctor's eyebrows pinch together. "I'm sorry. I should speak with the husband."

"Won't do any good," says Mary. "Whatever gets done is done by us."

"Girls, your father was here the night before last. You should talk to him."

"Was he drunk?"

When the doctor nods at Mary, she says, "Then you understand how things are. Best you tell us what we must do for our mother."

"Ahem, you have a point. Your mother needs a third transfusion and more sunray therapy. I prescribed vitamins C and A and a morphine regime that will let her rest and heal."

I ask timidly, "When can we bring her home?"

The doctor looks over my head at the nurse. "Perhaps another week."

Christmas break, days normally awaited with great anticipation, drag slower than any I can remember. Yet I barely notice the absence of my favorite activities—baking, tree decorating, and Mam's traditional New Year's Eve potluck party. And now, even though classes reconvened, I have not returned to school.

"You're going today," says Mary.

"Mam might come home. She'll need extra care."

"Mam won't abide you missing more school, so back you go."

"I didn't make a lunch."

"Don't give me your sourpuss." Mary unscrews the jar our mother hides in the pantry and removes a shiny nickel. "Buy whatever you want at the cafeteria."

Rose pokes in her head as I pocket the coin and shoulder my bookbag.

"Walk fast. I must find Mama Louise before the bell. She cooks medicines in her kitchen that make people well."

Once inside the building, we slink into the cafeteria. The cook's apron is stained as if he killed some poor animal to serve for lunch. He snarls,

"Get out of here. Kids can't come behind the serving counter."

I square my shoulders. "We're searching for Mama Louise."

"Out. No students allowed in the kitchen."

Rose and I back out as the janitor sinks his mop into a bucket of dingy water. "Mama Louise isn't here."

"Where is she?"

He glances over his shoulder. "You know her husband busses dishes at a fancy restaurant, right?"

"Mama said his boss is stingy. He pays her husband so little she must work instead of staying home with their daughter. That's why I stay in school, even when the other kids frighten me, because a woman can never predict when she'll be called upon to support her kids."

"Good advice." The janitor leans on his mop handle.

"Will Mama come to work tomorrow?"

"No, 'fraid not. A white waitress, no offense intended, said Mama's husband pocketed her tips. The owner threatened to phone the police if he didn't return the money. He didn't have no way to prove he wasn't the thief, so Mama packed up the family and skedaddled."

"She's gone? Without saying goodbye?"

"She asked after you. The principal's secretary said yo' momma was doing poorly, and nobody knew when you'd be back. Mama took me aside and said, 'Jacob, tell my little friend she must stay strong. Tell Katie I love her, and I'll miss her, but I got ta go.'"

I want to thank the janitor, but my words catch in my throat. Only when Rose and I reach our classroom, can I speak. "Everybody leaves me. You're the only friend I have left."

We hook fingers in a pinky swear and speak at the same time. "Friends forever."

That night, I keep my loss to myself. But a premonition haunts me. "Mary, there's a gnawing in the pit of my stomach telling me we should visit Mam tomorrow."

In the morning, I take Billy and Tommy to Mrs. Odell's. I hug Rose long and hard, hoping that will give me strength, then walk to the corner with

Mary and Ed and board the 7:45 bus.

The sun cuts through tree branches that have lost their leaves and sparkles on the freshly fallen snow. Three boys bomb each other with snowballs. A black Labrador bites one boy's trouser leg and shakes his head as if playing with a rag toy. But I can't smile.

Once inside the hospital, a warning nip creeps along my ear and down my neck as I follow Ed, who is following Mary, who follows the nurse.

"Wait here," says the mustached nurse. "Doctor will speak with you before you go in."

A young orderly rolls a gurney past us. The swish of air stings of alcohol and the putrid stench of sickness. Two doors farther in the hallway, an elderly man covers his face with his hands and rocks in his metal chair.

The doctor's deep voice startles me. He tugs the collar on his white lab coat then fingers the stethoscope hanging from his neck. "I'm still uncomfortable giving updates to you children, but we haven't seen your father for a while."

I say, "We haven't either. And we haven't seen our big brother Joe. Has he visited our mother?"

"Ah, not that I am aware. Check the nurses' station. They maintain a record of Mrs. Ryan's visitors."

"Thanks, Doctor," says Mary. "I doubt he's been here."

"Well then, your mother's condition has deteriorated, but it is best for her if you don't act alarmed. She suffers from sepsis, which is a serious complication of septicemia. I'm treating her with oxygen, but the inflammation spreading through her body can cause blood clots that prevent oxygen from reaching her vital organs."

Mary's brows pinch together. "What does that mean?"

"Ah, um, organs fail when their oxygen supply is blocked."

"Are you saying our mother might die?" asks Ed.

My vision darkens. As if handed a hundred-pound flour sack, I crumple to the floor until awakened by a cold, wet cloth on my forehead. The doctor stares at his watch while pressing his fingers against the inside of my wrist.

Ed leans close. I recoil from the lingering stink of the Lucky Strike he smoked while we waited for the bus.

"Your pulse is normal." The doctor shines a small black flashlight in my eyes. "Are you dizzy?"

"No, sir. I want my mother."

"Please walk to the nurses' station and back."

The floor moves sideways beneath my feet, but I'll not let anyone keep me from my mother. I lift my chin and place one foot in front of the other.

When the doctor nods, Mustache Nurse barks, "Come, children." She halts before the last of four beds and drags a white curtain along the metal bar. "Such a shame. Six weeks pregnant. No woman should suffer this. Men and their useless laws. What do they know about a woman's body?"

The silver canister beside the bed reminds me of Shamrock Gas Station's pumps. Its black hose connects to a transparent funnel-shaped device.

When Mary whispers, "Mam," our mother's eyelids flutter.

Only then do I realize someone taped the funnel to her mouth and nose.

"Five minutes." Mustache Nurse tugs on her white belt. "Don't make me leave my desk and chase you out."

The angry red spots have spread across Mam's body, and her voice is scratchy and faint. "Mother? Is that you?"

I fight the urge to run. "Is Mam talking to Nana? Doesn't she recognize us?"

Mary's eyes glisten. "I suspect she's confused."

Ed's thirteen, yet he stands tall like a grown man. He blinks his moist blue eyes and propels me forward. "Tell her it's us."

Mam's breath, a fast and fierce rasp, frightens me, but I caress her hand. *Praise be to you, Holy Virgin Mother. She's alive. Please tell me what I should do to help our mother get well.*

We lean close to hear Mam murmur, "Fear not, I will watch over you from heaven. Your father will care for you on Earth."

"We won't hear of you leaving us," says Mary. "You just need time to get well."

The metal hospital bed creaks as I crawl in, lay my head on Mam's chest, and listen to what sounds like raindrops pounding against an empty bucket. "You must get well. I need you. I'm not even nine...."

I wait for my mother's response, but the only voice comes from the patient in the next bed. "Have you kids seen that nurse? I want my orange

Jell-O."

Ed points. "Here comes Mustache, looking madder than a wet dog. We better beat it."

We plod home in silence. But as we climb the porch steps, Ed proclaims, "If father is in charge of our care here on Earth, we're in for a brutal dose of it."

When Nana passed one year ago, the music, stories, and kind words from both friends and people my grandmother hadn't even met confused and terrified me. Yet I came to understand those were acts of respect. When I ask why no one came to honor our mother, Mary mumbles a bit about the stain of having an abortion.

Now, at Roselawn Cemetery, I hold up my feet because the folding metal chairs sit atop Nana's grave. The white roses, lilies, and carnations draped across Mam's casket would please her, but I'm unsettled. Something else is terribly wrong.

This morning, I asked Da if we will bury the baby who killed my mother in the same grave as Theresa and Mam. He swore and threw his whiskey tumbler. The image of the golden liquid running down the wall and glass shards crashing to the floor still singes my brain.

Mam's wishes were to cradle her last-born child into eternity, but Theresa is alone in the tiny coffin someone dug up and placed on a fresh mound of rich, dark soil. I whisper to Molly, "Surely, our baby sister is terrified. Somebody needs to take her out of that box and put her in our mother's arms."

The undertaker, Mr. McCarthy, lingers behind the row of chairs set out for the family. He entwines his fingers and rocks on his heels. If I had the strength, I'd stomp right over and tell him he should try to look sad rather than bored.

Tommy bawls, "I want Mam." When Mary rocks him as if they are one, his puffy eyelids close and his breathing slows. Billy fidgets in the chair next to big brother Ed, who stares into the air above the coffin, his body ramrod straight.

I clench the Bible, the only one of Nana's favorite belongings I asked to have for my own. When I flip through the pages, the air swirls like tiny birds flitting past my face.

Joe twists his flat cap in his hands and paces, slow and stiff, behind the folding chairs. I swivel away from him and toward Father Bertram. The cadence of the priest's voice comforts me as if I were in a sailboat slipping over gentle waves. He sweeps his palm over Mam's coffin then raises the Bible toward the sky. His thin gray lips move, but my brain blocks his words. I visualize the unplugged kitchen wall clock, spun back to 1:25, the moment my mother died, alone in the dark, alone in the hospital, while I slept in my soft warm bed.

Father Bertram utters his final words, then Mr. and Mrs. Parker offer their sympathies and leave. Rose wraps her arms around me. "I'll come over later."

I'm so numb I can't lift my arms to hug her back. Thunder clouds hang low. The breeze rustles through the trees and blows across my bare neck. A chill settles in my bones. Is it grief that has Da bent over? Or is he drunk?

"My beloved wife, now my daughter..." Granda shudders as he stands, knocking the folding chair over backward. "Thirty-six years old. Too young to die and leave these kids motherless."

The first shovelful of dirt hits the coffins with a gritty thunk. I scoot forward in my seat. How easy would it be to slide into the hole and wrap my arms around Theresa's tiny coffin?

Easier than standing up and carrying on.

CHAPTER SIXTEEN

FEBRUARY 1932

Blades of grass stand up as frozen as the icicles hanging down from the eves on this Thursday morning when Mary announces we will attend Candlemas, and she'll allow no arguments to the contrary. While my sister collects our candles from the holders and kitchen drawer, I slip on a school dress rather than my Sunday best.

I put rolls of lime and orange Lifesavers in my coat pocket. Billy and Tommy think it's fun to stick their tongues in the center hole. While I appreciate how that keeps them quiet, I see no reason to have our candles blessed.

"Tradition," says Mary.

"What good will it do?"

"It's the light-at-the-end-of-the-tunnel sort of event, Katie. Lord knows we need a cure for the darkness we've been through."

Father Bertram says Jesus is the Light of the World, but Jesus deserted me, let my mother die, and Nana, Theresa, and Mrs. O'Shea before her. They are buried where there is no light, and there's no light in my heart.

No blessed candle will change that. I sink into a chair. I could argue neither Da nor Granda will go, but fighting with my sister takes more energy than I can muster. Mary takes after Mam in that there's no sense arguing once she makes up her mind.

Granda thumps and bumps his cane while making his way to the kitchen table and grunts toward Joe. He takes a seat and wheezes, "Try to keep the lads quiet. Your Da's in a bad way."

I say, "You don't sound so good yourself. Can you stay home?"

"Nah, can't abuse CF&I's kindness. My boss wasn't obliged to keep me on after I was such an eejit as to crash into that wheelbarrow. You know, Katie, I was talking to your grandmother."

"I look up to heaven when I talk to her too."

"I've watched you. Your fool brother Ed said you talk to the squirrels in our tree, but I knew." Granda groans as he stands. "Doc explained my arthritis is getting worse, but I got to go to work. I need to keep those paychecks coming so I can pay off this house before I meet my Maker."

"Don't say that. I couldn't bear it if you die." When I step into my grandfather's warm and loving arms, I notice he is less muscular than a year ago.

"I'm a lucky man, living to seventy-nine, but the doctor says my arteries are hardening and restricting my blood flow. Arteriosclerosis. Ain't that a big name for being too damn old? Katie, I'll put on my work boots while you make that sandwich."

After the door closes behind Granda, Da straggles from his bedroom. Joe rams him against the wall. "Where's the food money I gave yeh? These kids are hungry. Empty your pockets, yeh ballbag."

"Yeh didn't give me much."

"I gave Mam the same amount, and we ate just fine. She always put us first."

"I gave her my paycheck too." Da breaks free from Joe's clutch.

"Liar. You're a feckin waste." Joe digs in his pocket then hands several coins to Mary. "For the bus. Bring the kids and meet me at the Sunshine Diner after yeh get done at church."

Billy reaches for the paper menu and knocks over Joe's Coca-Cola. The brown liquid fizzes and trickles onto the floor. I wait for Joe to thump Billy upside the head for embarrassing him in the presence of the cute waitress. Today, Joe simply raises his hand to alert the white-aproned gal we made a mess.

"What can we order?" asks Mary.

"Whatever yeh want. This is an important talk we're gonna have."

"Malts?" Knowing we can afford ice cream only on special days, I wait for Joe's *no.*

He stares at the menu; doesn't even wink or call the waitress Babe as she takes our orders.

Tommy runs his tiny racecar along the battered table's metal-trimmed edge. Ed babbles about the winning run he made days ago playing baseball in the street until Joe says, "Quiet, please," instead of "Shut up, yeh little gobshite."

This is serious. I study Mary's face for a clue.

Joe lowers his voice. "Da was at the local with a woman."

I imagine my eyes are as large as an owl's. "Mam won't put up with that."

Ed rolls his eyeballs up in their sockets. "Mam's dead."

"I know, turnip brain, but she's watching."

"What's she gonna do?"

"Smite him dead with a lightning bolt."

"Holy mackerel, Katie. Do yeh believe everything Father Bertram says? You need to lay off church until yeh get your head screwed on straight."

"Enough, you two." Joe rolls and unrolls his flat cap. "Listen. The problem is we'll be caring for ourselves from now on out. Granda can make the house payment and pay the water, gas, and electric bills, but that leaves him short for food. Since Da drinks his entire salary, here's the plan. He gets paid on Fridays, so Saturday morning, while he's still passed out, whoever's up first skims his wallet. Leave him a buck. He won't realize what the story is. Ed, you'll have to contribute your newspaper route earnings to the grocery fund. And Mary, the fancy fabric you're buying, we can't have any more of that. If we're gonna survive, we need your babysitting money."

"What about your wages?" asks Mary.

"I'll be chipping in more. We'll each do our part. This won't be easy."

Two weeks later, Mary grits her teeth and grips the aluminum mixing bowl as if someone might steal it from her. The clang of the metal spoon reminds me of the Philly train engineer ringing his bell. How different would life be if we had stayed?

"Katie, I should've had you sneak Mrs. Murphy's rat poison from her gardening supplies. A sprinkle mixed with the powdered sugar on my cocoa cake and this woman of Da's will stand before Saint Peter begging to be let in the pearly gates before either of them figures out what we did."

Ed clenches his throat and makes puking sounds.

I cover my mouth and laugh. "Not funny."

My brother crumples down the wall into a mass of writhing arms and legs.

I tell him, "You could go to hell."

"Sweet Jaysus, save me from the devil." Ed folds his hands in prayer and gazes upward. "It was for a good cause that I poisoned her."

"Listen, dummy," I say. "Maybe this woman will become our stepmother and take care of us like we are her own."

Last week, Joe took us to the Colorado Theater, downtown Main Street, for a rerun of *Dracula*. Now, knowing how scared I get, Ed scuffles across the floor on bended knees and imitates Bela Lugosi's deep, threatening tone. "Bwahahahahaha. Save me, Katie. The devil's hand is upon my shoulder, forcing me down and down, into the center of the earth. I'm burning...."

"Get me Mrs. Murphy's deadly powdered sugar." Mary wriggles her eyebrows and shapes her hands into claws. "Pleeease...."

I shove my sister away and peek in the oven door. Earlier, I chopped rutabaga, onion, potatoes, and leftover brisket, wrapped the mixture in pockets of shortcrust pastry, then crimped the edges. Now, the juices bubble where the golden crust split. My pasties smell heavenly.

Mary followed Mrs. Kozak's New Year's Eve recipe and rubbed fresh thyme and chopped fennel into the chicken's skin. I chuckle. My Irish pasties sit alongside the Jewish hen waiting for the fallen woman Mary wants to poison.

"Close the oven door and go get the boys," says Mary.

"We should leave the little stinkers with Mrs. Odell so we can eat a calm and peaceful dinner like we're all adults."

"Best this woman sees us as we are, a shouting, blubbering mess of snot-faced boys." Mary winks. "She'll run screaming from this house. Then, I won't need Mrs. Murphy's rat poison."

Still using his Dracula voice, Ed shouts as I head to Rose's to collect Billy and Tommy. "It'd be a good thing we did, saving the woman's life like that."

An hour later, Mary opens the oven door. "My chicken shriveled, and your pasties burned."

"Guess you're getting your wish. Da's woman won't want to stay for dried-up food."

Billy, who says he is a big boy and must now be called Bill, climbs up two kitchen shelves as if it were a jungle gym and drops the open box of Grape-Nuts. I ignore him and glance toward the ceiling. Overhead thumps sound like a burlap sack of raccoons rolling across the floor.

Ed shouts at Joe, "Yeh bleedin' maggot, give me my card."

When Tommy bumbles past, I smell an all-familiar, stinking-to-high-heaven scent—just when I thought I had him potty trained. As I tug his waistband and peek down the back of his trousers, the front door opens.

In steps the woman wearing a heavy crepe peplum blouse with an exquisite cream lace caplet that clings to the curve of her shoulder and flares mid-arm. She poses as if to have her portrait done—points a high-heeled, top-stitched T-strap shoe out from the flounce of her copen- blue ankle-length skirt.

I bite my upper lip to keep it from rising in disgust. The red scarf tied around the woman's neck reminds me of my third-grade teacher reading *The Scarlet Letter* aloud last week. I should greet this woman. Instead, I say, "Sorry, I've got a mess." I steer Tommy toward the bathroom, help him take off his trousers, and shake his underpants over the toilet.

Holy Virgin Mother, please forgive what I am about to do, but I won't let this woman disgrace my mother.

A greenish-brown mound plops into the water. If caught, my punishment will be severe, but this woman must be driven off. I run my right index finger along the edge of Tommy's underpants and pick up a thin layer of poop, then force the smirk off my face. "Go tell Ed you need clean pants."

Naked below his manly, green-checkered, button-up cotton shirt, Tommy darts into the living room.

My big sister rarely swears like Joe. Today, she makes an exception. "Somebody get ahold of Bill. He's tracking feckin Grape-Nuts across my clean floor. Katie, get the bloody broom."

Ed and Bill thunder past as I use my unsoiled left hand to retrieve the broom from the closet beneath the stairs, then stall in the dark hall to make Mary more frantic than she is now. Tommy spots me and squeals with delight. It's a game we play. The more I whoop, "Naked boy on the loose," the louder he laughs and the faster he scampers. I don't wish to disappoint my brother, so I ride the broom and cackle like a witch. I've never come after Tommy like this. He shows his joy by shrieking and throwing his hands over his head.

As we roar into the living room, my mind fills with last November's newspaper photo of Norma Shearer holding her golden statue after receiving the best actress award for *The Divorcee* at the 4th Academy Awards ceremony. I remember it clearly because I had stared for hours, thinking if we had stayed on the train, I too would be in Los Angeles and could have put on my Sunday best dress and headed over to the Biltmore Hotel to see it for myself.

I halt at the feet of Da and his woman, lean my broom against the wall, and smugly angle my chin and cock my head to imitate Ms. Shearer. Then I reach out to shake the Scarlet Woman's hand. "How do you do? Welcome to our home." I resist laughing out loud about passing Tommy's poop to her and lift the crystal candy dish off the side table with my clean hand. "Have a peppermint." I wait until the woman slips a candy between her painted lips. "Made these from our dead mother's favorite recipe. Mam said peppermints work the best to overpower Da's stinky breath after he stays out all night, smoking and drinking with his mates."

The Scarlet Woman delicately slips the tips of her painted ruby-red fingers into her brassiere, removes a white linen, monogrammed handkerchief, and expels the peppermint.

I hide my snicker, skip into the kitchen, and scrub my fingernails across the carbolic soap until confident every trace of poop is washed off. Still, I have a creepy sensation from shaking hands, so I rinse again with steamy hot water.

Mary throws a dishtowel at my back. "Good Lord, your hands are corned-beef red. Help me set out this food."

"Will somebody put pants on this baby?" hollers Joe.

Mary winks at me. "Do it yourself, yeh maggot."

Da raises his voice. "I need all of yeh in the living room."

Mary slams the oven door. Joe clenches his jaw the way he does when holding back his words and hoists Tommy onto his shoulders. Tommy grabs a hank of big brother's hair for balance, and Ed and Bill move into positions beside Joe. My sister and I join the boys as if lining up before a firing squad, only I'm not sure which side has the guns.

"This is Margaret Ellen Kelly. I call her Maggie."

"That's not what I'd call 'er," mutters Joe.

Da's proud smile becomes a snarl. He raises his fist.

To my surprise, the Scarlet Woman steps between them and extends a hand as limp as wilted lettuce.

Ed shakes the woman's hand while Joe and Da glare at each other.

I experience a touch of guilt, then reason, Ed's not terribly clean, anyway. And Joe's bracing Tommy's bare bottom to prevent him from rolling backward off his shoulders, so there's no telling what's on his hands. My responsibility is to protect my sister.

I sniff noisily. "Dinner's burning." As Mary dashes toward the kitchen, I back out of the room. "I'll help her."

Joe saunters into the kitchen, peels Tommy off his shoulder, and sits him in the highchair. "Isn't that geebag done up like a dog for dinner?"

I glance toward the adults. "She can hear you."

"Tommy's going to play fireman's hose if you don't put drawers on him," says Mary.

"The queen has spoken." Joe lifts Tommy and pats his bottom. "Come with me, mate."

The Scarlet Woman enters and pinches Bill's cheek. "Aren't you a cute baby?"

He slaps her hand away then pats his chest. "I'm three. A big boy."

I wish I could faint, or vomit, or run and hide in my room. How can I dishonor Mam by eating with this woman at my mother's table?

Mary hands me the dried-out pasties, then removes the overcooked chicken from the oven. The poor bird's wings and legs hang loose, and the bones poke out its skin, but this is good. The Scarlet Woman will think we are dreadful cooks.

Instead of Mary's usual command—*Get your butts to the table*—she smiles graciously. "Supper's ready. Please, take your seats."

My lip rises in a snarl.

Da eats silently.

The Scarlet Woman swallows daintily. "Mary, I presume you are an experienced babysitter?"

Mary takes an enormous bite of pasty and chews as if hours might pass before she can speak.

"Katie, do you enjoy school?" asks the Scarlet Woman.

My chair nearly tips over as I lean out to catch the small metal drinking cup Tommy drops over the highchair's side. "I'm lousy at arithmetic, but Ed's worse. If you're replacing our mother, you should know she tutored him every day." I wait for Ed to protest my lie, but he's stifling a belly laugh. He understands I'm speaking badly of him to scare this woman away.

"Got work. Can't be late." Joe's chair screeches as he thrusts away from the table.

I point my fork at him. "Don't stomp your feet when you straggle in at 4:00 a.m."

"Why should I change my ways for an annoying pipsqueak?" Joe's voice drips with sarcasm. I'm pleased. He's playing along.

"Nice to meet you, Joe." The Scarlet Woman's tone is as cold as her eyes.

He ignores her then sneers when Da says, "Maggie and I are staying at the Minnequa Hotel until she moves in with us next week."

I turn to Mary and move my lips silently. "Moves in?"

Any other night, once I tuck Tommy and Bill into bed, the rest of us wheedle to play one more poker hand or finish our Monopoly game. Tonight, I just want to sleep.

Mary rises as if she has the aches and pains of the elderly. "I'm done with this day. Good night."

I leap from my chair. "I better go with my sister."

"Ah, yes. We should leave," says Da. "Get checked in at the Minnequa."

Snug in bed, I listen for the sawing noise my brothers make when sleeping. Mary's breathing is smooth and deep. The wooden floors creak, but I no longer worry someone has broken in. This old house's tired groans comfort me. The lone distracting sound is the tap, tap of teardrops plopping onto my pillowcase.

Mary touches my arm. "You're shaking like a leaf. Don't let that hoary bat bother you."

"It's not that."

"Then what?"

"Mary, I'm ashamed of my thoughts."

"Ashamed? You've done nothing worth sobbing your eyes out."

"I hate the baby who killed Mam. Father Bertram says hating is a sin, but I can't stop."

"Katie, infection killed our mother, not the baby. They used filthy tools."

"Why would a doctor use dirty tools?"

"This is just wrong. I shouldn't have to explain abortion when you're nine."

"Doctors shouldn't kill babies."

"Wasn't a doctor."

"Who did it?"

"Some woman in a kitchen or back bedroom. Remember the day Mam and Mrs. Odell borrowed Mr. Parker's car and said Mam had a doctor's appointment? That's when it happened."

"Killing is a mortal sin. Is our mother in hell?"

"No, no. It was too young to live. Mam didn't feel the quickening."

"Quickening?"

"She hadn't felt the baby move. Ensoulment hadn't happened. It didn't have a soul. She wouldn't have gotten an abortion if it had. Remember at the burial, Father Bertram said Mam's in heaven watching over us?"

"What if it was the sister I've been praying for?"

Mary stares at the ceiling. "We'll never know. Can't tell at six weeks."

"Is the baby inside the coffin with Mam?"

"Don't force me to tell you that."

"Why didn't we have a funeral for the baby?"

"Please, Katie. Don't make me say it."

"Can we go to the cemetery tomorrow?"

"The baby's not there."

"Where is she?"

"The woman threw it in the trash."

"Noooo! You're wrong. Mam wouldn't let her. She loves her kids."

Mary tugs me close, and we fall asleep in each other's arms.

CHAPTER SEVENTEEN

APRIL, 1932

Mary, Joe, and Ed are sitting around the kitchen table when I walk in after collecting Tommy and Bill from Mrs. Odell.

"Family meeting," says Joe.

"Without Da?"

"This meeting is regarding him and the woman. They got married."

Mary glares at Joe as if it's his fault.

A metallic taste pools in my mouth. "She's our stepmother?"

Joe pats his chest. "I'm sixteen. Don't need mothering. Listen, that's not my point. Da's gone completely arseways. He's been gone six weeks, could be he's not coming home."

Mary picks at her cuticle. "He'll be back. This is his house."

"That's the deal. Granda's name is on the deed, and he says the Kelly woman isn't welcome in the home he bought for his wife and daughter."

"Joe, why isn't Granda attending this meeting?" asks Ed.

"Still working, numbskull. He may take pity on them when he finds out she's pregnant."

"Pregnant? They just got married."

"Good Lord, Katie. Don't act so innocent," says Mary.

Mortal or venial? I'm thinking back to Father Bertram's sermon about which type of sin this is when Joe says, "Saw the new Mrs. Ryan at the local, done up like a two-dollar hoor and drinking like a fish."

Mary smacks Joe's shoulder. "And you weren't?"

"A single pint with me mate. But listen, Benny's fluff says the child might not be Da's."

"Scarlet Woman."

"Katie, we don't need your drama. Benny's bird says Miss Kelly received a marriage offer from another bloke, and he might be the father."

"She made a bad choice picking Da," says Ed.

I ask, "Are we gonna have another brother or sister?"

"Half brother or sister," says Mary.

"I'm hearing," Joe pauses and scratches his head, "she calls us unruly hallions."

"Could be none of this is true."

"Ed, the place where there's smoke, there's fire. She claims she can't tolerate a bunch of wild ingrates in her delicate condition."

"What's an ingrate?"

Joe playfully smacks Ed. "You, meathead. But she's saying we're all ungrateful buckets of snot."

I snort, "Why should we be grateful to the Scarlet Woman?"

Mary answers, "I thank her for taking our mean-arse-drunk of a father off our hands."

"On that, I agree, but money's as scarce as hen's teeth." Joe pulls out his pocket linings. "How do I feed yeh, buy clothes and school supplies, and get yeh to a doctor if need be?"

"Granda gives me money for food," says Mary.

"CF&I will never fire him, but as watchman, he makes half his former wages. I asked for more hours but don't hold much hope. The depression hit the company hard. Fellas laid off every payday. If I'm one, I'll drop out of school and get a full-time job."

"Don't. You graduate in a year."

"Katie, I just don't see any other options," mutters Joe as he rises from the kitchen table and flips on the radio.

The announcer says, "The good citizens of Los Angeles are ramping up for the July thirtieth opening of The Games of the Tenth Olympiad. We're excited about an opportunity to forget our woes during this Great Depression and focus on winning the gold."

I say, "If we'd stayed on the train, we'd be in Los Angeles instead of the middle of this big fat catastrophe."

No one cares if the house is tidied, or the dishes are washed. If not strong armed into clean clothes, the boys wear the same shirts and trousers until they stink worse than the racoon that died underneath the porch. I spread Welch's grape jam, then a generous layer of Skippy, advertised at the market as the latest creation in peanut butter, and slap the air-filled Wonder Bread together. I hope these sandwiches entice the boys to be a bit more cooperative. But Ed is so busy staring out the window he can't feel the hot glare I'm hurling toward his back.

"Yeh gotta get a gander at this," Ed shouts from the living room then thunders out.

I join him and Mary curbside as Da steps out the driver's door.

"Holy mackerel," says Ed. "A brand-new 1932 Ford Model B Two-Door Sedan. Must have cost $500."

"The last of your mother's savings, but this car's a beauty. Worth every penny. Filled 'er up at Shamrock Gas to bring good luck." Da opens the passenger door.

A black suede pump at the end of a silk-nyloned leg emerges below the hem of a moss-green wool skirt. Glossy red lacquered nails catch the light. The thing angled atop the Scarlet Woman's head resembles a vinyl record. I choke down my anger when Da takes her pale hand and assists this evil woman from the car. He never helped our mother off the bus, not even when the weight of Bill or Tommy in her stomach nearly toppled her off the rickety metal steps.

Da opens the car's trunk and strains to lift three large suitcases, a red leather makeup case, and a flowered carpet satchel. "Give me a hand, Ed. My back's killing me."

Mary rests an arm across my shoulders. "Appears Granda had a change of heart."

"Da's moving back in?"

"With the woman. Lord have mercy on our souls."

"Could be good. Miss Kelly can tend Bill and Tommy so we can go to school every day."

"Listen, Katie, Corwin lowered the age requirement to fifteen for switchboard operators. I look old enough. I'm on my way to apply. How hard a job can that be? Talking on the phone all day. We'll need cash if the Scarlet Woman gets sick of us and moves out and takes Da with her."

"We're his kids. He wouldn't leave us."

"Joe thinks he will. Don't worry on it now." Mary opens her coin purse. "I'll treat you to a malt at H.S. Kress."

The months drag, and many days pass without event. But last night, Da and his new wife had a ripping good fight, and the Scarlet Woman stormed out for the Minnequa Hotel with a suitcase in hand.

Tonight, Da sits on the sofa, nursing the whiskey in his tumbler. I'm perturbed because Joe and Mary didn't invite me to tag along on their double date. When I plunk yesterday's Luncheon Salad on the table, the coagulated gelatin and shriveled peas shimmy like a block of slime. The boys clench their throats and gag. I snatch the plate, thrust the gelatin salad into the trashcan, and grab the Grape-Nut flakes from the cupboard. Bill and Tommy cheer then slurp the cereal as if it's the best dinner they ever ate.

Da hauls Bill up by the armpits. "Taking me boy with me tonight."

"It's past his bedtime." I extend my arms, but Da heads toward the door.

Ed blocks his way. "Yeh can't take a three-year-old to the local."

"He's *my* boy. I say where he goes."

Bill struggles to wrench free. "I want to play marbles."

I beg, "Please, Da. He needs a bath."

Ed lunges at our father. Bill puts his arms around his big brother's neck, but Da swings with his free hand and knocks Ed to the floor. Our father hurries out the door to the car. Bill pounds his little fists against Da's shoulder, but our father flings open the passenger door and tosses him in the front seat. He scrambles to a seated position and presses his palms against the passenger window. My heart shatters when my precious brother's lips move as if saying, *Help me.* Da revs the engine. Ed stands behind the car and crosses his arm. But when our father rams the gear into reverse, Ed leaps to safety.

Tommy scurries up behind, clings to Ed's leg, and whimpers, "I want Bill."

I've never felt so helpless as when watching the taillights fade into the darkness.

"This is bad, Katie, but what can we do?"

"Go to the theater and find Joe and Mary."

Ed pats his trouser pockets. "We don't have bus fare."

We gather around the supper table. Tommy sucks his thumb. I am deep in thought when Ed opens the kitchen drawer and takes out a deck of cards. "Want ta play Beggar My Neighbor?"

"Not tonight. All this upset my stomach."

Ed loosens the string on his scruffy marble bag and kneels. Tommy chases the marbles as his big brother pretends to play against a boy who's plotting to win his entire collection, including the slag.

"Where's the local?"

Ed misses his shot. "Jesus, Katie. I don't know."

"We must rescue Bill."

"Are yeh bloody mad? Da will be buckled by now. He'd kill us on the spot for embarrassing him in front of his lowlife mates."

"It's midnight. If you're too chicken-lily-livered, I'll go."

"Katie, everybody calls their pub the local. Da could be anywhere."

"Joe knows."

"I'm sure he does, but when will he get home?" Ed extends his hand to Tommy. "Come on, little man. We're off to bed."

A key clicks in the lock, and the doorknob spins. I glance toward the clock through blurry eyes. But I don't care what time it is. I only care that Joe and Mary finally returned.

"Da took Bill."

"Took him where?" asks Joe.

"The local. Do you know where it is?"

"You bet your sweet arse I do. I'll bust his dial if he hurts that kid." Joe hollers, "Ed, get downstairs! I need your help!"

The boys run out. The night chill rushes in. I close the door, curl up on the sofa, and hug Nana's old lap blanket around me. Mary drags the rocking chair closer, and we wait.

I startle when the door flies open and the boys rush in. Bill's body hangs in Joe's arms like a wet blanket. "We can't wake him."

Our brother's head lolls to one side. Mary pats his cheek then massages his hands. Ed yanks off Bill's Buster Browns, bumps his lifeless feet together, then rubs his legs.

I press my palms in prayer. *No, no, no. Please, Holy Virgin Mother, don't take him.*

"Give him to me." Mary sits Bill in her lap, facing her. His head falls forward, against my sister's shoulder. His feet hang limp. She pounds his back as if burping a thirty-pound baby. The thumps get louder until he vomits slimy, half-digested Grape-Nuts in a brownish foam, then lets out a blood-curdling wail.

"Good job, Billy Boy," says Joe. "That's what I call bustin' a lung."

"Smells like beer," says Mary.

Please, Blessed Virgin Mother. Help us in our hour of need. I dampen a washcloth and wipe Bill's ruddy face.

"We caught Da charging his mates a nickel each to make poor Bill drink. That's how the arsewipe stays so bloody hammered after he blows his paycheck."

"What kind of man does that?" asks Mary.

"No man at all. He's a sneaky scut." Joe punches his fist into his other hand. "We can't let him take our little brother again, no matter what foul excuse he gives."

"Ever." When I brush Bill's sweat-drenched hair from his eyes, he looks up gratefully.

CHAPTER EIGHTEEN

OCTOBER 1932

As Rose and I turn onto our street, I envy my friend who will enjoy the peacefulness of entering a house in which only one other person, her mother, lives. When I step inside my home, the Scarlet Woman shrieks, "Where have you been? It's four o'clock."

I keep walking toward the stairs. "Got homework. I'm behind in math."

"These boys aren't my responsibility."

I drop my books with a thud. "Bill, get your ball. Let's teach Tommy to catch."

"Nah, he's too little." Bill, soon to turn four, flaunts his advanced age over his younger brother.

"We'll roll the ball to him." I enjoy playing mother, most of the time. Right now, I'm tired. *Please, Holy Virgin Mother, grant me strength.*

Granda stumbles in the front door and falls against the wall. He snarls at the Scarlet Woman's back as she scurries into the bedroom. "Got to be the luck of the Irish that brings that woman to our house. You know, Katie, that's the problem about being Irish. All our luck is bad." My grandfather's laugh deteriorates into a cough that rips up his chest and sends a spray of yellowed phlegm.

I back him up against the sofa. He falls hard and grabs his hip. "Jesus, Mary, and Joseph, burns like some arse-bite stabbed a hot poker through my thigh."

"You're home early." I lift his feet onto the footstool.

"Put my boot back on, girl. I'll be late for work."

"Granda, you just got home."

"I did? Aye, I get a wee bit confused these days." Granda pulls his dented flask from his work pants pocket as I remove the second boot. He takes a long swig then rests his head on the sofa back. The flask tilts in his limp hand.

I snatch it before the foul-smelling liquid spills. "Boys, we'll play ball later. Granda's not well."

Bill mimics an airplane bombing enemy territory. I stuff Tommy into the highchair. He squeals when Joe and Ed tromp in, good naturedly prodding each other. As if no one or anything else matters, the older boys huddle around the radio and rotate the dial until an announcer's voice blasts through.

"Yesterday, October first, the top of the fifth inning. Babe Ruth pointed his bat into the stands. When he connected, and oh boy, did he connect, the ball flew to the Babe's intended target, and he scored a home run."

Mary marches in the door and barks, "Ed, take Bill and Tommy upstairs. Joe, get the broom. The porch needs sweeping."

The boys mutter, but amazingly comply without uttering a single swear word while I set the table. Mary places last night's leftovers on the burner. The Milkorno porridge is even less appealing than yesterday.

Two hours later, Da lets the door slam behind him. Joe glares over the newspaper. Granda, asleep on the sofa, stirs and coughs.

Mary points to the pot of lumpy corn meal, powdered skim milk, with a sprinkle of salt, on the supper table beside the cold soda bread. "Da, you're late. Granda's sick, and your new wife has taken to bed because she's too delicate to help."

I eye the back door. If I slip out to Rose's, I'll avoid Da arguing back with Mary. But Da surprises me by hiking his trousers high on his waist and swaggering into the bedroom where the Scarlet Woman hides.

Voices escalate. Mary and I inch closer.

Joe jumps up. "Girls, I need yer help."

With the next cough, bloody pus shoots out Granda's mouth.

Mary grabs the dishcloth. "Oh, my Lord. He needs the emergency room."

I offer to get our father.

"Katie, he won't care. Granda is Mam's father."

Behind the closed bedroom door, Da shouts, "No, you will not. You're my wife. You'll do as I say."

The Scarlet Woman emerges with a hatbox dangling from one gloved hand and the red leather makeup case from the other. Da follows, wearing his hangdog expression and carrying the flowered carpet satchel and two suitcases.

Everyone pivots when a car honks at the curb.

"That's my cab."

I ask, "Where are you going?"

"To my sister in Aurora. I shan't endure having my child in the midst of this chaos."

Panic must have shown on my face because Da says, "It's okay, Katie. I'm staying."

"Not sure that's good," mutters Ed from the stairs.

"Granda's in a bad way, Da." Mary jabs out her palm. "We need your keys."

He drops the carpet satchel, digs into his pocket, then slams the keys into Joe's hand. "Be careful with my car."

Mary says, "Katie, you and Ed stay with the boys."

My brother trudges upstairs as if wearing concrete shoes. Rustling noises overhead tell me the younger boys are not yet asleep. I sit in the warm indention Granda's rear end made on the sofa and pray.

Please, Holy Virgin Mother, my grandfather needs your help. TB killed my Nana. Please don't let it take him too.

"When they put you in the hospital, you know you're going to die." My siblings gape. Cereal spoons freeze midair. Milk dribbles from Tommy's mouth. "If we don't see Granda today, we may never again."

"Shouldn't we wait for Da?" asks Ed.

"His drunken mug hasn't come around for three days," says Mary. "What makes you think he's coming back?"

I shake my spoon at Ed. "All the more reason to go today."

"I'll check on my job application," says Mary. "I'm babysitting the

Murphy kids this morning. Meet you at Corwin at one."

I give Ed a gloomy glare. "You know what that means?"

"Aye. We're stuck with the boys."

As we head down the street later in the afternoon, Ed plucks an oatmeal clump from Tommy's hair. "Can we take the bus?"

I snort, "Where would I get bus fare? Listen, Ed, we're going to have to carry the boys or visiting hours will end before we get there."

Once inside the hospital, Tommy and Bill fuss while we wait for the clerk to look up Granda's room number. When the nurse points down a dimly lit hall, I say, "Thank you, ma'am, but I've been here many times. I know the way."

A decayed flesh stench wafts from one room; moans and groans from another. "No children allowed," says a nurse as thin as a tree branch.

I read the nurse's nametag and stand tall, hoping she'll think I'm an adult. "Nurse Raile, we're with our sister who's sixteen and checking on a job application." Mary's fourteen, but surely Jesus will forgive such a dinky lie if it gets us in to visit our sick grandfather.

Nurse Raile points a knobby index finger toward a bench. "Sit and wait for your sister."

I gasp and grab my chest. "Hurts like someone stabbed me."

Nurse Raile stiffens. "Are you ill?"

"Yes. No. First my friend in Philadelphia, then my Nana, then my baby sister, then our Mam. I must see my grandfather before he dies."

"Goodness. We don't know he will die."

"I'm his favorite. He needs to see me before he goes."

Nurse Raile twists her scrawny neck and fixes on Ed. "How old are you, young man?"

"Thirteen, ma'am."

"Can you control these youngsters for ten minutes?"

"Yes, ma'am." Ed scowls at our brothers. "Yeh won't make a peep, will yeh, lads?"

Bill drags a dead cricket from his pocket and offers it to the nurse.

"Young man, you can't bring that filthy creature into this hospital. It's unsanitary."

Ed snatches the cricket, latches onto the boys' collars, and yanks them toward the bench. "Come with me, yeh little wankers."

Nurse Raile sniffs indignantly, then motions me to follow her into a narrow room with eight iron beds, their headboards against the wall. The overhead lights flicker. Creeping shadows paint the room with a ghostly pall. Each patient wears an oxygen mask attached by rubber tubes to a tall metal tank beside their bed. The room wheezes like a vast creature struggling for breath.

"Please, keep your voice low. These patients are quite ill. Like your grandfather, most have pneumonia, although his complications make for a more problematic recovery."

Mary slips up behind me. "What complications?"

"Are you the sixteen-year-old sister?"

Confusion flits across Mary's face. I nod so she'll recognize my need to tell this lie to ensure we are allowed to see Granda.

"Yes, nurse. I am."

"The doctor is in surgery and won't be available before visiting hours conclude." Nurse Raile lifts the clipboard from its hook. "Mr. Maguire has hardening of the arteries. This makes it difficult for the blood to deliver oxygen and nutrients. His broken hip and resulting chronic degenerative arthritis leave him in a weakened condition. Stay five minutes, then let him rest. I shall return to administer his medicine."

"Granda? Can I get you another blanket? A glass of water?" When I hold his hand, his mottled skin hangs and greenish-purple veins bulge. "Granda, please talk to me."

"Don't upset him," says Mary. "Tell him something nice."

"I-I love you, Granda. When you come home, I'll make you cocoa powder brownies, the biggest batch ever."

Granda gasps a ragged breath.

"He hears me."

"I believe he does." Mary pats Granda's shoulder. "We need you to get well. Katie and I will leave so you can sleep."

I kiss my grandfather's forehead. His skin is feverish against my lips. He doesn't move or speak, yet I feel wrapped in his love. As we enter the hallway, I am thankful the boys are quiet and still, the way Nurse Raile directed.

"Can I see Granda?" asks Ed.

"Sorry, he's unconscious," answers Mary.

"Aye, next time. I'll tell him what I've got to say next time."

On a gloomy night, a week later, I'm alone on the back porch steps searching the overcast sky for even a sliver of moonlight. Yellow light filters out through the kitchen window. The people inside are little more than eerie shadows moving about.

My thoughts return to St. Francis Xavier Church. Haunted by the bagpipe droning "Going Home," I hear feet scuffle as the pallbearers carry Granda from the hearse to the gravesite. Nana, watching from the heavy dark clouds, sent the single ray of sun that broke through when the bagpipes played her favorite song, "Danny Boy."

As the pallbearers lowered her beloved husband into the ground, Nana drew the clouds together, cutting off the light.

Loud cheers summon me to the here and now. "*Slainte!* Good health to you!" In my mind's eye, guests lift their glasses in honor of my grandfather's life. I hug myself for warmth. My sweater is too light, but I'm not going inside the house. Sadness swells as I remember how Granda was gazing heavenward, talking to Nana, when he ran into that brick-filled wheelbarrow.

If I had made heat packs and helped him when he struggled with the pain from his broken hip, maybe he'd still be with us today. I paid no heed when he said, "I won't make it to eighty." Now, it's too late. Who will comfort me when I'm sad and advise me when I don't know what to do? The others have gone to heaven, left me with this heavy, empty feeling that has me pinned to this porch.

The people inside are noisy with their goodbyes. Their voices slur as if leaving a grand party. The front door slams over and again.

Holy Virgin Mother Mary, it's me, Katie. I stand before you, most sorrowful. My thoughts are sins, my concerns for myself. Da is a danger to Bill, maybe Tommy too. I must shield my younger brothers, but I am weak, only a child. Holy Mother, I've told no one else except Molly, but my father frightens me. Guide me so I may set aside my fears and protect my brothers. I realize you're busy, but please, if you could, have mercy and answer my prayer because this is the worst fix I've ever been in. Amen.

CHAPTER NINETEEN

───── ❧ ─────

FEBRUARY 1933

I roam the market aisles, filling a wire basket with the items on Mary's grocery list. Four months have passed and I'm tired. Yet my faith is restored. The Holy Virgin Mother answered my prayers to keep the Scarlet Woman in Aurora.

I swat Bill's bottom. "Quit yanking my skirt. We've got enough, Mary. Let's go."

"Run get the twenty-five-cent bag of macaroni. That'll leave ten cents for candy."

I hike Tommy higher on my hip. "I'm worn out from lugging this tub o' lard."

"Don't let him loose," says Mary. "He snags everything off the bottom shelves."

"I'll get the macaroni." Ed calls over his shoulder, "And the candy."

On the bus, the peanut butter and molasses sweetness of a bite-size Mary Jane melts in my mouth as the motor's purr lulls me to sleep. I'm confused when Ed pokes me, waking me from a dream about Mam making creamy homemade fudge. I take Tommy's hand. He waddles, and I stagger down the metal steps.

After a dinner of leftover cabbage, pea, and noodle casserole, Ed rotates the radio knob until he finds *The Shadow*. Blood-curdling laughter fills the air.

I run to the bedroom.

I'm hunched into a ball when Mary yanks my blanket. "Climb in, boys. Keep them close, Katie. Da's leaving for the local. Odds are he'll take a run at snatching Bill again. Beer and bathtub gin can kill a little fella. I'll sit on the bottom stairstep until he's gone."

My brothers wriggle and squirm. "Sweet dreams, boys. Nobody's taking you from me."

I'd protect my brothers with my life. My inner voice says, *You wouldn't need to if Mam were alive.* Tommy's sweet, milky smell and Bill's, more like warm soda bread, help stave off the loneliness gnawing at my heart. I relax into the warmth of the boys' small bodies, lulled to sleep until a hand rocks me. I bat it away. "No, you can't have them."

"Katie, it's Joe. Your Scarlet Woman is in our living room with suitcases and a big trunk."

Da's voice booms. "You kids get downstairs."

Joe kneels and peers into my eyes. A warning nip tingles behind my ear. *Holy Mother, full of grace—*

"Listen, wee one, I need ta tell you something you'll not like. Miss Kelly and I just had words. I'm leaving."

My heart sinks into my stomach. I clench my teeth to still my quivering chin. "Please, don't go."

"I'm awful sorry, but that woman in Mam's bed brings out the violence in me. I turn seventeen this year. Time to make my own way."

"Joe, we need you. What if we can't stop Da from getting Bill drunk again?"

"I won't be far. Staying with me mates until I can afford a place of my own. Then yer all welcome to live with me."

I wrap my arms around big brother's neck. If I hold tight, he'll be forced to stay. He lifts me from the bed and rocks as he hugs me. The weightlessness makes me dizzy.

"Please, don't cry." Joe's voice cracks. "I'm ducking out the back."

"Get downstairs—now!" yells Da.

I leave the sleeping boys and meet Ed in the hall. Da will shout again if we go slow, yet I can't seem to move faster. Mary stands, ramrod straight, facing Da, Miss Kelly, and the bundle snuggled to her bosom. Ed and I step to our sister's side and slide a hand into hers.

"My wife and her child are moving in tonight. I expect you to treat them as family."

I take Mary's firm hand squeeze as a silent pact for us kids to stand

together, no matter what.

For the first few weeks after the Scarlet Woman returns with her baby, I dislike them both. I ask the Holy Virgin Mother to make this child wail throughout the night and be so troublesome Da will send them packing back to the sister in Aurora.

But this infant, curly hair the color of fresh milk and pink skin as soft as the inside of a rabbit's ear, steals my heart. Perhaps it's all my fault. I might have confused the Virgin Mother with my prayers. Or maybe in heaven there's no difference between a half-sister and a real one. Whatever the reason, I won't hold it against the sweet child in my arms.

But I can't control Mary, who jiggles the crib until Caroline howls, which makes the Scarlet Woman threaten to return to her sister, and Da take to the bottle even more.

Miss Kelly complains she must care for Bill and Tommy as well as her own child while us kids attend school. On this, she's unreasonable. Mary and I shop for groceries, cook, clean, and do the laundry, so watching over the boys while we're at school is this whining woman's single responsibility. Still, I think the arrangement is going fairly well, until Mary announces she accepted a switchboard operator job at Corwin Hospital, and since it comes with room and board, she's moving out.

My heart continues beating, but I'm not sure how since it feels as if my blood drained out my feet.

"Did you hear me?" Mary touches my shoulder. "Are you okay?"

"Nana, Mam, and Granda, then Joe..." I shift out of my sister's reach. "Now you're abandoning me?"

"No, no. It's not that."

I imagine falling into Mrs. O'Shea's ample lap and gentle arms, burying my face in the apron that smells of boxty frying up to a golden brown. I wait for the soothing balm that was her voice: *Don't fret, darlin'. Everything's going to be just fine.* It doesn't come, so I announce, "I should have stayed in Swampoodle with Mrs. O'Shea."

Mary reaches for my hand. "You know she's dead."

"Don't touch me. Do you expect Ed to take care of us? He's fourteen, and he's a boy. Don't you care about Bill and Tommy?"

"I'll work full time. By the time I'm eighteen, I'll be able to afford an apartment. Then I'll come for you."

"In three years? Don't bother," I say with more confidence than I feel. "I'll have everything worked out long before that."

I enter the boys' room, aware of Mary calling for me to come back. Ed squints up from teaching Bill to flip a marble. "What the bedevil is wrong with you?"

Tommy raises his arms. I hoist him and listen to Mary drag a suitcase from beneath our bed. My head throbs when the locks click open. More disturbing than nails on a chalkboard is the sliding of drawers, open and closed, in the room we share.

Ed's mouth gapes as I share the details of Mary moving out. "Holy, shite. How will we pull this off?" He whirls toward the click of the light switch and Mary's hurried footsteps on the stairs. "Isn't she gonna say goodbye to me and the boys?"

Bill's eyes redden. He wipes his nose on his pajama sleeve. Even though Tommy's too young to understand what's happening, he whimpers. I kiss his cheek and pat his back. "Ed, I'm scared."

"Me too, but we can't think that way. It's up to you and me to care for the boys."

For the first time in a month, the house is clean. Everyone else is napping or self-occupied. I'm alone on the back porch, grateful for the quiet. The afternoon sun filters through clouds as white as freshly bleached sheets. The leaves on our Mayday tree shimmy in the breeze. Mam said that's Indian spirits checking on the relatives they left on Earth, like when Nana checks on us, only she doesn't blow through the trees.

I spot a shady movement before I hear the thud. I squeal, leap, and rip open the back door.

"Wait, Katie! It's me."

"What the heck? You scared me, falling over the fence like that."

Joe brushes dirt from his trousers.

"Are you coming home?"

"Sorry, Katie, but I can't. Da's new wife, she and me can't be in the same room."

"I miss you, Joe."

My brother's not good at expressing emotions, but I feel his love when he ruffles my hair. "I brought you a surprise." He unfurls an immense burlap sack attached to a thick brown rope.

"I could use an electric vacuum cleaner, not a feedbag."

"How much would that cost?"

"The General Electric Deluxe model is $42.50 at H.S. Kress."

"Yeah, right. I'll run right out for that." Joe chuckles as he loops the rope over the tree's thickest branch, ties several knots, and tugs. "It's a swing. Climb in." He grabs the burlap, strains to pull me as high as his shoulders, and lets go.

I could fly over the treetops. I laugh and pump my legs until the Scarlet Woman shouts, "Katie, where are you? Your brothers awakened me."

My spirits sink when my Joe says, "I gotta go."

"No, please, no." I jump out of the swing and grab at his leg as he throws himself over the fence. When I say, "Please come back," my voice is a mere whisper so I don't imagine he can hear me.

The boys love the burlap swing. I push them but haven't gotten back in myself. I savor the thrill of my big brother propelling me high in the sky and want nothing to replace that memory. Joe's only been around once during the last three months, when he slipped back over the fence while I was hanging laundry and left a cowboy hat for Tommy's third birthday. Now the only way to distract that child from riding across my damp clean floors on the broom that doubles as his horse is to chase him with the mop and shout, "Get along, little doggie." This is as close as I come to having fun at home.

I often wonder if Joe is out there, peeking over the fence, watching for one of us kids to come out. I step out on the porch every chance I get then fight back my sadness because he's never there.

Ed and I settle into a routine of sharing what Da calls women's work. He cleans the windows with a solution that revives memories of Mam's warm vinegar pies. I like the scent but can't find time to bake, even though

Ed stepped up in a way I never expected from a boy. Besides delivering newspapers on his way to school, and again after he finishes his homework, he plays in the yard with Bill and Tommy while I mop and complete my school assignments.

When I interrupt his yardwork or home repairs, he helps me hang wet bedclothes on the line without so much as a grumble. And most surprisingly, without being asked, he plucks Mam's raggedy old dishcloth off the rack beneath the sink and dries the dishes while I wash. Still, this is the first time the house is as clean as it used to be before Mary left.

Once a week, Mrs. Odell brings us supper. Her lima bean loaf is somewhat tasty when she can afford tapioca. But even without the tapioca, the boys like it better than her liver loaf.

On the rare occasions when the new wife cooks, dinner is either burned or half raw, which upsets Da. I'm grateful he directs his anger at the Scarlet Woman, still, I feel a bit sorry for her. She's the closest thing I have to a mother, so I try to help. I'm taken by surprise when this woman who I thought hated me, says, "Dear, you may call me Maggie instead of Mrs. Ryan."

Happily, I accept my stepmother's act of kindness by setting aside my math homework and measuring one and a half cups of flour, adding a half cup of shortening and rolling out the dough to make her a water pie.

I'm drizzling a teaspoon of vanilla over the sugary water mixture I poured into the pie crust when Da comes home drunk, and Maggie makes the mistake of asking him to step into the living room. If Maggie had told me she planned an important talk, I would have warned her to wait until Da's belly was full and he slept off the alcohol.

I cringe at the sharpness of my stepmother's voice. "You're drinking up our money at the pubs."

"It's my money. I'll spend it like I want. Got lots of troubles, woman. I need a drink with me mates. You need ta lay off buying fancy dresses."

"I can't run a house on what you give me."

I recoil when Da bangs the wall. "I'm the man of this family. You can't tell me what to do."

Maggie screams, "You will not slink off to the pub every night."

Like a lightning bolt, Da's arm flies, sending Maggie reeling against their bedroom door.

I leap to my stepmother's aid, but Ed scurries downstairs and hisses, "Don't. He'll hit you too."

"He never has before."

"Likely he will this time. Get behind me."

I clench the banister and step backward, up two stairs, away from our father.

Da rips open the front door. It hits the wall with such force the Blessed Virgin Mother's picture crashes to the floor. He kicks the shattered glass then shakes his fist at Maggie. "I spent my last savings on that car because you couldn't abide riding the bus. I work as hard as a mule, and we've got these kids to feed. All this worry, I deserve a night out. Don't need some woman haggling me."

I plead, "Stop him, Ed."

"Not a feckin chance. Get upstairs with the boys."

The window shimmies when Da slams the door. Tommy wails because Bill nudges him away from the staircase edge.

"Katie, I said get upstairs," says Ed.

"Maggie's crying."

"So is Tommy, and it appears you're about to yourself." Ed stands on the bottom step, clenches both railings, and braces his feet as if to block me and the boys from coming down. "Go on up. I'll stay with Maggie."

CHAPTER TWENTY

AUGUST 1933

I speak to the sultry voice singing "Stormy Weather" on the radio. "Sorry, Ethel, you've got a lovely voice, but I'm sad enough. Feels like a bucket of water was dumped on my head. My mood's not such as I can listen to how crummy life is for you." I rotate the dial until "We're in the Money" breaks through the static. "Yep, the sky is sunny." I plaster on a smile. It's fake, my smile is, but I'm determined today will run smoother than yesterday.

When Bill and Tommy work themselves into a snit, I settle the dispute by telling Bill he can be the Lone Ranger first. But after fifteen minutes, they must switch, and he's Tonto.

The boys' laughter fills me with hope as I mix freshly grated Idaho potatoes into last night's leftover mashed. Mrs. O'Shea always said people can't stay angry in the presence of a golden boxty frying in a hot cast-iron skillet. I slap in an extra butter pat to make sure. It sizzles and releases its toasty aroma into the air.

Da emerges from the bedroom that used to be his and Mam's. I'll never get used to Maggie sleeping in my mother's bed. My father's jowls droop the way they do after an evening at the local.

Maggie slinks into the kitchen as if sleepwalking, a sign she has taken another Konjola dose. The label claims the vegetable extract strengthens nerves, and my stepmother says it helps her cope with the commotion made by seven people living in our small and meager house. But the liquid smells the same as the bootleg Da brings home, and there's no evidence it helps her deal with anything or anyone.

I take baby Caroline from Maggie and stuff her chubby legs into the scuffed wooden highchair. Bill and Tommy laugh and shove as they run in, demanding milk and peanut butter on toast. Ed walks in from his paper route and drops his canvas bag with a thump.

"Quiet," screams Maggie. "Your fracas upsets my system."

I hold a finger to my lips. "Shh, fellas. We'll have a picnic on the lawn."

Our stepmother can't tolerate the boys' normal scuffle and noise. And she can't abide Bill's shrieks and howls for help when he needs rescuing from his nightmares. I don't wish to think ill of Maggie, or have Maggie think unkindly of me. That's why I choked back my laughter when our stepmother swooned at the sight of blood dripping on the kitchen counter from the crow Ed shot with his friend's BB gun.

Maggie helps herself to a slice of toast. "I'm going back to bed."

I snarl at Ed like everything's his fault. "Thanks a lot." When I recognize the hurt on his face, I take a deep breath and calm myself. "I'm sorry. Even though I'm ten now, it's an enormous responsibility to handle three kids, with Bill being the oldest at age four. I can't do as much as our mother did. I just want to be a kid again."

Ed hangs his head. "I've done a few evil deeds to annoy Maggie, hoping she'd knock herself out with Konjola. Didn't realize the hardship that makes for you. I'll do my best not to anymore."

I nod my appreciation and drop a boxty into the sizzling butter.

Maggie, wearing a new smoky-beige silk dressing gown, reenters the kitchen. "Hand me my Konjola."

I act quickly to steer my stepmother toward Dr. Miles Restorative Nervine because it causes a mild mental fog rather than deep sleep. At least my stepmother takes interest in Caroline in that state. I say, "Yes, ma'am," but plop an effervescent tablet into a glass of water.

"Don't want that bubbly stuff," says Maggie.

I read aloud from the black print on the narrow khaki-colored box. "Reverses the signs of aging and eases frustrations annoying children cause."

"Perhaps you're right. That sounds a better choice." Maggie sips from the glass and saunters back to her room.

I congratulate myself for my cleverness and flip the boxty in the skillet. Caroline, perched in the highchair with a pillow behind her back, dips her fingers into the plastic bowl of Pablum Mixed Cereal. I tickle the pink flesh where her tummy sticks out below her t-shirt. "And you, cutie pie, can help me corral Bill and Tommy so they don't upset your mother."

Caroline claps her tiny hands as if delighted with the idea, but Ed mumbles, "Good luck with these hooligans. Come, lads, let's go outside and toss a ball."

In the morning, I pretend to sleep. I should wake my brothers and take them to Sunday services, but Bill had a restless night, kicked me awake more times than I can count. Getting out of bed requires too much effort, and dressing the boys and waiting on the corner, shivering on this cold January morning while waiting for a bus, is out of the question. When the stairs creak, I shift my back toward the sound.

"You're faking," whispers Mary.

"You came!" I pop up and cling to my sister.

"What's wrong? I thought I'd attend church with you and the boys but you're all still in bed."

"We haven't been going. I'm too tired, so I'm letting the boys sleep late. Besides, Da drank the food allowance, so we've no money to put in the collection plate."

Mary opens her pocketbook and removes ten one-dollar bills from a soft leather coin purse. "For groceries."

"I can't take your money."

"Sure, you can. Tomorrow's payday. I only need bus fare back to Corwin. I'll bring you more next week." Mary tilts her head. "Listen. Da and the woman are arguing. Tell the lads I love them but had to slip out. The Scarlet Woman won't want me staying for breakfast."

As we descend the stairs, I murmur, "Da won't either. He says you deserted us."

"Yeah, that's right," snorts my sister. "I'm the one who left this family high and dry."

"They're in the kitchen. Sneak out while I distract them."

We pause when Maggie says, "I cannot live like this. Your children are too noisy, too demanding, and always underfoot. How can I care for our baby Caroline under such a burden?"

Mary slinks around the banister and out the back door.

When I step into Da's view, he snarls, "Sweet Jesus on a stick. Can't a man and his wife have a private conversation?"

"Sorry, thought I'd fix pancakes so we can have a nice family day."

Da storms toward the front door then stops and hollers at Maggie. "I've got business with me mates. I'll finish this discussion with you later."

Five days have passed since Da and Maggie's last fight when I drag the round metal tub of bedding to the clothesline. I struggle to force a wooden clothes peg over the rope. A breeze slaps the wet sheet against my face. A rude awakening on this wintery morn. I rub my arms for warmth then hang the second and third sheets. But when I fling the fourth over the rope, the clothesline poles lean and the line sags.

"Help! Help me, Ed."

The back door slams as my brother dashes into the yard.

"The clothesline's falling over."

"Sweet Jesus, thought someone was killing yeh." Ed stomps toward the rock pile near the fence. "Women." He braces the poles and stretches the rope taut again.

I brush dirt off the two bedcovers that touched the ground. "I'll put these on Da's bed. He'll never notice a smudge or two."

"Yeh know he didn't come home again last night?"

"I thought Maggie might help a bit with the housework if I hid the Konjola, but she's finding it."

"Tell yeh what, Katie. I'll take over sweeping the floor after supper."

"Thanks." Love for him drives aside my despair.

Ed shuffles his feet. "Now, don't go getting all girly and weepy on me."

Even with his new pledge of help, I work as hard as an ant climbing Mount Elbert, knowing there's no hope of reaching the top. I believe my life can't get worse until my teacher takes me aside.

"If your grades fall more, I shall phone your mother for a meeting."

"She's dead."

"Oh, I'm sorry. Then, your father, dear."

"Good luck. Us kids haven't seen him since Friday night." My teacher never called me dear before, and I find no comfort in the endearment now. Still, I'm thankful the woman doesn't mention a meeting again.

CHAPTER TWENTY-ONE

JANUARY 1934

The result of last year's shouting match between Da and Maggie was a truce of sorts. Now, everyone seems to have settled on trying not to irritate each other. At this moment, Caroline is the only one distressed. My best technique to distract her from the pain is barking and saying her dog tooth is popping up, but the pesky canine tooth is taking forever to break through the skin. As I head downstairs with the boys, we smile when Maggie barks and the toddler giggles.

I take Tommy to the bathroom and scrub his face. He sputters and fights to escape.

I'm proud that after the lesson from the school's visiting nurse, we purchased a tube of minty Pepsodent and nylon toothbrushes. But I'm even prouder, since Mary's last visit, twice a month, I take the boys to church. Today is the first Sunday of the month, the day the Ladies' Auxiliary provides a free pancake breakfast with all the maple syrup a person might want.

Maggie is not usually awake this early. I wonder, then dismiss the thought she and Caroline will join me and the boys.

The clock reads, *8:12*. In three minutes, Tommy and I will head to the bus stop whether or not Ed has come down with Bill. I spit on my finger and pat a wayward curl on Tommy's head. He's a handsome little fella clad in the navy-blue knickers and white sailor shirt I selected at the church's clothing drive for the poor.

Da shocks me by stepping in from outside with his face washed, hair combed, and wearing clean trousers and a white button-up shirt. I'm baffled when he says, "Ed and Bill are in the car. Let's go."

"What the heck?" I whisper in Tommy's ear. "Da's taking us to church in his car?" I sniff my father's breath as he places his hand on the passenger door lever. The stink of whiskey comes as no surprise, but his hand is steady. Still, I hesitate.

Ed leans out the backseat window. "Katie, get in. Keep standing in the street and the good ladies will run out of pancakes before we get to church."

I push aside my uncertainty, climb into the front passenger seat, and settle Tommy on my lap. Thinking he'll be safe if I grasp him firmly, I wrap one arm around his waist and the other across his burly little chest.

The car is toasty from the sunlight on the windows. How long have they been waiting? I slip off Tommy's jacket, then my sweater, and lay both across the car seat. When I crank the handle and roll down the window halfway, a crisp breeze blows through my hair.

People wearing their Sunday best pass beneath gracefully swaying tree limbs.

Tommy points toward a boy who throws a stick for his lop-eared mutt to chase. "I want a dog for my birthday."

Mr. Parker glances up from helping his wife into their car and waves. I experience a certain contentment. No one will guess we have money problems when we ride in Da's fancy new car.

The car detours left. "Wrong way, Da."

He glances at me but drives on. I'm smart enough not to anger him when we're out in public, so I say no more. I peer over the car's hood. The orphanage looms ahead. I try to hide my trepidation, yet my arms involuntarily tighten around Tommy when Da enters the side street. Rose and I hadn't been brave enough to walk around back. Maybe Ghost Girl is there.

Of the many windows set into Sacred Heart's soot-darkened, red brick walls, I focus on the single open curtain and don't realize the car has halted until Ed speaks. "Da, why'd you bring us to an orphanage?"

A creepy nip crawls up my neck.

"We're meeting someone." Da fidgets with the steering wheel then opens his car door.

Ed folds his arms over his chest. "We're not going in. We'll wait in the car."

"Get out." Da snatches open the passenger door.

Ed and Bill hang their heads, scooch across the seat, and plant their feet in the gravel parking lot.

"Please, no, Da." The pulse in my neck beats like a drum. "The kids at school say the nuns keep dead people in there."

"Dead people? That's the damnedest thing I've ever heard."

"Tommy's scared to death." My arm is numb from clenching him.

"Get out, Katie. I'll have none of this."

I mustn't let my little brothers go inside. Tommy grabs my dress neckline when Da yanks us from the car. The fabric cuts into my skin. I lean against the car to steady my trembling body. "The boys want pancakes and syrup. We're leaving."

"We have an appointment with Sister Agnes."

I ran home the day I saw Ghost Girl at the basement window. Can I run that far carrying Tommy?

Bill makes the *wup, wup* sound, prelude to his grandest temper fits. I signal Ed he should take our brother's hand, but his glare is locked on Da.

Bill latches onto the door handle and climbs back in. He kicks and punches as Da drags him out. "No, no. I'm not going in there." Snot collects on the bow of his lips. The tenderness with which Ed picks Bill up leaves me weak-kneed.

Da puts his hands on my shoulders. For an instant, I think he will hug me and Tommy, but he spins us toward the orphanage and prods me between my shoulder blades. I dig my heels into the gravel, but my father flings me toward the walkway. Tommy shrieks when I almost drop him, but Ed scrambles to steady me.

The orphanage door creaks and swings open. A nun, as tall and wide as a man, rushes out, her black robes flapping like bat wings. "What is this disturbance?" Her steel-gray eyes penetrate like shards of ice.

I say, "We're going home."

"I want pancakes," sobs Bill.

Tommy wails, "Home, home."

"I apologize, your Holiness, but we don't intend to go in," announces Ed.

"Goodness, boy. I'm not the pope. Call me Sister Agnes Evellius." Her enormous, wrinkled hand slithers from her sleeve and opens the thick mahogany door. "Come. I have cookies."

The nervous twinge creeps along my neck again, but Ed hikes up his trousers and saunters in. "All this upset my brothers. A cookie might do the trick. But we're on the road to church, so just one, if you please."

We follow the nun along a dark hall. The heels of her black leather shoes click against the stone floor. Sister Evellius grasps the wooden staircase rail and hauls herself up. The banister creaks from her weight. At the top, the silver ring of skeleton keys she removes from beneath her scapular clang as she unlocks the door.

Reassured by sugar sparkling atop the plate of golden cookies resting on a small, delicately carved cherrywood table, I expel the breath I've held inside.

"Help yourselves, children." The nun's thin lips stretch across her teeth.

Hair rises on my neck again. I hand Tommy a cookie and select one for myself so we can get the heck out of there. My stomach burns as if I swallowed coal, so the cookie goes into my pocket beside Molly.

A framed picture of Jesus hangs on the wall. He holds his heart, wrapped in thorns and bursting with flames, in his outstretched hand and stares at the cookies.

Blessed Mother Mary, what did Jesus do to deserve this punishment? Wasn't hanging on a cross enough?

Da bends on one knee as if to look us in our eyes but stares over our heads. "Listen, kids. I got to give yeh some bad news. We stayed in the house because I used Granda's life insurance for the payments, but I'm months behind. We must move. This kind Sister will care for you until I'm back on my feet."

"What about your new wife and her girl?" asks Ed.

"We're moving into a hotel for a bit."

"You're dumping us and keeping them? We're your real family."

"Ed, they're family too."

"We were yours first."

"Da, Maggie needs my help with Caroline." I kiss Tommy's clammy cheeks. "She's so nervous...and not a good cook."

"I'm sorry, Katie," Da rises from his kneeling position. "You thought you were helping, but Maggie says the bunch of you make her too anxious. It's more than she can manage."

"More than *she can manage*? Ed and I do everything while she lays around all day." I swallow the bitter slime pooling in the back of my mouth.

Ed, who is approaching fifteen, is tall enough to glare directly into Da's eyes. "You're a feckin arse."

"Oh, my," says the nun. "Children, honor your parents, saith the Lord."

"Da, Mam won't like what you're doing to us." The room darkens and closes in. "You can't leave."

"Ah, yes I can, and I must." Da lowers his voice. "I'll be back in a couple of weeks."

"Go to hell!" shouts Ed at Da's retreating backside.

"This will not do," scolds Sister Agnes Evellius. "Thou shall not curse in the Lord's house."

Ed grits his teeth then spits his words. "This isn't the Lord's house. It's a prison for unwanted kids."

As Tommy pounds my shoulder, a wail roils up my throat. "I want to go home."

Sister Evellius rips Tommy from my arms. His cookie tumbles down the nun's black habit and shatters.

I tuck my trembling chin, so the boys won't see my panic.

Ed squares his body and crosses his arms. "Sorry, ma'am, but my sister and our brothers are not going with you."

The nun tightens her clutch on Tommy and storms away. He reaches over her shoulder, stretching his arms toward Ed.

Nobody takes Tommy from my sight. I seize Bill's hand and tug him along. The hall ends at a different staircase than the one we climbed to the nun's office. When my shoe catches on an uneven step, the nun jerks her head around. "What are you doing?"

"She just tripped, Sister Evilness," says Ed.

"My name is *E-Vail-E-Us*."

"Sorry, Sister."

The stairwell opens into a small dark room the size of our bedrooms. In the center sits a circular bench, upholstered in shiny fake leather strips dyed green, yellow, red, and blue. Lightheaded from doubt and dread, I sway and sit before I black out.

The nun demands, "Boys, come with me."

"Please, no. We've never been apart."

"We'll stay with our sister," says Ed.

"Thou shalt not."

"Sister Evellius?"

"What, girl?" The nun's eyes darken.

"My brothers are a handful." I realize we have no choice other than do as the nun commands. I jut out my chin as a signal for Ed and Bill to follow the nun. "May I hold the little one until you get his older brothers settled?"

The nun's long black sleeves envelop Tommy's face as she thrusts him back to me. "I'll send someone for the child."

Tommy shivers in his white cotton sailor shirt and navy-blue knickers. "I'm so sorry, baby brother. In all the commotion, I forgot your jacket in the car." I feel guilty giving my youngest brother such a lame excuse. Da dressed up, twitching as if bugs were crawling beneath his skin—I should have known something bad was going to happen and used my brain to prevent it.

Jesus peers down from the cross hanging on the wall. I shirk from his judgment while rubbing Tommy's icy legs. *Molly, it's a short dash to the parking lot. Do you think Da's still in the car, realizing he made a huge mistake?*

Feet scuffle toward me. A velvety voice says, "I am Sister Anne Beatrix. I've come to help you."

The kindness in her voice takes me aback. I sense I've seen this nun somewhere, her enormous smile and apple-red cheeks. The tiny woman, mere inches taller than my four-foot-six, extends her hands. I don't realize what's happening until she takes Tommy from me.

"What a beautiful boy. Someone will return for you."

My arms fall to my sides. Grab Tommy! Scream for Ed! What's wrong with me? Why can't I move?

The creak of a door closing in the distance breaks the spell. I rush through the hall, following the nun. Terror steals my breath and leaves me panting. Ahead, a wooden door thuds closed. I slink, then step inside.

Legs flailing as if running for his life, Tommy screams as Sister Anne Beatrix lowers him into a crib. He spots me and stretches out his little arms. "Save me, Katie!"

I snatch him from the crib.

"This transition is difficult, but Sacred Heart is your new home," says Sister Anne.

"It's not our home. Da will come for us in a few weeks."

"Ah, perhaps, but for the time being, your brother must sleep with the other little ones."

"Please, Sister." I rub Tommy's back. "He's never slept alone."

"He won't be alone. An orphan girl cares for our babies and toddlers."

"Tommy and Bill sleep with me."

"My dear, that's hardly proper."

"I protect them."

"From whom?"

I hesitate. Someone who works directly for the Lord will never let us go home, into our father's custody, if they know the truth. But if I don't explain, the Sister won't understand why I must protect my brothers.

"From whom?" repeats the nun.

"My father."

"Your brother's exhausted from all this commotion. He can barely hold his head up. Return him to the crib and let him rest."

"Sister, he's too big for a crib."

But when she nods at me as if she has faith I will do as she asks, I nod back and lay Tommy down. A small moss-green blanket hangs over the crib rails. I touch the soft yarn to my face and breathe in its soapy fragrance.

"Lovely, isn't it? A group of generous Pueblo ladies, they call themselves Knitting to Glory, creates them for our little ones."

I tuck the blanket around my whimpering brother.

The Sister smooths Tommy's curls. "He's a sweet child, isn't he? Walk with me. I want someone else to be aware of what you said regarding your father."

I follow this seemingly kind woman, someone I might trust to help me and the boys. But my heart races when I recognize the door before which we halt. "Sister Anne, if you don't mind, I'd rather talk with you."

The Sister knocks lightly.

"Enter," says the severe voice I already know so well.

The lamp casts long, thin shadows across the desk. I hang my head as Sister Anne recounts my revelation.

Sister Agnes Evellius' pencil-thin eyebrows climb high, dragging the tip of her nose with them. "And why do your brothers need protection from their father?"

Holy Virgin Mother Mary. I messed up. Should have kept my mouth shut.

"Sister Anne, you may leave."

What have I done? If Mary were here, she'd know what to say. Virgin Mother, I need your help.

"Speak, girl."

My jaw quivers. "Bill and Tommy sleep with me and my older sister, or did until Mary left us, and now it's just me. Anyway, I keep Da from taking Bill to the local pub. His friends each pay him a nickel when he makes Bill drink beer."

"You're a liar." Sister Evellius rubs her thumb the length of the large silver cross dangling on the thick chain around her neck.

"No, ma'am. I am not. That's how my father drinks for free."

"Bill is your second youngest brother? He's five?"

"Yes, ma'am, but he was three the first time we caught Da."

"Address me as Sister."

"Yes, Sister."

"No father would do such a despicable act."

"Ask Ed. He'll tell you."

"I don't need your brother to confirm your lies."

"I'm telling the truth."

"The Lord does not abide a liar."

"Neither did Mam. She taught me not to lie."

"Did your mother wash your mouth with soap?"

I face what Nana used to call a double-edged sword. The nun will take a truthful answer of yes to mean I lied. But that's not the case. Mam scrubbed my mouth with carbolic soap because I swore. Which sin is worse? I'm in trouble either way, so I lie.

"No, Sister Evellius. Mam never washed out my mouth with soap."

"Well, you deserve it now." The nun twists my ear, propels me into a small adjoining room with only a sink and toilet, and forces me to my knees.

Please, Holy Virgin Mother Mary, are you nearby? Of course, you're with these women of God. Are you going to let her do this to me?

Sister Agnes Evellius grasps a fistful of my hair, wrenches back my head, then grinds the soap against my lips, forcing them apart. The bar rams my tongue into my throat. When I gag, the impact of the nun's slap sends the soap sliding across the floor.

"Disgusting child. Clean that mess."

As I spit soapy slobber into the sink, the door slams. The lock clanks. "Wait, Sister Evellius. I'm cleaning as fast as I can."

"Lower your voice, girl."

The click of heels fades into the darkness. "Please, Sister, don't leave me in this bathroom." I smash my ear against the door. The only sound is my voice. I wonder if my mother sees what Da has done.

I crumple onto the cold white tile and remove my doll from my pocket. *Molly, do you think the Holy Virgin Mother understands what a mess we're in? Has she forsaken us?* I rest my head against the sink's base. *Go to sleep, Molly. No point in yelling anymore.*

CHAPTER TWENTY-TWO

THE FOLLOWING MORNING 1934

I'm curled into a fetal position, shivering when the tiny room floods with light and a warm hand nudges me. "Mam, is that you?"

"No, dear. It's Sister Christine Daniel."

"How long have I been in this bathroom?"

"I'm not sure, dear. You must have misbehaved."

"I want my brothers."

"Yes, I suppose you do, but it's five a.m. You must come with me." Sister Christine walks briskly.

I slow before each open door until the one that is closed draws me to it. I know well the hearty howl that surges above contented coos and muffled shushes. Shocked by the ease with which my touch opens the door, soundlessly, I step inside.

Ten small, narrow metal beds line the left wall, cribs on the right. Toddlers, blond and blue-eyed, redheaded and hazel-eyed, gawk. A mousey, brown-haired girl who looks fourteen lifts Tommy. My heart flip flops at the sight of his green eyes bright with fear. The room whirls. A strange girl has my brother.

A hand spins me from the cribs. "You are not allowed in this room. I instructed you to stay with me." Sister Christine prods me into the hall.

The snap of the door closing slices through my heart. "Please, my brother's frightened."

"Yes, dear, I suppose he is. He cried the entire night, but that is no longer your responsibility."

"I can settle him."

"I suppose you could. Nevertheless, you may not. We house the youngest separately for their safety."

"I'd never hurt a child."

"No, dear, I don't suppose you would. Still, it is not tolerated. He must orient to his new circumstances."

"Who's the girl?"

"Hannah. The nursery is her work assignment. She feeds and cares for our younger children, under Sister Anne Beatrix's supervision."

"There must be twenty children, too many for one girl. I have experience with my brothers and new baby sister, half-sister, that is. I'd gladly help Hannah. Please, Sister?"

"I suppose it might be possible." Sister Christine Daniel's blue eyes sparkle. Hope warms my chest.

"We may only ask. Sister Agnes Evellius assigns work duties."

The stone floor becomes sludge. My feet sink. I can barely move.

"Come, dear." Sister Christine directs me through a large door.

A moldy stink hits me in the face. Spoons scrape against bowls, and bodies shift on wooden benches.

Sister Christine nods toward a rectangular table at the front of the dining hall. "Help yourself to one ladle from the tall aluminum pot. Make haste. Breakfast concludes in four minutes."

The nun behind the table is taller than Sister Christine. Her tiny nose protrudes past her heavy black veil, reminding me of a turtle emerging from its shell. I bite my lip to stifle a grin, "Good morn—"

"No talking in the dining hall." The nun's rigid-lipped grimace is stern, yet her wide brown eyes are as soft and moist as a doe's.

At first, I think the room's odor comes from what looks to be about fifty girls squeezed into the rows of long tables and benches. Now I realize the repulsive stink is from the watery substance in the large pot. My hand trembles when I lift the ladle. Dark globules jiggle and spill onto the white tablecloth.

The Sister's red-knuckled fingers shoot out her sleeve and slap my hand. It doesn't hurt, but the gray substance hurls back into the pot. "Wasteful girl. Now, you have two minutes to eat."

I look to Sister Christine for direction, but she's gone. I wish one of the girls peeking over her bowl would signal me what to do. Five inches of wooden bench stick out in the second row. When I set my bowl before the small space, a slim girl, who looks about twelve, tucks the flare of her cotton skirt beneath her legs and shifts an inch.

I whisper, "Thank you. What is this?"

The girl fixes her stare on her empty bowl. "Oatmeal."

The nun bangs the ladle against the metal pot. "Ladies! The rules. No talking."

The slim girl murmurs, "You don't want to make Sister Mary Myrtle angry."

I slip a spoonful of the lumpy discolored slime into my mouth then purse my lips to prevent it from spewing out. And the boys thought my gelatin luncheon salad was bad. I force down a second bite, but there's no time for more. The girls file past the Sister and stack their bowls alongside the pot. The bowls lean and wobble. I fear my remaining oatmeal will spill, so I place my bowl on the table.

"We don't waste food," snaps Sister Mary Myrtle.

I imagine the fresh-baked freckle bread Nana and I nibbled as we watched soft-shelled turtles bask in the sun then cool their round bodies with a dip in Lake Clara. Unlike those sweet creatures, this nun, nose peeking out her veil, is a snapping turtle.

Sister Myrtle the Turtle dumps the remaining contents of my bowl back into the pot. "Take your position in line."

Unwilling to guess where my *position* is, I slip in at the line's end. I've already learned not to call attention to myself, so I cast my gaze downward and watch my shoes. We turn in to a large, musty, rectangular dormitory. A crucifix hangs crooked between two shuttered windows. Blood drips from Jesus' crown of thorns. A small, framed painting of the Holy Virgin Mother Mary hangs on the far wall.

In the distance, a church bell tolls. God is near.

Iron beds, similar to those in the hospital where Granda died, flank the center aisle, two deep and twelve in a row, forty-eight in all. The rod frames wobble and rattle when we sit. Unlike the soft blanket the hospital provided Granda, these shabby, dingy-white sheets drape over misshapen pillows and thin lumpy mattresses as if ghosts have come to rest and their evil spirits lie and wait. I imagine earthbound souls rising from beneath the bedclothes to scare the bejaysus out of me.

Should I claim one of the two empty beds? The girls on either side of the first bed appear to be about six. Near the other, they seem about eleven or twelve, about the same as me.

Everyone leaps to their feet and stands as stiff as rods when Sister Agnes Evellius enters and paces the room's length while tugging on the large silver cross hanging from her neck. She points her craggy index finger toward a wrinkled pillowcase. When the nun scribbles on her clipboard, a sense of dread overwhelms me.

"Why are you standing idle in the middle of the room?"

"I don't—"

"Think, girl. Don't you know to take the empty bed?" Sister Evellius jerks her head toward the older orphans and raps her clipboard. "Work assignments remain the same."

Sweat oozes from my pores. The painting of the Virgin Mother Mary appears to hover over the nun's head. "Sister Agnes Evellius, may I request—"

"*No*, you may not. Drop to your knees."

Fear collapses me. My knees slam against the stone floor. A bolt of pain sears my legs.

The nun glares. "How did that feel?"

Two responses rest on the tip of my tongue. I suspect either will bring more punishment down upon my head. I could go for sympathy and release my tears, but I hear big brother Joe growl in my mind. *Nobody in the Ryan clan, not even the girls, lets an outsider see us bawl.*

Or I could smile and reply I'm fine. But before I decide what to answer, Sister Evellius kneads her way up her silver cross. "You appear comfortable on our floors. Therefore, you will join Rachael in scrubbing them."

My hopes sink like a rock in a marsh, yet I'm eager to search for my brothers, so I rise.

"Did I say stand?"

I drop back to my knees.

The nun inspects the neatness of each girl and her bedclothes then raps the clipboard against the footrail nearest me. "Dismissed."

Does she mean me? Do I follow Rachael? Or remain on my knees?

Like bees eagerly wanting to escape to far away fields, the girls take flight. A tall, olive-skinned girl pokes my arm. She must be Rachael. Her long, dark waves bob in the distance. I rush after her, but when we step into a dimly lit stairwell, I stumble and grab the rail.

"Hush. The Sisters want us silent," whispers Rachael.

I place each foot lightly, but the stairs creak. Fear's icy sweat pools in my armpits.

Holy Virgin Mother Mary,
I was led astray in every way.

I sense the bottom of the pitch-black stairwell.

I renounce sin,
I renounce the devil.

My eyes adjust to the dim light. I see my hand on the banister.

Please, protect me from what lies ahead.

Great, fuzzy-edged shapes emerge from the darkness.

Free my soul from all that goes against the Lord.

When Rachael clicks on the light, I expel a desperate, *Amen.*

We come to huge tin cans of coffee, sardines, and evaporated milk as well as onions, peas, beets, and tomatoes preserved in quart jars on shelves. I wonder why the girls had to eat watery oatmeal when all this was stored in the basement. Certainly, my family never would have been hungry if Mam's pantry held a fraction of this much food. As we pass multicolored flour sacks and lima beans and potatoes in brown burlap bags, the heat of the enormous wrought-iron boiler sucks air into its bowels.

Whispered laughter floats overhead. Three girls carrying enormous baskets of soiled clothes descend the stairs.

"Hi," says the pretty girl with a long, slim nose. "I'm Zarah."

"Hi, Sarah. I'm Katie."

"Zarah," says Rachael. "Her parents didn't spell it right."

"They did too. It means princess in Hebrew."

"Nobody would dump a princess at an orphanage," snorts Rachael.

The girl with hair as dark as the nun's habits, whose tight curls appear electrically charged, shoots Rachael a warning scowl. "I'm Ethel, and this is my friend, Tazia."

Rachael pivots and tromps up to a splintered wooden door. The deadbolt screeches as she forces it open. "Get a bucket."

I cover my nose and mouth as if it were possible to block the damp, acrid stench. Zarah empties her laundry basket into a huge iron basin. Ethel and Tazia dump theirs into the wringer washing machines' steel tanks. At the second basin, Rachael fills our buckets then motions me to add the Red Devil lye and powdered soap flakes.

I recoil from the fumes.

These girls seem as if they could become my friends. Like when Elena and Elizabeth spent the night with me and Rose. Maybe this won't be so terrible. I raise my hand in goodbye, but the girls are intent on lighting the coal burners beneath the washers.

Rachael snarls, "Quit messing around. You're gonna get me in trouble."

At the day's end, we line up again. When the dining room door opens, I follow the girls to the wooden table holding the large aluminum pot. Supper appears to be the same rice gruel served for lunch, except corn kernels and tiny carrot bits float among the slimy cabbage leaves. After I take my seat, Sister Mary Myrtle drops a brown chunk before each girl. It thunks like a log. I copy the orphans who dip the stale bread into their gruel. With the last morsel, I scoop up a jiggling gray sliver that might be beef fat.

Sister Myrtle announces, "Dinner is over."

We orphans rise like soldiers under command, file past the serving table, and leave our bowls and spoons. At home, I complained about the eternal stream of dirty dishes. Here, there truly must be no end.

"Pick up the pace, ladies." The nun presses her leather strap against Tazia's back. "The Lord saith, whatsoever you do, do it heartily."

Silently, I expel the breath that fear had captured inside me.

In our dormitory, a younger child drops her shoe. The poor girl whimpers when Sister Myrtle raps her knees with a leather strap. I want to scream—It was an accident—but that would bring harsher punishment on us both.

When Zarah removes a folded nightshirt from beneath her pillow, I panic. All I have is the dress I've worn since Da dumped us in this awful place.

The Sister points at a small stack of clothes. I recognize the skirts and blouses, even my socks. Da brought my clothes? He must love me, just not as much as Maggie and her child. Did he take the boys home? Am I the only kid left behind? The only one he doesn't want?

The Sister motions toward the small, two-tier wooden shelves between Zarah and my beds. "The uniform and nightshirt are for you. Stack your belongings and get in line."

When I slide my flour sack dress onto the shelf, four pennies roll from the pocket and hit the floor. My pulse races as I hide the coins, the last of the money Joe gave me as a birthday gift. In school, Julia endeared her circle of friends with gifts of hair ribbons and juicy orange slices. These pennies could do the same for me.

"Bring your nightshirt," whispers Zarah.

"Did I hear talking?" We freeze when Myrtle the Turtle snaps her leather strap against her own thigh. "Fall in line and go."

Eight shower heads protrude from the ten-foot-long open stall covered with the same white tiles as Sister Evellius' bathroom. I shiver as if I am still huddled on the cold hard floor. But I'm not alone now.

Zarah points to the floor. "Stack your dress and underwear on top of your shoes and socks." She steps into the shower, soaps her hair and body, then offers me the lye soap bar. "Brace yourself. The water's as cold as ice."

I step away from the spray. "I'll wait until tomorrow."

"Better hop in," says Tazia. "We don't shower again until Thursday."

"What happened to 'cleanliness is next to godliness?'"

Tazia throws back her head and laughs. "The new girl is funny."

"That only has to do with floors, dishes, and laundry," says Zarah as our voices grow louder than the water flow.

"Enough chatter, ladies," orders Sister Mary Myrtle.

I scrub hurriedly. Goosebumps climb to painful peaks. Hannah smooths my hair and twists. Water splats onto the floor. I say, "Thank you. And thank you for caring for my little brother."

After drying my body, I wrap my hair. The towel's worn so thin that water still trickles down the curves of my neck and back, and my nightshirt clings to my damp body.

"Line up, girls," hisses Sister Myrtle.

We march back to the girl's dormitory. I watch the others place their clothes on the wooden shelves next to their beds and do the same. Then I stand at the foot of my bed, fighting to quell the quivering.

Sister Myrtle frowns as she inspects us from head to toe, then halts in front of Ethel, one of the girls I met in the basement, and tugs her collar. Ethel says Sister Evellius didn't deliver her to the Colored Orphanage and Old Folks Home because it's closing due to financial woes, and the Sisters would end up with her anyway.

While we showered, Ethel told us a family friend raped her mother when she was only thirteen. The horror of those recollections caused Ethel's momma so much pain she couldn't bear to gaze upon her own child's face.

Now that I'm older, Ed says I resemble Mam. Could that be why Da doesn't want me anymore? Don't he and Ethel's momma understand how much it hurts to be abandoned? At least Ethel's grandmother took her in, for a while. If only Nana hadn't died...

Betty, the redheaded girl who seems too timid to speak, closes the shutters. The naked bulb overhead barely lights the room. Sister Turtle flips the switch and shuts the door.

An instant before the latch clicks, someone coughs. The girls moan. The door swings open, and the overhead light flickers on. Fearsome shadows slink along the walls like banshees. Betty covers her mouth with her nightshirt's hem, but a second cough rattles up her chest and through the cloth.

"Take your positions, ladies," says Sister Myrtle. "In these close quarters, if one becomes sick, it spreads to all. My responsibility as your house mother is to maintain your health. We shall nip this in the bud."

"Nice work, carrot top," hisses Rachael. "Here comes the cod liver oil."

"Quiet, ladies. We can't have scarlet fever running rampant through the orphanage again." Sister Myrtle disappears into the closet at the room's end.

"Better not close your eyes tonight, Betty," says a scowling older girl.

I whisper, "My mother gave us cod liver oil plenty of times. It's not so bad, especially with a bit of sugar."

The scowling girl snarls, "Sugar? Aren't you a hoot?"

We quiet when Sister Myrtle emerges, clasping a large brown bottle. She fills the same metal spoon over and again. Some, mostly the younger, retch when she jabs the spoon deep into their mouths. Determined not to gag, I clutch Molly to my chest. But when the Sister rams the sharp-edged spoon between my pursed lips, it clanks against my teeth, and I yowl.

Sister Myrtle's yellowed nails dig into Molly's body. "Only after you repent and prove your worthiness shall you deserve to have this filthy doll returned."

"Please, I won't—"

"Another word and you'll never see this disgusting toy again."

Sister Myrtle stuffs my only friend into the darkest depth of her habit pocket. I'm crushed by despair but won't blubber while standing before this nun. Later, I'll cover my mouth with my threadbare blanket so no one can hear and shed my tears alone in the darkness of night.

After the nun extinguishes the lights and locks the door behind her, Ethel's drawl floats across the aisle from her bed near the Holy Mother's picture on the wall. "That uppity nun burned the stuffed rabbit my cousin brought. I reckon she'll do the same to your rag-baby unless you hide her, if you ever get her back."

"Why'd she burn your rabbit?"

"I tole my brother Sister Evellius whooped me with the leather strap, and he said he'd better not hear of that again. But these nuns don't care what he says."

I whisper, "Why are they so horrible?"

"Missy Myrtle the Turtle ain't no problem. Evilness is the one to fear. She'll make y'all drag big fat stones and build a border 'round her precious vegetable garden. Or lock ya in the mop closet until you can't suck air, like you're surely gonna die."

"Quit it, Ethel," says Zarah. "You're scaring her."

"She needs warnin'."

I curl into a ball and cover my head with the blanket.

"I hear you whimpering," murmurs Zarah.

"I'm scared for my little brothers. They've never gone a day without me."

"Got an idea." Zarah leans over the side of her bed.

"Shush yo' mouth," cautions Ethel. "If Rachael hear, she be snitching."

"Tomorrow." Zarah places her index finger to her lips and rolls back into her bed.

In my troubled sleep, I dream of when my family gathered around the radio, waiting for the organ's first spine-tingling note that announced *The Shadow*. I sense Bill crawl into my lap. Ed tickles my neck, making the tiny hairs stand on end. The Shadow emerges from the depths of wickedness and asks, *Who knows what evil lurks in the hearts of men?*

I wake with a start. I have more to fear than a voice inside a wooden box.

CHAPTER TWENTY-THREE

FEBRUARY 1934

I'm on my hands and knees, scrubbing the rectory's stone floor, when I notice a streak of blood behind me. Rachel says scabs harden into callouses, eventually, but they haven't yet. When I peel back my uniform skirt hem, Sister Evellius digs her fingernails into my arm and yanks me to my feet.

"I'm truly sorry, Sister. Molly wanted to see the blood on my knees."

"The Lord knows it's always something with you and that doll." Sister Agnes Evellius drags me to the basement door and shoves.

I clutch the splintery handrail to stop from tumbling down the stairs then descend quickly so the nun won't push me again.

We pass the huge iron sinks and duck under sagging ropes strung from wall to wall, on which my new orphan friends hang wet towels and bedclothes to dry. Fire burns in the enormous wrought-iron boiler. The black contraption weighing thousands of pounds heaves smoke and steam. Its many tubes, like filthy arms reaching out, frighten me.

Sister Evellius halts at the cleaning closet and selects a worn brass skeleton key from the ring she keeps beneath her scapular. It clanks and scrapes in the lock. She opens the door and shoves me from the back.

I gasp from the burn of lye and chlorine bleach and the damp musty stench of mold. The deadbolt screeches through its metal casing, sending a bone-chill down my spine.

"Molly and I aren't scared. You've locked us in this closet before."

The nun's shoe heels click toward the stairs.

In the dark, I bump the mop handles. They clatter and fall. I crush my ear against the door and listen for the rustle of Sister Evellius' tunic. Even the rosary that dangles from the brown rope tied around her waist is silent.

"Please, come back. I swear on Jesus' word, I'll do whatever you wish."

"Our Holy Father observes your disobedience. He awaits your repentance."

"Please, let me out. I'll kneel for as long as you want, longer than any other girl."

"God hears your lies. He wants you punished. As His servant, I must perform this task." Each wooden step protests under the nun's weight as she climbs.

A strangled sob clogs my throat. "Please Sister Evellius, I beg of you...."

The heavy basement door slams. I slide down the wall to the damp concrete floor and tuck my legs beneath my skirt. "Don't be frightened, Molly."

Sister Evellius says I'm too old to play with dolls. But I don't just play with Molly, I confide in her. This cloth doll that used to belong to Nana is the only belonging of hers I have left, except for the family photograph with *Easter 1929* written on the back.

From this day forth, I'll hide Molly inside my blouse. But I must be careful. The older children say the nuns bury those who are very bad in a single grave behind the fence.

CHAPTER TWENTY-FOUR

MARCH 1934

"My mother was strict. I dreaded her punishments, even when I deserved them. But Racheal, don't you think this is cruel? All we did was rest for a minute." The uncooked rice embeds deeper in my knees when I motion toward the second-floor prayer room window. "I'd jump just to get away."

"This is your fault," says Rachael. "Where's your head? Of all places, you had to spill your bucket on Sister Evellius' beloved rug?"

I rise and pluck rice out of my red wrinkled knees.

"Get down before she comes back." Rachael yanks my skirt. The force breaks the thread that secures the waistband button. It clanks against the stone floor as loud as a metal ball. We suck musty air between our teeth and freeze. "Keep lollygagging and you won't need to jump. Sister Evellius will throw you out."

"Liar." I speak boldly, even though my voice quakes with uncertainty as I lower back onto the rice-covered floor. "These windows don't open."

"Upstairs they do. The year my mother left me here, that nasty old Evilness threw Eugene, a sweet curly-headed boy, three years younger than us, only eight, out the—"

"I don't believe you."

"Why would I lie? Sunken, dull-brown eyes and pasty white skin. The poor kid looked like he'd seen the devil. I guess you could say the nuns whipped him to hell and back befo—"

"Hush, Rachael." A twinge of fear nips my neck.

"Wasn't his fault he moved so slow. His brain didn't work fast."

"You think you can fool me because I'm new."

"Ask the other girls. The poor kid's buried in the nuns' private vegetable garden. They dug a grave between the turnips and onions. Guess that's why they grow so well. Not that anyone who wasn't starving would eat a bitter turnip."

"Did you call the police?"

"Me? Who'd let me use the phone? Besides, I don't want to end up as fertilizer."

"You can't scare me."

"No, Katie? You were plenty scared when Sister Evellius locked you in her bathroom."

"My brothers and I are only staying until Da returns."

Rachael snorts, "Nobody comes for any of us."

"Da will the minute he gets on his feet. We have a home big enough for the seven of us."

"Shush," hisses Rachael. "Somebody's coming."

The hint of a smile on Sister Evellius' face gives me the courage to speak. "When you make assignments for next month, may I work in the younger children's room?"

"Absolutely not. We don't want the innocents to observe the evil of your rebellious ways."

"I'm almost twelve, Sister. I cared for my brothers, even when I was much younger."

"Do not speak of it again. You are better suited to scrubbing floors."

Before sunrise, while the room is still chilled from the night, I hurriedly change from my nightshirt into my uniform. I'm struggling with the tiny shirt buttons as Zarah leans close.

"Fiddle with your bedclothes when Sister Myrtle comes in."

"Won't we get in trouble?"

"Nah, act like you're making your bed perfectly smooth. She loves that. Stall so we can be last in line."

Sister Myrtle enters and walks the aisle.

My hand twitches as I fluff my pillow and press my blanket flat for the third time.

"Satisfactory, ladies. Take your positions in line. Mustn't be late for breakfast."

I stick close to Zarah but glance nervously behind me. It's anybody's guess what she has in mind, and I'm sure there'll be punishment if we're found out. Instead of following the girls to the dining hall, my friend detours sharply then murmurs, "I heard the guys planted Evilness' asparagus seedlings upside down and laughed about it. Now, they're all in the chapel, getting an extra dose of God's word."

We creep to the open doors. Cold sweat runs between the tiny mounds I proudly call my breasts. Ed makes eye contact then nods toward Bill. I take that as a sign my brothers are okay.

The boys' teacher, Sister Reparata, opens her Bible. "The Book of Thessalonians teaches us that any man 'who would not work, neither should he eat'. Now, bow your heads and pray for the strength and good judgment to follow our Savior's word."

"That's enough. We're gonna get caught." We scurry then pant with fear as we step inside the dining hall, coming face to face with Sister Turtle. Her glares bores into us.

"Sorry, Sister," says my quick-thinking friend. "The heel came off my shoe. It took me and Katie a moment to get it back on."

Blood pounds in my ears.

The Sister extends her neck past the edges of her veil and peers down her nose. "Get your oatmeal, ladies."

At six in the morning, Sister Evellius teaches our hour-long Bible Class. Every lesson's message is the same. We, the girls who sit before the nun, are filled with sin. But through the study of God's word and the actions of His son, a flicker of hope exists.

I doze during the godliness of charity. As penitence, Sister Evellius demands I donate an item of my clothing to the Women's Auxiliary drive for the poor.

"What beggar could be poorer than me?" I don't realize I muttered my thoughts out loud until Evilness' leather strap hits my knee. Then when "Holy shite," slips out between my lips, the nun assigns me to write Ephesians 4:29—*Let no corrupt communication proceed out of your mouth*, until I fill ten pages while the other girls spend the time in the sun-filled yard.

I'm envious and regret speaking aloud. Yet I must admit this is fair, and far less unpleasant than other punishments I brought down upon myself last month, like when I left my Bible on the chapel pew, which I didn't realize was a sin until Sister Myrtle made me kneel on rice and beg the Lord's absolution rather than eat dinner.

Now, Sister Evilness taps her pencil against the wooden desk as she waits for Sister Mary Myrtle to come in to teach the next two hours of reading, writing, and mathematics.

I speak in my most polite tone. "Sister, I was about to graduate from sixth grade and learned way more in elementary school than here."

"These lessons are adequate for where you girls are bound to finish up in life," snarls Sister Evellius. "To atone for this insolence, ponder your gratefulness for what we teach you while you take over the scrubbing of the cookware tonight."

The following day, once again my knees leave a thin, bloody trail as I crawl. If Sister Evellius notices, she'll make me start over, so I wring my stained gray rags and wrap them around my knees. The lye solution burns. My tears splatter like rain onto the stone floor, but I must be careful. Rachael has a reputation. I fear if she sees me cry, leave a dirty spot, or disobey the rules, she'll twist the story and gain favor for herself.

The floors in the hallways, dormitories, dining hall, vestibule, and chapel seem to run for miles. But this is good because when the boys pass I will tell Ed to check for my notes in the tiny nook behind the Blessed Virgin Mother's sandaled foot. The notebook paper folded in my pocket crinkles as I dip my rag into the bucket. We scrub the chapel floor on Mondays. How simple it would be to leave a note every Monday if I trusted Rachael not to snitch. I'm considering the risk, deciding if confiding in her would bond our friendship or break it apart when she speaks.

"Sister Reparata caught your elder brother playing with his marbles and threw them into the boiler's fire."

"I've got another." I dig in my pocket for the yellow swirl Ed gave me after he won others from the neighborhood boys. "I'll slip it to him when we pass in the hall."

"Nope. Won't happen." Rachael rocks back, balances with her buttocks on her heels, and smirks. "A farmer took your stupid brother and five others to the San Luis Valley. Early lettuce crop."

I ignore Miss Know-It-All and scrub faster. If I reach the end of this hall within the next few minutes, I'll slip Ed the yellow swirl when Sister Reparata marches the lads past the chapel. My stomach churns. How long will he be gone? Who will watch out for Bill?

Yet Tommy is a bigger worry. He turned four, so Sister Anne should move him into the dormitory with Ed and Bill. But for now, my only way to find out if he's alive is to creep into the toddlers' room or sneak a peek out the window during the youngest children's outdoor playtime. I gauge the distance and increase the speed at which I scrub. I don't notice the heels clicking until black leather shoes halt where I crawl.

"Ungrateful ward. I observe your carelessness. Rushing instead of doing your best work."

The heat of Sister Evellius' scowl beats upon my shoulders. When I make the mistake of peeking up, the nun places the toe of her shoe on my hand and shifts her weight.

"Please, Sister. I beg your forgiveness."

"It is not my absolution for which you must beg." Sister Evilness bears down. "When you finish, do not enter the dining hall. Kneel outside and recite the Confiteor until I come for you."

When the nun releases the pressure of her foot, I expect relief, but a greater pain, as swift as a lightning bolt, shoots up my arm.

The nun's heels click through the stone hallway.

Rachael scrubs her way up behind me. "Be glad Evilness didn't step on my hand too, or I'd give you a punishment of my own."

"I'd tell her it wasn't your fault."

"You made a fuss for no reason. Doubt you'll ever see your brother again."

"He'll come back when they finish the harvest."

"Ya think so?" snickers the snitch. "Sister Christine Daniel says he's the best worker. There's talk about this farmer keeping him."

I fix my glare on Rachael's head as we set the buckets and rags inside the cleaning closet. Are you lying? Or just scaring me? I think we're friends, but sometimes I'm not sure. I scowl at Rachael's back as we trudge toward the dining hall. You like us begging for what you've overheard. But none of us can imagine how you find out what the nuns are thinking, saying, and doing behind closed doors, or whether these things are true. Do you make up stories, so we'll owe you?

Rachael and I take our places behind the girls filing in. After all forty-seven enter, I nudge the door partway closed so they won't see me face the wall and kneel. I don't want the other orphans to overhear me either, so I keep my voice low.

> *I have sinned exceedingly in thought, word and deed;*
> *through my fault, through my fault,*
> *through my most grievous fault.*

I remove Molly from my pocket, shape her tiny hands into prayer, and rest my forehead against the wall.

> *Therefore, I beseech Blessed Mary ever Virgin,*
> *Blessed Michael the Archangel...*

My voice quavers. I should speak up, but I'm so tired. My eyelids glide shut. When my arms fall to my side, Molly tumbles onto the stone floor. The click of heels penetrates the numbness of my brain. Louder. Closer. I push upright from the wall and grab Molly. The doll's arms and legs flail as I strike my chest three times and raise my voice, true and clear.

> *Blessed John the Baptist,*
> *the holy Apostles Peter and Paul and all the Saints,*
> *to pray for me to the Lord our God. Amen.*

Sister Agnes Evellius grasps the leather strap from her habit's folds and thwacks my thigh. "You think I didn't know you were sleeping? Follow me. The Lord believes cleaning the boys' toilets will instill gratefulness for the kindness I bestow upon you by allowing you the work of scrubbing floors."

"Sister, may I ask one question?"

The nun harrumphs indignantly.

"Is my brother coming back?"

"Where'd you get such a silly notion? Of course, he is. Where would he go?"

CHAPTER TWENTY-FIVE

SEPTEMBER 1934

I wait in the visitors' reception room beside the chapel and smooth a crease in the skirt I selected from the Auxiliary Women's donation bin. It's important to look my best. This afternoon is special, only allowed because thirty days have passed since I last misbehaved.

I recognize the soft scuffle of Sister Myrtle dragging her left foot, so I don't bother peeking out but squeal with delight when Mary follows the nun in. We laugh and whirl in each other's arms.

"Ahem, ladies, I shall show you out."

"Don't trouble yourself, Sister," says Mary. "I know the way."

"You may know the way, but I bolted the door."

We follow Sister Myrtle and wait for her to sort through the keyring attached to her rope belt. When she opens the door, I squint from the sun and take Mary's hand as we step toward the sidewalk. "Let's wait for the boys."

"Katie, it's just you and me. The big nasty nun said since I'm only sixteen I can't take more than one at a time."

"Sister Evilness probably thinks you'd keep us if you got us all out at once."

"I wish I could." Mary bites her lip. "But we'll not let anyone ruin our afternoon. We have three hours. Let's go downtown and have some fun. Quick, there's the bus."

I extend my arms, palms open, and run to catch freedom in my hands. As I scramble up the metal steps, memories flood my mind. The times I rode the bus with Mam and the boys never felt this good.

I call out over the passengers' heads. "Hello."

Those who glance up appear surprised. Four grandmotherly ladies, leaning across the aisle deep in conversation, raise their heads and chuckle.

"Hello. Welcome to this bus," responds the elderly woman with ruby red lipstick and frizzy cold waved hair that sits on her head like a gray football helmet.

"Take a seat," says the driver. "I don't have all day."

"Sorry." Mary nudges me.

"I have nothing to be sorry for. This is the best day of my life." Sunrays glint off the red and gold leaves of fall. The bus passes boys playing baseball on a dirt field. That's where Ed and Bill should be.

"What do you want to do first?" asks Mary.

"Eat fried chicken and creamed corn. And drink a malt."

"Does the Sunshine Diner suit your tastes?"

"And a hot dog and a cinnamon bun with white sugar icing so thick it drips off the sides."

We take a table near the window. "Mary, the last time we came to this diner, Joe told us about Da taking up with the Scarlet Woman."

"Oh, my Lord. Do you want to leave?"

"No, I have good memories too."

As we eat, Mary shares how, as Corwin Hospital's switchboard operator, she hears callers reveal secrets they wouldn't be happy to learn she knew, like when a married council member asked Nurse Willoughby to meet him behind Grays' Coors Tavern after the town hall meeting.

We laugh until Mary says, "I guess you guys are getting on okay now that you've settled in.

"No, Mary, no. It's awful. I get punished a lot. Ed and I hide notes behind the Holy Virgin Mother's foot. It's a great risk but our only way to communicate. I'm worried about Tommy and Bill. I beg you to get us out."

"My job pays too little to rent a room in town. Maybe just you if we sneaked. The head nurse would fire me if she found out."

"I'd sneak or lie or whatever else you say to do." I slurp my strawberry malt. "But I must stay. Who'd watch out for the boys?"

"You're only eleven. Let Ed. He's four years older."

"He does his best, but I can't dump the responsibility on him. Especially Tommy. He's a tough little guy but too young. And Bill appears lost, kind of glassy-eyed. Besides, Ed's often gone, working on farms and ranches."

"I'm sure you're right. You all need out of there."

My mouth is full of crispy fried chicken when I ask, "Why doesn't Joe come for us?"

"He and I disagreed on a few things, but I'll take another run at making him see this situation my way. For now, let's head to Sweeter Than Sweet and buy a small bag of candy you can share with our brothers."

The following morning, I lick my lips as if I still taste the cinnamon bun I ate for dessert. My heart will break if I lose the blue and pink flowered silk scarf Mary bought me at H.S. Kress. I tug the ends, smile because the knot is secure, and pat the six hard candies in my pocket.

Six is a lot. If I give my friends each a candy, they'll like me better. But I can't do that. Mary bought the candy for our brothers. I could give three to the fellas and the other three to Zarah, Tazia, and Ethel. But what about Rachael? I don't need her breaking our friendship. I should give a piece to Hannah. She still slips Tommy an extra biscuit when she can.

As I follow the line of girls to breakfast, my stomach growls. I lean close to Tazia. "Today, Sister Turtle will serve us plates mounded with fried eggs and toast."

"Quit. You're torturing me."

"Or pancakes with butter melting between the layers and maple syrup dripping over the sides."

Tazia smacks her lips. "I dream of my mother's mushroom ravioli. Evilness says Jesus suffered on the cross, and we must honor his sacrifice through our own suffering. But I think the old bat is just horrid, crueler than the devil."

Sister Evellius slips up behind and slaps the back of Tazia's head. "Ungrateful girl. Such a filthy mouth. No wonder your parents didn't want you."

"That's not true."

I gasp and shake my head in tiny jerky movements to stop Tazia from saying more, but she continues. "Dad committed suicide because he lost his job. My mother said none of what happened was my fault. She couldn't keep me because he left us broke, and she feared I'd starve."

Evilness whacks Tazia's knees with her leather strap. "Watch your mouth, ignorant child."

I wince, dip my hand in my uniform pocket, and give Molly a squeeze. Rachael says the nuns prefer bony knees because they don't bruise as easily as soft flesh. My mind screams, *Stop hitting my friend!* but speaking out brings more abuse.

I've also learned not to jump at every strange noise, or flinch when the nuns appear from who knows where. If I do as told, Evilness is the only nun I need fear. I feel sympathy for the others. After Mam died and Mary moved out, I cared for the boys and cleaned, cooked, and kept up with the laundry, even though the boys dirtied everything faster than a toad could hop across the yard.

When Maggie moved in with baby Caroline, there was no way I could handle all the chores. These five nuns are responsible for one hundred and twenty kids. And on the days the Monsignor or Father Faolan come, the entire orphanage must be as perfect as if the pope were arriving for a visit. I understand why the nuns are strict. If only their punishments were less severe...

Sister Evellius interrupts my thoughts. "Katie, you may go to class."

"If you don't mind, Molly and I will stay with our friend."

"Do as I say before I toss that filthy doll in the boiler." Sister Evellius glares down her nose's length and tugs on her heavy cross necklace.

I dash to class. But it's impossible to focus on conjugating Latin verbs or calculating how many miles a person can drive at thirty miles per hour because images of the punishment Tazia must be suffering consume my thoughts. I wish I had given her a candy to comfort her, wherever she might be. Or maybe I shouldn't get attached—avoid the pain and emptiness of when my friends are taken from me.

When Sister Myrtle releases us to go to our work assignments, I tug Rachael's arm. "Hurry. Evilness probably locked Tazia in with the mops."

We fling open the basement closet door, sigh with relief, and load our buckets with rags and lye. As Rachael and I trudge back upstairs, she says, "Tazia might be someplace worse."

"Let's find her."

"Katie, you're crazy."

"I'm gonna check on Tommy, make sure no one's taken him, then search for Tazia."

"I'm warning you. The nuns will lock you up, maybe in the root cellar with those horrible flesh-eating rats."

"Stop scaring me. Nuns wouldn't do that."

At the top of the stairs, I veer left, and Rachael turns right. She says families interested in adopting healthy young boys visited yesterday.

Please, Blessed Virgin Mother, don't let my brothers be gone.

I slink against the walls. Sometimes, on warm days such as this, Sister Anne Beatrix lets the youngest orphans play outside. If I make my way to the third floor without getting caught, I might find a room with an open door, one with a window that faces out back. And I might catch sight of Tommy.

A door creaks. I squeeze into a small alcove then bolt into Evilness' office. Sweat beads on my forehead. I must be quick. If found, no explanation I could give would spare me the leather strap, or worse.

The window high on the wall behind Sister Evellius' desk overlooks the play yard, but I'll have to climb onto the swivel chair. Will my feet leave imprints on the padded seat?

A huge black Bible that appears to be a hundred years old sits where the cookies had been the day Da abandoned us. On the cover, gilded in gold, Jesus points to his Sacred Heart. I hoist the Bible. It must weigh ten pounds, much more than I expected. My hands shake and the frail table tips. I catch it before it crashes on the floor. Careful not to disturb the swivel chair, I place the Bible beneath the window. Jesus stares up at me.

Should I flip him face down? Then, he can't breathe. I slip off my shoes and place my feet along the Bible's edges and not on Jesus. *I beg your forgiveness. My stinky feet on your Father's Word. Surely this is a sin.* My threadbare socks slip, so I step up again and hook my toes over the Bible's edges. At four inches, the Bible raises me sufficiently to peek over the windowsill.

Tommy and another boy leap from one hopscotch square to the next. The window is thick glass, but in my mind, I hear my brother laugh. Dizzied with relief, I step off the Bible and return it to the table with the spine facing the window.

Help me, Jesus. Which way did it face? I spin the Bible toward the desk.

"May I see you in my office?" asks a man's voice in the hall.

Sister Evellius responds, "As you wish, Monsignor."

I am petrified. Where can I hide? Why didn't I pick up on her heels tapping? Surely, Evilness hears my heart pounding. I peek around the doorframe. In a swish, the black fabric disappears. I snatch my shoes and creep along the hall. I must sneak downstairs before the girls take their seats in the chapel for afternoon prayers. I'm almost past the Monsignor's quarters when a bony hand grabs my shoulder. My blood runs cold.

"Why are you sneaking through the halls?"

I resist Sister Evellius' strong grasp. My mind offers a hundred excuses—none good.

"Speak up, girl." The nun drags me downstairs, toward the back door. "I have the perfect place for you to repent your devious ways."

I sigh with relief. Any punishment in the yard is better than the mop closet. I walk willingly. Sister Evellius jangles her keys then bends to unlock the root cellar padlock. Fear nips my neck. I glance over my shoulder. Is this where the nuns put the very bad children to die?

Evilness motions for me to open the wooden hatch. It's hopeless to resist. My knees shake as I descend the three log steps. When the door crashes shut, I duck, barely avoiding it slamming against my head. I huddle against the dirt wall and wait for my eyes to adjust. A single thin stream of light sneaks in where a bevy of furry bodies scratch the root cellar door. I pity these tiny creatures. Just like me, they want out. But when the rats squeak and hiss, I toss a potato, and the rodents scurry as if they know a way out.

Needle-sharp teeth chomp and grind, sending a shiver along my spine. The reek of decayed rat flesh, feces, and damp earth overwhelms me. I cover my and my doll's noses with my hem and silently message her.

Don't be frightened, Molly. They're just eating potatoes. They're hungry too. Be very quiet and listen. The boys have weed duty today. If one comes close, we'll tap on the door to get his attention. Maybe it will be Ed. Wouldn't that be lovely, Molly? He'd let us out quicker than a wink.

Beady eyes glow as red as hot coal. Two rats gnash their teeth. The larger lunges, and I swat it away. *Holy Virgin Mother Mary, I have sinned. But standing on the Bible in Sister Evilness', I mean Evellius' office, was that so terrible? Isn't it my duty to ensure Tommy's okay?*

Listen, Molly. I hear the boys!

I tuck my doll inside my waistband and crawl toward the cellar door. A rat scurries over my fingers and disappears into a small dark hole. I swallow my scream and listen for Ed, but it's Sister Christine Daniel I hear.

"Robert and Willard, pull the weeds near the gate. The rest, take a corner and work toward the center."

Sister Christine doesn't call Ed or Bill's name, but surely, I'll detect their voices. Shovels clang against rocks, and rakes scrape the ground. One boy asks another for help.

Dust and fear fill every breath I draw. The dirt walls close in, seeming to come closer and closer, I unfold my legs and stiffen my feet to keep them from squishing me. My skin crawls as if covered with attacking ants, and my dress sticks to my hot, clammy body.

As the temperature in the root cellar rises, I doze, then wake with a jerk when Sister Christine calls out, "Good work, fellas. Return your tools to the shed and clean up for dinner."

The boys are leaving, Molly. I know you want to shout for help, but I'm afraid. The rim of sunlight grays at the trapdoor's edge. Molly, this is all wrong. Jesus loves the little children. He wouldn't want us locked in here, forgotten, possibly to die.

My stomach grumbles. I brush off a potato and sink in my teeth. Once past the strong taste of dirt and peel, the white flesh tastes delicious. I chew until the padlock rattles and Sister Myrtle peeks in.

"Come, Katie. The girls are in line for dinner."

I climb out into the darkened yard.

"Put that doll in your pocket and wipe your face. You're a mess. Sister Evellius won't be happy about that."

"She put me in there."

"Ah, well, let's not dwell on that."

"Sister Mary Myrtle..."

"Yes, my child?"

"Enormous rats with big pointy teeth live in the root cellar. I feared they'd eat me alive."

"Oh, my, well..."

"And Sister Myrtle, it stinks to high heaven in there."

"Watch your language, child. Sister Evellius wouldn't like you to speak that way."

"Yes, Sister. Ah, no, Sister. She wouldn't like it one bit."

"Katie, your heart is good. I understand your need to ensure your brothers are well, but you get yourself into trouble doing so. Sister Christine says it upsets the boys when you are punished on account of them."

"Are you saying I shouldn't check on my brothers?"

"Either that, child, or devise a means by which thou shall not get caught."

Two weeks pass without spotting Tommy or Bill, or talking with Ed. But I'll see them today. As I enter the chapel, I direct my eyes away from the Blessed Mother's sandaled foot for fear someone might suspect I'm searching for a note.

The boys sit on the chapel's left, girls on the right. Rachael says the priest demands this because as he stands behind the pulpit, the boys are to his right, and everybody knows the most useful people find a place at the right hand of God. I don't care where anybody sits as long as I see my brothers. I crave to hug them or at least touch their hands, but such action will result in punishment. The most I can wish for is a glimpse into their eyes.

Sister Myrtle clutches my arm. "It's best you stay with me. I can't have you placing me in an embarrassing light again."

Yesterday, I made that mistake. Sister Evilness must have felt especially thankful because her dinner prayer droned on and on. At long last, she concluded, "We thank You, our Lord and Savior, for feeding these girls' souls with Your Word, and their bodies with this nutritious soup."

By the time we said, "Amen," the watery gray cabbage gruel was cold rather than lukewarm. It hadn't registered in my mind the *yuck* I was thinking emerged from my mouth until Sister Myrtle the Turtle smacked my shoulder, which caused me to knock over my bowl and propel slimy cabbage leaves across the table. Now, she marches me along the center aisle and into the front pew, so I'll cause no embarrassing moments like yesterday.

Father Faolan motions for us to sit. The nun's attention appears to be on the sermon, so I search for my brothers as best I can without moving my head. I'm consumed by thoughts of how I might message Ed until the reverend's words catch my interest.

"'When my father and mother forsake me, then the Lord will take me up. Psalm 27:10.' I read this verse so you understand God shall never abandon you. Children, can you sense Him by your side? And in your hearts? Bow your heads and thank Him for this promise He makes.

I close my eyes. *Lord, I thank You, but my younger brothers need You more than I. The time You might spend on me, please be with them instead. Thank You, O Lord.*

I stretch my neck and catch a glimpse of Ed. He cocks his head toward Bill then Tommy at his elbow. But when his shoulders droop, I know he senses how hard it is for me to return his smile.

"Our Lord observes you, children," says Father Faolan, "innocent waifs, offended by your parents. Instead of ensuring your welfare, they do harm that causes you to stumble and fall. By no fault of your own, your parents abandoned you. Such parents will suffer for their offenses. The Lord God shall ban them from His holy light."

Please, Lord, it was my father who left my brothers and me for a new family. I beg of you to let my mother stay in heaven with You and Nana.

Father Faolan's voice builds to a feverish pitch. "And what doth the Lord saith to the father and mother who, through their actions, teach their children to abandon their own, as they themselves abandoned those poor waifs God entrusted in them? He sends His message through the written Word, Matthew 18:6. 'But whoso shall offend one of these little ones which believe in me, it were better for him that a millstone were hanged about his neck, and that he were drowned in the depths of the sea.'"

Terror strikes. I hug Molly against my chest so she can hear my thoughts. The priest said all children go to heaven. But Mary said the baby Mam made die couldn't go because it didn't have a soul. What greater offense could a mother commit than to prevent her child from going to heaven? *Please, God. Don't make Mam leave.*

Father Faolan raises his hand heavenward. "Take comfort. You are in the lap of our Lord's love. He shall never forsake you. Please, rise and repeat Psalm 27:10 with me."

My voice wavers. "'When my father and mother forsake me, then the Lord will take me up.'" I message Molly with a soft squeeze. *After lights out, we'll talk about what we just heard.*

CHAPTER TWENTY-SIX

❧

DECEMBER 1934

Sister Myrtle controls which girls spend the hour after Sunday supper playing board games in the meeting hall and which polish the silver chalice and every candleholder in the orphanage. I stack my clothes neatly, remain motionless during bed inspections, and restrain my responses to, *Yes, Sister,* and *Forgive me, Sister* to gain her good favor.

The room arrangement places the girls' tables in the front and the boys along the rear wall. While the nun doesn't allow me near my brothers, the boys and I exchange smiles and nods, often sneaking a wave when a misbehaving orphan consumes Sister Myrtle's attention.

Two Sundays ago, Bill didn't look himself. His sparkling blue eyes were shrouded and dull, and his head jerked at every sound as if he feared someone might sneak up on him. I search for Bill at every turn but haven't seen him since Sister Evilness directed me and Rachael to give particular attention to scrubbing the meeting hall, then locked the door and allowed no children inside. It didn't appear any boys were to be allowed in tonight.

Rachael says two men hauled in an enormous pine tree and three ladies carried boxes of Christmas decorations. Yet a person can never be sure of what she claims to know.

Rachael's mother works as a housekeeper at the Columbian Hotel in Trinidad, ninety miles south, near the New Mexico border. They lived in a single room the owner provided. Her six brothers and sisters attended school, but Rachael was four, so she stayed with her mother. The owner said her presence interfered with Mrs. Funkhouser's work, and she must either quit her job or send Rachael away. For me, being the child your mother doesn't keep explains Rachael's need to exaggerate and tell tales that cause us girls to cling to her every word. I get aggravated and lose my patience, but mostly, I forgive her. In this case, however, Zarah says Rachael might be telling the truth because last year's Christmas party was grand.

As we file from the dining hall, Rachael elbows me. "Those ladies are from the Pueblo Women's Aid Society."

Ethel's tiny corkscrew curls dance as she swivels her head. "Quit actin' all into yourself. You ain't knowing them."

"Yes, I do," Rachael hisses. "The chubby one was in the car when I ran away, and they caught me at the Union Depot."

My mind whirls. An orphan can run away? Blood pounds against my temples. Rachael must have spent a week locked in the mop closet for punishment. At least they didn't bury her out back. I'd have to be smarter and sneakier, and run faster. Ed could carry Bill, or maybe Bill can run fast enough. I could carry Tommy. But he must weigh forty-five pounds. Felt like a hundred last time I lugged him to the market and back, and that was almost two years ago. Still, there must be a way.

"I'm talking to you," mutters Zarah.

I halt in the middle of the hall. "Sorry. What'd you say?"

"Will your father come to the Christmas party?"

I shrug. "How would he know of it?"

"Sister Christine notifies whoever signed the papers to leave you here."

"The bank took our house. Da and his new family moved into a hotel until he gets on his feet, but I can't remember its name."

"Catch up, my friend," says Tazia. "Not a good time to get in trouble, with the party coming up."

Once inside our dormitory, we stand at the foot of our beds, as still as statues of saints, while Sister Myrtle announces, "Ladies, I have a surprise. The kind women of the Pueblo Society sewed you each plaid flannel pajamas."

Grins spread across our faces.

"Be quick with your showers. I stacked the new nightwear on the bench—small, medium, and large. As soon as you're dressed, form a line in the hall. These generous women also brought homemade sugar cookies and popped corn for you to string and decorate the Christmas tree."

Rachael smiles smugly. "I told you so."

A hum of delight fills the meeting hall. A tall woman, whose glasses ride halfway down her nose, holds out a plate. "You may take two."

The cookies are twice the size of my palm and sprinkled with sugar tinted either red or green. I take one of each. A buttery cinnamon scent tickles my nose. Every crunch creates a sugar explosion in my mouth. *Holy Virgin Mother, please, make sure the boys get cookies. Especially Bill. He looked awfully blue last time I saw him.*

A shorter woman, wearing a white ruffled apron, points toward tables at the far side of the room. "Please, girls, find a seat."

A thick bright-green fir tree, at least nine feet high, stands at the front of the room. The girls' "oohs" and "aahs" become background noise to my thoughts. I have returned to my family's first Christmas in Pueblo and the spindly fifty-cent tree. Mam had been so proud of surprising us kids. I now realize it was the best tree we ever had.

Huge bowls of fluffy white popcorn sit on several long tables. Others hold colored papers, scissors, watercolors, paintbrushes, and glue pots. I would help make decorations for this magnificent Christmas tree just as I had our first Pueblo tree.

"I'm stringing popcorn," says Rachael, "so I can eat my fill."

Pulled from my memories, I think I'll be plenty full after eating the two big cookies. Besides, I'd rather cut out stars and tiny pine trees and paint designs on paper bulbs.

"Have a seat, dear."

Bewildered by a silky voice that reminds me of Mrs. O'Shea, I peer into the golden-flecked eyes of a rosy-cheeked woman who left the bluing rinse on her hair too long.

"Would you like a cup of Kool-Aid, dear?" When I nod, the woman says, "Select your colored paper. I'll get you a cup. Cherry or grape?"

"Grape, please, ma'am."

"The children call me Auntie G, and I'd love it if you would too."

I can't tear my stare from the woman as she walks to the drink table and back. Last week, a husband and wife adopted a girl. Would this woman want me?

"Here you go, dear." Auntie G hands me a cup and slides a large lump wrapped in a paper napkin across the table. "Put this in your pocket." She winks and lowers her voice. "An extra cookie for later. I hear the food isn't that great."

I slip the cookie in beside Molly. No one has treated me this kind since Mama Louise. I must ask before I lose my chance. "Auntie G, do you like boys?"

"Boys are a bit much for me. You know how they are, dear. Snails or worms, always slimy, crawly creatures in their pockets. I much prefer girls." Auntie G chuckles as she hands me small scissors and a glue pot. "Make any decoration that suits your fancy."

This is not the answer I hoped for. Auntie G might adopt me, but not my brothers. Still, I want this blue-haired woman to like me. "I prefer girls too." I consider telling her I'm still sad about my baby sister who lived only ten days, but Zarah, Ethel, Tazia, and Hannah plop into the empty chairs and shuffle through the colored paper.

Their intrusion irritates me. I want Auntie G to myself. But I don't ask them to leave because these girls are my friends.

Auntie G lifts a brown plastic radio from a large shopping bag and plugs it into the wall. It squawks and buzzes as she rotates the dial. When the air fills with "Silent Night," calm washes over me. The girls quiet. But when "Jingle Bells" plays, we laugh and sing along while cutting out stacks of decorations.

Auntie G cuts lengths of ribbon and demonstrates punching a hole with the wooden paintbrush. We thread the ribbons and tie knots at the ends. The stack of multicolored decorations grows. Rachael and Betty climb ladders then toss strung popcorn to each other. The homemade garland spirals the tall tree. My friends and I hand up decorations then hang the rest on branches within our reach.

Everyone acts happy, but my fellow orphans must have the same question as I. Why does the Lord separate children from their families? I reach for Molly, safe in my pocket, hoping she will message me, but she remains silent. I guess she doesn't know the answer either.

Four men struggle beneath the weight of enormous boxes. When they unload brightly wrapped packages and arrange them beneath the tree, even Evilness smiles.

Each package has a nametag. There's a rectangular box labeled "Bill Ryan" and a two-inch puffy package with Zarah's name. Yet sadness builds in my chest. Fifty gifts rest beneath the low-hanging boughs, and a hundred and twenty children live at Sacred Heart. Others must have had the same worry because when the men return with the huge boxes again filled higher than the brims, we cheer and clap our hands.

But when Sister Evellius says, "Line up, girls. Time for bed," grumbling drowns out the last refrains of "We Wish You a Merry Christmas" playing on Auntie G's radio.

Our spirits rise again as we file out. The wobbly table outside the meeting hall sags beneath the weight of turkeys, huge sacks of yams, and smaller mesh bags of ruby-red cranberries.

Zarah whispers. "You'll see your brothers tomorrow. We open presents and eat Christmas dinner together."

When Sister Myrtle steps into our dormitory, redheaded Betty hops out of bed and flings open the shutters. I squint into the sunlight, excited for the day. We dress in our new uniforms, freshly starched white blouses and navy-blue gathered skirts provided by the Catholic Welfare Bureau.

"Single file, ladies," says Sister Myrtle.

"Like we go anywhere any other way."

Zarah pokes Rachael. "Hush. Not a good day to cause trouble with your snot-mouth."

As we enter the dining hall, our heads swivel toward a resounding clang. "Oh, my. Sorry. I didn't mean to drop the lid." From the pot that normally contains each morning's disgusting oatmeal, Auntie G fills the ladle with steaming cocoa and empties it into our battered tin cups. The air fills with a sweet chocolate aroma, and the room buzzes as if it is an enormous beehive.

Before each orphan's designated seat sits a muffin the size of a man's fist, white icing drizzled on its mounded golden top. As Rachael stuffs a huge bite into her mouth, I inhale the sweet blueberry scent and eat slowly, letting every buttery crumb melt in my mouth while remembering Mary's muffins, smaller, but every bit as delicious.

The boys are lined up in the hall by the time we approach the chapel. Ed touches my arm with his chapped hand. "Got an idea. Tell you at the party."

I slide into a pew. Scuffling sounds from the chancel distract me from wondering what Ed wants to tell me. I swallow a laugh as Sister Reparata crushes down on the shoulders of a child costumed as a cow, and the cow sinks onto all fours, pretending to nibble the hay spread alongside the makeshift wooden manger.

Mary and Joseph stand beside a swaddled doll, and a sheep settles at the foot of the manger.

Father Faolan begins the story of Christ's birth with such enthusiasm I wonder if he thinks this is our first time to hear it. And when the magi enter draped in bath towels dyed red, gold, and royal blue, Father's voice soars and his hand shoots into the air. "Where is he who is born the King of Jews?"

The sheep jumps to his feet and pushes his furry face to the top of his head. "Katie! It's me, Billy Boy."

Sister Turtle snaps her head toward me as Sister Reparata swoops in from the alcove and heaves Bill off his feet. A vision of him locked inside the mop closet flashes in my mind. *Blessed Virgin Mother, please, help him. He's terrified of the dark.*

I lean forward as if I could reach my brother. Sister Myrtle blocks me from rising as Bill wriggles and squirms, trying to escape Sister Reparata's clutches.

"Your brother will stand in the corner with his nose touching the wall," says Sister Myrtle. "Do not worry. She won't restrain him long. The Christmas spirit is upon us all."

After Father Faolan offers the final prayer and the last boy strides out, Sister Myrtle leads us girls into the meeting hall. The room, set up with tables and chairs, smells of pine and sugary bakery treats. The apple cider line is long. We admire the poinsettia tablecloths sewed last year by Laura and Violet. Groups of three or four children cluster by the tree's base, searching for the gift that bears their name.

Bill stampedes in, waving his arms. "Here I am. I didn't get punished long."

Tommy breaks away from Ed. "Katie!"

I bend and kiss Bill's cheek then lift my youngest brother Tommy. Gone is the sweet and milky scent I expect. He has the dusty, sweaty smell of a growing boy. My knees buckle. Ed grabs my elbow then wraps his arms around us all.

We sit cross-legged in a circle on the floor. That's when I notice the gash on Tommy's leg. Prepared to curse the nun who hurt him, I ask, "What's wrong with your leg?"

"Bill stabbed me."

"Yeh deserved it," laughs Bill.

Tommy scoots closer and lowers his voice. "He was grinding the butter knife he stole against the concrete step. I said he'd never get it sharp enough to cut anything, so he stabbed my thigh. It's a wee bit infected."

Bill rolls his eyes. "Quit acting the mot. It's getting better."

"I miss you boys so much." A knot rises in my throat. "I worry constantly." I squeeze each brother's hand then warn Bill. "Don't cause trouble. The nuns will keep us apart, forever."

"We won't be in this stinkin' place forever," says Ed.

"You're fifteen, four years older than me. You know better than to think we'll get out before we turn eighteen."

"Da's coming soon." Ed glances toward the bare ankles that stop at the edge of our circle.

His dogged belief frustrates me. "Our father's not—"

"Mary!" Bill leaps up. We scramble and hug our eldest sister then rearrange ourselves into a larger circle.

"The new switchboard operator got herself fired," says Mary. "Our supervisor made me work extra hours. That's why I didn't visit last month."

I say, "We're thankful you came today. Da never visits, and we don't see Joe much."

"You guys look okay."

"Life is hard here, Mary. Tougher than the worst that happened at home. Still, most of the Sisters are nice, but there's a couple..." I raise my skirt and reveal the scars. "Got these scrubbing stone floors on my hands and knees."

"Why don't you use a mop?"

"I've been locked in a closet with lots of mops, but Sister Evilness won't let us use them."

"What do you mean? Locked—"

Ed pokes Mary's arm. "Shh."

"You must be the elder sister." Sister Myrtle peers down at us. "We are pleased you joined us for this festive day. Will your father attend?"

"Da passed the invitation on. But no, Sister, he's not."

"He's taking us home soon," says Tommy.

"Ah, yes, perhaps. Listen closely. The ladies from the Women's Aid Society will call names..." Sister Myrtle's voice trails off as she works her way through the throng of youngsters.

Mary opens her pocketbook. "I brought money so you can buy a treat."

"Keep it." Ed motions toward the nun's back. "They take it."

"Nuns don't steal from kids."

"The farmer out on Route 50 gave us fellas each a fifty-cent piece as thank you for how well we slopped his hogs and cleaned the pens." Ed glances over his shoulder then leans closer to Mary. "Sister Reparata overheard us planning what we'd buy. We got quite a lecture about it being the Lord's money, and the leather strap to boot. Took a week for the welts to heal."

"Leather strap?" Mary glances at me as if expecting me to say our brother is making this up. "Why didn't you tell me before now?"

"As long as they're not hitting little Tommy, it's better to keep quiet."

"Oh, my. Not certain what good it'll do, but I'll talk with Da. He's drinking right through his paychecks."

I motion to Bill and Tommy. "Get another cookie. We're having an adult conversation."

"I'm sure Da's flat broke," says Ed as the younger boys scurry to the dessert table. "Living with the Scarlet Woman and her child at a hotel must cost more than our house payments did."

Anger shoots through me like a hot flame. "Our father doesn't give a rip about us. Has Joe earned enough money that we can live with him?"

"Well, that's another problem," says Mary. "The hospital pays me a higher rate if I give up my room. So, I moved in with Joe, thinking I could save money."

My hopes rise. "How much do you have? Can you take us now?"

"I was working on it, but Joe's getting married, starting his own family. His girlfriend moved in, which cut into our savings." Mary picks at a cuticle. "She and I had a spat over that. I might have slapped her."

"You *might have*?"

"He kicked me out. I'm back living at Corwin, sharing a dinky room with another girl."

Ed's shoulders cave toward his chest. "We're never getting out."

I say, "Just take Bill. He's not safe."

"Can't. The hospital doesn't allow kids in our rooms."

"Listen, Mary. This is serious. Something rotten is happening to him."

When Auntie G's sweet voice rings out, "Katie Ryan," I approach the tree, force my quivering lips into a smile, and accept my gift.

Tommy bolts back from the cookie table. "Open it, open it."

I slip off the ribbon.

"Don't be so glum," Ed whispers. "I was planning to tell yeh, I'll leave when I'm eighteen and find employment that pays enough to get you and the boys out."

"In three years? Ed, that's no plan. Besides, what kind of job can you get that will pay enough to support the four of us?" The ribbon slips from my fingers and floats to the floor.

Bill rips the box from my hands and tosses the lid aside. He yanks out a red flannel stocking with a snowman embroidered on the cuff and dumps its contents into my lap. Out tumbles an ornate silver comb and brush set. He digs to the bottom of the stocking and pulls out a handful of cellophane-wrapped anise squares, the same candy Rose and I bought at Sweeter Than Sweet.

Holy Virgin Mother? Is this a sign? Does Rose walk by searching for me? Will she help me escape? "Mary, do you think Rose knows I'm trapped in this orphanage?"

"She's gone."

"Gone? Gone where? We're best friends. Rose wouldn't leave without saying goodbye."

"The house is empty."

When Auntie G calls his name, Bill presses against his stab wound and rises to collect his gift. He limps back, leaving a trail of ribbon and ripped wrapping paper. He hoists a green hand-carved truck over his head as if showing the other children that *Bill's Delivery Service* is painted in bright gold on the doors.

I wipe my eyes, but there's no restraining the tears that flow.

"Why are yeh blubbering?" asks Ed.

"That's the saddest thing—ever."

"You must be kidding. After all we've been through?"

"Don't you get it? Somebody we don't even know made that truck for our brother. Painted his name with their very own hands. What gift did Da bring? He couldn't even spare an hour to wish us a Merry Christmas."

Ed's lips move, but I don't hear him speak. I pray, *Take me, Lord. I'd rather die and go to heaven with Mam and Nana than struggle to carry on. I can't take any more.*

Auntie G raises her voice over the buzz of children opening presents. "Tommy Ryan."

When Ed whisks Tommy onto his shoulders, he shouts, "Giddyap!" And on the return ride, he waves a soft package wrapped in red snowman paper. "I got a present."

Mary stands and straightens her skirt. "Sorry, kids, I picked up an extra shift because of the holidays, so I have to skedaddle back to work."

Ed hugs her briefly then kneels and makes truck noises alongside Bill and Tommy. I pray Mary will turnabout and come back, but she disappears through the throng of laughing orphans sharing their excitement over the gifts they received. Ethel, tall and lithe, takes her place beside the Christmas tree. Voices crest in harmony, singing "Joy to the World."

I stand silently, my hands hanging lifeless at my sides.

Holy Virgin Mother Mary, I'm sinking into the darkest hole. I confess, I didn't appreciate how good I had it, wasn't thankful for how much Mam and my grandparents did for me, for us. I'll survive. I have friends my age, the friends I've wanted all my life. And Ed can survive okay. Tommy, I'm not sure. He seems fine, but whoever is hurting Bill might go after him next. This orphanage is not a safe place for them. Please, Virgin Mother, tell me what I must do. I await your sign. Amen.

CHAPTER TWENTY-SEVEN

JANUARY 1935

Begrudgingly, I emerge from a dream about Mam's New Year's Eve parties, fresh-baked pasties, roasted chickens, and powdered-sugared cakes. Our window edge glows like a golden halo. Betty flings open the shutters. When she raises the window, black smoke pours in, bringing a stench that smells like dirt and cigars.

Rachael hangs over the ledge. "The coal pit's on fire! Maybe the entire basement!"

"Run!" screams Hannah.

"My brothers!" I yank Zarah's blanket. "Help me get my brothers."

Red-faced Sister Mary Myrtle stomps in. "Betty, Rachael, remove yourselves from that window. Into bed, ladies. The issues are under control."

The girls scramble back under their bedcovers, but I stand my ground. "Please, Sister, I must get my brothers."

"They are none of your concern."

"How can you say that?"

"Your brothers are fine. Bill is extinguishing the fire."

"He's only six! Just a kid!"

"Calm yourself." Sister Myrtle points at my bed. "You're frightening the other girls."

"Did you notify the fire department?"

"No, Katie. Firemen are too large."

"Call my brother Joe. That's what he does, puts out fires."

"Young lady, we are well aware of how to extinguish this fire. Your brother Bill is strong, yet small enough, to slip through the coal chute."

I clench Sister Myrtle's upper arms. "He could burn to death."

"Remove your hands. Your brother is spreading the coals. They'll cool and extinguish on their own. Return to your bed. If Sister Agnes Evellius hears you screaming, she may decide the mop closet is a better place for you." Sister Myrtle steps toward the window. "Betty, close the shutters, immediately."

The nun's habit swishes. As the door lock clanks in place, I reopen the window and lean out. Two nuns lurk in the shadows, a safe distance from the thick clouds of smoke.

A boy dragging a shovel emerges from the narrow coal chute opening. "Fire's out below!" Cinders spark like firecrackers when he digs into a pile of red-hot coals on the ground. He yanks a handkerchief from his trouser pocket and wipes charcoal soot off his face.

"Bill's safe!" I wave furiously, but my brother motions me back in. He and another boy continue flinging shovelfuls of coal as I close the window.

Three days pass. I fidget while waiting for our father to enter the visitors' room beside the chapel. When he does, his head hangs as if Father Faolan's Bible reading came to pass. Da's spine is bent, and his shoulders sag as if a millstone hangs about his neck. He lowers himself into a chair facing me. He appears to suffer the burden he would carry if his son had burned up and died. Does his apparent remorse make my disgust for him unjust? Is my satisfaction in witnessing his shame a sin?

Da holds a pink bakery box in one hand, and with the other grabs his lower back. "My joints ache."

"Ache?" What a fool I am to think he's feeling guilty. "Bill could have died."

"Terrible that happened, but he's a hero, don't you think? Just a kid—putting out that fire. A chip off the old block, I'd say."

"Where have you been? You said you'd be back as soon as you got on your feet, but you haven't even visited us."

"I'm moving slow these days." Da lifts the lid, releasing a buttery sugar scent.

I ignore the fresh-baked cookies stacked inside the pink box. "When

Sister Mary Myrtle said you had come, I thought you were worried Bill might need a doctor. But you're just talking about yourself."

"The pain keeps me awake most nights." Da tilts the box toward me.

"I don't sleep much either. Every strange noise terrifies me that someone might be hurting Bill or Tommy."

"All those years shoveling coal at the rail yard. Then working as a rod turner for CF&I—hard, hot, back-breaking."

I recoil from my father's pungent alcohol breath. "Listen, Bill crawls into Tommy's bed and weeps, and Tommy comforts him all night. What else can he do? None of us knows because Bill won't say what the story is. If you can't afford four of us, at least take Bill."

"I've got the hotel's cheapest room, about the size of a closet." He fingers the pink box on his lap.

I mumble, "Believe me, I know about closets."

"Doc says I have an ulcer. Can't eat much."

"Are you hearing what I'm telling you? Except for food donated by the Women's Auxiliary and the Pueblo Community Chest, Bill eats slimy cabbage, occasionally a carrot or onion sliver or shred of meat in a liquid the nuns call soup. Breakfast is a foul-tasting lumpy mush. Whatever you feed him will be better."

"I can't afford a larger room."

"Da, what's wrong with you? Us kids slept together on that nasty mattress in Philly. Bill doesn't need anything fancy. He just needs a safe place."

"Used up my savings." Da picks up a cookie then returns it to the box. He wipes the crumbs that cling to his fingertips on his trouser leg.

"We know you drank up our money before you lost the house." I feel a bit of hope when Bill walks in. How can anyone not care about this sweet blue-eyed lad?

Tommy steps out from behind and hesitantly heads toward the pink box.

"Are you taking us home, Da?" Bill cradles his gauze-wrapped hand.

Tommy's eyes widen as he snatches a cookie. "You're my Da?"

"How's that make you feel, Da? Your son doesn't recognize you." Anger butts against the inside of my skull. I expect my head will explode. I have more to say, accusations to make. Instead, I ask Bill, "Are your burns healing?"

"A tad crispy, but I got a week off from shoveling coal and stoking the boiler. Evilness put me on the list to go slop hogs at the farm, but kindly Sister Anne talked her out of it."

Bill grimaces at Da. "Did yeh come to take us home?"

"Now that's a question I've been asking the good Lord to answer," says Ed.

Our father squirms, scratches his head, and plucks a yellow citron sliver off a cookie. "Ahem, ah, well, sorry, boys, but I can't."

"Let me tell you a thing or two." Ed shakes his finger in Da's face. "I believed Mam when she promised to watch over us from above. For the first year, I trusted she was right when she said you'd care for us on Earth. Appears our mother was mistaken on both accounts."

"I haven't forgotten you. That's why I brought cookies."

"Well, aren't I fortunate?" Bill extends his bandaged hand. "Sister Reparata thanked me with an entire glass of milk. Would have been grand if you'd brought the cookies then. I could have dunked mine in that rare glass of fresh, cold milk. Oh, boy, how I love to dunk my cookies."

Da, head still hung low, shuffles to his feet. "I've got to go, kids, but as soon as I get on my feet..." He leaves without glancing back, still carrying the pink bakery box.

The room falls so quiet the echo of his footsteps can be heard, softer and softer. The key clanks in the front door lock. Is that to keep him out? Or us inside?

A tear forms in the corner of Tommy's eye. Bill's head hangs as he expels a sigh of hopelessness. Ed marches to the door and turns the doorknob violently until Sister Anne's voice filters in. "Just a moment, children. I'll get the right key."

Later that night, as I kneel beside my bed, Sister Myrtle's glare chills me. She's angry that we girls made too much noise getting ready for bed.

O Lord, hear my prayer. You are my refuge. The Bible says you love children. But my brothers and I, through no fault of our own, ended up in an unsafe place. I prayed to the Blessed Virgin Mother, yet we remain. Please, rescue us. Or show me the way. Amen.

Monday morning, I cringe from the screech of Sister Mary Myrtle's chalk against the blackboard. She writes in her sprawling hand, *To forgive, to pardon.*

I forgive Da for dumping me, but not for abandoning Bill. His thoughts were for himself instead of the horrible things his six-year-old son must endure. If Da is to be forgiven, someone else will have to do it. Not me.

White dust lights on Sister Mary Myrtle's black sleeve. She raps a wooden pointer on each word. "*Ignosco, ignoscis, ignoscit.* Tazia, please recite then give us the plural."

I tug a loose thread. My skirt seam separates. When Sister Myrtle dismisses class, I raise my hand. "I beg your patience, Sister. My side seam ripped. May I use a sewing machine?"

The Sister frowns. Rachael motions for me stop talking and leave. I turn away from her and back to Sister Turtle.

"Perhaps after the girls finish their work?"

"I think not." Sister Turtle swivels her head. The veil slaps against her pallid cheeks. "It's not allowed. Machine repairs are costly."

"My mother taught me on our Singer."

"You know how to use a machine?"

"Mam sewed dresses and women's coats in Philly, ones that sold for a high price. Before she died, my sister and I saved our money and bought our own Singer."

"Humm, you are a hard worker."

"Thank you, Sister. Does that mean you will allow me?"

"What have you sewn?"

"Nightgowns and dresses. Rompers for Tommy and shirts for my other brothers. I'm a tad slow at making handstitched buttonholes but sew a seam as fast as Mam, and she was a professional."

"I assume you would find sewing more pleasing than scrubbing floors?"

"Yes, Sister. I believe I would."

"A seamstress who turned eighteen leaves the orphanage Friday. I shall speak with Sister Evellius. For now, you and Rachael, run on and scrub the floors."

I scold myself, *Stupid, stupid.*

"You'll be sorry you opened your big mouth," says Rachael.

"Already am. What was I thinking? How will I check on my brothers if I'm trapped in the sewing room? Or leave notes behind the Blessed Virgin's foot?"

"More than that. Come on."

I follow Rachael down the basement stairs. Zarah, scalding whites in the iron sink, rubs her nose, red and runny from bleach fumes. Ethel and Tazia drop huge laundry bags onto the cement floor.

Tazia grins. "Did you check out the handsome new boy?"

"Outward appearance don't add up to a thing," says Ethel. "My momma had three slick lookers, all no-counts."

Rachael opens the mop closet door. "He's seventeen. Be gone in a few months."

"We shall marry."

"Sure," says Rachael. "You're just what he wants, a fourteen-year-old wife."

"Italian women are known for the spells we cast on men." Tazia dumps soiled clothes into the washing machine.

"Kinda had my eye on him myself," says Ethel. "Momma borned me at thirteen. Not that she wanted me. But whatcha gonna do when a man holds a knife to your throat?"

"He'll take me, and only me."

I can't believe what Tazia is saying. "You'd leave us?"

"He will have an important job, and we shall never put our children in an orphanage."

"Girl, yo' mind is running wild. You don't know nothing 'bout him." Ethel holds Sister Evilness' white undershirt on her head so it drapes over her shoulders and sings "Here Comes the Bride" while strutting toward the boiler.

The stairs creak overhead.

We stare toward the thump, thump, bump as enormous cloth bags tumble down the stairs. Two fellas smile embarrassedly, drag the flour bags across the room, and prop them against the concrete wall. When the electric washing machines emit their metallic clang and grind, Rachel and I retrieve our buckets and follow the boys upstairs.

"Are my brothers okay?"

"As good as any of us," answers the boy named Gilbert before they walk away.

Rachael whispers, "Before we got interrupted, I was saying I like you. You're the only person in this whole rotten place who ever gave me a gift."

"Only a penny."

"Still, except for the auxiliary ladies, you're the only one. Anyway, I'm warning you."

"Of what?"

"Monsignor Docher, the fat gray-haired priest who comes on Fridays to get some sewing done and meet with Sister Evilness. You'll recognize him. He's got an enormous snout like a pig and pasty-white skin that sags so you can see the blood vessels inside his bottom eyelids. Bloodhound eyes, but that's not the worst. Violet renamed him Monsignor Douche Bagger."

"She might end up in hell for that."

"Douche Bagger belongs in hell's deepest, darkest caves. Pay attention, Katie."

"He's a monsignor, a man of God—"

"Who traps girls on his lap and slips his filthy hands up their skirts."

"Noooo. The Sisters wouldn't allow that."

"He pretends he's tickling, so watch yourself. We're late. We'll be spending time inside the mop closet if we don't get the dining hall scrubbed before the lads come for their lunch slop."

As we dunk our rags and scrub, the boys approach. While Rachael gawks at Tazia's potential husband, I work my way toward Ed.

He steps out of line. "We gotta get the feck out of this prison. I'm thinking we could call Mr. Parker and he'd come get us in his car."

"Who's going to ask Sister Evilness to use the phone?"

From farther down the line, Tommy waves furiously. "Kaaatieee..."

My name echoes in the stark hall.

"Shite." Ed ducks his head. "We're in trouble now."

Sister Christine's heels click on the stone floor as she scurries up to us. "Did I hear voices?"

Ed scuttles back in line, and Tommy watches his feet. As my youngest brother marches past, our fingers brush. A tear falls from his eye. I drop to my hands and knees and make large, slow circles on the floor as the boys walk away. My breath catches. I expect punishment when the nun leans down to me.

"Scrub faster, Katie. Sister Evellius is not far behind."

Several nights later, as I lie in my bed, the dormitory is so quiet I'm sure I'm the only girl awake. Laughing inwardly, I remember the day Ed hid the golf club inside his trouser leg. I sniff as if smelling the sweet juice that sprayed when I whacked the orange with the putter until a scurrying sound whips me from my thoughts and into root cellar recollections. When a hand tugs my foot, I squeal.

"Quiet," mutters Rachael. "Wake Zarah and Ethel. I'll get Hannah and Tazia. Meet me in the linen closet."

Rubbing sleep from our eyes, we squeeze into the closet at the room's end. When we sit, wooden shelves poke our backs.

"Quick, Tazia, close the door," hisses Rachael.

The light from a single match cuts through the pitch black, lighting the closet just enough to illuminate Rachael as she pulls an offering candle out of her armpit.

"Did you steal cigarettes again?" asks Zarah.

"Bigger than that," says Ethel. "See how her pajama shirt pokes out— like the Lord sent the big titties she's been praying for."

We giggle as Rachael pulls out a bundle wrapped in a linen dishtowel. "I skipped a corner in the nuns' dining room, so Evilness sent me back. Could hardly believe my luck, eight large buns sitting on the table."

"Why didn't you take them all?" asks Tazia.

"Somebody'd notice if all the buns disappeared. Besides, I only needed six. One for me and each of my best friends. So, I cleaned that slovenly corner then snuck these handsome golden buns inside my shirt, ran back, and hid them under my pillow."

Zarah snorts, "Explains why these beautiful buns are a bit flat. Nice work, you sneaky thief."

"Heavenly." Orange marmalade squirts between my teeth.

"Darn tootin'," says Ethel. "My Grandma Sally made 'em Sundays after church. Ain't nothing better, excepting her sweet potato pie."

"We could go to hell for this," says Hannah.

"Here, let me save you from the devil." Rachael grabs Hannah's bun.

She snatches it back. "You girls aren't going anywhere without me, not even hell."

I say, "Thanks for choosing us, Rachael."

"You are my only friends."

Tazia's eyes widen. "You do realize, we shut ourselves up in a closet?"

I chuckle, "It's fun when we do it to ourselves."

"Them other girls gonna lose their religion when they find out we didn't share. But that won't compare to the whoopin' you'll get from the good Sister." The lard Ethel sneaks from the kitchen and combs through her hair glistens in the candlelight. "And Sister Myrtle, she'd be laying little baby turtle eggs."

"Don't leave a single crumb or we'll be hauling boulders tomorrow," warns Tazia.

"There're worse things." Hannah lowers her voice, deep and eerie, as the melting candle wax threatens to saturate the wick. The flame flickers, barely emitting sufficient light to see each other. "Like the caves of Los Hermanos Penitente, the meeting place of the Repentant Brothers."

Zarah shivers. "Where's that?"

"In a canyon near Del Norte, three hours from Pueblo. Who cares where it is? My point is, the brothers nail live men onto wooden crosses, just like Jesus. They atone for their sins by beating themselves with leather whips."

Zarah tsks, "What's that got to do with us?"

"If you weren't interrupting, you'd know. If beating themselves doesn't do the trick, these goons kidnap girls and beat them too."

The whites of Ethel's eyes gleam like two dinner plates. Hannah trembles, and Tazia hugs herself. The candle flickers one last time.

"Criminy, it's dark in this closet," says Rachael.

I whisper, "Let's go back to bed."

After a restless night of dreams filled with men hanging from wooden crosses and blood spurting around the nails that anchor their hands and feet, I stare, bleary-eyed, at the words as Sister Evellius writes a Bible verse on the chalkboard. The stem of the T climbs tall and firm. Its arm bends heavenward. The out stroke of the C swirls like an ocean wave. Each letter is perfectly formed.

The nun presses hard against the chalkboard and writes: *1 Thessalonians 5:19—In every thing give thanks: for this is the will of God in Christ Jesus concerning you.* Her voice drones, "Through our words of gratefulness, the Lord knows us and accepts His lambs into His kingdom. Take this verse into your minds and souls. For what are you grateful? For what do you give thanks? Front and back, don't leave any lines blank."

Tazia looks at me and rolls her eyes until only the whites show.

"The sun shines upon us," says Sister Evellius. "It proves to be a glorious day. When completed, I shall grant you time in the yard, that is, after I approve your work."

I press my pencil against the top line and will my hand to move. The pencil appears frozen in time. But freedom on a warm day comes as often as visits from the Easter Bunny. I'm determined to partake in this unexpected kindness.

Zarah scans the room as if searching for something worthy of gratitude. Rachael, bent over and chewing on her bottom lip, scribbles as fast as light. I admire that about my friend. Whatever the situation, whenever called upon, Rachael gets the job done. Ethel bites her eraser then writes furiously.

The heat of Evilness' stare bears down on me. My pencil moves.

> *1. I am grateful for a bed.*
> *2. I am grateful for a blanket.*
> *(Be nice if it were thicker.)*
> *3. I am grateful for our tasty food.*
> *(Sorry, Holy Virgin Mother. That's a lie, but I must fill this page.)*

4. I am grateful I no longer sleep on a thin lumpy mattress on the floor.

Sister Evilness glares when a sob balloons in my throat at the thought of squeezing in with Mary and my brothers.

5. I am grateful my mother taught me to sew.
(That got me out of scrubbing floors.)
6. I am grateful Nana taught me to make buttonholes.

My lips curl up ever so slightly as I work toward the bottom of the page.

7. I am grateful Mrs. O'Shea taught me to cook.

When the boys and I get a place of our own, I'll fry a giant pile of golden boxty with crispy edges. I can smell them now. Mary and Joe will come over, and we'll eat like a family again. Our lives will be perfect.

The chalk screeches as Sister Evellius writes on the blackboard, August 23, 1935. "Put your name and the date in the left-hand corner."

I have the weirdest sense of floating in space. Can today be my birthday? I'm twelve?

Mam baked me a chocolate cake five months before her death. The multicolored candles dripped wax on the whipped frosting mounded like miniature snowdrifts. Did I thank my mother? Everyone got a birthday cake after Granda bought the house. The first year, it was a big deal. If I'd realized the cake for my ninth birthday would be my last, I would have thanked her a million times. Three years since she died. The best I can do is thank her now.

8. Mam, I am grateful for your love and my birthday cakes.
9. Mam, I am grateful for your pork and bean and bologna casserole.

I'd never complain if I could eat it again. First Rachael and Tazia, then Zarah and Ethel, place their lists on Evilness's desk. I flip my paper and write faster. As I approach the bottom of the page, my sewing room friends, Laura and Violet, rise from their seats.

> *10. I am grateful for sunshine.*
> *11. I am grateful to have made the good friends I prayed so long to have.*
> *(But now, my brothers and I must find a safer place.)*
> *12. I am grateful for time outside with my friends.*

I lay my pencil down and take my list to Sister Evellius.

The nuns' lips move as if reading every line. She inspects, top to bottom, then flips the paper over.

I pray she'll hurry. There can't be much time.

The nun makes a large red check in the righthand corner and slaps my list atop the pile.

I rush outside and peer heavenward. I run toward the friends who are waving for me to join them near Sister Evilness' vegetable garden. For this, I am truly grateful.

CHAPTER TWENTY-EIGHT

SEPTEMBER 1935

I stifled a hallelujah when Sister Myrtle told me Joe arranged an outing to the Colorado State Fair. Now my thoughts whirl as I settle in at my assigned sewing machine and plan how to best convey the urgent need for him to rescue us. The foot pedal clinks against the concrete floor. The machine races. Sister Reparata will make me rip out any pucker in Monsignor Douche Bagger's shirt and sew it again. My hand trembles so I ease the pressure.

Perhaps I can convince Joe not to bring us back. I must pack. I don't have a suitcase, not even a paper sack, but my plaid pajamas could be rolled inside a dress and tucked beneath my arm. If caught, the punishment will be extraordinary.

I press the foot pedal and stitch the shirt's hem. I'm confident, when Joe knows the truth, he will take me and the fellas into his home.

A second outfit underneath might do the trick. The boys won't be going back to the chapel today, so it's too late to leave a note behind the Virgin Mother's foot to tell Ed to have the boys do the same.

I break the thread with my teeth. Joe's nineteen or twenty, I've lost count. Either way, he's old enough. But we've been in the orphanage nearly two years. If he planned to rescue us, wouldn't he have done so by now?

I slip the shirt onto a hanger. If Monsignor Douche Bagger wasn't getting fatter, his clothes wouldn't need repairing so often. I glance at Laura and Violet's bony elbows then rub the sharp points of mine. My empty stomach grumbles. The Monsignor must eat the same food as the nuns rather than what they give us orphans because none of them are skinny.

I pin the tear in a boy's nightshirt. Joe kicked Mary out when she slapped his wife. Can't blame him for that. Family first. But me and the boys are family, flesh and blood, and we haven't done anything wrong. The nightshirt smells of sweat. Da didn't want us after he married the Scarlet Woman. And now Joe has a wife. Maybe that's why he doesn't want us.

When I reminded Mary how little we survived on in Philadelphia, she glanced at her gold watch, fidgeted with its delicate black, double-thick corded wristband and said, "Nearly time for my shift on the switchboard," then abruptly left.

I visualize the skirts, sweaters, and shoes Mary bought herself when we were supposedly saving for the Singer. Her clothes are even nicer now. Clearly, Joe is our last hope.

Later that night, I flip-flop in my bed like a grounded fish. Never has the sun taken this long to rise. Still, I must have fallen asleep because when Betty slams open the shutters, I leap. My eyes burn, and my temples throb.

Sister Myrtle harrumphs and tsks then paces the aisle as we change into our day clothes. When she pivots toward the door, I slip on the yellow flour sack dress donated by the Women's Auxiliary, and over that, a white blouse and the least worn of my two uniform skirts.

"What the heck?" asks Zarah.

I press my index finger against my lips then slip Molly into my pocket. I finger my soft plaid flannel pajamas, feel the love with which the Pueblo Society Ladies made them, and leave them and my second uniform for the next poor orphan girl.

Sister Myrtle's eyes bore into me. "No breakfast for you today. Your brother plans to feed you at the fair. Wait in the visitors' reception room."

I barely contain my excitement. "Thank you, Sister."

"One more thing."

I yank my uniform skirt hem in case the yellow dress shows.

"I appreciate how steadfastly you toil."

"Thank you, Sister Mary Myrtle. I do my best."

"I hope you have a lovely day."

These kind words leave me speechless. I curtsey then berate myself. Sister Myrtle's a nun, not a queen. I bolt through the halls and down the stairs like a mouse avoiding a house cat. My spirits sink when none of my brothers await me in the visitors' room. Remembering Da's offer of cookies instead of a home brings a flood of disappointment. Then, I hear a sound I will never forget, the long strides and heavy footsteps of my eldest brother. I jump into Joe's arms.

He spins me until my feet fly, the same as before. "Wow, you've grown."

"It's been a year since you—"

"Sorry. Wrong of me. I was saving to get you out. Then, the baby came."

Bill and Tommy tackle Joe from behind. He laughs and pats their heads. "Take a gander at you. You're little men."

Ed pumps Joe's hand and gives him a manly hug. "Where the feck yeh been?"

Joe pushes back his flat cap and scratches his head. "I was just telling Katie—"

"Mary keeps us up on what's going on," says Ed. "Once a month, she brings us candies and the news."

That's a stretch of the truth, yet I nod my approval and think—Well done, Ed. Lay on the guilt. Joe tugs his cap brim until it rides against his eyebrows. "Sweet Mother of Jesus, you're making me feel awful. Has Da checked on yeh?"

"Haven't seen hide nor hair of him since he brought those feckin cookies," says Ed. "Don't want to waste time talking about him. Let's go to the fair."

My brothers and I cheer until a "Hush," from the hall quiets us, and we scurry out to where Sister Christine waits to unlock the heavy wooden door.

"Have a glorious day, children. May the Lord be with you."

The bus lets us off at Colorado State Fair's entrance gate. Three men on a wooden platform strum guitars behind a cowboy singing "Tumbling Leaves." The roller coaster clangs and roars. I scoop up wide-eyed Tommy before he's swallowed by the frenzy of stampeding legs.

"Five years old. You're getting big, nearly broke my back." I kiss Tommy's cheek then point to the banner hanging from a concession stand. *Fried Sausages 5¢.* "Joe, we're hungry."

My grinning, bobble-headed brothers rub their stomachs.

I can't remember any experience more wonderful than this taste of freedom.

As the kids wipe sausage grease off their faces and slurp orange drinks, Joe asks, "What next?"

"Cotton candy." I lick my lips.

"Rodeo." Bill circles his hand as if to rope a cow.

Ed rams his body into Bill. "Bumper cars."

"Zoom, zoom." Tommy mimics jerking a steering wheel to the right then the left. "Race cars."

"Sorry, lad. No race cars at the fair." Joe points toward a dirt track. "Harness racing?"

The boys groan like a single wounded animal. "Noooo."

"Okay," laughs Joe. "You boys arm wrestle. Winner's choice."

Ed fakes a squeal of pain and lets Bill twist his arm toward the ground. "Rodeo it is."

As we climb the bleachers, a raging bull bucks the cowboy clinging around his neck. The massive animal kicks all four legs at once and spins in the air. When he lands, he paws the brim of the cowboy's hat. Three wildly costumed clowns wave frantically and charge the bull. The crowd roars when the cowboy and his hat are saved to ride another day.

A teenager, thin with brown hair hanging in his eyes, climbs the bleacher steps, shouting, "Peanuts! Hot roasted peanuts. Two for a nickel."

"Please?" Tommy tugs Joe's sleeve.

"Whatever yeh kids want."

I open my small paper bag and inhale the warm, nutty scent. When Tommy pops a whole peanut into his mouth and chomps, I realize he's never had one roasted in its shells. I extend my palm. "Spit it out. Want a peanut plant growing in your belly?" He giggles when I pat his stomach. I break the soggy shell in half, and like a momma bird, drop two peanuts into his open mouth.

We leave the steer wrestling and pass a monkey wearing a red velvet vest and pulling a wooden wagon carrying a perky black and white dog with one floppy ear. Joe nudges us to hurry. We laugh and scramble to select the bumper cars we think will go the fastest. We crank the steering wheels and ram the tin cars into each other. Ed howls with delight when

238

Joe's fender falls off and the man runs out and hammers it back on.

Our grins curve upside-down when big brother says, "Sorry, kids, but I have a shift tonight. Pick one more, Wonder Wheel or Rocket Ride, then I'll buy ice cream. Or would yeh rather have a Coors malted milk?"

"Rocket Ride and chocolate ice cream in a sugar cone!" shouts Bill.

Contentment warms me. Then, a chill freezes my heart. I can't remember when I last saw Bill's face light up this way. Will I ever see it again?

After the silver rockets return to ground level, we climb out. Tommy says the ride upset his stomach, but not so much he can't eat ice cream. The boys gobble the last of their cones as we board the bus. In minutes, Bill and Tommy fall asleep.

I waited for the right moment to reveal the spare outfit I wore underneath, but that moment never came. Now, I fidget in my seat, wondering whether to beg or demand Joe take us to his home. I decide to tell him the truth.

Joe bites his lip as I describe how we slave, the food we eat, and the severity of Sister Agnes Evellius' punishments. He nods when I give examples of the kindnesses shown by Sisters Mary Myrtle, Christine, and Anne and explain that only happens when Evilness is not around.

Ed sits silently and listens until Joe asks, "How's school?"

"I'm sent out to work horse ranches and pig farms. We're gone for weeks mucking barns and hauling shite. Bill and I, and other boys seven and older, anyway we're supposed to be seven, they send Bill because he's big for his age. But what I'm trying to say is we help with planting season then work the harvest. Sister Anne Beatrix is a good teacher when we're there, but we're not learning much because we're gone."

"Joe, the girls have lessons four days a week. An hour of Bible study and two of reading, writing, and arithmetic."

"Katie, that's way less learning than when you were in regular school."

"I got in a bit of trouble when I said that to Sister Evilness. She says we have scant need for formal education given the positions we will assume in life."

"Mam wouldn't like that."

"Lots going on Mam wouldn't like."

"Can't believe Mary didn't throw a fit," says Joe.

"Wouldn't do any good. Might make our lives worse. Bill needs rescuing first, and quickly. He crawls into bed with Tommy and cries most the night."

"What does Tommy do?"

"He holds Bill until he falls asleep. But that's backward. Bill's older, nearly seven. He should take care of Tommy, not the other way around."

Joe's eyebrows pinch together. "Ed, can't you get him to say what's wrong?"

"Nah. Some evil's got ahold of him, deep inside. He can't let it out. He's rattled."

"Bill's always clung to you, Katie," says our eldest brother. "You must know more."

"I wish I did. A big sister should protect her little brothers. But it's impossible. The nuns separate us girls from the boys, so we won't go down the wrong path, toward a life of sin. Only path I'm interested in is the fastest route out."

"Katie, you're gettin' off track," says Joe.

"Oh, yeah. Sorry. The boys and I sneak a word when we pass in the halls. Ed and I hide notes when we can. Big trouble if we get caught. The Christmas party is one of the few times we can say more than a few words to each other. Bill says he's just sad. But it's more than that. Joe, we're all sad. Our Billy Boy is a softy, but this is worse, and he's not spilling the beans."

"What about Da?"

"He claims to live in a closet-size room at the Minnequa and can't take Bill. Makes me so mad I could spit. He has room for the Scarlet Woman and their kid, but not us."

"She divorced him. Left his drunken arse. She and Caroline hightailed it back to Aurora to live with the sister."

"So, he has no excuse."

"Katie, you know how Da is. He's always got an excuse."

The bus clanking to a stop awakens Tommy and Bill. They rub their eyes as we stagger down the metal steps. Nobody speaks until Joe bangs the orphanage door knocker.

Silently, we each hug Joe.

"I promise yeh I'll talk with my wife." Joe tilts his flat cap and rubs his forehead. "I'm low on the fire department's totem pole. Don't earn much, and we got little Shirley. Shite, I'm in a tough spot."

I can't believe he would say such a thoughtless thing. "You're in a tough spot? Really, Joe?"

Sister Anne opens the door. A yellow beam of light casts shadows across Joe's face. I turn my back on him and follow my brothers into the orphanage.

CHAPTER TWENTY-NINE

OCTOBER 1935

Sister Christine Daniel loves the Lord first, but baseball runs a close second. Of course, she doesn't proclaim this in Sister Agnes Evellius' presence, but I know it's true. From the first game through the playoffs, Sister Christine lords over the donated radio, a Cathedral Style 1931 Philco, Model 90.

"I will sprinkle water upon you, and ye shall be cleansed of your filthiness." Sister Christine scrubs the speaker cutouts with a damp cloth and polishes the wood until candlelight reflects in the oily glow. She recounts sitting at her father's side, cheering for the Detroit Tigers. That is why, except for the Sacred Heart Angels, the Tigers remain her favorite team, and why Sister Christine wants the radio in perfect condition for their battle against the Chicago Cubs on this warm Monday afternoon, October 7.

I don't much care for baseball, but Bill does, even more than Ed. I'm confident the boys will gather around the radio for this final World Series game. I shoot my hand in the air when Sister Myrtle selects which girls may also listen to the game and thank the nun profusely when she chooses me.

The boys gather close to the radio and wager items they don't have, footballs and leather helmets, hot dogs and candy bars. As dictated by Sister Christine, we girls sit a respectable distance behind the boys. I won't get to talk to my brothers, but we share smiles and signal each other. For now, that has to be enough.

The boys are tense and quiet. Announcer Hal Totten's voice sounds like a whispered warning coming out of the radio. "In the ninth inning, the game continues to be tied."

Then, Goose Goslin hits a single into right field, over the head of second baseman Billy Herman. The Detroit crowd goes wild as Totten describes Cochrane racing around third and heading home for the winning run. The orphan boys jump up, fake punch each other, and cheer as if they were at the game.

Sister Christine beams. "Gentlemen, this is a sign. The same fate awaits our team.

Sister Christine coaches the orphanage's team, the Sacred Heart Angels. Six-year-old Bill is the youngest, but he holds his own, thanks to being taller than most boys his age and the time he spent with Ed and the lads playing in the street outside our home.

When the Angels lose their first game against the Fighting Irish of St. Patrick's School, Sister Christine says it's because her boys have no gloves. Before the Championship game is played, she applies the pressure of the Lord, brings sufficient guilt upon the opposing coach that he relents and lets her trace his team's baseball gloves on the butcher paper she brought along.

Every Sunday, a parishioner wishing to gain Father Faolan's favor brings him pineapple skillet cake with butter and brown sugar topping. As I move the button to accommodate his expanding waist, Sister Christine walks in, hands filled with paper patterns.

Ed and Bill follow, dragging a lumpy and torn mattress.

"I have business that needs my attention. Your brothers know which parts of a hand need protection, so I leave them to show you how to shape the gloves." Sister Christine hesitates. "Only a week until our game against the Pueblo Orphans Home. These gloves will do the trick."

Ed watches until the door closes. "We'll get laughed off the field."

"The other team won't find it so funny when you don't let them score." I intend my words to cheer Ed, but his shoulders slump, and his eyes gloss over with hopelessness. I glance away to save his dignity.

"We were doing okay before Mam died." Ed runs his fingers through his hair. "Our own house, own bedroom. Had enough food, even a leather baseball glove. I wonder what Da did with my glove. Think he sold it? Did yeh ever suspect that once again we'd be as poor as we were in Philly?"

"Never thought our father would abandon us." My tears are large and hot, albeit few. I must be strong for the boys.

"Nobody cares about us except us," says Bill.

Ed stomps his foot. "I'm done with this. Turning sixteen next month. I can make a solid wage working as hard as I do for the nuns and get us all out of this feckin place."

"Bill, drag the mattress into that corner." I glance at Laura and Violet. The whir of their machines prevents the girls from hearing me. "Ed, did something new happen to Bill?"

"What do yeh mean?"

"Rachael said he was in Sister Evilness' garden, sitting on a boulder with his head in his hands instead of picking the nettles she sent him after."

"Sister Evellius caught Rachel the Snitch snatching an apple from the nuns' dining room. Now, she's in the mop closet doing penitence."

"Can't say I'm surprised." I debate telling my brother about the jam-filled buns.

"The truth is harsh, but I'm tellin' yeh not to take what Rachael says as gospel. She makes up stories to keep yeh beholding."

"She told me Bill resembles her youngest brother, so I don't believe she'd lie about this."

Violet slips Bill a Tootsie Pop. He unwraps the paper, runs the sucker beneath his nose, and takes a deep breath. "Gosh, this is awful nice of yeh."

Hiding candy from the nuns is next to impossible. It's uncanny how they sniff it out. As I watch Bill twirl the pop in his mouth, my mind swirls around how I might repay Violet until Ed's whisper breaks up my thoughts.

"He misses you and Mam and Da. He's glum. Feel that way myself, but I'm better at setting it aside. The only thing different, anyway, I thought it was strange—I was trying to cheer him by pretending to snatch his tiny bread pudding square. We scuffled a bit and knocked the bowl off the table. Guess what happened next."

"A visit with Sister Evilness and a long discussion of your evil ways."

"Yep, but that's not what's important. We were headed toward the office of Evilness when the Monsignor poked out his head. 'Twas a week ago today, last Friday. Bill turned white as the dead and grabbed my arm then dragged me down the hall like a wolf was snapping at our heels. But he won't say what set him off. That night, he crawled into bed with me instead of Tommy. My pillow was wet in the morning. He'd been crying, and I didn't even wake up. Got to tell yeh, I feel crummy about that."

"Get it out of him tonight. We'll have the mitts cut out and stitched when you come back to show us where the stuffing goes, and you can tell me what he says."

"I'll do my best." Ed raises his voice. "Come on, lad. We've wasted enough time with these birds. Let's get out there and weed Evilness' garden."

My worry subsides when Ed lays his arm across Bill's shoulders and my brothers lean against each other. But once they disappear into the hall, I worry about what Ed will tell me after their talk. I stab the mattress with a metal seam ripper. When we find out who's hurting Bill, they'll have to deal with me. I dig into the opening, grab a handful of cotton batting, and fling it. "So there!"

Laura's eyebrows rise. "Quite a mess you've made."

Violet points. "I don't think you can make baseball gloves from that disgusting mattress."

"Gonna try. It's important to my brothers."

"And Sister Christine," chuckles Laura. "I made seven rompers from the bag of rags Sister Anne brought me. Soon as I put snaps on the crotches, I'll help."

"Me too," says Violet. "Maybe Sister Christine will let us go to the big game."

We pin the glove patterns onto the blue striped mattress case and cut around the edges.

The following morning, we sew the gloves, leaving a slit for stuffing. By five in the afternoon, I realize Ed might not show. Hoping he'll barrel into the room at the last minute, I sweep material shreds and loose threads into the dustpan as slowly as I can.

"Sister Christine's working the boys hard, pitching, batting, sprinting," says Violet. "Don't worry. She'll send him down tomorrow. She plans on winning that championship."

It would comfort me to tell my friends that it's not the game worrying me. But my brother is a proud lad, and I couldn't betray him like that. So, I spend the day deep in my own thoughts.

Midmorning the following day, I bear down on the sewing pedal. The needle thrusts faster and faster. Every few seconds, I peek toward the door because the Monsignor might arrive at any minute. Nervous over that and anxious from waiting to see Ed, my fingers move with the cloth and the needle catches my skin. I'm sucking blood when Sister Evellius steps inside. My heart pounds. Laura and Violet think the same as I—we do our work and keep our mouths shut. So why has Evilness come to the sewing room?

"Katie, are you finished? The Monsignor prefers you fit him with this cassock."

Watermelon best describes the Monsignor's shape. The robe is big and loose. There's no reason for a fitting, but I can't refuse. I snip the thread, gather up the cassock and a pin cushion, and follow Sister Evellius.

The Monsignor sits in his desk chair, rocking slowly. His broad smile plumps his cheeks but doesn't reach his squinty eyes. "No need to stay, Sister. Katie has fitted me previously." He slips off his jacket.

I begin to say he's mistaken. Instead, I bite my thumbnail and stare at my scuffed brown shoes until I hear the office door close and the swish of him putting on the cassock.

He smooths the black fabric over his stomach, straightens the fuchsia piping, and works his way down the thirty-three, cloth-covered buttons. "What do you think, Katie? Run your hand along this seam. Is it puckered?"

The seam hangs true and smooth. How do I respectfully tell him he's wrong? I tug the hem, careful not to touch him. "It's straight."

"You are quite the little seamstress, aren't you, my dear?"

"My mother taught me."

"You don't think it fits too tight? I do like my sweets."

"Me too. My mother gave my friend and me pennies for anise at Miss Betsy's Sweeter Than Sweet Candy Shoppe." I lower my eyes again. "My apologies, Monsignor. I talk too much."

"No, no, dear. It's a pleasure talking with polite young people such as you. Do you like chocolate? Miss Betsy brings me fresh-made candy every Sunday." The cellophane crinkles as he reveals four squares.

I draw in the rich chocolate aroma and rub my tongue against the roof of my mouth as if tasting the sweet, creamy fudge. Three years have passed since I made candy to celebrate Mam bringing Theresa home from the hospital. Even while flooded with horrible memories of my baby sister's death, I really want some fudge.

"Come, let's read the Bible together." Monsignor Docher sits and pats his thigh. His stomach takes up most of his lap.

I perch awkwardly at the edge of his knees. I fear sliding off until he steadies me with one hand on my knee and offers a chocolate square. As the fudge softens in my mouth, he lifts the open Bible from his desk. "Matthew 19: 13-15. Are you familiar with these verses, Katie?"

If I open my mouth, softened fudge will ooze out, so I shake my head.

"'Then were there brought unto him little children, that he should put his hands on them, and pray.' Katie, do you know what Jesus said?"

I roll the chocolate with my tongue and shrug.

"'Suffer the little children to come unto me and forbid them not.'" His moist, fleshy fingers massage my knee. "'Embracing them and laying his hands upon them...'"

I squirm as his hand creeps toward my inner thigh. I cross my ankles and pinch my legs together. Melted fudge oozes down my throat.

"'When he had imposed hands on them, he departed from thence.'"

I position my arm across my lap to halt his advance.

He flips to a page marked with a red ribbon. "Psalms 118:16. 'The right hand of the Lord is exalted.' As clergy, I sit at His right hand and do His bidding."

I wriggle free from his grasp. "Sister Christine wants the baseball gloves ready for Saturday's game."

"Ah, yes, Sister Christine. I worry she loves baseball too much."

"She's very pious." I step backward. "And kind."

The door swings open. "Monsignor, is the repair to your liking?"

Thank you, Holy Virgin Mother Mary. First time I'm happy to see Sister Evellius.

"Ah, yes, Sister, it is fine." The Monsignor whisks the fudge off the desk and into his pocket. "Um, I shall go now. I'm overdue at the church."

I scoot around the Monsignor, past Sister Evellius, and dash into the hall. Upon reaching the bottom of the stairs, I run into Ed's arms.

"What the bejaysus is wrong with yeh?"

"The Monsignor gave me fudge and read Bible verses."

"Brutal. Aye, that would scare the devil outta me."

"He put his hand on my leg."

"Yer leg?" Ed raises his fists. "Dirty wanker, I'll take a go at 'em."

"It was nothing, really."

"Then why are yeh shaking?"

"Just being a ninny, I suppose."

"I'll knock his pan in. He won't be touching my sister again."

"He's a man of God, Ed. He didn't intend anything bad."

"Well, if yer sure. But tell yeh what," Ed licks his lips, "if the good Monsignor returns with more fudge, I'd be happy to collect it for yeh."

I punch Ed's arm. "Were you headed to the sewing room?"

"Aye, I was. Let's get those gloves padded. Sister Christine's all worked up about the championship game against Pueblo Orphans Home. She says we must establish the superiority of a Catholic upbringing."

"How's Bill?"

Ed grimaces. "He wet the bed, but Bill's popular, so nobody snitched. When Sister Reparata discovers a lad has committed this dreadful crime, she pours the water pitcher over his head and makes him wear wet clothes all day. But that's not what worries me most. When I get the chance, I slip away from my detail and check on our brothers. Fridays are a problem. Bill disappears."

"Be careful, Ed. It won't help if you get locked up."

"The weird thing is Sister Christine had me deliver a fruit bowl to Sister Evilness' office. Stretched the limits of my religious upbringing not to gobble the big fat juicy peach on top."

"Ed…"

"Yeah, yeah. Anyway, it gave me time alone in the hallway, so I searched for the window that scares the piss out of Bill. Must be an inner chamber. Came across Ethel in serious pain, kneeling on the rice with her nose smashed against the good Sister's wall. Anyway, I asked if she'd seen our Billy Boy. Poor girl shook her head and kept praying up a storm. Then, as luck would have it, I ran into Sister Reparata carrying a pile of white shirts. So, I asked if Bill was with you."

"And?"

"She stuttered, got flustered like she knew where he was, but all she said was no boys have assignments in the sewing room. Keep your eyes open. Something's going on."

Sacred Heart's Angels will play the Pueblo Orphans Home Miners at Central High, Mary's former school. Recalling how I longed to be a student there drags me down, so I force myself to think about the excitement surrounding this final game. The stakes are high. In addition to the awarding of blue ribbons and paper certificates, the reigning team will celebrate at H.S. Kress with hot dogs and Black Cow floats.

Sister Christine wrangles the loan of two orange school buses and makes a list of orphans who will fill the bleachers. I am first on the list as a thank you for my good work on the baseball gloves, and she assigns my friends to the same bus. We sit in the rear seats and practice cheers until the team climbs aboard wearing uniforms, with *Angels* embroidered in purple across the backs, donated by the Rotary Club.

I wave.

My brothers acknowledge me with a somber tip of their chins, as if they are men engaged in a serious enterprise.

I had asked Sister Christine for the favor of allowing Tommy to attend the game. She said she was sorry but couldn't break the rule. For safety, only children six and older were eligible for bus trips.

As we approach the bleachers, a rare occurrence happens. We are allowed to sit wherever we want. The object of Tazia's dreams, the handsome, dark-haired fella, left the orphanage the day he turned eighteen, yet she's undeterred in her quest for a boyfriend. She takes a seat beside Ed's friend and brushes his hand as she settles in. Tazia, now fifteen, more than two years older than I, seems to understand how to get a boy's attention.

What Nana called the green-eyed monster claws inside my chest. I'd like a boyfriend too, but I'll be gone soon.

A six-foot, chain-link fence encloses three sides of the field. How hard could it be to slip behind the dugout and keep walking? Rachael, Hannah, and Ethel wave me over. Zarah pats the space beside her.

The Angels bat first. The ball thrown by the Pueblo Orphans' pitcher is low in the strike zone. Ed hits a grounder toward third base and runs to first. Fans suck in their collective breaths as the third baseman fumbles the ball. Sacred Heart orphans cheer from the bleachers as he slides safely to first base.

The next player moves Ed to second base with a solid hit. Tension increases as the next two Angels strike out.

Bill tromps to home plate, takes his stance, and bunts. The pitcher scoops up the ball and throws it to first base.

The umpire clenches his fist and as if he's holding a hammer, delivers a quick sharp low through the air and shouts, "Out!"

We groan.

The Sacred Heart Angels don the new gloves and jog onto the field. Ed lopes to first base while Bill, with his shorter legs, runs to center field. I beam with pride. The blue and white striped mitts look fine, from a distance.

The first Miner raises his bat above his shoulders at a perfect forty-five-degree angle and stares down the Angels pitcher.

"Miner, Miner. Dig a hole to Chiner," shout the kids in the Sacred Heart bleacher.

The Pueblo Orphans Home batter doubles over and laughs so hard he drops the bat.

"Whatcha got on your hands? Your momma's apron?" yells a Miner from their dugout.

The Orphans Home fans laugh and jeer. We chant, "Hey, batter, batter."

The boy takes a mighty swing, but all he gets is air.

"One, two, three. Strike the bum out!" I shout the loudest of all the Sacred Heart orphans. I sense Sister Myrtle's stare but ignore her and clap my hands. The sun warms my neck and shoulders. I inhale the scent of freshly cut grass. Nothing is going to ruin this day.

The Angels' pitcher strikes out three Miners. The boys grin and smack each other's backsides with their homemade gloves as they return to the dugout.

In the eighth inning, the score is tied, each team having tallied three runs. The fans are restless.

In the final inning, Ed is fourth up. The bases are full. He taps home base, sets his feet, and raises his bat. The *crack* of the well-worn wooden bat against the ball resounds through the air and brings the crowd to silence. The ball's cork and ground rubber center does its job, propelling the ball farther than the wool-filled balls the Sacred Heart boys use in practice and over the Miner's third baseman's head. As it rolls between the outfielder's legs, orphans and nuns alike leap to their feet and scream, "Run! Run!"

Not a sound is heard from the Pueblo Orphans Home players or their fans as all four Angels round the bases.

The final score is Angels seven, Miners three. The players walk the line and shake hands like gentlemen until the Miners' catcher says, "Did your momma make those gloves out of your boxer shorts?"

Before a single Angels' player retorts, the Miners' coach rips the boy's leather mitt off his hand and smacks him in the head. Our players snicker, but Sister Christine shushes them and huddles the team as my friends and I board the bus.

After the boys clasp hands for a final cheer, Bill and another chap, who appears to be eight or nine, claim the bus seat over the rear wheel to enjoy the bounciest ride. The rest of the Angels follow, smelling of sweat, dirt, and grass, replaying the game, and congratulating themselves on their big win.

Once in motion, Sister Christine stands and grasps the safety pole. "Gentlemen, you have much of which to be proud today. As individuals, you used your skills and played your very best. As a team, you worked like a well-oiled machine. Most importantly, you never let a teammate down. You had the other fella's back every time. You are the finest team I have worked with, and I thank God for every one of you. Please, bow your heads and express your gratitude to the Lord, our Savior."

The bus quiets. I sense the pride Mam must feel for her sons and hope the boys sense it too. I thank the Lord for my brothers and open my eyes.

Some players rest their heads against the windows. Other boys sit quietly, wearing huge grins. The corners of Bill's lips still curl up as his head bobs in sleep. Who would guess what his life is like; what our lives are like?

Ed walks the aisle toward me and my friend. "Trade seats, Tazia. Robbie's got an eye for you, wants you to sit next to him."

Tazia smiles, gets up, and leaves.

Ed scrunches into the seat beside me. "Bill and I were charged with building a border beneath the back corner window so Evilness could plant some blessed plant."

"And?"

"It happened again. Bill turned deathly white and wouldn't go near the window." Ed peels dead skin from an old blister on his hand. "The way he trembled, nearly shook right out of his shoes, you would've thought we'd come face to face with *The Mummy* himself."

"Did you ask why?"

"He said stuff that shouldn't happen to any kid happens in that room. Then, he clammed up."

CHAPTER THIRTY

FEBRUARY 1936

I sit in Sister Evellius' office, expecting the worst. I don't know what I'll be punished for, but it's coming, as sure as I am sitting on this wooden bench.

"Boys, your sister is waiting for you," says Sister Christine outside the door. "Return to the dormitory immediately after you are dismissed."

When my brothers step inside, they appear as confused as I. Bill's face is milky white, and Tommy's hands fidget inside his pockets.

Ed mutters, "What's going on?"

I shrug. "I figured I messed up royal and was in for the lecture of my life, maybe a stay in the mop closet. But that can't be it because you're all here."

We squeeze in on the bench, cross our hands in our laps, and sigh with relief when Father Faolan enters. His strongest punishments come in the form of assigning Bible readings that last until the offending orphan falls asleep. My brother Ed has been known to fake a snore.

Father Faolan rolls the chair from behind the desk, sits before us, and wrings his hands. His smile doesn't hide the worry in his eyes. "This is never easy to tell a person, especially a child."

My breath catches. Tommy trembles, and Bill takes my hand. Ed stares straight ahead.

"I believe you know your father was living at the Minnequa Hotel. You may not have been aware he suffered from cirrhosis of the liver."

Ed makes the motion of tipping a glass to his mouth. "From his drinking?"

"Um, well, perhaps. I'm not a doctor, so I cannot say. Five days ago, he underwent surgery for stenosis pylorus."

I ask, "What's that?"

"A complication of his chronic ulcer."

"When Da finally visited us, he said he couldn't eat much." I press against my stomach. "But that was a year ago."

Father Faolan clears his throat. "Ah, well, your father suffered abdominal pain and swelling. Liver disease made surgery a necessity. Unfortunately, he went into a hepatic coma."

Bill's face wrinkles with confusion. "A what?"

"My son, he was unconscious, in a deep sleep."

"Can we visit him when he wakes?"

"It is with great sadness that I tell you your father is with our Lord in heaven."

"He died?" asks Ed.

"Ah, yes. I am terribly sorry, children. Your father passed this morning at 1:18. Such a shame, a mere forty-seven years old."

Multicolored dots obliterate my vision. Bill makes quick gasping sounds. Little Tommy draws him close.

"Please join hands. We shall pray." Father Faolan bows his head.

Ed crosses his arms over his chest. "Why didn't Joe or Mary come tell us?"

I clamp onto the sides of the bench to keep from passing out. "They don't care about us."

"Children, your elder brother and sister are busy with your father's burial arrangements."

"There's nobody left to come for us." I swallow the sour slime that burns up my throat. "Will we attend..." *the funeral of the man who abandoned us?*

"Yes, Katie. The service is for family only, but Sister Christine Daniel offered to accompany you."

Bill wipes his tears on his sleeve.

"Come on, boys. We're done." Ed steps toward the door.

I block his way. "No, Ed. We stay together. That's all we've got."

Father Faolan motions for us to join hands. "O God, You are my guidance and strength. Do not abandon these children in their hour of need."

Bill and Tommy close their eyes and lower their heads. Ed and I make eye contact, but he quickly looks away. I stare at the bald patch in the center of Father Faolan's bowed head.

Shadows flit over the soil in shades of gold and black like swallowtail butterflies. Nana said the souls of dead Irish seek to return to their homeland and cannot know peace until laid to rest among their own. Could this be her spirit in the crisp breeze, moving through the branches above my head? But Nana wouldn't leave them alone in heaven—ten-day-old Theresa, Granda, the two infants named James that I never met, and Mam and the unborn child who caused her death. I feel so alone.

Joe says the funeral home donated the white rose and jasmine spray that adorns Da's pine casket. When Mary asked if we should pay, he answered, "No. The flowers are left over from an earlier funeral. It's the least Mr. McCarthy could do given the business our family's brought him.

Mary, our brothers, and I fill the six chairs set up by Mr. McCarthy, who now shuffles his feet and glares at his watch. Sister Christine, hands clasped as if in an upside-down prayer, seems to listen intently. I've never met this priest, and from the words he speaks, I can't tell if he even knew our father. As he begins a recitation of Psalms 24, I study the boys' faces.

Ed's is stiff and angry. Joe glances around as if searching for an excuse to leave. Bill's shoulders quake, but he's dry-eyed. Tommy rests his arm across his brother's shoulders.

I wonder what expression others see on my face. I can't picture what my loss looks like, not the loss of this man who lies in the plain wooden casket, but the hope I held in my heart, hope he would come for us and swear he loved our mother more than the Scarlet Woman. I visualize him with tears in his eyes as he confesses the fool he was to abandon us, his real family, in favor of the Scarlet Woman and her child.

The image disappears like a puff of smoke. Da chose his second family over the boys and me. I've thought of him as dead more than once since he abandoned us. This resentment I doubt I'll ever overcome.

I rely on priests for comfort, but this one's words wound me. "Keep my soul and deliver me. I shall not be ashamed, for I have hope in Thee. Amen."

After the way our father treated us, left us in such a harsh place, how can this priest ask God to say Da should not be ashamed. And why should the Lord welcome and keep his soul? I stand, smooth my skirt, and lean into Mary's arms. "You haven't visited in months."

"Sorry, been working a double shift."

I whisper, "Did you get my letter?"

"What letter?"

"I put it in the mail basket yesterday."

"I didn't get it."

"Tomorrow, probably tomorrow. I guess I should have waited and brought it with me today. I panicked. Mary, mail me your response quickly. Just a note, but seal it tight. If you don't receive it, you must take off from work and come so we can talk."

"Can't you tell me now?"

I sense Sister Christine moving closer. "No, it's not safe."

"We should return to the orphanage," says the nun.

CHAPTER THIRTY-ONE

JUNE 1936

After two weeks with no response, I give up hope. I drag through each day as if a shawl of rocks lay across my shoulders. Every night, I awaken from a dream of being buried in a hole so deep that I can't dig out. Now, sitting before my lukewarm bowl of oatmeal, I am unable to lift my spoon.

Sister Myrtle taps my shoulder and glares. "Follow me." The nun stops just outside the dining hall and removes an envelope from her habit pocket. "Most unusual for an orphan to receive mail."

I pray my emotions do not show on my face. My hand trembles as I take the envelope then spin away from the nun's anger. "Excuse me. Sister Reparata needs me." But instead of going to the sewing room, I slink to the chapel and slide into a pew. I break the seal and smooth the letter inside a prayer book so any prying eyes will think I'm reading verses.

That my sister Mary received my message qualifies as a miracle. The Holy Virgin Mother must have absolved me for the sin of stealing Sister Evellius' envelope. But the issue of no stamp? While slipping it into the mail basket, I prayed the postman would deliver it anyway. But in my dream that night, a gnarly hand threw the letter into the trash, and I fell out of bed grabbing it. The rest of the night, I prayed for divine intervention, for someone who would affix a stamp onto the envelope.

God, Jesus, Holy Virgin Mother, or guardian angel, whoever took care of the delivery, I thank You with all my heart. Maybe it was Mam? Or Nana?

In my letter, I set a date, time, and place to meet, Pueblo Union Station, the very spot where my family first arrived. Mary wrote back,

"Train tickets will cost all the money I have. Meet me at the Greyhound Bus Station instead." After twice reading my sister's note, I folded it into a small square, caught the edge aflame, and dropped it in the prayer candle jar.

Mary has visited only once since she sent her response, but I'm not worried. She's working overtime shifts to make our plan succeed.

Yesterday, I signaled Ed to look behind the Virgin Mother Mary's foot. When I checked, my note was gone. But we haven't spotted each other today, so there's been no opportunity for him to double-blink to indicate he received my message.

Now, I clasp the iron bedframe and heave myself upright. The tick-tock of a clock reverberates inside my head, marking off the seconds. I press against my temples when Betty bangs the window shutters against the wall, letting in sunlight so bright it burns my dry eyes.

"Katie, what's wrong?" asks Zarah.

I flash my *everything-is-fine* smile.

At breakfast, I force myself to eat. Oatmeal clings to the sides of my throat. The lumps won't go down. I need energy and calm nerves for what lies ahead, so I gulp water to flush down the lukewarm oatmeal. When dismissed, I trudge behind the other girls, upstairs to Bible class. The effort leaves me as drained as if I had run.

"Proverbs 6:6. 'Go to the ant, thou sluggard; consider her ways...'" Sister Evilness' voice buzzes like an annoying bee rather than the silence of a tiny ant. "Girls, burn this lesson into your minds. To win our Lord's favor, consider the ant working tirelessly and model your efforts as such."

Later, as I mend shirt after shirt, my head bobbles, and my foot slips off the pedal, jerking me awake. Laura and Violet's machines roar like the train that brought my family to Pueblo. How different would our lives be if we had never gotten on that train? If we had stayed in Philly?

When Sister Reparata releases us for dinner, Laura and Violet join the brigade of marching feet. But I need a moment to think, so I step inside the chapel.

Small, identical blonde-headed girls rub rags in large slow circles over the wooden pews. The air smells of pine seed oil. When they notice me, their hands whirl. Sunlight beams through the stained-glass window and reflects off the pew as if it were made of glass. I wonder if I should tell the twins, it's not I who cares whether they put full effort into their assigned job. "Are you new?"

When the twins nod, yellow curls bounce over their saucer eyes.

"Who put you here?"

"Sister Christine Daniel."

"Strange. She's the boys' room mother. She wouldn't want you missing dinner. Hurry and catch the girls who just marched past."

"Will the nun punish us?" ask the twins in unison.

"No, Sister Christine is the kindest. If she returns, I'll tell her I released you for supper."

Luminaries flicker. The Blessed Virgin Mary shimmers in their light. The wood is warm against my legs as I slide into the first-row pew. Glassy-eyed saints perched on the walls bear in on me, watch me. The punishment will be quick and severe if Evilness finds me in the chapel, but I must talk to God.

In the name of Jesus Christ, I pray. Please, have mercy upon my brothers and me. I ask for Your protection in what we are about to do. It's bound to be a sin to run from the house You built for these women of God and a sin to abandon the duties the nuns assign in Your name. Still, I beseech You, keep us from harm, as it is from harm that we run.

A large white globe hangs above the altar. Jesus' painted plaster body appears to sweat beneath its glow. Mini lightbulbs over each confessional booth cast unearthly shadows. I imagine being locked inside until I repent my many sins.

Holy Virgin Mother, I failed you more times than I can count. But I want you to know, I tried to do right by you, to behave as the Sisters demand and keep my complaints to myself. I hope you noticed, I quit swearing.

Footsteps in the hall grow louder. I crouch lower than the pew's backrest until they move past the chapel.

Holy Virgin Mother, what if I mess up and we get caught? I wanted to do this legally, have Joe take us out, but he hasn't come around since Da's funeral. He didn't offer to take us home then, so that door is closed. Mam always said God helps those who help themselves. So that's what we're doing. I'm terrified. Please, be with my brothers and me tonight. Amen.

I cross myself and enter the empty dining hall. Mealtime has ended. I bustle to the showers.

Tazia dries with a threadbare towel then perches on the slatted wooden bench. She has pretty feet and is meticulous in their care. When Tazia turns eighteen and sashays out, she claims the first thing she'll do is paint her toenails firetruck red.

Hannah splashes Zarah. My friends' laughter reminds me of our clandestine meeting in the linen closet, telling tales and eating the orange marmalade buns Rachael stole from the nuns' dining room.

"Want me to braid yo' hair, Katie?" Ethel holds up a wide-tooth comb. "Yo' got hair thicker than most white girl hair. I can make it nice."

Nobody has styled my hair since Mam bobbed it. I sense her presence.

Say yes, Katie. Braided snug against your head is perfect for what you will do tonight.

"Thank you, Ethel. I would love that."

Zarah dries her face and meets my eye. Can these friends I wanted so desperately and now love so much sense I'm leaving? My heart aches as if I've already left. I long to hug each of them, but the risk is too great. My friends might guess I'm worried and nervous and ply me with questions. Besides, Rachael says Sacred Heart's walls are giant ears. Tonight is the last time they'll overhear anything I say. I crawl onto my thin mattress and tug the threadbare blanket to my neck.

Zarah murmurs, "Goodnight, Katie."

I struggle to keep my voice from cracking. "Goodnight, my friend."

Guilt weighs heavier than the biggest lie I ever told. It's a great betrayal, leaving my friends without saying goodbye. But the responsibility falls to me. I must get Bill to a safe place.

Friday, always Friday. Tomorrow, the Monsignor comes for the fitting of his new white shirt. I know this because I laid out the pattern, cut the cotton fabric, and stitched every seam and buttonhole as carefully as if making it for someone who deserved a nice shirt. Now it hangs, starched and ironed on a metal hanger, awaiting his arrival.

After his fitting, the Monsignor will take Bill to the corner room.

CHAPTER THIRTY-TWO

―――――― ∽ ――――――

JULY 1936

No clocks in our dormitory. No watches on anybody's arm. How will I know when midnight comes? Will the boys be on time? Mary had written, "Meet me at 3:00 a.m."

I wait until the air stills then rise from beneath the bedcovers and put on my newest dress. As a thank you for the quality of my work, Sister Reparata had allowed me the first choice of the brightly dyed flour sacks donated by the Women's Auxiliary. Green with ballet dancers swirling among red roses, the dress is three weeks old.

Holy Virgin Mother, Father Faolan says I can do all things through Christ. I'm not so sure. Please stay by my side.

Silently, I slip my white uniform shirt over the ballerina dress.

Deuteronomy 31:7 says to be strong and of good courage. Holy Virgin Mother, I just vomited in my mouth.

I take my blue uniform skirt off the shelf then hesitate when Zarah rolls over in bed.

Holy Virgin Mary, please let my friend know how sad it makes me I couldn't confide in her, and I'm so very sorry I didn't say goodbye.

I button the waistband and smooth the fabric. It's time.

As I tiptoe to the door, Ethel murmurs, "Momma," and flips onto her stomach. I freeze and wait, wondering if I'm the only one who hears my heart pounding as loud as a marching band's bass drum. I clasp the doorknob with a sweaty hand, too frightened to rotate it. When displeased, Sister Mary Myrtle locks the dormitory door.

I should have listened. Did the lock click?

A whimper escapes my lips when the doorknob spins. I tighten my grasp and lift because that takes the weight off the hinges and the door doesn't scrape.

The hall is as black as a cave. I miss a step in the stairwell and grab the banister to stop my fall. Carrying my worn, brown, lace-up shoes, I glide in stockinged feet. I eyeball the length of the dark hall leading to Sister Evilness' office. A strip of light escapes beneath the door. I pass on tiptoes and descend the next stairway. The chapel doors stand open. Shadows shift in the flicker of the lighted globe above the altar.

The basement door will clank if I shut it, so I leave it open just a crack and descend the final set of stairs. Are the boys hiding in a corner or behind a door—waiting and wondering? The darkness closes in. I am overcome with dread. Maybe I'm too late.

The basement is unearthly quiet. I pray for some small sound, a cough, a scratch, then I'll know the boys hide in the shadows. We've waited since Da's funeral at the end of February for this, a plan that can only work in the summer, when the boiler is not lit.

I work my way toward the window on the far side of the storage shelves holding preserved beets, green beans, and other vegetables from Sister Evilness' garden. Thick slime and the stench of rotted onions escapes through one jar's shattered glass.

I pass the iron sinks and massive washing machines. Warmed by reminiscences of the day I first met the girls who became my friends, I almost smile.

Holy Virgin Mother, why did I have to lose my family before my prayers for friends could be answered? Is it too much to ask for both? Am I being punished for my greedy thoughts?

The mop closet looms to the right. That I won't miss.

I open the heavy brown drapery. The only glimmer comes from the full moon. Cobwebs, black and heavy from coal dust, dangle off overhead pipes. When they brush my face, I clasp my hand over my mouth.

The boiler looms as ominous as a black monster. I flip over the bucket that sits near its base and set it in the darkest corner. My knees quake as I perch on its edge.

The monster's giant mouth, where Ed and Bill feed it coal, hangs open and blocks the coal chute opening through which we will escape. I rise and force the door closed. Its latch clanks. I cower in the dark and pray the sound did not awaken the nuns.

In the note I left behind the Blessed Virgin Mother's foot, I told the boys to glide along the halls in socked feet to avoid making any noise. Still, scurrying down the steps is bound to cause the wood to creak and groan. I imagine my brothers holding their breaths then gasping puffs of air. There is no way three boys can be as quiet as I. They should have opened the basement door by now. Surely, they got caught.

My brothers would never reveal that I'm in the basement. Yet it's simply a matter of time before the nuns check my bed and come searching. Fifteen minutes then I'll sneak back to the dormitory.

A thump jolts me out of an exhausted haze. The boys? Or nuns? Should I find out or remain in the shadows?

Someone trips and crashes into the iron sink. "Holy shite!"

I know that hushed voice.

"What the bloody hell? I don't remember the sink sticking out so far." Ed yanks a match box from his pocket, one he stole along with a pack of cigarettes, when the van driving the boys to their worksites stopped for gas. I warned him his punishment would be worse than any he's had if the nuns find out, but now I'm glad he snagged the matches. The flame casts ghoulish shadows on the boys' faces.

I extend my arms to hug them, but Ed shifts away. "No time for mushy stuff. Evilness is roaming the halls."

"I thought something happened."

"Was a close call, Katie." Ed tousles Tommy's hair. "We ducked into the chapel and hid in a pew. Pinched this lad's nose 'cause he had himself wound up for a sneeze."

Tommy grins sheepishly. "I'm good now. Let's get going."

"Whoa, sport," cautions Ed. "Let's talk this through. Should be shovels beside the chute. Don't knock 'em over."

"Bill's always blundering into a wall or door," says Tommy. "It'll be him for sure."

When Bill rams Tommy, I grab his collar. "Knock it off."

"Listen up, yeh meatheads." Ed's voice is no louder than a sigh.

We lean close and strain to hear. "No deliveries since the weather warmed, so there's no coal in the chute. But it's dirty in there, and darker than the darkest night."

"Shh." I raise a finger to my lips. "What was that?"

"Rats use this chute," says Ed.

Rats! Tiny hairs rise on my neck. I can't do this. The nasty creatures might be in there, waiting.

"When you get out, run past the vegetable garden." Ed glances over his shoulder. "Back of the cornstalks, there's a place where the chain link broke loose from the pole. We'll crawl through the opening. Wait on the other side, but not too long. If you see or hear the nuns, run like a banshee's coming for your soul. It won't be pretty if we get caught. Yeh gotta get to Mary."

"Breathe shallow and move slow. Our climbing will loosen coal dust, just like when I put out the fire." Bill winks at Tommy. "Could choke you, make you cough or sneeze. And sound echoes in the tube."

"It's steeper than I thought." What had I been thinking? We can't get out this metal chute without making all sorts of racket. We'll wake everybody. I clench my fists against my thighs to stop the trembling.

"I'll go last so I can shove yer butts should yeh slip. Katie, go first so yeh can yank Tommy up."

"You're stronger, Ed. You should go first. Easier for me to push Tommy than haul him to the top."

"Makes sense. You'll be black with coal when yeh climb out. That's good. We won't get spotted so easy. No telling who might be watching."

"Keep your dirty clothes on until we're sure nobody's coming after us," I say. "Good camouflage."

"Okay, we're on our way." Ed sticks his head up the chute. He scrunches his wide shoulders but still makes a rubbing sound as he struggles to fit through.

I nudge Bill forward. I hope it's fear that makes me think I hear the clank of keys.

Bill's shoe soles are slick, and he slips more than Ed. My head swirls as he claws the metal tube's sides. The sound will carry to the floor above. And the footsteps overhead are real.

"Tommy, do you need help?"

"Nah, not me. I climb like a monkey."

I ignore the creaking sound of a door opening at the top of the basement stairs and force my youngest brother, more roughly than I intend, into the chute. He climbs as easily as scrambling up the slick sides of a children's slide. I stick in my head and shoulders. The opening narrows the higher I climb.

Please, Holy Virgin Mother, give me strength.

Tommy's foot slips. He careens toward me. I brace my legs and thrust his bottom upward. He regains momentum.

"Sweet Jesus, lad." Ed grunts as he hauls Tommy over the top. "You're heavier than you look."

Moonlight illuminates my path to freedom. I'm frozen by the marvel of it until Ed sticks in his head, blocking all my light. "Yeh comin' out? Or gonna spend the night?"

I smash my arms and legs against the slick tube and shimmy-walk to the top. A hand stretches toward the opening, clenches my wrist, and yanks. The jolt of pain feels as if Ed ripped my arm from its socket. I gulp air as he drags me to safety. "I heard footsteps on the stairs."

Ed heaves me to my feet. "Run! Light on in the basement."

We dash across the yard and through the cornstalks. Ed separates the chain link. Bill dives through headfirst. His trouser leg catches, crashing him face first onto the ground. I rip his cuff free.

"Did yeh hear that?" There's panic in Ed's voice. "A clank, like the lock on the back door?"

Tommy steps through the chain link opening unscathed. Ed and I follow.

Bill raises his arms over his head and spins. "We're free."

"No celebrating yet. The Sisters could be on our heels." Ed points to the outline of a human blocking the light shining through an overhead window. "Move!"

We run until Tommy gasps and clenches his knees. "My legs are too short."

"Listen," whispers Ed. "Somebody's near the fence."

I suck air into my lungs and wave the boys on. We run and run. My chest burns. Just as I think we've taken a wrong turn, I see the sign—a greyhound leaping on a black background. I gasp, "Ed, there are no buses, only cars."

"Buses should be out back. We need to find Mary."

I warn, "We've coal dust all over us. Anybody with eyes can tell we're up to no-good. We should clean up first."

We slip inside the terminal and past a man wearing a suit and vest. He tilts his Homburg, lowers his newspaper to his lap, and scowls at us.

Ed opens the men's room door but blocks me from following Bill and Tommy. "Girls over there."

"I'm staying with you."

"Okay, but let's be quick. Lads, take off your top layer and wash up a bit."

My knees go weak when the bathroom door swings open. A tall man with bloodshot eyes, his tie hanging loose, stops at the mirror and runs his fingers through his Brylcreemed hair. I grip the sink, fill my hands with water, and splash my face. The man glances but doesn't appear to notice I'm a girl.

While he's in the last stall, we tuck our oily, blackened outer clothes under our arms and scoot.

I squint into the shadows. "Do you see Mary?"

"Hopefully, hiding at the back of a bus."

We duck behind the circular wire map rack when two policemen saunter up to the ticket counter clerk. "We're watching for runaway orphans, a thirteen-year-old, brown-haired girl and three boys."

"Sorry, officers," says the clerk. "Haven't seen them."

"Didn't think they'd come to the bus depot," says the wide-shouldered younger officer. "Orphans wouldn't have ticket money. Probably hitchhiking. Just in case they show up, phone the department."

"Of course, officer," says the ticket clerk.

We slink along the wall until Bill points outside. "Two buses have their engines running." Black smoke, stinking like rotten eggs, rolls out their exhaust pipes.

I caution my brothers, "Act normal. Don't draw attention to yourselves."

"We're ready for our great escape," murmurs Ed. "If only we had tickets."

I stifle a scream when a hand grips my shoulder.

"Hush. It's me," whispers Mary.

My knees buckle with relief.

"Coppers headed this way." Mary opens her handbag and removes tickets. "Quick. Second bus. Denver."

I huff, "That's not far enough away."

"Then on to Oregon."

"Oregon?"

"Portland. I've got a job waiting at the Oregon Shipbuilding Company on the Willamette River. Now, quit yakking and board that bus."

Bill places his foot on the first step as the officers, talking and laughing, round the corner. The older man rests one arm on his paunch and whacks his billy club against the metal garbage can, sending the lid clattering to the ground. The sound hits me in the chest like a gunshot.

A swirl of dark cloth catches my eye just before a woman hails, "Officers." I hear evilness in that voice. Cold sweat pools in my underarms.

Ed grabs Tommy by one arm and the seat of his trousers and hurls him onto the greyhound bus. In the front row, a man hunkered over a brown paper bag, an amber bottle spout sticking out, pulls his legs from the aisle as Mary and I scramble up the steps. Ed and Bill almost knock us over hurrying to get down the aisle.

"No running on my bus," growls the driver.

The boys throw themselves into the rear seat behind an elderly couple. The silver-haired woman pivots as if she might scold them then loops purple yarn over a metal knitting needle. Bill angles her large bag to block the view of where they hide. The young man and woman across the aisle appear so interested in each other that they don't notice the scuffle. An elderly man shakes his head and frowns at my brothers.

"Never had an eye for a copper," says Mary. "Might make an exception for the broad-shouldered fella."

"No time for that." I strong-arm Mary into the only remaining empty seat in the back of the bus, three rows in front of the elderly couple. The gray plastic is cold against my clammy skin. Tommy curls up on the floor across from where Bill and Ed have crawled under the seat.

"This'll be a holy show," says Ed. "Must have been Sister Evilness chasing us."

"The baseball nun is on her tail." Mary crams my head down on the seat, but I peek out. My temples throb.

Sister Evellius stops before the first bus, rises on tiptoes, and peers in the front window. When she knocks, the driver opens the door.

My breath snags. Will Evilness board this bus next?

"The baseball nun's coming this way," mutters Mary. "And so is that handsome young fella in blue."

I sense movement from where Ed and Bill hunker beneath the back-row seat, but they are well hidden. Across the aisle, Tommy's red shirttail might as well shout, *Here I am!*

My mouth is dry, yet I whisper fiercely, "Tommy! Your behind is sticking out in the aisle."

Mary rams me to the floor. I think my eyeballs will explode from the pressure in my head.

Sister Christine steps onto the bus. "I'll only be a moment."

"No problem, Sister," says the driver.

When I poke my head up, Mary knocks me back down with a sweeping motion of her arm and drapes her coat over me. The wool traps the stale, oily stench from the bus floor. I gag.

"Morning, Sister," says the drunk in the front seat. "Don't mind this. It's my medicine."

"May the Lord heal you." The nun's footsteps, muffled by the rubber mat, come closer.

From the folds of Mary's coat, I peer between the metal seat frames until the sound moves past and halts at the rear of the bus. Tommy, eye's wide as saucers, makes a tiny wave at me, then curls back up in a ball with his rear end clearly visible. My stomach cramps, and bitter slime burns its way into my throat.

I watch in amazement as the nun extends her hand as if tucking Tommy's shirttail into the back of his trousers. "May the Lord watch over you."

The silver-haired woman glances up from her knitting. "And you as well, Sister."

Confused about what's happening, I wipe sweat beads off my forehead and listen to the swish of Sister Christine's habit and the soft scuffle of her shoes. When she pauses beside Mary, I swallow the vomit in my mouth.

"Have a glorious trip."

Mary's fingernails dig through the coat fabric as she pushes against my back. "Thank you, Sister."

The metal steps creak beneath the baseball nun's feet when she steps off the bus. Cool, damp air swooshes in with the closing of the bus door. The interior lights dim. The bus backs slowly away from the curb. I shift my sister's coat off my head.

Mary smiles. "Handsome fella. A shame we're leaving."

The bus rolls forward. I peek over the window frame as Sister Evellius squints and tugs the heavy silver cross that hangs from her neck. The brakes hiss and squeal when the bus rolls to a stop at the corner.

No, no. Please, Holy Virgin Mother, make him go.

The gear shift grinds. The engine strains.

Hurry. Please, hurry.

I count telephone poles: one...two...three. Faster and faster, the world blurs until the sun's glow surges above the horizon. When I gaze toward the clouds, their fuzzy edges light with gold. I take that as a sign Mam and Nana are looking down, and they are pleased.

I don't know what we will face in Oregon, yet I am not afraid. My family is with me.

AUTHOR'S NOTE
2023

My mother Katie used to say we Irish are not always easy to love. Our family history includes examples of why that might be true. Still, I admire and respect my relatives who squabbled, disagreed, and suffered intermittent, even broken relationships while loving, providing for, and protecting each other.

As parents, the adults were stern. By today's standards, their punishments could be considered harsh. Still, they paled in comparison to the practices of certain nuns. The siblings agreed no child should endure the life of an orphan, yet gave credit to Sisters Katherine, Anne, and Daniel, whom they described as the only saving grace to their lives in the orphanage.

With the greatest respect, I remain in awe of those who rise above difficult childhoods, as did my mother and her siblings. The common thread is a strength that grew out of necessity and a commitment that what had happened to them would never happen to their children. It did not, and it might be said that is the greatest measure of their success.

This is not to say my mother, aunt, and uncles were unscathed by their experiences. They were, but it is important to note they were not undone. Unlike many of the orphans whose tragic stories are revealed in news reports, the Ryan kids survived to marry, have families, and live full, interesting lives. I dedicate this novel to them.

ABOUT THE AUTHOR

Dr. Pat Spencer has lived in three countries and seven states. She loves to travel and has spent time in South Africa, Botswana, Zambia, Zimbabwe, Namibia, Spain, France, Croatia, New Zealand, Australia, Italy, Greece, Mexico, the Galapagos, and the Bahamas, as well as Alaska and the Hawaiian Islands. She has road-tripped across the continental United States several times. Pat enjoys getting to know people and learning about their culture.

Dr. Spencer is a retired professor and California Community College president. Pat lives in Southern California with her husband. She speaks to service and community organizations concerning human trafficking, the writing and publishing processes, and her books. When not writing, Pat golfs, reads, walks on the beach, hangs out with family and friends, or frequents book clubs and writing groups.

Please visit her online.
Website: https://www.patspencer.net
Facebook: https://www.facebook.com/pat.spencer.9849/
Instagram: https://www.instagram.com/drpatspencer/
Twitter: https://twitter.com/DrPatSpencer

Dear Reader,

Thank you for choosing Golden Boxty in the Frypan. If you enjoyed it, please submit a review on the site at which you made your purchase. I appreciate hearing from you. I love visiting book clubs. If you are not local, I am available to join zoom and other online meetings. Please visit me on Facebook or my website at http://patspencer.net. You can also sign up for giveaways and other authorly news.

Sincerely,
Pat Spencer